THE CASE  1

Sandorf Passage books are available to the
trade through Independent Publishers Group:
ipgbook.com | (800) 888-4741.

National and University Library Zagreb Control Number: 001197362

Library of Congress Control Number: 2023946514

ISBN: 978-9-53351-437-6

Also available as an ebook;
ISBN: 978-9-53351-440-6

Co-funded by
the European Union

NATIONAL ENDOWMENT for the ARTS
arts.gov

The European Commission
support for the production
of this publication does not
constitute an endorsement of
the contents which reflects the
views only of the authors, and
the Commission cannot be held
responsible for any use which
may be made of the information
contained therein.

This project is supported
in part by an award from the
National Endowment for the Arts.

NATIONAL
CULTURE
FUND OF BULGARIA

This book was translated with the
support of the National Culture
Fund of Bulgaria.

Republika
Hrvatska
Ministarstvo
kulture
i medija
Republic
of Croatia
Ministry
of Culture
and Media

This book is published with financial
support by the Republic of Croatia's
Ministry of Culture and Media.

THE CASE OF CEM

VERA MUTAFCHIEVA

TRANSLATED FROM BULGARIAN BY ANGELA RODEL

SAN-
DORF
PAS-
SAGE

SOUTH PORTLAND | MAINE

TRANSLATOR'S NOTE

WHAT FIRST DREW ME to Bulgaria was not the literature, but the music: the brassy female voices, the funky lopsided rhythms, the squealing bagpipes. Le Mystère des Voix Bulgares sounded like a choir of (albeit deafening) angels when I first heard them as an undergrad at Yale. When I finally got over to Sofia in the mid-1990s to follow these sounds to their source, it's not surprising I ended up marrying a Bulgarian musician. But luckily this particular wooden flute player was also a poet who introduced me to another divine chorus of Bulgarian voices: the vibrant, turn-of-the-millennium literary scene. Poetry was the dominant genre at the time, and the explosion of postsocialist literary experimentation found its expression in avant-garde performances.

Yet as a reader I have always been a fan of novels—the fatter and more historical, the better. My idea of a perfect afternoon is to curl up with a tome of Iris Murdoch, Robertson Davies, or Dostoevsky. I asked my then husband for recommendations of classic Bulgarian novels. He thought for a moment, then said:

The Case of Cem. I was stunned by what I found in this historical novel published in 1967 at the height of the Cold War by the prominent Ottomanist Vera Mutafchieva.

On the surface, *The Case of Cem* tells a straightforward tale: upon the death of Ottoman Sultan Mehmed the Conqueror in 1481, his eldest son, Bayezid, takes the throne. However, discontented factions within the Ottoman army urge Mehmed's second son, Cem, a well-educated and experienced soldier, to oppose his brother's ascension and to suggest the two split the empire. Bayezid refuses, setting off a ruthless power struggle. Cem is forced into long years of exile and finds himself essentially a hostage, a pawn for European powers as they try to slow the Ottoman Empire's expansion and even to take back Constantinople. Cem wanders from Syria, Egypt, and Rhodes to Rome, where he is held by Pope Innocent VIII, before finally being passed on to King Charles VIII of France. Cem dies in Neapoli in 1495 under mysterious circumstances, but even death is no end to exile; several more years pass before his body arrives back home to its final resting place.

But the book's structure is anything but straightforward: Mutafchieva presents the story as a series of depositions by historical figures before a court, bringing medieval history and modern "courtroom drama" together in a way that is extremely experimental for Bulgarian (and I daresay world) literature of the time. In The Case of Cem, we hear firsthand from Mehmed's grand vizier, Pierre d'Aubusson (grand master of the knights of Rhodes), and many others. Yet the one character who never speaks directly to the court is Cem himself; he remains silent, not unlike the Balkans themselves, who were often voiceless victims in the tug-of-war between East and West. The closest we get to Cem is through the Persian poet Saadi, Cem's companion and (as becomes clear as the novel progresses) erstwhile lover. Saadi is hands down the most sympathetic character in the book—the greedy, ever-scheming Westerners look quite craven by comparison—leading me to wonder how Mutafchieva managed to get such positive queer representation past the communist censors of that era. Perhaps because Saadi was Persian and not Bulgarian? Although Cem's story is intriguing, fit for a History Channel special, why should Cold War-era Bulgarians or contemporary readers of English care about the fate of a medieval Ottoman prince? In the foreword to the novel, the author herself raises this question, and uses her insight as a historian to offer a convincing answer: "What brings us back to Cem today? In the case of Cem, which unfolded over a whole decade and a half at the tail end of the fifteenth century, the politics of the East and West were sketched out with utter clarity, with naked simplicity. Later some would call this 'the beginning of the Eastern Question' and they might be right...."

In addition to the big historical questions about individual agency that it raises, The Case of Cem is also a very personal exploration of emigration and loss. More than one Bulgarian critic has pointed out that Mutafchieva wrote the novel about a young prince in exile only a few years after her own brother, Boyan, defected to France in 1963. Under socialism, Bulgarian defectors were generally not allowed to return and had very little contact with relatives behind the Iron Curtain. Authorities often punished loved ones left behind by denying them jobs and educational opportunities, or forcing them to collaborate with the secret police (a trap Mutafchieva found herself in). Not unlike Cem, defectors were often used as pawns by competing governments in propaganda campaigns, and a few, such as Georgi Markov, were even assassinated. Some scholars see Mutafchieva's *The Case of Cem* as a veiled critique or interrogation of Cold War East-West tensions and politics disguised in medieval trappings, which adds another layer of richness and relevancy—especially given the divide that remains even today within the European Union, as many eastern member states such as Bulgaria continue to struggle with corruption, populism, weak democratic institutions, and a feeling of "second-class citizenship" compared to wealthier western EU members.

The novel also put me, the translator from Bulgarian, on unfamiliar footing. Mutafchieva immediately throws the reader into Cem's world, peppering the text with Turkisms she does not define or explain. Although the Bulgarian language retains quite a few Turkish borrowings, due to its 500 years in the Ottoman Empire, the author constantly uses terminology that is not familiar to the average Bulgarian reader. As a translator, I have tried to preserve this aspect of Mutafchieva's writings and leave many of the Turkish terms in, since they provide a strong sense of atmosphere, while the context generally makes clear what these unfamiliar words mean.

Although Mutafchieva was a highly respected historian, she clearly did not feel bound to one-hundred-percent historical accuracy in her fiction. She freely changes certain names and other historical details of the text; the first-person narrators are at times unreliable (if not downright deceptive), which adds another layer of complexity to their "testimony" before the court of history. Despite its historical grounding, at the end of the day, *The Case of Cem* is a work of fiction, and I respect and even marvel at the imaginative approach the otherwise fastidious Ottoman scholar Mutafchieva took in her tale of an exiled prince and his European wanderings.

Mutafchieva's brilliant psychological portraits of these "witnesses of history," especially the poet Saadi, pushed me to break one of my most ingrained translator's habits I have faithfully stuck to for more than a decade: translating a book in order. As I approached the end of the book, after nearly two hundred pages of being in Saadi's head, following his thoughts, I couldn't bear to let him go. I did not want to translate his final sections, so I jumped ahead out of order, and only when I had translated everything else I possibly could did I go back and finish Saadi. Since I never had the honor of meeting Vera Mutafchieva before she passed away, I felt as if Saadi was my coauthor of this translation, the cocreator I found myself in constant conversation with. The Persian poet is also a singer and musician, so perhaps it is not surprising that he drew me in, just as Bulgarian voices drew me into the wonderful world of translation so many years ago.

FOREWORD

CEM'S NAME IS long-since forgotten, even though centuries ago it was on everyone's lips. Back then—centuries ago—novels and poetry were written about Cem, they would have featured him in inserts, if in his day newspapers had existed and those newspapers contained inserts; as it was, wandering bards sang Cem's praises. In the seventeenth century, there was no topic more loaded or exciting than Cem Sultan, or Zizim, as he was called in the West.

As is often the case, Cem was merely an excuse for writers and poets, the canvas upon which they embroidered their whims. To the seventeenth-century world, Cem was a hapless prisoner and the cruelly betrayed paramour of bored and similarly imprisoned noblewomen; to them, Cem was a victim of court intrigues—a crystal-clean young man duped by others.

This was not, in fact, Cem Sultan, but the hero of the seventeenth century. He could have borne any other name equally as well, but Zizim had an advantage: it was Oriental, shrouded in mystery, notorious.

The romantic victim Zizim's fame came and went. The eighteenth century arrived with new kinds of heroes, while the ninteenth ushered in others more different still. What brings us back to Cem today?

The fact that Cem has not yet been discovered, for example. True, he was exhumed four years after his death, to prove that he was dead. But for us, what is important is not his death, but his life—the life no one wants to describe, the true one.

We also return to Cem because he was not simply a pathetic victim. Cem's fate demonstrates that certain truths are not new; they do not hold only for today—there are great and eternal truths that history continually illustrates. For example, the fact that a complex dependency exists between a person and their homeland, one that has not yet been precisely defined. ("A stone weighs heavily in its place," one saying goes, while another counters it, "No prophet is accepted in his own country.") This truth cannot be overcome; as long as there are people and homelands, the fate of the exile will always be a topic of interest.

We come back to Cem today for yet another reason. In the case of Cem, which unfolded over a whole decade and a half at the tail end of the fifteenth century, the politics of the East and West were sketched out with utter clarity, with naked simplicity. Later some would call this "the beginning of the Eastern Question" and they might be right....

Let's assume that the "Eastern Question" did not begin with Russia's advance toward the warm seas and the West's efforts to block this advance, but rather with attempts by that very same West to inhibit the development of the European East, leaving it behind, even condemning it to centuries of suffering. The liberation of the newly conquered Balkans would never again be as easily achievable as it was during the time of the case of Cem. The West did not fumble this opportunity by accident. Some think it resulted from bad strategy. That's not true, the strategy was actually rather good.

We owe quite a lot to this. In the most general terms, we owe to it our delayed development; let's not even mention the suffering, as sentimental considerations have no place in history.

Now this is the main reason we keep coming back to the case of Cem. We have long been told that what happened in the Balkans, and ended in their "Balkanization" (a term, which, if not offensive, is at the very least condescending), is a question of historical fatalism. "What can you do?" they like to say. "Who's to blame that the Balkans are on the doorstep of the East and take the full brunt of all those barbarian invasions?" We understand your pain," they love to say, "but geography is geography, beyond human will."

They really do understand us. But why should we keep quiet about the fact that we understand a few things ourselves as well? For example, that in the Case of Cem (as in all historical cases), we should not look for either historical fatalism or geographic predestination. Beyond those, human will truly was at play—the human will of a series of people who were guiding the Eastern Question in its very beginnings. They were more than happy to welcome both geography and fatalism—and to use them very skillfully.

Actually, the whole business is not so complicated. We know as well as others that history plays no favorites. Since we have been doomed to all that which has euphemistically been called "historical determinism," we have no need to accept such euphemistic speech. Our sad advantage is that we can discover the truth about the Case of Cem.

The witnesses in this case are long dead, but thanks to contemporary legal proceedings it is not difficult for the dead to speak, especially where a major suit is concerned. They will hardly resist; their part is easy. They must merely await the judgment of history. Such a sentence harms no one, as it is suspended and in absentia.

PART ONE

TESTIMONY OF THE GRAND VIZIER NISANCI
MEHMED PASHA ABOUT THE EVENTS THAT OCCURRED
BETWEEN MAY 3 AND 5, 1481

A VOICE AWOKE me before dawn. I raised my head, frightened—they don't wake up the grand vizier over trifles.

Now sitting up, I tried to see who had barged in. In the darkness I could barely recognize him: one of the sultan's *peiks*, a halberdier from his bodyguard.

"What is it?" I asked the peik. Mehmed Khan often beckoned us at the oddest of hours, as if he himself never slept.

"Pasha," the peik replied. "Mehmed Khan has gone to his eternal rest in the bosom of Allah this night."

My heart sank. We all know fate follows its own path and brings a man that which he least desires, but this was too much: Mehmed Khan could not have chosen a more unsuitable hour for his death.

Everything that pushed me to do one or the other thing that I did between the third and fifth of May—at that time it was not yet exactly a thought, to say nothing of a decision. Right then I only knew Mehmed Khan should not have died, that his death would change too much in my life, in the lives of all of us, of the empire and the world. This series of still-groggy concerns led me to order the peik, "Be silent! As the grave! Who else knows about Mehmed Khan?"

"Me... and the sultan's valet," the peik said, white as a sheet. He knew that his admission had doomed both of them to death.

"Stay here!" I called to him over my shoulder. Because I had to take care of the valet.

I gave orders to Yunus, my Sudanese mute.

As I dressed, the mute returned with the other man. He was holding him by the collar.

"Finish them off right here, right now, in the tent! Just roll up the carpet so you don't stain it. Then hide them under my couch; we'll bury them tonight."

While I was wrapping my turban around my head and tightening my sword belt, Yunus killed the two men and hid them as I had commanded.

"Come on!" I signaled to him to follow.

I recall being surprised that day had not yet broken. The short time between the peik's news and his death had seemed like hours to me. I looked around. The camp was sleeping. *Good thing it's asleep*, I thought. The tents were staked one after another in the distance, as far as the eye could see. Two hundred thousand men—gathered from Serbia to Persia, some followers of the true faith, others not, mobilized of their own free will or by force—had hurried to steal a final hour of sleep before the campaign. Yes, rumor had it that we would march today of all days.

Where to, you ask? I don't know, and clearly you don't either —in the intervening five hundred years you have not managed

VERA MUTAFCHIEVA

to learn where exactly the Conqueror had planned to lead his troops on that morning, which he did not live to see. I notice that this blank spot in your knowledge irritates you. But we were used to it, uncertainty did not alarm us, because the great Sultan Mehmed II always found his way through it. The man whose battle luck never deserted him.

I nodded again to Yunus, and we slipped between the tents. Through the canvas I could hear the soldiers' deep and calm snores in a hundred different voices. All of these men, who had grown up and gone gray in battle, gladly left their fate in the Conqueror's hands. And now he was gone.

I won't even attempt to explain to you what his death meant to us. The time of the Conqueror was unlike any other time and you, who supposedly know the sultan's empire so well, cannot imagine that once—even if only for a short time—things were different.

Broadly speaking: in our time and in our part of the world, people swore by two prophets—Muhammad and Jesus. But Mehmed Khan had his own prophet: victory. In its name, he stopped at nothing. Even our blessed clerics, before whom great ones such as Osman and Orhan had paused, could not stop him. The Conqueror took all their lands with a single word and turned them into estates for his *sipahi*, his cavalry, so as to have an army such as the world had never seen before. And so he got his army—but along with it the undying hatred of our clerics.

But Mehmed Khan was so powerful that he could turn his back on such hatred; even his back—which was as broad as it was tall—inspired respect.

For the Conqueror, there was no such thing as believers and nonbelievers. Everyone who wanted to serve him, who could serve him, was accepted in Stambul, what you know as Istanbul, and Topkapi. Mehmed Khan—when Rhodes held out against him—announced to the entirety of the Old World that he sought a great master who could design a successful siege of the knights' island. Out of the dozens of Germans, Englishmen, and Frenchmen (it was amusing to see them in Topkapi, fawning with their scrolls of paper, pandering in their clownishly bright clothing and feathers, shouting over one another in all imaginable tongues), some Master Georg from Prussia won the prize. Mehmed Khan followed his sketches, sparing no gold, and showered as much gold again on Georg himself, whose last name no one ever learned—there was no need.

The Conqueror had succeeded in convincing us (or at least forcing us to swallow our objections) that victory must be prized above all, and that we would never reach it if we kept stumbling over prohibitions, fear, or pangs of conscience. Unprejudiced—that was your word for Mehmed Khan. During his time there were many unprejudiced people (contrary to your opinion of us), but no one took this quality to such heights of perfection as the Conqueror. And so, in that early predawn they slept in our camps in two neighboring tents, or even in one and the same tent, our men, believers and heretics—only the name of Mehmed Khan had brought them together.

Would there be a victory without Mehmed Khan? I thought, confused. I still didn't know what I was going to do, but I needed to decide quickly.

The two *baltaci* axe men standing in front of the sultan's tent moved aside—I had the right to see the sultan even uncalled.

The tent was filled with a faint glow. The light inside was red due to the carmine canvas. I walked the dozen steps to the curtain, behind which lay our master's bed, on my tiptoes—as if I were coming to steal or worse. I pulled the curtain aside in the same way, like a thief.

Mehmed Khan was lying motionless on his tiger skins, but even at first glance it was clear that his stillness was not sleep. There was something strained, tortured, and alarmed in his face, as if in his final moment Mehmed Khan himself had realized he was leaving us at such an inopportune time.

I leaned over him.

In the pictures you showed me just now, Mehmed Khan did not look much like himself. You can see that the painters, since they could not astound you with the sultan's beauty, at least wanted to portray him as imposing. But he was not at all like that, I can assure you.

Above all—he was laughably short. They say such men, the laughably short ones, are terribly touchy. Mehmed suffered on account of his diminutive stature. In my every meeting with him, I noticed how he—the ruler of half the world and a threat to the other half—always sat up ramrod straight on his couch, keeping his counselors on the floor in order to tower a whole head above them.

There are short people who are well apportioned, their petiteness passes as exquisite. But my master was not one of them. He was freakish—may his soul rest in peace! As if Allah had taken the flesh needed for a tall man, yet had made him small, squashing him from top to bottom. Mehmed Khan could not interlace his fingers across his belly; his feet never touched the floor, they would swing in the air during every one of his frequent, sultanesque outbursts of anger or mirth. Because in this man, one emotion would most suddenly replace the other—sometimes it seemed to me that in his stocky body there was too much blood, it blustered in its insufficient vessel, causing spasms that were completely impossible to foresee.

Our lord's face would have also been freakish—may God forgive me!—if the Conqueror's terribly agile, sharp, deep mind had not animated it. Indeed, a clever man can never be completely ugly, it's impossible. In fact, even though God had granted our sultan a face that was wider than it was long, despite the fact that beneath it hung a flabby gullet that sagged down to his torso, even though on this face the overly thin and hooked nose and mouth, with its upper lip as thin as the lower was fat, looked disproportionate, while his eyes looked like holes in a target—despite all of this, Mehmed Khan was not ugly in the face.

That morning, stretched out on the tiger skins, his head thrown back and his thin, wire-sharp reddish beard jutting out, Mehmed Khan looked terrifying to me. Likely because of his expression.

I took his hand—I still did not want to believe the worst. It was heavy and moved in its entirety, without bending. Then I became frightened I had stood there too long. With difficulty I pulled my thoughts together, and with even more difficulty I focused them in one direction.

"Yunus," I said when I was again outside, noticing in horror that the camp was stirring awake. "Bring me Mehmed Khan's porters."

They soon arrived with the sultan's gilded litter. I made them go into the tent while I muttered some nonsense about Mehmed Khan's illness and how it hit him harder if he tried to get on his feet. Their faces only fell when we got inside, and I, trying to project ironclad calm and decisiveness, ordered them to load Mehmed Khan into his litter as if seated.

It was torturous. The corpse was twice as heavy, and Mehmed Khan even without this doubling had never been light. We somehow shoved him through the little doors, but he resisted; he had already gone cold. And so, bolstering him around the middle, with his filigreed robe tossed over him, we pulled aside the curtain. But not all the way. Through the crack I wanted the sultan's face and one hand to be visible.

His hand bobbed slightly with the porters' first steps and—seen from afar—it looked as if Mehmed Khan was greeting his troops.

I would not wish for anyone to be in my shoes that May morning. I rode to the left of the litter; from time to time I bent toward the little doors, as if reporting something or taking orders; the sultan's baltaci rode in front of the litter—I deliberately chose all of those who perhaps suspected the truth—and behind it came two battalions of Janissaries.

Passing through camp was nevertheless the most dangerous moment. Here were those who would rise up in rebellion as soon as they learned of our ruler's death. I passed between the tents as if on embers. Those thousands of tents felt like an endless canvas city and filled me with fear. Up ahead, an hour away, the minarets of Skoutari gleamed white, and beyond them—on the hills on the opposite bank—Stambul itself swam up out of the morning.

"Allah, give me strength today!" I called.

After such fear, I let myself slump in the saddle as if crushed; I felt exhausted. But then I startled: What past danger was I talking about, when the real danger was only now beginning?

You will object that for a first adviser and a second-in-command of the empire, such a day is always hard—the day when one power gives way to another. You are right to a certain extent, but in our case this process was more peculiar and much more difficult. Here, as a rule, the army rebels after every sultan's death; here, everyone who has dreamed of donning the vizier's robes spreads his entire worldly wealth among the Janissaries and the clerics so as to win them over, predisposing them, using this very day of interregnum.

Few of our grand viziers have survived such a day; they can be counted on the fingers of one hand. No matter how I tried to keep up my courage, I didn't believe I would be among them. Not hope, but something else now urged me toward Stambul. In the few hours I had for myself, I, Nisanci Mehmed Pasha, had the power to decide the future of the empire. More precisely: to protect and continue the work of my great lord.

I was not the only one who suspected the danger that threatened his legacy; it was widely known. I could not count on someone else (besides myself, begging your pardon) deciding to sacrifice his life to avoid the inevitable: a return to the times before Mehmed Khan.

As I already said—our clerics were hard-hit by Mehmed Khan's laws. They would take advantage of his death. And they had just the thing to wager on. Perfectly legally, without any violence. They were betting on Şehzade Bayezid, Mehmed's eldest son.

I am glad that history has confirmed my opinion of Bayezid, I never dared to utter it aloud. Incidentally, you know more about Bayezid than I do; I never saw him on the throne. But he seemed off to me even as Şehzade. I couldn't say why I felt loathing for him; he behaved perfectly well with both me and all the other pillars of the state. Much was said about his talents—he was an excellent bowman, unsurpassed; he had a deep mastery of theology and astronomy.

Rumor also had it that while the Şehzade's talents were plain to see, indeed almost on display, their flip side—his vices —remained hidden. But no one would ever guess they were there. That then-young man had one great quality: self-control. He never let loose his anger or foolish mirth in front of others, as his father liked to do; Bayezid never let on what he preferred and what irked him. This oily perfection was precisely what disgusted me about him. Not only me, of course, even though history has painted me to be his one and only opponent.

Shortsighted, that was what I thought of them all—the Janissary aghas, mullahs, some of the old or deposed viziers —who were in awe of Bayezid. A fellow like him—as I saw it—would betray even his own mother (incidentally, I should note that she is unknown to this day; Bayezid never showed her any respect, never named her, while Mehmed Khan himself had long forgotten his youthful dalliances). The clerics clearly hoped that a devout believer steeped in the theological sciences would raise them out of the humiliation and poverty the Conqueror had relegated them to. These hopes of theirs led me to believe that his piety, too—just like everything about Bayezid—was no accident.

My estimation of our future ruler is not something I have cobbled together today, with the hindsight of history. I held it even then, when Mehmed Khan sent his sons away as *beylerbeys*, or provincial governors, one to Amasya, and the other to Konya.

This has been interpreted in different ways: he was afraid of a sonly conspiracy and internecine war, or the sultan wanted his young sons to learn to govern. I suspect I have understood the real reason. Mehmed Khan was so firmly melded to life and to everything he took from it, everything he still meant to get from it, he did not want to have his final judgment always before his eyes: sons waiting for their father's death so as to become rulers themselves. And here's another detail for you: Mehmed Khan kept his grandsons as hostages in Stambul, which makes me believe the rumors to some extent. Mehmed Khan did not leave things to chance; he always took charge of his own fate and—even at the height of his powers—he never missed an opportunity to further secure himself.

Despite my loathing of Bayezid, whose ascension—I had no doubt of this—would set us far back, I was obliged to inform him of the day's sorrowful news and to hold the capital until he could come to take up power.

Very simple, at first glance. Even if a revolt broke out in Stambul, I would be blameless; it was inevitable. So what worried me then? you ask. I can't hide it; it came to light only a day later: I did not want Bayezid for a sultan.

You suggest it was not my business to choose a sultan for the Ottomans. I know this. But we were far too bound to the deeds of Mehmed Khan, we had given him our best years, our blood. Who could convince me that something that had cost me so dearly was not my business?

I also admit that on the morning of May 3, I was still struggling to outwit fate. The fact that I hid Mehmed Khan's death should not be seen as disobedience to the Şehzade Bayezid. On the contrary, he should thank me for putting off the Janissary revolt until his ascension to the throne.

When we reached Skoutari on the Bosporus, I purposely made the porters and baltaci get on the barge along with the litter. The two battalions of Janissaries followed us in several large skiffs.

The streets were nearly deserted—the army was still encamped at Hunkar Cayiri. At the time, few civilians lived in Stambul; the city had not recovered from the long sieges and the conquest. The few passersby bowed low to the ground before the litter; the Conqueror's heavy hand bobbed as if in greeting. Feeling faint, I led my horse and prayed for us to reach Topkapi as soon as possible.

The guards in front of the palace hurried to open the gates. We passed through the three empty courtyards—even the troops usually stationed at court were in Hunkar Cayiri—and finally I found myself in front of Mehmed's private chamber.

In the third courtyard I was again alone with Yunus and the baltaci. I ordered them to unload the corpse and place it on the sultan's bed. I felt as if a mountain had lifted from my shoulders when I turned the key twice in the lock of the sultan's private chamber.

Outside, the porters, the baltaci, and Yunus were waiting for me. Without a word, I pointed them toward the new treasury. I knew there was nothing inside—Mehmed Khan had not succeeded in transferring his treasure from Yedi Kule. Now everyone who had accompanied the sultan on his final journey filed one after another into the dark vestibule of the treasury. I turned that key and hung it on my belt next to the other one.

Done!

Only then did I realize how my legs and arms were trembling. I was shaking. What had I gained with all this effort? A lot. Time. I had to use my winnings wisely.

I wrote the letters myself in the *divanhane*, the receiving hall. I had never written anything so long; there were scribes for this sort of work.

After I finished the first letter, I sat there for a long time in the twilight of the divanhane. I gathered my strength for the second letter, for my death sentence. Whichever of the sultan's sons took the throne, he would not forgive me for writing both of them at the same time, for playing both sides.

I almost decided just to leave the first—to Bayezid. *Why not just stop here?* I thought, knowing very well that I would not stop. Bayezid's success spelled my doom in any case. I was a member of the sipahi after all. Hadn't I taken part in Mehmed Khan's measures against our clerics? You might say that my decision was not so fateful; my song had already been sung.

When I realized this, I felt relieved. I quickly cobbled together the second letter. Short, only a few words. I tucked it under my turban and went out with only one scroll in my hand. I immediately found the messenger I needed: a trusted man, unschooled in letters. He needed to ride quickly, changing horses at every way station, to Amasya. "At every way station!" I repeated. According to my calculations, that would make an eleven-day journey.

The second messenger took me much longer to find. They all seemed unworthy of being entrusted with my life—until I realized that Yunus would be the best man for the job. I released him alone from the treasury, stripped him naked, and stuck my letter to his black skin.

"Dead or alive," I whispered in Yunus's ear, yet it felt like I was shouting and all of Stambul could hear me. "But better to make it to Konya alive. Don't change horses only at the way stations, but every three hours. Avoid meeting anyone, hide as if the earth had swallowed you up! You'll be in Konya in a week. Here is plenty of money; slip it to whomever you need to. Don't you dare hint that I sent you, you hear? You don't know me, you belong to no one! In Konya you'll look for Cem."

From the early morning I hadn't dared to let that name (Cem!) even slip into my thoughts, even though I had wheedled Allah for help, for the sake of Cem, for the sake of Mehmed Khan's great deeds. "God, watch over the black mute. Watch over your soldiers. What is the displeasure of a few hundred mullahs and kadis who have had their juicy bone taken away from them? You don't need prayers, God, but rather victory for our faith. And we will give it to you."

Truly, I have never prayed as fervently, with my whole heart, as I did that day. And immediately I must add: God did not hear my prayers. Perhaps Mehmed Khan's audacities and our clerics' destitution had indeed infuriated Him.

During the hours that followed, I was no longer alive—I had turned into a numb stick of wood. I walked around amidst people, I answered their questions, but I was not there. My entire mind was with Yunus.

God punished me, verily, for my meddling in these worldly events, but He also spared me something: the waiting. It ended on the evening of the very next day.

Shut away in my residence (I made sure not to be seen outside), I could hear the clamor rising from afar—almost imperceptible, you could mistake it for thinned silence. But I was already all ears, so it didn't fool me: an army was entering the streets of Stambul? What army? The one from Hunkar Cayiri, there was no other. The camp had learned of Mehmed Khan's death and they had hurried to the capital, so as not to miss out on the looting and burning. All my attempts to divide Asia from Europe were in vain—the day before I had already ordered not a single boat to cross the strait in either direction.

I anticipated that by evening I would find myself in a better world as the first victim of the revolt. But Allah wanted me to pay for my sins with yet another night of agony. All night I could hear the screams from the Jewish and Greek quarters; all night I watched the reflection of the fires on the Bosporus. Fleeing didn't cross my mind—my residence was surrounded by Janissaries. But even if they had not been there, I wouldn't have run. Why? Only to die a week later, on the orders of the new sultan?

As unbelievable as it may seem to you, I did not attempt to escape for another reason as well: since things had taken this turn, I truly did need to go. Because I was part of Mehmed Khan's time, because I would have no place in a differently ordered empire under Bayezid. They would not have tolerated me, and I would not have tolerated them.

I met my death—I daresay—calmly. My only regret was the thought that perhaps I had dragged in my fatal wake the one whose triumph I would have gladly perished for; I was afraid I had misled Cem, the hope of Mehmed's soldiers. If you can convince me that it was not my deed that launched him on his journey, then I will not regret that I was called back from oblivion.

But you remain silent. It seems that you do not know who the prime force behind Cem's revolt was. Or else you suffer no pangs of conscience over a long-dead old soldier.

I'm finished. I cannot be a witness to what happened after May 5, 1481. They killed me at five o'clock in the evening.

TESTIMONY OF ETEM, SON OF IZMET,
ABOUT THE EVENTS
THAT OCCURRED BETWEEN MAY 8 AND 22, 1481

THE BLACK MUTE was brought to me at noon on the eighth. He was brought by Ahmed, baltaci to our master Sinan Pasha, the beylerbey of Anatolia.

"What made you think to catch this fellow, much less bring him to me?" I asked. I was the *baltacibashi*, the head of the guard, and I didn't take kindly to being disturbed for any reason.

"He's hiding something," Ahmed replied. "Search him yourself and you'll see, for God's sake!"

"So why is he silent as a stump?"

Ahmed elbowed the wretch, and the latter opened his mouth wide to show his cut-out tongue. "Since he's mute, since he's running like hell, and since he swerved toward the woods right before he reached the city, what would you think, huh?" Ahmed said.

"True." At last I started to vaguely catch on. "Only viziers keep mutes.... Shut that mouth of yours!"

I grabbed the mute by the shoulders and gave him a good, hard shake. He cringed, obviously expecting a beating. But he kept silent, how could he not keep silent? He had no tongue, after all.

"Untie his hands, let him show us with signs. Where were you going, huh?" By the way the mute hung his head and huddled into himself, I could tell: he knew he didn't have enough brains to try to weasel his way out of this and so would take a beating. Enough of this haggling!

"Listen!" I lifted his chin with my fist so he couldn't hide his eyes. "I'm going to ask, and you're going to answer. Did the sultan send you? Or the grand vizier?"

A lot of good my questions did! The mute just stared like an idiot.

"Strip him and stretch him! He'll remember right quick whose servant he is!"

I went to get my bruisers, but Ahmed called after me. "Baltacibashi, a note fell out! It was under his shirt."

Well, well, a note! But why entrust it to a mute? There are Tatars for such things. Clearly someone did not want it known that they were sending a note. And Ahmed had caught him so quickly the mute didn't have time to swallow the message.

I left the two of them there in the cell, while I ran to my master's *kahya*, his steward.

"Is the pasha at home? I have something to report."

"He's home," the kahya said. "Go in."

As for Sinan Pasha, in case you're asking, he was the real deal. They say he used to be a Greek. They took him when they were rounding up boys for the Janissaries. Later he made his mark and became an agha, and as agha he got into Mehmed Khan's good graces during the battles for Stambul. He was a Greek, after all; he was right at home, he knew the language, the roads, so he helped a lot. Then Mehmed Khan gave him—what's the word for it again?—not his own daughter, but the daughter of the woman who had borne Bayezid to Mehmed Khan. The sultan had later given her to some bigwig, and she'd had a daughter by him. So, without being of royal blood, she was still Şehzade Bayezid's sister.

After the wedding, things really took off for Sinan Agha, to the point that he became Sinan Pasha and bounced around as the governor of a few sanjuks until he finally got the Anatolian beylerbeylik. During the time you're asking about, Sinan Pasha must've been around fifty. What else can I say about him?—he wasn't an easy master to serve, demanding as well as stingy, may he rest in peace. That's why I was hoping if I brought him some really important news, he might loosen up his purse strings a bit, if you catch my drift.

I found him napping in the *selamlik*, the men's hall. He'd run himself ragged for several days rounding up the Yuruk tribesmen (we'd already sent the sipahi to Hunkar Cayiri) and was facing a journey of his own—in a day or two he himself would set off on a campaign.

"Pasha," I said, "we've caught a runner, a mute. We found a message on him, so I've brought it to you."

Sinan Pasha jumped off the low couch and grabbed the note out of my hands.

"Call the kahya!" he ordered. I called him.

"Read!" he commanded.

No one ordered me out, so I stayed and listened.

"To my glorious master. Today on the fourth day of the month Rabī' al-Awwal in the year 886, the most sublime Sultan Mehmed

Khan Gazi went to his divine rest. His death has been hidden from the army, which is encamped at Hunkar Cayiri. I remain at the command of my glorious master."

"Who is this glorious master?" Sinan Pasha snatched the message back and peered at it, as if trying to read it. "Isn't there any name? Who wrote it and to whom?"

"There is no name," the kahya replied.

"But how?" Only now did Sinan Pasha realize what he had heard. "So Mehmed Khan has died, is that right? Could this be some kind of trick?"

"It's the truth, that much is clear," the kahya said, "since-someone was in such a hurry to report it, and in secret, no less."

"I think I can guess why it's a secret. If they were telling Bayezid, my kinsman, why would they hide it? They're telling someone else. The question is who? Do you know?"

I figured it out before the kahya. We soldiers might be simple, but we have a better sense of these things. Rumors had long spread through our ranks that Mehmed Khan had not yet decided whom to leave his empire to and for that reason had sent both of his sons far away. The nobles and the mullahs strongly supported Bayezid, while Cem was our man, the army's choice. So Mehmed Khan's mind was divided.

As soon as Sinan started shouting, I immediately thought, *The letter is for Cem.* But I kept silent. Now that Sinan Pasha is no longer with us, I can tell you. I hoped he would not guess whom the letter was for; otherwise things would be bad for Cem. But for all the pasha lacked in brains, he made up for in loyal stooges.

"Those Stambul blackguards are calling for Cem," the kahya told him.

"Well now!" Sinan Pasha's mouth hung open. "How dare they. Don't they know they're playing with fire? This country has laws, as well as those who enforce the laws."

Too bad, I thought to myself, *such is Cem's luck. Of all the pashas in Anatolia, his letter had to fall into the hands of the only one who supports Şehzade Bayezid. And why? Is it because he has such a great love for his country? No, it's because he'll become the sultan's brother-in-law, that's why. But it is what it is. This business is not our business.*

Sinan Pasha and his kahya had drawn aside and were whispering. I couldn't hear the plans they were hatching, but at one point my master turned to me.

"Etem," he said. "Finish off the mute immediately. No need to torture him; everything is clear. This very day you and the kahya will ride for Amasya with two dozen men. You'll find Şehzade Bayezid and you'll give him this letter. I'll arrive four days from now in Hunkar Cayiri. Tell Bayezid Khan that he can always count on my sword."

And so it came to pass. By that evening we had set off. The kahya carried the message, and I had to guard him on the journey, lest he somehow be killed!

Later, when Bayezid Khan became our sultan, I often thought back to our days and nights on the road to Amasya. I realized, to a certain extent I, too, had helped Bayezid Khan take his throne. I pondered it with a sense of guilt; it gnawed at me. Did I really not know what awaited us under Bayezid? Why didn't I do anything, why didn't all the soldiers not do anything to stop him? For days on end a man rode ahead of me carrying that important letter to the Şehzade—I could have knocked him off just like that and then taken to my heels.

It's easy to look back in hindsight, after it's clear how everything played out. Besides, look at it through a true believer's eyes: how could a good Muslim raise his hand against divine law? By law, the throne was Bayezid Khan's; it was his right. Who was I, Sinan Pasha's baltacibashi, to meddle in such big things?

So I rode behind our pasha's kahya, protecting him. We arrived in Amasya without incident. This was on May 12 at midday. As it turned out, just a few hours earlier a messenger had arrived from Stambul carrying the same news. By the time we reached the streets of Amasya, they were swarming with people. Everyone had come out to see how Bayezid would pass through the city, dressed in black. That was our custom.

The crowds were thick before we reached the Şehzade's residence, since he had already come out. It was then I saw Bayezid for the first time, before that I had only heard tell of him.

The sultan's son left his residence on foot, barefoot no less. This last bit, they say, was not normal, but he did it to show the deep humility of his grief. The Şehzade was wearing a black robe without any decoration, which reached to the ground and was belted with a cord. His turban was also black.

We managed to squeeze our way forward, so I saw Bayezid up close. I must say I had also seen Mehmed Khan—he always rode at the head of his troops when rallying them for a campaign, thus every one of our soldiers knew him. Bayezid Khan did not look like his father at all. He was also short, but not fat—he was shriveled, as shriveled as a hermit. That's probably why of all the manly pursuits, he had only mastered archery, which didn't take much strength, nor much courage—you're far from the enemy, after all. While we watched the procession, the Şehzade's

VERA MUTAFCHIEVA

bare feet struck me as ridiculous. It was clear he wasn't used to going barefoot; he stepped as if walking over a thorn patch. His feet resembled flutes—as thin as could be, with pointed heels and narrow soles. Downright womanly. Same with his hands. He had crossed them over his belt, which added the finishing touch to his dervish-like look. And in the face Bayezid Khan was also an absolute dervish or mullah. Pale, somehow pensive. They say he had quite the sharp mind, so much so that it drained his strength. But then again, Mehmed Khan was no fool, yet he had a neck like a bull!

Be that as it may, we watched the procession, which, after making the rounds of the wealthiest quarters of Amasya, returned to the residence. We followed along after him.

We waited with our kahya in the courtyard, with the servants. Bayezid had few servants, and even fewer horses. Rumors among the troops had long since had it that the Şehzade was tightfisted, and there appeared to be some truth to this. Otherwise, why wouldn't a sultan's son keep a few dozen horses, hm?

They did not feed us, nor water our horses—everything in that courtyard in Amasya was as miserly as you can imagine. So we milled around on the cobblestones, waiting for our kahya, and he took quite some time.

When he came back down the stairs, his head was swelled to bursting. He was clearly overjoyed that he'd picked just the right time to show the new sultan how well he served him.

"Give me one man. He and I will catch up with Sinan Pasha in Hunkar Cayiri," he told me with urgency.

"But what should we do?"

"Stay here. You'll go with Bayezid Khan to Stambul."

"Why?"

The kahya glanced around and then whispered in my ear, "Don't you get it? Bayezid Khan is holding you as hostages to ensure Sinan Pasha's loyalty."

"As if the pasha would give a rip if Bayezid slaughtered us. Why aren't you staying with us?"

"I've got an important task. I'm carrying a letter. And you know what it says? Three words. Bayezid Khan thinks I'm illiterate, so he wrote it in front of me. 'Strangle Cem quickly.'"

The kahya peered at me, narrowing his eyes. He might have thought that I'd be shocked and sorry for Cem—after all, I'm a soldier and the son of a soldier.

"Mind your own business," I told him. And that's the truth—what should I care? "Bayezid Khan knows best."

"That's right. That's what I say too," the kahya agreed. An hour later he and a guard rode away.

But Şehzade Bayezid waited until the evening to set off for Stambul. He readied his troops as if for battle. He had many men. I doubt Mehmed Khan had known how many soldiers his supposedly stingy and pious son kept. And they didn't look shabby at all, Bayezid's men.

As for us, Sinan Pasha's baltaci, they scattered us among the others. If I tell you we rode for Stambul day and night—nine days and nights in all without stopping—you'd think it a lie. But that's how it was; we slept in our saddles. For us soldiers, it was grueling. But that's how the Şehzade rode too. Then I saw with my own eyes that Bayezid was not who the army took him to be—he was not "Granny Bayezid." I don't think even Mehmed Khan—may he rest in peace—would have survived such a ride.

VERA MUTAFCHIEVA

And not once during those nine days did Bayezid's expression change, not once did he allow anyone a glimpse into his pious little soul. Say what you want, but this is no small thing.

On the morning after the tenth night we were in Skoutari. Bayezid did not pass through Hunkar Cayiri, even though the detour cost him a few extra hours. I realized why: he was looking to avoid all dealings with the army until after his coronation.

From the banks of Skoutari, Stambul looked peaceful; only two or three neighborhoods had been burned down. Şehzade Bayezid's troops spread out along the banks—everyone wanted to get a glimpse of what awaited us in Stambul. Bayezid ordered two of his aghas to cross over and tell the palace that the new sultan was waiting before his capital.

The two of them didn't look as if they appreciated this honor—they were afraid. But still, they went. How the Şehzade had the patience to wait for them, I don't know—even I had started sweating by that point.

Right ahead of the aghas, across from us we could see a commotion. People, Janissaries were running toward the pier. What was all this now? Had they come to destroy us or welcome us? But the whole business soon became clear, because a procession appeared, coming from Topkapi Palace. "That can't be a bad sign," I told myself.

The city's leaders, along with the Janissaries and plenty of townsfolk, piled into whatever they could find at the pier—boats, ships, rafts. In an instant they covered the Straight such that you couldn't even see the water. And how could you have seen it? In the very front rowed the boats of various viziers. Then Şehzade Bayezid ordered his men to get in.

I boarded one of the first boats, as it happened. We were rowing just behind the barge carrying Bayezid, horse and all. When our boats met others coming toward us in the middle of the Straight, a hullabaloo rose to the skies. Hollering at the top of their lungs, the people of Stambul welcomed the Şehzade, who had today become sultan. You might say that all our fears and haste were in vain—Stambul had proclaimed Bayezid as our *padishah*.

Oh, what a weight lifted from my shoulders! Even though, as I already told you, I was far from thinking Bayezid was a boon for us, nevertheless everything was as it should be, by law. What are we humans? Grains of sand at the feet of Allah. Once he has made his will clear, we had best uphold it. That's what many others told themselves as well, I realized, so they enthroned Bayezid as our sultan, may his days be long and glorious!

Bayezid Khan, accompanied by Ishak Pasha (he had taken over as grand vizier after Mehmed Pasha had been killed a week earlier), stepped onto a gilded barque, while the people cheered all the louder.

On the far bank we lost sight of the sultan. He rode ahead, while we stayed behind; they didn't even let us into Topkapi. They told us to sleep in the little Greek houses that had been abandoned after the victory, because Bayezid Khan had ordered that no soldier leave Stambul until he had taken the throne. So I had to wait in the capital that day; I could not return to my master. Thus, I also saw the great celebrations.

First off, Bayezid Khan ordered the start of preparations for his father's funeral. They say that by three weeks after his death Mehmed Khan was in very bad shape—May is a warm month in

Stambul. In any case, they sealed him up in a lead casket, gilded the outside with gold, and that was that.

That coffin was completely covered in expensive rugs. The viziers carried him, and among them was Şehzade Bayezid, again dressed in black and barefoot. While the nobles glittered in silk and gold brocade, their sovereign looked like an Anatolian beggar. And the people saw something holy in that; they hurled themselves prostrate before him and kissed the soles of his feet. Some even brought the sick out of their houses to bask in his blessing.

Well, there was no blessing to be had. Bayezid Khan only played at being a saint; everyone knew he wasn't. But the mullahs were pressing close around him, they didn't let him out of their sight for a second. I remember there was always a crowd of sipahi and Janissary aghas around Mehmed Khan; he always looked like he was riding out on a conquest, while Bayezid Khan's suite from the very first day resembled a madras: priests and scribes, every sort of dervish scum, may Allah forgive me!

Let's just say Mehmed's burial was no lavish affair. Bayezid was clearly rushing. As soon as the coffin reached the cemetery, several of his men tossed a dozen basketfuls of small coins to the crowd, while Bayezid Khan retired to Topkapi to continue his mourning.

That same evening, we learned that the mourning period wouldn't last long, even though divine law demanded three days. Bayezid ordered that his accession to the throne be announced the very next morning. He was rushing, like I said, because the first rumors about Cem had already reached Stambul.

They were vague. Who knows if there was any kernel of truth in them? They said Cem had refused to lay down his life before his brother's throne, in defiance of the law. These rumors alarmed Bayezid Khan, thus he hurried along his own accession.

The next day, the mufti brought another crowd and declared Bayezid our lawful ruler. This time the sultan was no longer in black; they had dolled him up so he looked almost handsome with that white, brooding face of his, with his thin eyebrows and red beard.

We feasted our eyes on our new padishah, and he again ordered his men to toss us small coins, and the deed was done.

From here on I don't have much to tell. I stayed in Stambul, because the sultan did not free his brother-in-law's hostages right away. Bayezid Khan was clearly afraid of Cem and didn't trust the Anatolian pashas. The last thing I saw was Ayas Pasha setting off for Anatolia with the Janissaries.

Here in the capital they still didn't believe Cem would actually meet his brother's troops in battle, but Bayezid was not asleep at the reins. That's how it is: one man might count on his luck, and everything falls into place on its own, while another man lives always on his guard, he doesn't dare close his eyes to doze off—he has to arrange every little thing himself, to earn everything with his own sweat and blood. Bayezid was of the latter type—nothing simply fell into Bayezid Khan's lap.

So much for my tale; it tells you next to nothing. But we were the small fish, we didn't have a hand in the sultan's dealings. Now you say that the great era of Mehmed was built on people like us, that Mehmed Khan shocked the world because he depended on us and our goodwill. Likely that's true; you read books, you know best. But we didn't know it. Otherwise, we might have done things differently.

FIRST TESTIMONY OF THE POET SAADI,
CEM'S DEFTERDAR

SURELY THE FIRST thing you'll ask is how I, a poet by calling and profession, came to serve Cem in this most unsuitable post of *defterdar*, or bookkeeper. I would like to immediately disabuse you of this misconception: with Cem, there was no such thing as an unsuitable post; with Cem, there was no post not held by a poet or a singer. Unbelievable, yet perfectly true. It seems that I will have to briefly describe to you that strange court in Karamania—the court of Şehzade Cem.

Back when Mehmed Khan sent his younger son to govern Karamania, Cem was just twenty years old. For you, that is almost a boyish age, but in that devout empire, a person of twenty was already a father, a soldier, or a statesman, in short, a man.

When it came to my master, Cem, this was not entirely true; Cem looked younger than all of us, his peers. Sometimes at our parties, when Cem effortlessly drank us all under the table over the course of an evening, he liked to say with a laugh that he was getting younger and would keep getting younger, that he would outlive us all because his blood was not purely Turkish. Indeed, Cem was half-Serbian, on his mother's side, no less.

If you ask me, Cem had far more foreign blood than Turkish. He very distantly resembled his father, the great Conqueror. Perhaps in the aquiline hook of his nose or in his overly thick and jutting lower lip. Everything else was different.

Cem was tall—a trait few of our folk can boast of. Tall, broad-shouldered, with a narrow waist and hips, wiry, agile—back in our days in Karamania, Cem always reminded me of an unbroken stallion.

His face was also foreign to us—too light, wheat colored as we like to say. The reddish, tightly curled hairs that had surrounded the face of our deceased sultan had in Cem transformed into smooth gold. Like every true believer, my master always covered his head, but I—his closest companion for nearly two decades—often saw him bareheaded, and I must admit that my eyes never feasted on another beauty such as Cem, with his long silky locks, with his not high but wide and slightly angular white forehead, with the delicate arch of his almost joined eyebrows, which were darker than his hair. As for his eyes—suffice to say they were like the morning sun dancing on rushing water.

I understand—this is inexplicable to you. Your poems and songs tiredly praise female charms, as if all the beauty in the world comes together in woman. How blind you are! Is there anything more captivating than a man, than a young man, not yet coarse and heavy, whose every fiber quivers like a bowstring, who delights in his every movement, for whose springing step the world seems to have been created?

For you, such admiration passes as sick and shameful because you fill it with an expressly carnal content. Now I am the one who does not understand you; after all, we belong to different worlds. In our world, woman was something (not even someone) with which you could commune in a single and very simple way, with no choice, no searching, and no preference. We bought our women before seeing their faces. Sometimes we would get lucky—their faces would turn out to be tolerable. More often than not, things didn't go well. But in both cases, we were to be pitied, believe me, even though you overrate the advantages of the Muslim family. In both cases, we had to live side by side with an unfamiliar, unwanted object that had been foisted upon us. She produced children and to some extent this justified the nights wasted on her; she kept silent and this made the alienation tolerable. Nevertheless, the enormous, empty, insurmountable alienation remained, laden with hatred and hard feelings.

Most of us put up with it—those who had nothing to give and did not wish to receive anything in return. Besides, at that time we were a nation of warriors. The concept of "home" did not exist for them; they had no thoughts or dreams to share, only victories—you can splendidly share a victory with the warrior in the next tent over; after battles, chases, and hunts they did not have leftover rushes of emotion. An army of warrior-dervishes inundated the Old World. During its short breaks from war, this army raped, and only wed when the sultan dispersed it—then the army bought wives.

You may notice that I speak of "them" and not "us." We—Cem's court—were not soldiers, for all that Cem was our victorious army's idol. We were bards. We did not know the blissful exhaustion after a battle, yet we still experienced passions—joys and sorrows. We looked to project them onto someone else so that they would come back to us—deeper, richer—and be poured out in poetry.

That someone else could not be a woman. Our women were always willing, repulsively easy. Our disgust at the accessible diverted us, it led us back to our very selves. You find it unnatural, but we had to choose between two unnatural extremes: the isolation of our masculinity or the isolation of our spirit. We were poets, and thus our spirits would have frozen in solitude, so we preferred the former.

Forgive me for drawing you into ruminations so unseemly for you and your time. But you can count on me: Cem's closest, most steadfast, dearest companion. In another time, my role would be filled by the hero's wife or his beloved—only love causes you to feel through another person's senses, to suffer his pain and to think his thoughts. Let me not insult your hearing: I alone experienced such love for Cem. Thus, I knew Cem better than he knew himself.

During our time in Karamania, Cem was already a husband and father. He had bestowed this happiness upon one of his father's slave girls; I don't know her and have nothing to say about her. Cem himself saw her only rarely. She lived with his mother, the Serbian princess, in a residence outside Konya and looked after Cem's second child. His eldest son was being held by Mehmed Khan in Stambul.

Cem's court was located right in the old town, in the palace of the Karamanian prince whom the Conqueror had recently vanquished. His nobles, insofar as they had not been slaughtered, continued to serve our glorious empire.

The Karamanians were not part of our court's inner circle. Soldiers and statesmen, they helped Cem bring order to the province and force it into submission. During that time, we—and I mean the court—lived in a way rarely seen in our lands. We lived through thought and word, through beauty drawn from the East's most exquisite works.

From that whole East, bards and poets streamed toward Konya to be heard by Cem, to earn his high esteem or to win a prize. Cem kept a few of them with him (and here fate smiled on me). And since Mehmed Khan did not spoil his sons with a large allowance, Cem doled out to us the ranks of scribes, inspectors, counselors. We were not offended by these posts; they allowed us to be with Cem and to live the life I have described.

I cannot complain that fate has treated me cruelly. I truly suffered alongside Cem's suffering, I met my death by drowning at the age of thirty-eight, but I lived an extraordinarily colorful life for a true believer—you will become convinced of that yourselves by the end of my tale. And yet, when I turn back to my past, I feel its best part was there, in that strange little court of Şehzade Cem.

There were twenty of us, all young men. Most were poets; the singers among us were primarily itinerant bards who stayed a few weeks in Konya before continuing on their way.

Our days started late, that's what set them apart from soldiers' days. The sun was alredy high when we slipped out of our rooms one by one and slowly gathered in the palace's shady courtyard. Usually we found Cem already there; he slept quickly, as he liked to say—I've always envied him for that ability. We would all be somewhat tired after the sleepless night, our heads would be heavy, our every gesture sluggish. But Cem rose with the sun; he would gallop around outside Konya for a few hours and then come back to wake us up.

It will come as no news to you that Cem was one of the best wrestlers in the empire—this is a well-known fact. At the large fairs in Karamania, which draw in mountain shepherds as well as soldiers from three or four sanjaks away, I saw Cem beat them all in several rounds, one after the other, without taking a rest. And because some of us hinted to him that any tough would let himself be pinned beneath the knee of the sultan's son, Cem started going to fairs in disguise, without his suite or his honor guard—he wanted to earn his victory.

I only saw him defeated twice at those fairs. And both times Cem took it badly, as if his calling were to wrestling and not to poetry or statecraft. He loved being the best everywhere and in everything. Vainglory, they might say. But Cem wore it better than a silver-trimmed robe, because our young master seemed born for fame and success.

And so, in the mornings when we found Cem in the inner courtyard of the palace, our workday began. But it was not a workday—every one of our days in Konya was a holiday, a great holiday of the spirit.

Above all, we read—what readers we had! Ottoman poetry at that time was fragile, it was just taking its first steps and only a few made a living with it then. We lived and breathed Persian poetry—that eternally gushing font of wisdom and free thought, that unattainable model of exquisiteness.

Cem had a particular love for it; I have never met a man who was so intoxicated by poetry. To Cem, it was much more than song and incomparably superior to dance. Thus dancing girls rarely came to our court—Cem claimed that dance was an unclean art, its beauty easily slipped into lust. In the same way, he dismissed music—it was too broad, he would say; it excites you without passing through your mind, and it touches human superficiality above all. I always noticed: as soon as a bard began to sing, Cem lent an ear not to the voice, but to the words. The words! "There is no art more difficult and more precise, more elusive and more indirect, one that is simultaneously as far and as near to man as words"—that's what Cem would say. Words were his love, his sorrow, and his reward.

I remember our first task after Cem took me in. I was twenty-four then, and already well-known. Anyway, our first joint task was a translation of a Persian *diwan*. The Şehzade felt unsure in his Persian, so we worked together. I will never forget the solemn concentration with which Cem searched for words amidst his meager new Ottoman language, so as to pour into them the abundance of the Persian tongue.

We dedicated our translation to Mehmed Khan; he was known as a patron of exquisite speech, and he himself had written poems. And what poems they were. May Allah forgive me, but I have never heard more pathetic verses.

But the Conqueror couldn't stand a field where he had not tried his hand, thus he left his mark on poetry, too, under the pen name of Avni the Almsgiver. You might say that Mehmed Khan gifted us his works out of the kindness of his heart, but in his case, it didn't come from some internal need, no. In our culture, respect for the written word is simply a ruler's obligation.

The day Zeyneb Hatun, our one and only female poet, visited us is burned in my memory. The old woman was living in far-off Adana, or rather, was living out her life. With no family, no children, and no grandchildren, we took Zeyneb to be the incarnation of the unearthly word.

Her face, too, looked unearthly in its deep concentration; she did not hide it as did the rest of our women, as if trying to say with this that she stood beyond all temptation and desire, that she was not a woman, but rather a weapon in the hands of God.

Zeyneb had left Adana expressly to spend a few days in the poets' court, to bestow her blessing on Cem: "May God let me live to see the day when upon the throne of Osman, son-in-law of our first poet, Jalal al-Din Rumi, sits another poet: Cem Sultan!"—this is how she greeted my master when he helped her out of her litter.

I was next to Cem at that moment. I saw how the blood surged beneath his milky skin at this bold prophecy. Celebrated by three sultans, respected and praised, the old woman had allowed herself unheard-of license: while a ruler still lived, she had wished the throne on his son. And on his younger son, no less. And from the way Cem changed color several times, as if he were struck dumb, yet without lowering his adoring eyes from Zeyneb Hatun, from the way he nearly carried her in his arms—so carefully did he grasp the tiny old woman and set her on the ground—from all of that I realized that Zeyneb had uttered aloud Cem's innermost desire.

Until that day, neither I nor my companions from the court of Konya had given much thought to Cem's future. We didn't think about the future at all. Mehmed Khan was still in the prime of his life; he seemed immortal, riding the wave of our victories. Somehow unconsciously, beyond my loyalty as a faithful subject, I wished longevity on the Conqueror so that our happy days at Konya would last. Yet nevertheless—I realized for the first time that day—these days would come to an end. What then?

Then Cem, our idol, the model of youth, charm, and talent incarnate—Cem would be strangled. Don't speak to me of the law and crimes, don't remind me of the lessons of history! No power on earth could convince me to meekly accept such an end—a forced end—to something created to live and shine to the extent that Cem was. What benefit to our great empire could we possibly speak of if a twenty-year-old poet, a wrestler who seemed forged of gleaming bronze, was sacrificed for its sake—would this not be a sacrifice of thriving life itself?

The days Zeyneb Hatun spent with us passed like a dream. My newfound worry never left me for a moment. It was as if this universally revered old woman had spoken an evil omen and muddied the translucent cheer that hung over our court.

This worry weighed least of all on Cem; likely it was not new to him. Cem sat for hours with Zeyneb Hatun, listening to her poetry; Cem told her of his awe of Hafiz, a controversial poet whom many, including even the sublime Zeyneb, did not acknowledge.

The two of them were a wondrous sight during those days. The old woman—wisely exquisite even at her advanced age— and the magnificent, golden youth. You could not mistake them for teacher and student, to say nothing of mother and son. They were two laborers toiling together in the field of the word, lit up by the same fire, close beyond measure—as a mother and son could never be. I remember feeling jealous: Zeyneb was more to Cem than I was.

She soon took her leave. It was not seemly for a luminary such as herself to eat at the sultan's table for too long. Zeyneb retreated to her isolation and left me to my worries.

I dared not share them with Cem, since they surely had long since gnawed at him, and with great effort he had chased them from our cloudless days. Yet I tormented myself. I sought examples from the lives of great men; I was ready to turn all of history on its head so I could find some solution for Cem.

At one point I thought I had grasped a thin thread.

Do not laugh at what I will now say; try to understand us. We were not bandits, nor even soldiers. We lived with the conviction that we were bringing pure beauty into the world. We were not satisfied with a solution that would bring injustice, violence, or shame—we strove to reconcile our harsh law with our thirst to live. We needed to feel that we were in the right—this sets the poet apart from the man.

It was evening, one of our many evenings. We were again in the closed courtyard. It was summer, and the fountain gave off damp coolness. Fire from the torches flowed in its liquid streams, the water whined and begged for rest. The serving boys poured Shiraz wine into our cups, the dense scent of musk and perfume hung heavily over the paving stones—there was no breeze to dilute it.

We were lying around the fountain on pillows and skins, listening to Haydar reading. He was reading, not singing, yet he accompanied himself on saz—none of you know the magic of saz and verses, it goes beyond that of any song.

I was next to Cem. I could see the words possessing and overtaking him. Cem's pupils froze, while his skin seemed to grow thinner so as to absorb the words more easily. I saw how every swallow of wine passed beneath the smooth whiteness of his neck, flowing into the whole of Cem along with the poems.

And suddenly, more sharply than ever, I realized that Cem was a brief visitor among us; it would only take a single huff—the death of Mehmed Khan—and that bright fire would go out, and upon the earth would remain a large dark stain: the place once occupied by Cem.

"No!" I almost shouted aloud as the truth sliced through me like a spasm. It took me some time—Haydar's voice reached my ears as if from afar—to get ahold of myself.

I tilted my cup so I could see its bottom. Haydar finished. The others started chattering; some praised the reader, others were unsatisfied—Haydar hadn't given his all, they said. Cem kept silent; he was always the last to return from the land of poetry.

"Have we not had enough poetry this evening?" I asked, surprising even myself.

"Why do you say that?" Cem looked at me, as if just awakened.

"I feel like hearing something else," I said. "Something strong and not made-up. History, for example."

"Alexander again?" Cem's hazel eyes were laughing; he found my weakness for all things Alexander amusing.

"No," I said. "Something Byzantine. About the victories of Constantine Porphyrogenitus."

I knew very well that this Constantine was not famous for his victories, but I needed his name, just his name.

"You just rolled that off your tongue!" Cem laughed. "Por... how was it again?"

"Porphyrogenitus." The carefully learned name shot from my lips. "It means 'born in the purple.'"

"And what does 'born in the purple' mean?"

The others laughed.

"It's quite simple. The Greeks, like many other nonbelievers, have a law: the throne is inherited not by the eldest son, but by the first boy born after his father's accession, thus born to the royal purple, that's what it means. A man can't be a ruler"—I felt my voice rising to a shout—"if he is born to mere mortals. The difference between him and those born to the purple is the difference between the earth and the sky. When royal blood flows to you from both sides, when from your very first day..."

I could not go on. Cem was staring at me as if he would hug me or hit me. The others were flustered, likely by the feeling that I had thrown a stone into the calm waters of our existence.

"So what of it?" Cem said after some time. "This is a Christian law, is it not?"

"Yes." My throat was dry. And I thought about how Cem never said "nonbelievers," but "Christians." Perhaps he carried some unacknowledged awareness of his Christian half?

The serving boys again darted among us, pouring more wine; Haydar and the others began arguing, then someone started reading again. But I was watching Cem—Cem was not there.

When the night had almost given way to dawn—one of our countless happy nights in Konya—we wandered back to our rooms. The servants began gathering up the torches and a bluish twilight fell over the court. Dazed by the wine, by excitement and anguish, I was beneath the archway when I heard footsteps behind me. It was Cem.

"Saadi," he said. "Come here."

We returned to the courtyard and sat on the stone edge of the fountain. Its streams no longer flowed with fire, but with a bluish-silver glow.

"Saadi," Cem said. "You know what you have meant to me."

"Why 'meant'? Cem, my friend, do not shut me out! I don't want..."

"Stop! Just tell me, Saadi"—Cem placed his hand on my shoulder, and I could feel his warmth conquer me—"Tell me: why did you say that? I don't want to think that among my closest companions there is someone who is testing or watching me through you. If I allow for such suspicion, I am lost. So why did you say it?"

"For your sake," I wanted to answer. "Don't you see? I am looking for a way to save you from your doom. Because the sun would go out along with you..." That's what I wanted to say, but instead I said, "I must have had too much to drink, master. Ever since I had that fever, wine has gone to my head. I shouldn't have said it.... And yet, it is the truth. Forgive me if it was unseemly, but do not let doubts into your heart. I am not an enemy ear—I want to be the stone beneath your feet, Cem, my friend, such that you tread on me on your way to salvation."

I was almost crying. Wine was to some extent to blame for this business. Yet Cem did not seem to hear the last part of what I had said.

"So it's the truth, you say...." he began dreamily. "I've always thought we had something to learn from the Christians. Why, Saadi, do they have more of a sense of justice; why do they not accept the might of the single divine judge? Surely death cannot be the solution for anything whatsoever—it is simply an end. The end of good or evil, but not a judgment, not an escape."

He was talking about death in general, but thinking about his own death.

Don't be surprised that Cem uttered thoughts unseemly for a Muslim—indeed, he quite often said such things. I am afraid he was poorly acquainted with our divine law. This was due in part to his mother, the Christian, but it was due in a much larger part to the Persian poems. It is well-known that the Persians are heretics—they drink wine and pay far too much heed to earthly joys and sorrows. It is not for nothing that our clergymen rail against Persian verse—nothing undermines faith more than it does.

"Yes," I agreed quietly, as if I, too, were now afraid of eavesdroppers. "Death is not a solution. As long as he is alive, a man must seek another way. There is no way such seeking could be a sin, is there, my lord?"

Cem did not reply.

I have understood from Nisanci Mehmed Pasha's testimony that history considers him—the executed grand vizier—as the prima causa in Cem's rebellion. I would very much like for that to be the case, but it is not. It was not Nisanci Mehmed, who had not seen Cem since he was fourteen, but I who planted the seed of insurrection in Cem's soul; it was I who gave the push it so hungrily awaited.

I had vaguely sensed that Cem rebelled against the thought of the necessity of his death; I had seen how Cem trembled bodily at Zeyneb Hatun's bold blessing. But she still had not provided a justification for a rebellion against the law. I whispered this justification to Cem; he never would have undertaken anything if he had not felt himself in the right.

Forgive me, I must ask for a rest. Everything you have heard so far—the memories of our days and nights in Konya, the recollections of Zeyneb and Haydar, long-since deceased, and most of all, the memory of Cem and me trading a few words by the water —it all weighs heavily on me. More than what follows: the naked suffering.

SECOND TESTIMONY OF THE POET SAADI
ABOUT THE EVENTS
BETWEEN MAY 21 AND JUNE 15, 1481

AS YOU HAVE already learned, it was not the black mute who brought the news to Karamania. A sipahi, among those mustered at Hunkar Cayiri, jumped on his horse as soon as he heard the rumor and rode straight to our capital. Given that he didn't dare stop to change horses, and given that he had to rest at night, he lost a lot of time. So Cem learned of his father's death after Bayezid. This is far from the only example in which pure chance has decided the outcome of world events.

Since I had been present during all the important steps in Cem's life, God willed that I be by his side at that moment as well.

Our day had begun as usual. When we came out into the courtyard, we found Cem already there, invigorated from his morning ride. I went to him and kissed his shoulder, feeling the warmth radiating from his nearness. Ever since that night when the two of us spoke about Cem's inevitable death, I treasured our every hour together.

Cem is still here, thank God, I thought. *Cem is still warm!*

He gave me an affectionate glance, as if to remind me that I didn't need to greet him as my master.

"Saadi," he said, "I have heard nothing of your new diwan."

"Şehzade," I replied, "forgive your humble servant for being afraid to insult your hearing with an unfinished work."

Cem's happily distracted gaze was already jumping from Haydar to others and beyond.

"Friends," he said, "tonight we shall hear Saadi's new verses. That's an order!"

We had just sat down around the fountain and started chatting when a guardsman ran up.

"Şehzade," he said to Cem, "a messenger has come. He's looking for you."

My whole body bristled. This was it... this was it! My months-long nightmares were coming true. I only needed a single glimpse of the messenger—he was a simple sipahi, half-dead from the ride, covered in dust and sweat—to be certain.

I noticed that Cem was thinking the same thing. He went pale beneath his light tan; Cem could not utter a word.

"What is it?" Haydar broke the silence.

"Which of you is Cem Sultan?" the sipahi rasped, and from the mere fact that he called our master "sultan," everything became terrifyingly clear.

"I am!"

I was afraid I would faint.

With difficulty, the sipahi got down on bended knee. He lowered himself onto the cobblestones—dirty and exhausted as he was—and looked up at the Şehzade as if raising his face to the sun.

"It's the sultan," he whispered, clearly overwrought, "our lord and master. Steel your heart for bad news! The most glorious Mehmed Khan is no longer among the living. Take up the reins of our army, lead us where your father did not! The sipahi, the first pillar of our empire, are yours, my sultan!"

He had clearly rehearsed his short speech—it didn't come naturally to him. "Perhaps he's been sent by someone." I clutched at a straw. "The sipahi sense what Bayezid has in store for them and have backed Cem. Merciful God, please let it be so!"

"Stop! Stop and get up." Cem interrupted my prayers with an eerie indifference. "The Ottoman throne has an heir. Why have you not submitted to Bayezid?"

"Where will your brother lead this empire?" The sipahi was no longer whispering. "Down the mullahs' path, that's where! You all remember, don't you"—he now turned to the rest of us—"how the army lived before the times of the great Mehmed: without bread, without land. So the mullahs could have more. Will you abandon us to such indignities again, Cem Sultan? Who won glory for the Ottomans, who conquered the world? We, the footmen of the faith. We want you for our sultan, Cem!"

He was sent to us, I silently rejoiced. *You heard my prayers, God!*

Now Cem changed. The deathly pallor left his cheeks, and his eyes sized up the dusty sipahi as if trying to decipher what lay behind his outburst: treachery, conspiracy, loyalty?

We stood there like stones. And suddenly I heard my own voice—it was as if from a dream, as was everything on that day: "Master, you are obliged to hear your army. My purple-born master, do not leave our military glory in the hands of castrated dervishes. Your death warrant has already been signed, you have nothing to lose. Save the empire, Cem Sultan; it is your right!"

Yes, I said this. I admit it.

"My right," Cem repeated quietly. And then unbelievably loudly he said, "Do I have this right?"

"You do. You are fighting not only for your own life—it is expected of you, sultan. And who is Bayezid?" I continued, out of my mind. "The son of a slave girl, a bastard..."

"Leave me." Cem cut me off with disgust.

One by one, shaken to the core of our souls, we poets filed out of the courtyard. Now Cem needed soldiers.

Haydar caught up with me under the archway. "Saadi, what did you say?"

"The truth," I replied in despair. "Just the truth."

"It is against the law, your truth."

"The law is thought up by men, and so men can change it. Would you accept Cem's death?"

"No!" Haydar did not have to stop to think. "But Cem will run away, he will hide. You were doing more than just saving his life."

"He would never agree to run away. Cem is not made to hide. Haydar, could we, his closest companions, ever abandon him?"

"No." Haydar again shook his head. "Believe me, I will be Cem's first soldier. Despite the law."

We embraced. It felt like an oath.

It was almost noon before Cem finally ordered us to gather. We found the courtyard crowded: the Karamanian beys, aghas from Cem's troops. Dressed as if for a holiday, in all their regalia and medals. Yet their faces did not reflect the same magnificence—they were stern, almost glum. Cem stood out among them; he glowed with a new, unfamiliar light, more handsome than ever. As if the whiff of power alone had transformed him.

As soon as he saw us, Cem waved—come here! We noticed that our gait was no longer the same. We were not approaching our friend, but our sovereign.

"Put on soldiers' uniforms," he ordered us. "Get them from the guards."

This was a first for us. Haydar painfully squeezed himself into a pair of pants that were too tight for him; huffing and puffing, he buckled up a belt with sheaths for daggers and a saber. At any other time this would've earned him a good ribbing, but now we only hurried to help him suit up. "I present to you: Haydar Agha!" He joked, but nobody laughed.

Outside in the courtyard Cem was giving a speech to the Karamanians. I caught only the end of his speech—it stunned me.

"We cannot deprive our royal brother of that which he has taken—Rumelia. Because we do not wish for a fraternal war, we do not want to spill the blood of true believers. Even though he was not born under the purple, Bayezid has managed to usurp part of the empire, and I will not dispute his claim to it. But here, in Anatolia, the cradle of our glorious nation and the House of Osman, I will continue the deeds of Mehmed Khan. I will not allow Bayezid's rule in Anatolia! I shall revive our first capital—Bursa—and will lead the sipahi toward new conquests, so that each cavalryman shall have his own village. Let Bayezid return the land to mosques and imarets in Rumelia. Here in Anatolia we will continue the empire of warriors!"

Cem, my friend, I thought. *If you don't know, why don't you ask? A man should always demand the everything, so that he ends up with at least half. And why do you announce to your chieftains that you yourself are looking to split the empire? Is that the banner that will lead soldiers to victory? Why should Bayezid's blood stop you—do you really think yours would stop him?*

"I don't like this business," Haydar whispered in my ear. "Look at the beys."

I looked at them. Indeed, they didn't know what to think. They had hoped Cem would lead them to victory, so that the military law would stay in force. Now I suspected that their heads buzzed with less-than-pure thoughts: "Since Anatolia can be for the Anatolians, why can't Karamania be for the Karamanians?"

And what's more: from the very first moment, the older warriors saw Cem's struggle as somehow boyish, not well thought out. They quickly chalked this up to Cem's reputation—he was an excellent wrestler and a talented poet. But it was no longer a question of sparring and verses; far from it.

"Onward to Bursa!" Cem finished. His eyes were shining and his face blazed with inspiration. He didn't notice at all how the local leaders had received his speech.

"I don't like it," Haydar said again. "We should have gone about this business in an entirely different way."

Forgive me for going on a tangent, but I'd like to tell you something about Haydar. I used to wonder how a person like him could be a poet, and a good poet, at that—he was not the least bit fanciful, but instead grounded, simple, and precise in his reasoning. They say he came from a village, and if you ask me, it's true—it was the basis of all his strengths and weaknesses. Haydar's sober recommendations irritated me, yet—without meaning to—I always took them to heart. *Who knows*, I often thought afterward, *if Cem had chosen Haydar as his confidant instead of me, would things have happened as they did?* What Cem loved about Haydar was his poetry, but he would never show his true self to Haydar.

The Karamanian leaders left the courtyard in silence—they went to give orders and saddle up. I knew they would talk among themselves as soon as they were out of the courtyard. Haydar, who had been keeping an eye on them the whole time, immediately stood before our master in his too-tight, ridiculous pants.

"Sultan," he said, "allow me to go with them."

"Why?" Cem turned to him, his face still blazing.

"We need to know what they are up to. We are dependent on them."

"Haydar," Cem replied with impatience, "I am amazed a poet would suggest that. I trust my troops and their commanders."

Haydar merely shrugged. I was afraid that, as always, he would turn out to be right.

We set out in the late afternoon. Yakub Agha's sipahi rode in the very front. After them came the Karamanians, half tribesmen, half troops; their commanders led them, as focused as always, clearly reluctant. Then came Cem's suite of hastily recostumed singers and poets. Keeping ourselves in our saddles was pure agony; my whole crotch ached as if I'd been dropped from a great height straight onto my ass. As for Haydar, he swayed lazily; he'd already foisted his shield off onto an arms bearer so it wouldn't weigh him down.

We arrived at Bursa in three days and found the gates barred to us. A siege was out of the question—we were only four thousand men.

This first obstacle left Cem disconcerted. He had believed that all cities would welcome him with open arms and rejoicingly acknowledge him as their sovereign.

"Saadi," he called me to him, "we'll try to parlay. Go with Haydar and Yakub Agha and tell the governor of Bursa that the city will again become our capital. The dust of Osman, who lies in Bursa, will find peace when he sees its old glory restored."

"Look," Haydar told me on the way, "Cem needs to give us clearer instructions."

"His orders are clear enough to me as they are," I replied with irritation.

"They're not," Haydar insisted. "The governor will ask us what we want from Bursa—soldiers, bread, or meat. And whether we'll pay him. And we'll tell him that Bursa will be the capital. It's a weak move."

As much as Haydar's petty chatter annoyed me, it was thanks to him alone that we did not return empty-handed. Indeed, the governor—some old and feebleminded pasha put out to pasture here by Mehmed Khan, who got rid of his incompetent commanders in this way—met us with hostility. "We'll talk of that later," he kept saying. "It's never too late to declare Bursa the capital. Let's first see Cem as ruler and see Cem's empire!" Then the pasha underscored how Bursa had suffered from the battles between the Thunderbolt's sons and how they didn't want to find themselves in such a predicament a second time. Let Mehmed's sons resolve their argument on the open battlefield before the city, or better yet, far from it. Only then would Bursa, too, declare its loyalties.

And with that the governor would have sent us on our way if Haydar hadn't jumped in.

"We agree, pasha," he said, "but you must also agree that we've been on the march for three days. We will leave Bursa in peace, but in exchange Bursa will feed us in secret."

The pasha thought about it a moment and clearly saw the benefits of Haydar's suggestion. So, when we returned to the camp after dark, we led a long, fully loaded caravan.

News of our mission's failure to secure the city had preceded us, brought by a strange messenger: Seljuk Hatun, the favorite aunt of Mehmed the Conqueror. We found her with Cem. Seljuk Hatun was very old—she seemed as old as the House of Osman itself. But from her dark-yellow, wrinkled, shriveled face peered eyes that were youthful in their wakefulness.

Seljuk Hatun had come to our camp as soon as she heard Cem was nearby. Her weakness for the sultan's second son was well-known; Cem had always been the darling of all the living members of the Ottoman dynasty. Now he was sitting by her like a child, shamefaced, but knowing that much would be forgiven thanks to his charm.

"My aunt has told me," Cem said, turning to us, "that Ayas Pasha's troops have taken up beyond the city. Tomorrow will be the decisive battle."

"Decisive battle," Seljuk Hatun echoed mockingly. "There's nothing decisive about a battle between two armies of 5,000 men each, hm?"

I noticed that she did not at all act in a manner fitting a woman of the royal house. She did not mince her words, but spoke like an old soldier.

"This is only the beginning, I'll have you know," she started lecturing her nephew. "If he loses tomorrow, your brother will send ten times 5,000 soldiers. And if he loses those as well—expect a hundred times 5,000. Since you've made your decision, don't waste an instant; send messengers all around Anatolia and gather under your banner all the troops who are not already at Hunkar Cayiri, hm?"

She had a habit of always ending her sentences with that "hm?" which was not a question. Cem listened to her, all rapt attention; it was clear he was mulling over her advice. Thus I found his answer completely unexpected.

"No! I will not call for troops. The best of them are already in Hunkar Cayiri in any case. They were served to Bayezid on a silver platter. I would have to come against his army as an unlawful heir to the throne. The troops know only I will maintain the privileges they received from my father; they will come over to my side during the first battle. Hear me well, Seljuk Hatun: I want to rule not as self-appointed, but as anointed."

The whole time he spoke, the old woman was shaking her head as if to emphasize that Cem was spewing complete and utter childish nonsense. She kept silent, then finally spat, "If anyone else had spoken to me like this, I would have told him flat out: you're cracked! But it is none other than Cem who speaks thus, and Cem was born with a star on his brow. The heavens—not your mind or your strength—will not allow you to be vanquished."

The old woman turned to us, only now deigning to acknowledge our presence. "There are such ones, people who succeed in spite of all the rules. The lucky ones. Cem bears that great luck of the Ottomans. Let us hope it does not desert him, even though Cem talks nonsense."

VERA MUTAFCHIEVA

Insulted, Cem's face blazed up. And again his soft but firm words stunned me. "I cannot be any other way, aunt, or else I would become Bayezid. And why should I? Bayezid already exists—there's no point in me imitating him. Let the troops decide! The loser will suffer their judgment. I don't want to beg anyone. I, son of the great Conqueror, am within my rights."

We saw off Seljuk Hatun that evening, and in the morning the battle with Ayas Pasha began.

You'll forgive me if I don't dwell on the battles; that is not my job. Here in the East we have special bards for military stories and poems, and I am not one of them. I took part in Cem's battles as a self-taught soldier, thus to me they seemed more terrifying than a slaughterhouse, and I do not wish to recall them. In any case what is important to us are not the battles themselves, but their outcome. And I can tell you straightaway that the first battle against Ayas Pasha's forces ended in our absolute victory.

Well, what do you know, Haydar was wrong—he had predicted our defeat, hadn't he? Cem's words, the ones the old woman found so foolish, came true: the sipahi led by Ayas Pasha switched over to our side.

An hour later, when the pasha was fleeing for the forested hills—with barely three hundred Janissaries left of his forces—I saw Cem up close. Our master did not hide his happiness; he laughed loudly, joking around with the turncoats in a most nonlordly manner; he tossed his fur-lined broadcloth jacket over the shoulders of their military governor; he hugged each one of them individually.

Our army—now around ten thousand strong—was eating an afternoon meal when a crowd approached from the city, led by a few dozen of the city leaders. As soon as they drew near, we recognized the governor of Bursa as well. It was clear without a word: Bursa was opening its gates to the victor.

The victor! This word intoxicated Cem more wildly than Shiraz wine. Cem was still in his spurs and chain mail of delicate rings, surrounded by his commanders—surrounded by us.

With some newfound grandeur, he let those city leaders kiss his feet; with a voice no longer filled with laughter, he ordered the leaders of Bursa to rise.

I knew him very well and can confirm: if Cem had won that victory by force, he would not have been so triumphant. Cem wanted to impose himself with his name, with rumors of his exceptionalness.

We entered Bursa the next morning. Cem had ordered his troops to rest well and get themselves back into shape. He wanted to reawaken in our old capital all of its wounded pride—to present a sultan and an army worthy of Bursa.

When I remember it now, there was something unbelievable about our Bursa days. About the very way they welcomed us.

The whole of Bursa was out on the streets, down to the babes in arms and the infirm. From every window, balcony, and wall hung carpets, embroidered cloths, even silk blankets, robes, and towels—the city was bedecked to the tips of its dozen minarets. And what weather! May. Lush walnut and fig trees peeked over the stone walls; the grapevines reached out young, shiny green tendrils. The nearly black cypresses pierced this drunken, jubilant greenery, amidst which heavy magnolia blossoms glinted white and the acacias shone yellow. And the lilacs? Why have you not seen Bursa in its May lilacs?

Amidst that whole spring holiday that covered the centuries—the stony grayness of Bursa—ran another spring. Our master, whose suite did not include anyone over the age of twenty-five, lit up Bursa with his joy. Young, handsome, talented, adored by God, Cem had reached the pinnacle of human happiness.

True, fate did not smile on him alone; other Ottomans—Orhan, Murad, Bayezid the Thunderbolt—had also reaped victories and led chains of slaves and caravans piled with loot to Bursa. But God had not given to any of them such happiness at the age of twenty-two; he did not unite for anyone else victory and youth.

The Old Palace welcomed us. I shivered as I stepped across its threshold. Stambul is exceptional—there is no city like it. But for us Ottomans, Bursa is even greater still: a holy place. Here lie the remains of our first sultans. The Old Palace bore witness to our earliest history: how a half-savage tribe of herdsmen gave rise to an empire that threatened the whole world.

Everything in the palace at Bursa was made of stone—that's how I remember it: a dense, impressive coldness. It clearly showed that the palace was built by rulers who did not value the lilacs, but rather grasped everything by force, power, and conquest. Cem stood out so clearly against it, like a golden agate in a rough granite cliff.

During those days, Cem was tirelessly in action, giving commands; he was focused, eternally concerned. He was learning how to rule. After Cem declared himself sultan (the second in a week!)—albeit skipping the elaborate ceremonies—he ordered silver coins with his seal to be minted and a prayer for his well-being to be read every day in the mosques.

And nothing more. That's all it took to become a ruler in our lands, and for that reason he has gone down in history as Cem Sultan. A sultan whose power was limited to one city and eighteen days.

During those days, soldiers were coming to Bursa. With every new arrival, Cem gave us a look that said, "I told you so!" I honestly don't know whether he noticed that these soldiers were not nearly as numerous as he had predicted and as we had hoped. They were ragged bands of 20 to 50 men, nomadic Turkmen or Yuruk clans who had come to our capital—to the heart of the rebellion, as they likely thought—with their wives, herds, and children in tow. With such a ragtag force you could hardly hold on to power, let alone seize it.

We had gathered no more than 15,000 warriors when—it was already mid-June—news reached Bursa: Bayezid Khan II was approaching our capital with the troops from Hunkar Cayiri.

"Do you know what that means?" Haydar asked me. "Those are the elite forces of the empire, all of them. Of course, they gathered in the Conqueror's name for new conquests, and Bayezid received them ready to go."

"Who knows?" I countered. "Perhaps half of them will see their future with Cem Sultan."

Haydar didn't think this was likely. "Why do you imagine that soldiers think so much?" he said. "Once they've been rallied and led off to war—that's that."

I didn't need to hear Haydar's words to feel alarmed. Only Cem was untouched by worry. He spent the day with his troops, talking to their commanders, planning the impending battle. There was some kind of madness in his attempts to forget the

VERA MUTAFCHIEVA

truth—the number of his brother's troops, the experience of their pashas, Bayezid's lawful right to lead and win this battle. Cem—the glittering darling of fate—stubbornly believed that reality was obliged to step back and gift him with an unbelievable victory.

Toward evening, the scouts in the mountains sent word that Bayezid had pitched his camp three hours from Bursa; Bayezid wanted an open battle.

We were outside the city walls when Cem learned this. I could see that this confounded him—he had hoped for a long siege, during which all sorts of changes within Bayezid's army were possible. It would help skew attitudes in our favor; Cem was not ready for a direct fight.

On the road to the Old Palace—we were going back—Cem was silent, lost in thought. But just as we were before the doors, he turned to me. "Please, Saadi, go call Seljuk Hatun."

I NEVER LIKED going to bed early. For a well-nigh ninety-year-old woman, the bed is like the grave. Once again that night, it promised me no rest. In the morning, the armies of my brother's grandsons would go to war. How could I sleep before such a morning, hm?

When they told me some Saadi had come looking for me, I was just mulling over my nephew's foolishness in making fratricide the law of our house. I believe that Mehmed Khan had the best interest of the empire in mind, but to me the best interest of our family was no less important. And even the humblest shepherd knows that a breed improves if you let the finest animal from each lambing reproduce. So from whence this certainty that the firstborn is necessarily the best? Why did Mehmed himself need to castrate the House of Osman by pruning all its side branches?

That's men's reasoning for you, I thought back then, and I still do now. A woman would never stoop to the narrow-mindedness of men. What I'm trying to say is that internally I denounced this idea of Mehmed's, which had been proclaimed as law.

Anyway, they told me this Saadi was looking for me. I didn't remember exactly who he was—likely one of those depraved boys who surrounded Cem. It was plain as day that Mehmed, like all of us, our whole family, had too great a weakness for his younger son, so he let Cem live amongst that dubious rabble simply because he liked it. I have personally always thought this was beneath the honor of a sultan's son and was a bad influence on him, hm?

I told them to let this Saadi person in, and so they did.

He looked exactly as I had expected—like a girl ripe for marrying. I despise these types most of all.

"Seljuk Hatun." He bowed to me and began speaking more plainly than his appearance would lead me to anticipate. "Cem Sultan asks you to honor him with your presence this very moment."

The little one is in quite a rush, I thought as they dressed me. I did not enter into conversation with this Saadi; it was beneath me.

Cem was waiting for me in Orhan Khan's chambers. As soon as I entered the room, he rushed over and led me to the couch. He piled pillows around me and put a blanket over my legs—the night was chilly. I must tell you that Cem always had a knack for engulfing you with attention and putting you at ease—very few of our men have this skill.

He was pale and feverish. *Is this any business for a boy such as him*, I said to myself because I pitied him. I remembered him as a child: translucently fair, honey blond, like an exotic treasure worked with a fine chisel and delicate brush.

"Seljuk Hatun," he began, without trying to hide his emotion, "I asked you to come on terribly important business, fateful even." (Look, those pretty boys of his must have taught him to speak like that.) "You are the living conscience of our clan; you shall be the arbiter in the struggle between Bayezid and myself." "What arbiter?" I cut in. "The only arbiter in a battle is force." "And what is right!" Cem said sharply. "Seljuk Hatun, you are the oldest of the Ottomans. I'm begging you, convince Bayezid of how destructive a fraternal war would be for the empire. We still haven't recovered from the feuds between the Thunderbolt's sons. Tell Bayezid that I do not wish for his death, nor for his Rumelian holdings—let him keep them. He is also a man of flesh and blood, and he is also my father's son. Let us live as brothers, equal and amenable rulers of the two large halves of the Ottoman Empire."

Can you see now where dubious friendships, closeness with half men—with poets!—lead a person? What nonsense Cem made me speak in his name!

"Cem," I said. "What you're saying is laughable, you must understand. What rational mind would allow the splitting of a great empire? Would it even be great if it was divided? Fight! It is your only choice, no matter how repugnant I find fratricide."

"It is still less repugnant to you than to me." Cem cut me off heatedly. "How would I be better than Bayezid if I suggested he die instead of me? Seljuk Hatun, you are our aunt, you are the one who must bring about the resolution that will allow both of your nephews to live."

"I'll try," I replied. It was clear to me that Cem would not rest until I promised him this. I've known a lot of men in my day, make no mistake: they all think they have been called to set the world aright, while they can't even manage the simplest task—managing their own houses, wives, and servants.

Before I had even spoken, Cem took both my hands and pressed them to his chest. That was the strange thing about the boy—even when he did plainly ridiculous things, Cem still won you over. It was hard to deny him anything.

I could feel it inside me—as he was ordering them to ready me a carriage with the softest of springs, while he was assigning me a suite of companions and guards—how with every passing moment I was committing myself to my task. Just a few minutes ago I would have laughed out loud at his ravings, but now I was thinking it through, trying to translate his words into more sober language.

"Seljuk Hatun," Cem said, hugging me before I got into the carriage, "all of my thoughts go with you. May God bring you back with good news."

We traveled for several hours, but I recall nothing of the journey. I was absolutely lost in my worries. The guards stopped us near Bayezid's camp. The agha recognized me—I had lived long enough that all our notables knew me, generations of our state's leaders. They took me straight to Bayezid.

I hadn't seen Bayezid for a dozen or so years. Or rather, I had not bothered to see him. I found him the same: as gaunt as ever, even though the time had come for him to fill out.

"Blessed be the hour in which the honorable Seljuk Hatun crosses my threshold," he welcomed me.

"I'm sure you can guess why I have come to see you in the middle of the night, Bayezid." I purposely did not call him "khan," just as during my whole conversation I did not use this title with Cem. I wanted them to understand that for me, the two simultaneous sultans were simply my brother's grandsons.

"No, I can't guess, Seljuk Hatun," Bayezid said and looked me calmly in the eye.

THIRD TESTIMONY OF THE POET SAADI ON THE EVENTS OF THE NIGHT OF JUNE 20, 1481

IT WAS JUNE 20. I will remember that date until Judgment Day. Three evenings earlier I had observed my master as he waited for the old woman to return: Cem was like a man possessed. He paced through the palace of Orhan Khan, walking and talking to himself out loud. "Anything else would be pure madness!" I heard said several times amidst his quiet conversation with his thoughts.

The old woman returned long after midnight. They led her in, propped up by two servants—she was exhausted. Despite that, she found the strength to glare at me with loathing, and I should have left, but I stayed to listen. And so she relayed to Cem what she had said and the reply she had received. I shall not repeat what you already know.

Cem had been standing as he first began listening to her. Then he felt around for a pillow, pulled it over, and sank down; his legs had given out. *Merciful God*, I thought. *Is this how a military commander looks before a battle?*

He was crushed. You will ask: What else had he expected from such a diplomatic mission? I was asking myself the same thing. But Cem truly had no sense of real-life interrelations, so perhaps he had sincerely expected Seljuk Hatun to prevail.

"It's finished," he said when his aunt had fallen silent. "The divine empire will again be bathed in blood. Why did my father not slice apart this knot while he still lived? I would have died meekly if I had known that this was his will."

"Enough chatter!" The old woman cut him off, her exhaustion making her peevish. "I've just had to listen to how Bayezid would've died if the law had demanded it, now you. If the two of you are both so ready to die, why do you keep me up all night, hm?"

"No, I won't die!" Cem interrupted her every bit as sharply, and this was very typical of him—to swing from one extreme to its opposite. "Bayezid should not get his hopes up."

The old woman shrugged; she was getting tired of Cem's boyish outbursts. She made to leave.

He kissed her belt with more than reverence. I realized that he was saying goodbye to the House of Osman.

"Farewell, aunt," he said, his voice wet with tears. "I know that as long as you live there will be someone to pray for Cem."

"Come on, now! You're not to the point of prayers yet!" And her desiccated arms with their stiff joints found their way to Cem's shoulders.

"Saadi," Cem said as soon as we were alone, "before dawn we'll leave the camp before the city. We will set out for Yeni Shehir field."

"Is it wise to tire your soldiers before battle, sultan?"

"I don't want Bursa to pay the price for their loyalty to me. We'll fight on the open field. Call for Yakub Agha!"

I called Yakub, who was sleeping in the other wing of the palace. I was not present at his discussions with Cem, as I had other tasks to attend to. That conversation should be taken as the beginning of the end of the battles between Bayezid and Cem.

When I returned to my master, I found he had made a strange decision. Cem told me that he thought our troops should be split into two divisions (later I learned that he had been following Yakub Agha's advice). One would set out for Iznik to strike Bayezid's troops from the rear, while the other would head to Yeni Shehir to begin the battle. Cem entrusted this latter division—the better part of our troops—to Yakub Agha.

"Master," I dared to object, "I don't understand. We have few troops as it is. Why would you want to divide them?"

"Precisely because we cannot depend on numbers, we need to resort to trickery. Don't try to dissuade me, Saadi. You know how much I value you, but we are men untried in battle. So when it comes to war I will listen to Yakub Agha. It is his profession."

And so everything came about as Yakub had planned. That very night our troops set out in two different directions. On June 20 the Battle of Yeni Shehir took place, but no one attacked Bayezid from the rear during that fight—our men hadn't made it in time…. At the very beginning of the battle, both sides made minor sorties. While Bayezid was still positioning his troops and Cem was trying to oppose him with a meager line of cavalrymen, Yakub approached us—our master's small suite—his horse foaming at the mouth.

"How it shows that his profession is war," I said, since the *aleybey* looked to be in his element.

"My sultan!" He called from the saddle, reining in his horse with difficulty. "If we hesitate, all is lost: Bayezid will array his forces many rows deep and will set aside some ten thousand light cavalry to attack us from both sides. Don't lose time, sultan! Allow me to lead out all of the sipahi right now and we'll sweep away Bayezid before he has had time to dig in!"

Yakub Agha displayed the most terrible impatience—he danced around us on his stallion, hollering that every moment spent waiting was an indelible loss.

"Go," Cem ordered quietly.

I had my doubts as to whether he still believed we would win. Not even a poet but only a true madman would think that our 15,000 sipahi could do anything but drown amidst the ocean of troops before us.

That was the moment Yakub had been waiting for. His horse carried him off like a blizzard. During that time, we climbed the hill on our side of the river to follow the course of the battle.

We watched our sipahi seek out a ford and find it. Yakub's horse waded in before them—the aleybey was leading his men with confidence. The sipahi were hurrying, even in the river —after all, they were trying to save every second. And when they came out on the other bank, they rushed straight toward Bayezid's camp.

It struck me as strange that their arrival caused no great alarm: our enemies continued positioning their forces. Was Bayezid so self-confident that he considered our best troops nothing but chaff?

Yakub Agha was now just an arrowshot from the camp. We waited with bated breath, expecting shouts, moans, and clangs—the solemn rumble of battle. Until our sipahi cavalrymen—our hope and our pride—silently did not plow into, but instead mingled with Bayezid's troops.

Silence...

I will never forget that silence, in which I could hear our very breathing. There are thoughts so monstrous that they need time to be grasped; at that moment we were struggling with just such a thought: "Treachery!"

Cem slowly turned and looked at me—his gaze was terrible. It was not despair that burned within him; that is too weak a word. Horrified horror, infinite disgust and agony—Cem expressed all this and more.

"The Karamanians!" Haydar broke the silence. I envied him. None of the abovementioned emotions roiled our poet from the village at that moment. Haydar just watched the Karamanians, our last bulwark—he had written all the others off.

And the Karamanians really were collapsing. Their small bands that had pierced the enemy here and there were already falling back in disarray, rushing to reach the riverbank.

"We finished before the battle even began." Cem didn't realize he was talking to himself aloud.

"Stop them! Try to stop them!" Haydar yelled to him not as if to a sultan, but to a snot-nosed kid, and spurred his own horse down the hill.

"Stop!" Cem screamed at him, and with that he made clear to us that any further resistance was out of the question. "Come back! We have been betrayed...."

And without another word he headed back to his tent.

I may be wrong, but to me it seemed that Cem—after his initial horror—accepted Yakub's betrayal almost with relief. As if it freed him from any blame over losing the battle. Perhaps Cem saw fate itself at work in Yakub's treachery and surrendered to it.

I noticed that he was making an effort not to break into a run. Cem was holding on to the last shreds of his sultanly dignity. It held until he reached the tent. I didn't hear whether he ordered them to pack up; Cem swung a leg up into the saddle, grabbed the reins of his black mare, and pointed her toward the sunset.

Riding at a wild gallop, we covered by midnight what should have taken two whole days—the journey from Yeni Shehir to the Armenian Highlands. Only the Karamanian troops followed us, shedding bundles and weapons the whole way to lighten their load. We rode as if the devil himself was on our tail.

You have not heard of the Armenian Highlands—it is a sinister mountain range, a wasteland, without a single spring. We crossed it at night under the goggle-eyed, staring stars, in a deathly silence broken only by our horses' footsteps and the curses of the Karamanians.

There in the Armenian Highlands, Cem suffered a new blow to his sultanly pride. We had plunged nice and deep between the sheer cliffs of a pass when Turkmen attacked us—they're a desert tribe even more savage than the Karamanians, who make their living from plundering and killing. They attacked us as if we were a defenseless merchant caravan.

The fight was brief. I remember the Turkmen's predatory faces, twisted with avarice as they hurled stones at us and beat us with crude staffs. They hung on our saddles to make the horses stumble so they could wrest away some bundle. I saw how the Karamanians formed a wall around Cem to lead him out of that slaughterhouse; I saw how they threw down their last remaining bags so as to distract the wild men, doling out blows left and right the whole time.

To call our nocturnal adventure in the Armenian Highlands "hell" would be too lofty. It was an ignoble, boorish brawl between the half-naked and the buck naked, yet another bitter insult to my purple-born master.

Our company emerged from the other side of the pass unrecognizable; we looked like a band of beggars on horseback, even though no beggar has ever had a horse. The Karamanians' conscientious efforts had not saved even Cem's cloak—Cem was now riding in his shirtsleeves, numb from the desert cold. A bright sacrificial torch wandering in the dark.

Cem...

I went to him and tossed the body cloth from my horse over him—it had miraculously survived. Cem looked at me with resignation and huddled in the blanket, shivering.

"My friend Saadi," he said. "As soon as we stop, you shall bind me. I am wounded in the thigh."

This was the last thing we needed. I knew how dangerous a wound was in the desert; it could get inflamed and fester, full of maggots. Yet we did not dare stop.

After the pass, the Armenian Highlands disintegrated into low hills. Tossed willy-nilly in our path, they tormented us much more than the mountain itself had with all its dangers. We climbed and descended endlessly, exhausted, spent. We all thought we would not live to see the dawn, even though it, too, frightened us with its uncertainty.

At the very front, at the head of our whole ramshackle band, rode Kasim Bey. He was left as ranking commander after Yakub's treachery. Kasim was the last living offshoot of the Karamanian princes, and the twenty-odd clans he led continued to follow Cem and to protect him in his retreat. Kasim also knew the Armenian Highlands, as well as the deserts before and beyond them. We were entirely at Kasim Bey's mercy, but he did not betray us.

We were climbing what seemed like the thousandth hill when I heard him say, "The border is near, my sultan."

"The border!" The word pulled Cem from his stupor and he reined in his horse. "Are you sure, Kasim Bey?"

"Yes, below us is the Tigris River. Beyond it, Syria begins."

"Stop!"

"Why?" Kasim Bey asked, astonished. "We can only rest easy after we cross over."

"Stop! I need to bind my wound. Help me, Saadi!"

I helped Cem dismount. He weighed far more than usual when, leaning on my shoulder, he began to hobble. I didn't understand why he pointed me off to the side, down the slope. Then I caught on: he wanted us to be alone.

When Cem tried to sit, he simply fell. The stress, the exhaustion, the lost blood—all of it had sapped him.

I slid his boot off very carefully and poured it out—it was full of blood. I had to cut his trousers to roll them up, as they were stuck tight to his leg. I sprinkled a pinch of gunpowder in the wound—it wasn't deep but it was ugly, with ragged edges, a wound from a horse's hoof (Cem's pride was not spared even this)—and I bound it with cloth from my turban, as I had no other.

The whole time Cem leaned his back against the cliff, his eyes closed. I didn't know whether he was sleeping or had lost consciousness.

"Ready," I said as I finished. "You'd best not put your boot back on."

"Saadi." Cem suddenly grasped my hand. "Saadi, I am afraid."

"The most fearsome part is behind us, sultan. We have reached the border."

"It is the border I am afraid of."

Was he delirious? His dilated eyes shone feverishly; he was unlike himself.

"Saadi," he went on, "do you really understand what the border is? We will cross not only the boundary between two countries. It is much more.... Until this night I have been at home, upon the land of my father and my grandfather. Until today I have had rights, albeit contested. By crossing the border, I will give them up of my own accord and I will step beyond the law. As of tomorrow I will be an exile, Saadi.... The word 'exile' scares me, Saadi."

"My sultan, do not torture yourself with weighty thoughts. You are leaving the empire perhaps for a few days, a week at most."

"Even so. I will seek help from our enemies, and then I will be in their power. How will I be able to convince anyone that I have not paid for their help with treason? Who would believe I have not won my throne at the expense of my country? Saadi, perhaps it is best for us not to cross over?"

"Sultan, it is too late for such thoughts. You know your brother is at our heels. Tomorrow morning this whole countryside will be swarming with ambushes at every turn; they will hunt you down like a wounded doe, Cem. Since you've started this, you're left with no other choice: make an alliance with Bayezid's enemies—he has them and will always have them. You will not succeed here. The enemy is everywhere, betrayal stalks you, and we are still dazed. From Syria you can negotiate without rushing and seek out allies."

"You think so?" He looked at me sadly. "Yet I am afraid. It seems easier to me to die this very night in my own land, betrayed and forgotten, than to hurl myself into negotiations, alliances, intrigues as of tomorrow morning. I am not cut out for such things, Saadi."

Strangely, only once during all those later years did Cem ever return to these thoughts. After that night in the Armenian Highlands, Cem seemed to try with all his might to convince himself and the world that he was right, that hundreds and thousands of people backed him, and that he was leading a huge struggle. But at that moment, out of our men's earshot, sitting in the dark, whispering in a choked voice, Cem showed how he understood the horror he was facing, realizing fully how irrevocable crossing a border is. Perhaps Cem would not have laid himself so bare if not for the fever and the extreme exhaustion that unyoked his will and freed him from all inhibitions.

"Sultan," I hinted at one point, because I could hear the men on the road growing restless, "they are waiting for us. We must go."

I leaned down, grasped him under the arms, and led him back. Cem was limping, leaning on my shoulder, more trusting and helpless and dear to my heart than ever before.

"Saadi," he said as if reciting a mournful refrain before we reached our men, "I am afraid this night has divided my life in two. I am afraid of the border, Saadi."

But the border was imperceptible. There was something insidious about that—if you ask me, all fateful boundaries in a person's life are just as insidiously imperceptible. You are on this side until a certain point, and then a short while later you come to your senses—already beyond it. The irreparable has occurred, yet you weren't able to grasp the moment it happened.

I deeply loved Cem, but I don't think what I'll tell you now is biased: Cem's spiritual greatness lay in the fact that he noticed and took note of this border in his life. History accuses Cem of thoughtlessness, of ignorance of the world's games. It imagines him as some green young man blinded by ambition—a puppet in the hands of those wiser and more farsighted than him. But I alone—the only person Cem shared a few words with in the darkness of the Armenian Highlands—can attest: Cem was all too aware of the decisive steps in his life and struggle.

But don't blame Cem for the fact that not everyone who is aware of things is able to change them. History is not made by individuals.

I AM QAITBAY of the Mamluks, sultan of Egypt and Syria. I presume you have important reasons to disturb me. While my reasons for answering you are as follows: I would like to cleanse Cem's memory of the filthy insinuations made by scum—from the scorn of the generations, as you put it. It is not your place to judge our sovereignly acts. We stand not beyond but above the laws of the world.

I, Qaitbay, do not agree with history's assessment of our ruling house. Indeed, we are not Arabs, but Circassians; indeed, one of my distant forefathers was a simple mamluk—the mamluks were something like Janissaries, but they served not the Turkish, but the Arab sultans; and indeed, that distant forefather of mine, having risen through the court ranks, seized the sultan's throne through murder—he killed his sovereign. But that does not give you the right to call our whole house "Mamluks" and to constantly remind the world that our roots lead back to the sultan's stables. Actually, you can call me anything you like. I know very well that it is precisely because we bore blood younger than the faded blood of the Abbasids that we managed to rule for centuries over an empire that was alive only in name: the Arab Caliphate. And the Caliphate is something grand and holy, the equivalent of the Roman throne for you infidels.

At the time I'm talking about, yet another threat was looming over the Caliphate: the Ottoman Turks. I must admit, at first they didn't worry us—we'd seen bigger threats. The Seljuks, for example. The Crusaders who left a chain of ridiculous dukedoms, baronies, and principalities doomed to self-destruct in Syria, Palestine, and the Greek islands. In short, we weren't too alarmed at the appearance of a new breed of savages in Anatolia. That's how it was until the Conqueror.

You can praise his grandeur all you like—that's your opinion. We, the rulers of the world in Mehmed's day, judged this confrere of ours much less generously. In our opinion, Mehmed was too petty to be truly grand; he was painfully prideful in the face of every enemy. Mehmed dedicated decades to his wars with Skanderbeg—an Arnaout, a runaway sultan's Janissary turned mountain brigand. But Mehmed would not rest until he put an end to him.

Mehmed poured unheard-of efforts into defeating the Knights of St. John, the one-time rulers of Palestine, who later could barely hang on to Rhodes. I wouldn't risk my name over such a foolish grudge for all the money in the world. Who cares about those half monks, half beggars, half pirates dug in on some miserable island? But since Mehmed had once clashed with them and once had lost, he could not rest until the end of his days. I see

VERA MUTAFCHIEVA

that you are still mystified as to where he had meant to lead his army on that morning of May 3. I'll tell you: against the knights. And against me. Because Mehmed suspected that it was I who was helping them with supplies to withstand the Ottoman sieges. To what extent that is true, I, Qaitbay, am under no obligation to confirm.

I would not even have told you all I have so far if it did not illuminate that which happened between June and June of the aforementioned years: my meddling in the struggle between Mehmed's sons.

I won't hide the fact that this situation was advantageous not only for me, but for all rulers in the world and, more precisely, in the Mediterranean. It came right on time, on the eve of a new assault against the West and its friends; it would distract the new sultan (whoever he might be) from his father's dying wishes.

Go ahead and ask me: why, in that internecine war, did I place my bets on Cem—after all, he was the one lauded as the living continuation of his father—and not on Bayezid, whom we knew to be sickly? Because that's how things worked out, I could say. But since all of this is so far in the past, there's no point in lying. I bet on Cem, sensing that he was the weaker of the two. Superiority does not always depend on strength.

Shall I start from the beginning?

When they told me Cem had crossed the border into my lands, I immediately ordered for him to be met with honor and brought to my capital, and that Kasim Bey and his Karamanians should go back and whisk away Cem's family, who had been left behind in Konya.

So, he arrived in Cairo accompanied by a small suite and was installed in the palace of my *divider*—our grand vizier. After two days to rest and tend to his wounds, Cem came to see me. It was a pure courtesy visit—we did not yet know each other; besides, we had nothing to discuss. We still did not know what was happening beyond the border. Then I only offered Cem my hospitality, assured him I would not hand him over to his brother even if Bayezid set such a condition, and generally expressed my hopes of seeing him on the Ottoman throne.

While I spoke the young sultan did not look me in the eye. His resignation seemed excessive to me. I knew him only fleetingly then, so what I took as resignation was simply the fact that Cem was still crushed and needed time to pull himself together. I understood this at our second meeting—now that was a true meeting between two sovereigns. With dignity and restraint, Cem laid out his views about his struggle with his brother, about the future of the Ottoman state and the Mediterranean. He offered me peace—peace until the end of his life, because he could not promise anything after his death—if I would take his side against Bayezid.

"Could my royal guest possibly be considering ending the conquests of the late Mehmed Khan?" I asked him.

"No," Cem replied. "Thank God the infidels still hold sufficient land. We soldiers of one and the same faith should not go to war against each other."

"And yet your father won his greatest battles against Muslims: the Karamanian beys, Uzun Hasan. Mehmed Khan even fought against me."

"I would not raise a hand against the caliph. You have my word as sultan."

Cem was not the first ruler fate had brought me face-to-face with. But I must say this: only in my conversations with him did I feel certain that I was hearing the truth and not simply some royal game of cunning. Cem offered no pledge in exchange for his promises, because at that moment he had nothing to give—he did not swear oaths up to the heavens. Yet behind his words, who knows why, one did not suspect any treachery.

During that conversation of ours we didn't really decide much of anything. I did not wish to commit myself before it was clear whether Cem would succeed. Rumor had it the lands near our border with Bayezid were restless, so he didn't dare pull his best forces out of them. Konya was practically under siege, even though it had not resisted Bayezid. But the mere fact that Kasim Bey had slipped into the fortress without bloodshed and whisked away Cem's family looked sufficiently suspicious to Bayezid.

To temper his impatience, I invited Cem to visit the holy places: Mecca and Medina. In any case, a battle for Karamania was out of the question until Bayezid withdrew his forces—Cem had barely three or four thousand men, and my friendship did not extend so far as to giving him my soldiers.

Cem happily accepted my invitation. It was clear he was drowning withering away in Cairo. Yet he didn't set out for Mecca until the late autumn of 1481, because his wound worsened and took a long time to heal. He spent a whole four months in our holy places.

During that time events did not stand still; many things in Anatolia had changed. Messengers frequently came to Cairo. From them I learned above all that Kasim Bey had crossed the border several times. When he returned, he was filled with new hope; he said things were working out fully in Cem's favor. A series of Anatolian sanjak-beys—those were the leaders of the sipahi—had openly opposed Bayezid and were waiting for his brother as a savior. The most important among them was Mahmud Bey, the governor of Ankara.

Cem returned to my capital in the winter and immediately threw himself into preparations. Now he was visibly changed: close attendants of the Anatolian Beys swarmed around him, convincing him that he was not alone and exiled. I started to ask myself if I hadn't acted thoughtlessly by allowing the decidedly more competent and better loved of Mehmed's sons to wait in peace for his lucky destiny. Whatever else he might be, he was a son of the Conqueror.

If anything has stuck in my mind from those times, it is the day of my parting with Cem Sultan. At the time I didn't know it was forever.

Cem's forces were to head out early in the morning. They numbered only several thousand, but Cem had wanted to show them off to us in their finest form. They rode behind their sovereign, colorful and varied, yet all eager for battle.

I have no talent for description like your poets there, which is a shame—it is a shame I cannot describe for you Cem Sultan on that morning when he drew his horse close to mine to take his leave. I felt he was already distant, his mind far away where battles would decide his fate.

I will never forget his final words either. He uttered them loudly, with much grandeur: "The goodness I found under my royal brother's roof is emblazoned with golden letters in my memory. May Allah strengthen our right hands and grant us victory! Then Qaitbay, caliph and sultan, will learn what a sultan's gratitude truly looks like."

Then Cem, still sitting in his saddle, kissed my shoulder, and I hugged him in contradiction to all protocol—after all, I could have been his father.

At that moment I heard behind me noise, shouts, and among them a female voice. We both turned toward it. A woman was struggling to make her way through the throng of guards. We could not see her face nor guess her age. From her clothing I could tell she was no peasant. She was carrying a small child, a year or two old.

I shot Cem a quizzical glance; clearly the woman was coming to see him off.

My royal friend's face was tense. He followed the woman with his gaze and suddenly I thought he would leap from his saddle. But he didn't; he remembered he was before his army.

The woman reached us. Without saying a word, she lifted the child up high and placed him on Cem's saddle. As she did this, her yashmak slipped back and she stood before us barefaced.

This was the first time I saw the Conqueror's second wife, Cem's mother, the Serbian woman. I was struck by their likeness—the same light face with light eyes. Much later, when she and I had to fight for the same thing—for Cem Sultan's freedom—I came to understand their hearts were also alike. She was a remarkable woman, that is the truth.

Her appearance at that hour deeply disconcerted her son. He did not take his eyes from hers even as he held the child, without letting go of the reins.

Our women are different, thus you will not understand how strange what happened next seemed to us. The barefaced woman wrapped both arms around Cem's thigh (she could not reach any higher) and pressed against him with her whole body. She did it so fervidly, as if she would never let him go. She closed her eyes, her lips pressed tightly together, her entire being drank in this final nearness with her son. A truly devout Muslim woman would not have made such a spectacle of herself, would not have placed her maternal anguish on display before thousands of eyes. But we, God knows why, did not find her indecent. Everything the two of them did—I only determined this many years later—held some great human purity.

Cem very gently pulled his mother off and placed his hand briefly on her hair as they silently gazed at each other. Then the woman said something to him in her strange language, and Cem raised the little boy up high so the whole army could see him.

The men started shouting their loyalty to their leader, swearing they would be victorious. But I contemplated those three—mother, son, and grandson—three offshoots of a foreign blood, incomprehensible to us. I watched how they did not hide their sorrow and hope, how they were not afraid to show weakness.

Hear me now—I was sultan and caliph—you can learn much more about people when you see them from above: Cem Sultan's misfortune was rooted in the fact that he was all too human.

From here on I can be useful to you only with respect to the news that was coming to Cairo, as I did not witness Cem's wanderings in Anatolia. We learned that Mahmud Bey, the governor of Ankara, really did go over to Cem's side, and a series of other sipahi leaders also did the same. Upon hearing this, Bayezid headed toward Aidos, while Kasim Bey, dragging his Karamanians in tow, united with Cem and Mahmud to lay siege to Konya. But before that my royal friend signed the following agreement with Kasim: to resurrect the Karamanian beys' obliterated state and to place Kasim on its throne.

I mused that Cem was now promising things he did not have. I also didn't like the fact that he was announcing agreements of this kind—the Ottomans would not forgive him for breaking up their young empire. That is, in Anatolia things were not working out in Cem's favor; I was sure this would be the case, even before I knew for certain.

News of his failure came much later, after two months, in the summer. The siege of Konya had failed, as was to be expected, mostly because Bayezid had his troops inside the fortress defending it, while Gedik Ahmed, Mehmed Khan's leading military commander, dealt Cem the heaviest blow. By some miracle, Bayezid had spared him after keeping him locked up for half a year—the devil only knows what bargains they struck during that time, but Gedik Ahmed came out of prison as a fierce supporter of Bayezid. I personally can guess the reason that pushed the old commander toward Bayezid. Ambitious and a master of his profession, Gedik Ahmed had foreseen that if he served a warrior sultan, as Cem was famed to be, he would always play second fiddle. Whereas with Bayezid, who never showed any propensity for military business, Ahmed Pasha would keep his position as the leading Ottoman commander.

Very simple, right? You're fooling yourself if you think up there in the highest ranks, among sultans and viziers, the calculations are more complex than among neighbors and craftsmen.

As soon as Ahmed Pasha arrived in Anatolia, he ordered Mahmud Bey's whole family—all his wives and children—to be captured and taken to Istanbul. And Mahmud Bey, frantic, raced after the Janissaries who had taken his wives and all. He stumbled right into the clutches of Suleiman Pasha, the governor of Amasia and was beaten and killed, and his head was sent to Bayezid. Because of this idiocy, Cem lost his most promising military commander and his best troops.

By midsummer we learned that negotiations had begun between the brothers. If Cem had held them earlier, before the siege of Konya and Mahmud's defeat, who knows how they might have ended. But now Bayezid had won victories, and his response was harsh: "The empire is a fiancée—she cannot have two grooms! (You have likely noticed his fondness for folk sayings; with them Bayezid demonstrated his nearness to the people.) Let my brother cease to stain his cloak with the blood of true believers and end his days in Jerusalem, outside of our borders!"

Bayezid's saying was followed by swift action: Gedik Ahmed Pasha set out for Cilicia—on the very border of my lands—where the remnants of Cem's army were hiding, to finish off Cem's rebellion once and for all.

We waited impatiently for news. I was not worried for the caliphate—Bayezid was in no mood for conquests at that moment. Every morning I worried that I would learn of Cem's death. It had become inevitable. Rumor had it that all of his allies, with the exception of Kasim Bey, had deserted him and Cem was again wandering with just a few thousand men through Cicilia and Lycia by the sea. Twice, upon his mother's insistence, I sent messengers to offer him my hospitality. His mother insisted upon it.

Why do I underscore this?

Because there is no friendship between rulers. I felt for Cem, but I could not keep a pretender to the Ottoman throne at my court when that throne was legally occupied by his brother. I had to maintain some ostensible decorum in my relations with the Ottomans. So if I offered refuge to Cem, I only did it with the full belief that Cem would not accept. I knew him by then. Cem hated charity.

My messengers disappeared. Gedik Ahmed guarded the border well.

A few more words—about the day I was told that Cem had sought refuge elsewhere. I recall that I felt relief above all. I would no longer be party to this troubling business. And immediately thereafter: guilt. I carried it to my grave; it was the reason for all my later attempts to help Cem, my very vocal and demonstrative attempts. They were doomed in advance, and I knew it. I did it only in an excruciating attempt to convince someone—perhaps a mother, perhaps myself—that I did not betray my alliance with Cem.

Subconsciously, I was afraid Cem would be standing beside my deathbed, holding me accountable. Cem did not do this; he had forgiven me. Out of everything he went through, it seems I was the least of his cause for bitterness.

Someone else refused to forgive me—his mother, even though she never uttered a word of reproach. After all, she and

Cem's wife and his son lived off my table for many years; they were counting on me for Cem's salvation. His mother realized this and thanked me with deep bows—they were surely difficult for the daughter and wife of a sovereign. She swallowed back her reproaches, but I could sense them, because they echoed my own pangs of conscience. If I had at some point offered Cem not only shelter but also troops, if I had stood solidly behind him, many things would have worked out differently. Perhaps Cem really would have been sultan. And what's more, perhaps I would not have been the last caliph of the Mamluk line. Because Bayezid's heir—Selim the Grim, surely you've heard of him—put an end to the Arab Caliphate.

Incidentally, these are the words of the last Arab caliph.

VERA MUTAFCHIEVA

YOU DON'T KNOW Lycia.

I don't think you could find another place in the world that would more accurately reflect our thoughts and our torment than Lycia during the summer of 1482.

The mountains of Lycia are completely bare. They say once, back in the times of the Phoenicians and the Hellenes, they were covered in cedar trees. But as you know, cedar is especially well suited to ships, so over the course of the centuries the cedar trees of Lycia sailed away, carrying the impatient thirst of travelers, merchants, and pirates upon all the seas of the world.

Back then, in 1482, not a single trace of a tree or bush was left in Lycia. Floods, storms, and desert winds had not only stripped its mountains bare, they had turned them into some heretofore unseen, sinister desert. Lycia loomed over us with its blood-red, wind-whipped sands; Lycia descended toward the shore in huge slabs, like an enormous rooftop upon which no horse's hoof could gain purchase; Lycia groaned and whined with the whistling through its countless narrow gorges—Lycia was a scorching, inescapable torment.

We wandered aimlessly through this Lycia—several thousand defeated men who had lost faith in their luck. God only knows why we kept wandering, rather than staying in one place; one part of Lycia did not offer us anything more than any other. Everywhere we looked, our eyes met nature's same refusal to help, shelter, and comfort us.

And yet we plodded on. Following goat paths, we made our rounds of the rocky peaks, descended into the passes, and scrabbled up the sheer slabs with the last of our strength. We dipped our rocklike hardtack in a spring beneath a scree, resting for an hour or two. We grazed our horses in some hollow covered in desert lichen, we slept on the bare stony cliffs. A long caravan of human shades roving through Lycia, not knowing what it was looking for.

No, we did know something: sooner or later Bayezid would find out that we were here, in the merciless land of Lycia. Then Bayezid would not even bother to attack us. He would encircle the mountains with a chain of loyal troops and would wait. He would wait a month or a year, until we completely collapsed in exhaustion, until the desert winds dried up or infected the springs, until our horses dropped and our bread ran out. And then Bayezid would win, without having shed his brother's blood.

There wouldn't be any blood. Our corpses littered beneath the cliffs would be completely desiccated. Our skin would crackle, stretched tight across our ribs, while our eyes would be deeply sunken, and dry as well.

Every one of us was haunted by the specter of his own death in those intolerable June days of 1482. For this reason we were quiet. Our caravan wound through the gorges like a sick snake —soundlessly.

You are too far from our time, everything is different for you. You do not know that purely male triumph after a victory your hands have wrought. After a battle from which you remember the enemy's face, from which you have carried off a looted weapon or stolen away an enemy horse. Our victories were of the senses, which is why for you joy after such a victory is alien.

But there is another thing that sets us apart as well: the resignation that came after being routed. It was not meekness or lack of faith, but merely the realization you have failed and must accept that which follows from your defeat: torture, hunger, death. This is exactly what we were thinking in our days in Lycia—we had lost, now all that was left was to await our end. There is no mercy for the defeated and we did not expect any.

I don't know what would have happened to Cem if Kasim Bey had not followed us here as well. It was not Cem but rather Kasim who refused to resign himself to our defeat. For a few short weeks—while we reaped short-lived victories in Karamania and Anatolia—Kasim had imagined himself as the one who would resurrect his disappeared country. Kasim had made an agreement with Cem that the territories of the Karamanoglu would once again be free after Cem won. Now Cem could relax into the arms of death—even after his death, the Ottoman state would live on. But Kasim knew his death would be the end of Karamania, the absolute finale.

I observed how he watched over Cem day and night. He tried to convince Cem that not everything was lost, that Mahmud

Bey's defeat was a pure coincidence, and that Bayezid's victory was groundless.

Cem listened to him with an indifference that made my hair stand on end. It was as if Kasim was speaking not to him, but simply howling out his anguish and hopes at the sands of Lycia.

That's how I'll always remember the two of them during those days: Kasim tense with resolve and Cem, dead to the world, brooding. That's how it was until the hour when the Rumelian reached us.

It sounds unbelievable. Yet someone had made the trek from Adana, where Bayezid kept the bulk of his forces, searched us out, and found us amidst the jumbled rocks.

It was dusk. Nightfall in Lycia did not bring peace as it did elsewhere. The red cliffs there cut into the red evening sky even more oppressively, while their dense shadows covered the valleys, turning them inky black and cold as the grave.

We had unhitched and unsaddled our horses, as we were making camp for the night. The men were lined up in front of the spring—surely the only spring within a day's ride. Each of them scooped up water with his cup or skin, thirty spoonfuls, not more. It had to suffice for both the rider and his horse.

The stranger crept down to the spring somehow from above, from the cliffs. We later learned he had kept to the ridge the whole way—as much as one can speak of a ridge in Lycia—hoping to spot us. I noticed him even as he slid down the scree, half on his feet, half on his ass. At first the sun lit him up in red and he looked unreal. I remember saying to myself, *Now the visions are starting. Nothing in the desert is as real as the visions.*

As he slid lower, into the shadows, the stranger convinced me that he was a living, breathing man. Rags hung from his shoulders, the remnants of a sipahi uniform; his boots were so worn that his toes stuck out of them, as if they had been gnawed through. I rushed straight at him with my hand on my knife; the knife had become an extension of my hand—just look what war does to a man.

As soon as he spotted me, the stranger put up his hands, as if to say that he had no malicious intentions. More of our men gathered around us. We hadn't seen another living soul in weeks, unless you count the desert shepherds, who from time to time would appear on the crest of a ridge, only to disappear a moment later.

"I'm here to see Cem Sultan," the stranger croaked. "Does Cem Sultan live?"

This guy must be mad, I thought. His eyes flashed wildly; his whole being exuded tension and threatened to erupt in a shriek.

"Come on." I purposely grasped him by the hand. I knew madness was best blocked by human touch.

Cem had gotten to his feet. Strange, even something as minor as the appearance of a stranger amidst that caravan of dead men was enough to liven up his face.

"Is it a messenger from Bayezid?" he asked.

I was stunned that the thought of Bayezid still raised his hopes.

"Bayezid can go to hell," the stranger cursed. "I'm from the Rumelian sipahis. And you, my sultan, if you agree to speak with Bayezid's man, you can go straight to hell, too!"

Every man was within his rights to reply to such words with a blow, it was completely justified. Cem did not strike out at him.

"Speak!" he said.

"My sultan!" the sipahi shouted unnecessarily loudly. "Anatolia betrayed you. The Anatolian sipahi do not see the noose they have slipped around their own necks. So let them hang. Why don't you turn toward Rumelia, my sultan? Here, only the Karamanians have followed you, because the Ottoman state is their enemy. The House of Osman has many enemies in Rumelia—Greeks, Bulgarian, Arnauts, Serbs. Only in Rumelia will the revolt against Bayezid succeed."

The sipahi fell silent, his strength spent. I looked at Cem. He only grew offended now.

"Is this how low we've fallen?" His voice was sharp. "Is it possible that I will fight not against my brother, but against the power of the Ottomans themselves? Is that what the Rumelian sipahi suggests to me?"

"Not that," the stranger replied, almost reasonably. "But in a struggle, a man uses allies. Think about Musa Celebi, the Thunderbolt's son. He found allies in Rumelia."

"And how did things end for Musa?" Cem said.

"Badly, I know. But you are not Musa."

"Why am I not?"

Cem said it as if in passing, but I was not fooled: in the days after our defeat Cem had found it terribly necessary to hear who he really was.

"Even the mere fact that you are half theirs, that your mother is one of them, will rouse the infidels to your side."

"I want the word of the Rumelian sipahi, and not the Christians of Rumelia," Cem said coldly.

"Listen! We were Mehmed Khan's strength, because the mosque's lands spread widest of all through Rumelia, because everyone of us lives in a village that until yesterday belonged to the waqfs and which tomorrow will again fall into their zealous hands. We shared in your father's sin against Islam. There will be no forgiveness for us. Tomorrow half of the Rumelian sipahi will be left without land and livelihood—what man would not rise up to defend his home, his bread, and his realm? The sipahi from Anatolia will stay sipahi, no matter whether Bayezid or Cem rules—that's why they betrayed you. But we are done for if Bayezid prevails. Why did you bet on Anatolia and concede Rumelia of your own accord? What do you want to be sultan of—this bare desert and its rocky cliffs, with their Yuruks and Turkmen? Have you ever seen Rumelia, my sultan?"

"No," said Cem. "Our father never allowed us to go to Rumelia."

"And with good reason!" The impudence of this half-mad sipahi knew no bounds. "A man cannot see Rumelia and not desire it. Cross over, Cem Sultan!"

"We shall speak later. Feed him with whatever we have. Come with me, Saadi. And Kasim Bey."

Our men led away the messenger, while we sat down where Cem had been sitting shortly before that. We were silent. Cem was leaning back against the sand with an empty stare.

"What do you say, friends?" he asked at last. "Do I have the right to again seek a way out?"

"How could you not?" Kasim Bey replied quickly. "Are you even hesitating, my sultan? Rumelia has offered you its loyalty."

"Anatolia, too, offered me loyalty, did it not?"

"That man was right: Anatolia doesn't have much to lose if Bayezid rules. Karamania and I will suffer, for example. But the sipahi from Rumelia really will be in dire straits. You'll find allies there as well."

"Does an alliance with infidels not frighten you, Kasim Bey?" Cem shot up at him.

"What does it hurt for you to take chestnuts from the fire with their hands, my sultan?"

"And why should we assume that they will not see through our machinations, Kasim Bey?"

"They don't have much choice," Kasim Bey answered emphatically. "Just as I have no choice either. Why did I have to believe you would honor your agreement with me if you won? I believe it. What else do I have left? They are also obliged to believe you, that is the simple truth."

I knew nothing irritated Cem more than hearing those truths known as "simple." To him, they were not merely simple, but animalistic. He always thought human truth should be something far more complex.

"Fine," Cem said after some time, his voice bitter. "Since we have arrived at simple truths: What is the advantage for you if I shift my rebellion to Rumelia?"

"Very simple," the last Karamanoglu replied with dignity. "While you distract Bayezid's forces in Rumelia, I will easily free my land. And then what you agreed to will be, my sultan: the Karamanoglu state will live again."

"Indeed," Cem admitted. "It really is funny that the first thing on your mind takes such a long time for my mind to grasp.... You are free to go, Kasim Bey. I just ask you to call the Rumelian."

The latter looked reborn. The excitement, our men's attention, and likely the water as well had brought back his strength. Now I could also see he was a wiry, hardy man with an intelligent face. He didn't look mad at all.

"I must tell you, my sultan," he began without waiting to be asked, "the three sanjak-beys who sent me: from Çirmen, Filibe, and Dimotika."

"As I suspected," Cem replied. "Precisely those sanjaks had the most waqf lands until my father's new laws. And what exactly are they offering me?"

"They are offering you a chance to leave Lycia—it's a death trap. Using routes of your own choosing, you cross into Rumelia. As soon as Bayezid finds out you're no longer here, he'll pull back his troops. Then we, too, will go back to our sanjaks. And you will give us a sign that you're coming. They want nothing more from you."

"It's not the first time I've heard that promise. The Anatolia sipahi used it to call me from Cairo. Only to run away during the third battle. What will happen if the Rumelians also decide Bayezid's rule is not so terrible after all?"

Flustered, the sipahi fell silent. Either he didn't know how to answer or else he knew he would again spout some insolence. Now recovered, he was clearly awed by his sovereign.

"It couldn't be worse than Lycia, my sultan," he said at last. "And don't you see... how shall I put it?... If you need to seek shelter, I mean, it'll be easier for you there with them."

"With whom?"

"With the infidels," the sipahi mumbled cautiously. "They are gutless, as we know. To them murder is a mortal sin, that's how they are. They will have mercy on you—you're half theirs."

I was afraid Cem would explode. Even I, his closest companion, could never foresee what the consequences of reminding Cem of his roots might be. Sometimes he took it almost as a compliment, while other times he blazed up as if backhanded across the face. Now the latter seemed to be the case.

"I am fully a true believer," Cem said with an arrogance completely unnatural to him. "I am amazed my father's own soldiers would push me toward a long-forgotten kinship. I will fight and I will win as an Ottoman, mark my words!" Cem's voice changed. "Can you leave tomorrow morning?"

"I can."

"Take a horse; they'll give you some hardtack. Tell the sanjak-beys that I am in agreement with them. Let them wait for me. I will do everything humanly possible to make it to the border of Rumelia. Then I, in turn, will wait for you."

"Have faith in us, my sultan." The man almost sobbed, touched by such trusting magnificence. "What Rumelian sipahi would not follow Cem? Our sun! The living hand of the departed Conqueror!"

Cem stood before the Rumelian, solemn, not noticing how some slight madness crept into those promises too easily given, into that tearful praise.

And during those days in Lycia I had grown so consumed with the thought of my own death that the image of my own corpse was constantly before my eyes, lying beneath the cliffs, dry as a long-felled tree, quiet and peaceful—above all peaceful, free from the need to move and to suffer. It now seemed unbearable that the hour of sweet oblivion was slipping away from me and again I would be forced to live. Believe me if you will: you need to have spent a summer in Lycia, to have been defeated and part of a doomed army, to have been a poet and in love, and to have witnessed your beloved's suffering, to understand how undesirable life might look.

I recall that before he left, the sipahi told us his name and rank: he was the aleybey of Viza, Ismail by name. I watched him ride off. I felt exhausted. I lay down on the sand and stared up at the night sky—above Lycia it was pitch-black.

Cem was sitting next to me. If I had reached out my hand, I could've touched him. Yet I did not want to. I sensed that all my devotion was not enough to wrench Cem out of his solitude. *How many things, God?* I thought. *Ambition and pride, responsibility in the face of history and irresponsibility toward one's children and mother, will and helplessness. How many things you have piled on so as to make man the loneliest creature in the world.*

I hadn't yet fallen asleep when Cem laid down next to me, huddled under his blanket. He was frozen from the nighttime cold, yet was not shivering. I tucked my cloak under his shoulders and pressed against his back to warm him. Cem did not say a word. Only as I was drifting off did I hear: "Saadi, I weighed all the options. We really must go after Rumelia, but the path to it passes through Christian lands. Terrifying, isn't it? But the aleybey spoke the truth—they are another world. That's why we defeat them, because to them mercy is law, while their primary obligation is to help those who are suffering. Mama has told me as much.... It might very well be true, Saadi, that I am half theirs. Our unscrupulous cruelty is foreign to me, our underhanded means in the name of a great end. Perhaps I am a bit of a Christian without knowing it?"

"You are not!" I wanted to tell him. "You are neither ours nor theirs. A poet never belongs to anyone but only to the eternal, great, and weak family of poets. Our homeland is not of this world, Cem"—I wanted to tell him—"Here we will always be exiles.... Don't fool yourself, my friend, that anyone is capable of pitying someone besides himself. This is the poet's old delusion. Let us die this very night, Cem"—I wanted to beg him—"in hopes that we will finally find our way home."

But I kept silent. Dear God, why did I keep silent? Why did I not spare Cem that life and everything that life did not spare us; why during that night in Lycia did I not put an end to Cem with my own hand, so as to leave alive the memory of that twenty-year-old poet cast from gleaming bronze, blond, charming, and weak?

Why do we fear early death, my friends? Don't we kill ourselves much more completely by living?

FIFTH TESTIMONY OF THE POET SAADI
ON THE EVENTS OF JUNE 25, 1482

A JOLT AWAKENED me in the morning. Cem had leapt out of bed very suddenly. He exuded uneasiness—a decision had been made, now he needed to act.

"Saadi," he said, "call Suleiman."

"Which of our Suleimans, my sultan? We've probably got two hundred of them."

"The Frankish Suleiman."

I headed toward our camp—several thousand men sprawled out right on the sand. It warmed them for the first half of the night, and during the second half painfully sucked away their own pathetic warmth. Thus in the morning they looked like dead men who had reluctantly crawled out of their graves. I walked among them, wondering why Cem needed the Frank of all people.

Let me say a few words about him. I believe that among us there was no man as full of bitterness and disappointment with life as Frankish Suleiman, whom no one liked to talk to nor share a meal or a blanket with. Suleiman had come to us years earlier. Mehmed Khan had just entrusted Karamania to his younger son and was himself furiously battling the knights of Rhodes. The Conqueror used Cem for his negotiations with the knights, as he did not want to be personally involved. Then Cem was in Lycia for the first time, on its shores across from Rhodes. It was there that he accepted the knights' envoys.

One morning, when the caravel with such envoys had just sailed off—the negotiations had come to a standstill, as Mehmed Khan was stubbornly haggling to impose an annual tax on Rhodes—they brought a foreigner before Cem's tent. He was middle-aged, around thirty, blue-eyed, with shoulder-length hair, dressed in the black robes of the Order.

"He must've missed the boat, and now he'll beg us to give him some skiff," I said to myself.

"I seek refuge," the foreigner said clearly and coldly. He stared at us without blinking as the interpreter translated his words.

"What? Why?" Cem was taken aback and didn't manage to hide it.

"Under all laws I have the right to refuge," the foreigner said, as if giving orders. And he added, "I swear I have not committed a crime and it is not fear of punishment that leads me to you. I am seeking refuge!"

"Efendi, sir," replied Cem, who was still a boy then; clearly he could not find a more suitable way to address this foreign fighter. "I don't know how to look upon your action. Refuge, you say.... Is someone pursuing you? Why have you run to us of all people, we who are enemies of Rhodes? What prevents you from going to some land of your own, to Christians? In the suite or at the court of Şehzade Cem there is no place for a living nonbeliev-er; our laws are strict."

The foreigner listened to him with light scorn in his eyes, almost with contempt.

Realizing his words were quite harsh, Cem added more softly, "If you like, we can help you reach your own shores. Since you are not on good terms with the knights, and they are the enemies of the Ottomans, it follows that we should help you, does it not?"

Cem turned toward his suite with a questioning glance; he had gotten himself good and mixed up. When had we ever seen such strange business?

"It is no accident that I seek refuge precisely with you," the foreigner replied. "I do not wish to return to Christian lands. I no longer believe."

These last words of his were heavy with hatred, as if he were angry at someone for the fact that he himself had lost his faith.

Cem was startled—he was eighteen years old, the sultan's son, the favorite of the House of Osman, but at that time, Cem still knew nothing.

"Fine, fine," Cem gave in easily. "I will ask the higher-ups. They will fix this business. And you, efendi, don't worry! You'll see that Muslims are people, too."

"I am not afraid," the man replied morosely, completely un-moved by the Şehzade's benevolence. "And since a nonbeliever cannot live at your court, I am ready to accept Islam. Right now."

Then Cem really did have to consult his advisers. As you know, most of them were Karamanian beys or else like us, ev-ery bit as young and inexperienced as Cem, so it didn't take us long to think it over: let this foreigner convert to our holy religion and remain at our court. What could it hurt? Plus, we might need him later.

When we relayed Cem's decision to him, the foreigner got down on one knee and laid down his knife. Then witnesses to the ritual were selected. As you might expect, Cem picked Haydar and me. The whole thing was over in half an hour. I remember the man's words as he struggled to wrap a turban around his head because his long hair kept getting in the way: "Call me Suleiman! That's Solomon in your language, isn't it? I'm like Solomon the wise man himself. Because I am wiser than all of you put together."

So that's the kind of man he was, Suleiman, whom I sought out that morning in Lycia. Brazen to the point of insolence, cold, impenetrable, bitter at the whole world. At our court in Karamania he took up the role of armorer, since he knew quite a bit about weapons. He did his job well; his armory gleamed with cleanliness and order and, on the whole, he kept to himself. Only one night, when he somehow ended up among a company of high-spirited poets around the fountain, when the Shiraz had loosened his tongue—which still hadn't quite learned Ottoman—Suleiman finally spoke.

"Blessed are the small in spirit," Suleiman had said.

"Meaning?" I asked, being drunker than he was.

"Just that. Very blessed."

"Do we seem so trifling to you, Suleiman?" I should have been offended, but I was drunk after all.

"Very much so. You are children and like all children you cannot find joy in your own childishness."

"And what sets men apart from children among Christians?"

"The fact that they are sunk up to their necks in shit"—pardon me, but those are his words, not mine—"And that they can buck and struggle all they like, but there is no escape."

"You don't look all that dirty to me, Suleiman. To me, you smell"—I sniffed at him drunkenly—"like pure perfume."

Through the haze of the Shiraz, Suleiman glared sternly at me. He now seemed sober.

"If you have ever believed as I once did, and if you had seen after that what I have seen, for you, Saadi, even though you are a poet, shit would be far too mild a word."

I don't recall what I replied, surely something foolish. And that was my conversation with Suleiman; I don't believe anyone else spoke more with him. He clearly didn't like turning back to his past. Our cheerful court clearly irritated him, while Suleiman never hinted at his future—both to himself and to us he looked like a man without a future.

While I walked among the soldiers looking for him that morning in Lycia, I wondered why our master needed him of all people. Cem had not shown any particular fondness for him; like all of us, Cem avoided close contact with Suleiman.

I found the man on the very fringes of some group of Karamanians who were performing their morning prayer. Suleiman, lying down propped on his elbow, was watching them with his usual cold contempt. Seeing me approach, the Frank's expression did not change. To him, I was no better than a bunch of half-savage Karamanians. I relayed Cem's order and the two of us—after Suleiman had gathered up his cloak, his body-cloth, and his bag of hardtack—headed back.

Cem was waiting for us with impatience—I knew very well the signs of impatience in him.

"Suleiman." He turned toward the Frank. "Today I will entrust you with more than my life."

The Frank only bowed slightly.

"Today you shall go to the knights, and you shall request in my name that which you once sought from me: refuge."

Suleiman did not respond. I noticed how his face grew more hateful than ever, how his eyes narrowed as if before a fight, and how he lowered his head and spread his feet wide. What had gotten into him?

"My sultan," he replied after an eternity, "it is not your servant's place to question, but I will ask so you do not rebuke me later: How did you get it into your head to request refuge in Rhodes?"

"I am not obliged to explain myself to my servant, Suleiman, but I shall explain to you: our true goal is Rumelia. Yet we are not birds who can fly over land, are we? The first island to the north of us is Rhodes."

"Go to the shah of Persia or the Egyptian sultan, my lord."

That crackpot uttered this like a spell.

"Go to the devil himself if you wish, but don't set foot on Rhodes. I have been there. Haven't you ever wondered why I would prefer to my own people those who in my homeland are known as pagans and beasts?"

"Suleiman," Cem said very carefully, "your past is your own business. I understand that a man might be embittered, disappointed, that an insult or a heavy loss might have forced him into exile. But that should not make us blind. Not everything in the world begins and ends with the individual, Suleiman. I am not giving myself over into the hands of pirates. I am asking for refuge from the grand master of a monastic order. I know the laws of their faith—I would never seek shelter among people whose laws were unknown to me."

As Cem made this speech, the Frank transformed before my very eyes; his long-hardened coldness melted. Then Suleiman spoke as if he was defending the very meaning of his whole life.

"My sultan, it will be difficult to dissuade you, but that which you speak—forgive me, my sultan—is pure foolishness. Don't tell me about the knight monks until you have lived among them. And after you have gone to live there, it will be too late for warnings."

"Suleiman, you see the world through the prism of your person-al affront, and I don't blame you. But why can't you understand that—even if you are right—the Order will not act with me as they would with every other? I am the sultan's son, after all; be-hind me, as you heard last night, stand all the sipahi of Rumelia. Let's imagine that these knight-monks have no heart. They will still have reason. They would not discredit an order whose goal is to spread the law of mercy throughout the East before the whole of the Christian world. So you see, Suleiman, I am counting on their cold, hard reason."

The Frank looked to be shrinking beneath my friend's fine words. Likely Cem's magnanimity, Cem's statesman's sense was killing him, and he felt guilty for trying to plant suspicion in his soul. He stood for a while longer there under Cem's gaze, then tossed his head back and said with incomprehensible despair, "My sultan, you do not want to hear me, even if I were to swear my loyalty to you all day long. I have no talent for speaking, and besides it does not behoove a man to malign his blood and the family who raised him. I beg you for just one thing: ask the grand master for a letter. Let him promise on paper not only to allow you into Rhodes, but to allow you to leave of your own free will."

"Well, now that's truly ridiculous." Cem was laughing now. "I will ask to enter the port of Rhodes, surely. But to let me leave? What a strange request, Suleiman. You can't possibly be hinting that he would turn me over to Bayezid? Then Bayezid would continue my father's wars and Rhodes would be his first victory. The Order is the enemy of the Ottomans, Suleiman, so I am not seeking refuge there by accident."

Cem kept smiling as every not particularly crafty person does when delighted by some sudden crafty thought that has come to him. While Suleiman was watching him with pity, as if there was a dangerously sick man in front of him.

As for me, in case you're asking, I also did not understand the Frank's alarm. Cem was convincing in his reasoning.

"Master, give me whatever orders you wish," Suleiman finally said, "but I will not return without the letter I spoke of."

"Go, Suleiman!" Cem ordered him, leaving this final impudence unanswered. "You shall receive a letter from me, Haydar is writing it. Three hundred of our men shall escort you to the shore—you'll find a boat there. Let's hope God makes the wind blow at your back."

"And let's hope, despite the wind at my back, that I shall return, my sultan." The Frank's eyes lit up with derision. "I don't believe the Order will be overjoyed to see a runaway Turkified knight."

VERA MUTAFCHIEVA

"Suleiman, stop!" Cem yelled to him anxiously, as if the Frank had taken off running. "Do you think you are in danger? You truly were one of them, but now our law protects you. Perhaps there are some of our men there, runaways, whom the Order has sheltered, hm?"

"All true, my sultan." The Frank did not look frightened. "One runs here, while another runs there. And with that he ceases to belong to his own people, yet does not begin to belong to the others."

"I don't understand." Cem wrinkled his nose.

"I hope you never understand," Suleiman said this simply, without malice. "I only wanted to explain one thing to you: whoever has run away once should never try to find the way back—it does not exist."

"My friend"—how easily Cem used this word!—"if my choice has fallen to you, it is because you know their language. I never thought for a moment that you might be in danger on Rhodes. Tell me: Do you wish to serve as my envoy?"

"I have already accepted, my sultan," Suleiman said. "Even if harm threatened me, or precisely because it does. But I beg you to remember: if I do not return, it will certainly not be due to my own free will; rather I have been arrested or killed. I hope my death will at least serve as a lesson that you are far too trusting."

"No!" Cem was truly scared now. "Don't you think you would be paying too high a price to convince me?"

"Too high a price?" the Frank echoed, and this time, for the first time, his words moved me. "What are you saying, my sultan? What is the worth of the life of a man without a homeland?"

And without waiting another moment, Suleiman the Frank went over to Haydar, who was finishing the letter to the Order.

"I can't even recognize him." Cem was thinking aloud.

I had never realized our man Suleiman could speak for so long and that he might might do—what? "So you see, Saadi, what hardships do to a man? Even one as young as Suleiman. All it took was a few months of wandering through the Armenian Mountains, Egypt, Lycia...."

"I'm afraid that is not what has shaken him, my lord," I replied. "I am afraid that Suleiman has experienced something far more terrible than Lycia. I think the memory of it torments him."

And with that, our conversation ended.

After that, Suleiman set off, followed by three hundred of our men. Even from afar he did not wave goodbye to us. He was riding with his beard pressed to his chest, as gloomy as foreboding incarnate.

"Our armorer looks pretty down in the mouth this morning," Cem joked.

"When has he ever looked any different?"

FIRST TESTIMONY OF PIERRE D'AUBUSSON, THE GRAND MASTER OF THE ORDER OF ST. JOHN OF JERUSALEM, ON THE HISTORY AND STATE OF THAT ORDER

ACCORDING TO YOUR and all laws, I am under no obligation to give testimony—no man can be forced to bear witness against himself, that's what the law says. I am afraid this hearing of Cem's case will end in a new accusation against me, yes, against me above all. Why do I think this, you ask? Because I have long and sad experience in this regard.

They first began blaming me long ago, more than three centuries back. In various writings, from novels to political treatises, I was painted blacker than the devil himself, I was ascribed all the characteristics of a true monster.

Forgive me for reproaching posterity—it is generally thought to be faultless. But have you not noticed that on the one hand, I am accused of the seven deadly sins, while on the other, history points to me as the most prominent grand master of the Order? Which of the two is true?

Don't answer me, I already know: both are true. The truth is that in my day, a statesman could not rise to greatness without taking on not only the image, but also the techniques of the beast.

You object that this assertion is far-fetched. Shall I recount for you several of my contemporaries who left an enviable mark on history?

I was a contemporary of Louis XI. He tried to cobble together the feudal statelets between the Rhine, the Pyrenees, and the ocean into something that would serve as the foundation of the modern French state. With extraordinary scheming and a farsighted flair for statecraft. Very well, then, who was Louis XI? A freak, begging your pardon for the term. While still a young man, he rebelled against his father and even fought an actual war against him; once on the throne, he didn't shy from any means—dagger, poison, denunciations, and torture. Louis XI's imprisoned opponents spent years in cells that were eight by eight feet. They ate, slept, and did their business in such cages. Horrifying, isn't it? And Louis loved to wander between those cages and hold sarcastic conversations with his unwilling guests.

On top of everything, he was a buffoon—a person who got a rise out of making a mockery of people and of his own dignity. He would visit his lands dressed as a simple craftsman and coquet with the citizenry even while tripling their taxes. That was Louis XI in brief, who has gone down in history as the unifier of France.

I was also a contemporary of three popes: Sixtus IV, Innocent VIII, and Alexander VI. I am excluding Innocent from my record here, since he was a personal friend. The other two were each more vile than the next. Each of them openly supported a mistress or mistresses, and fed anywhere from two to six bastard children. They delighted Rome with carnivals and bullfights. That's how our spiritual leaders at that time looked, only to reach a supreme image, embodied precisely in Alexander VI, Rodrigo de Borgia, the father of Cesare and Lucrezia. Need I describe him for you in detail? Has any criminal intrigue been uncovered in Italy since the fifteenth century in which the Borgias did not have a hand? Incidentally, on the eve of the Reformation, our clergy showed—with all their might— what they were capable of.

I was a contemporary of Lorenzo de' Medici, the tyrant of Florence, who spent his life in unbelievable rivalries and wars; I was a contemporary of Ladislaus V, who killed John Hunyadi's elder son and threw the younger in prison; I was a contemporary of Cesare Borgia, who resurrected the papacy's worldly power through a series of wars—he was a most typical heir to the Renaissance, lover to his own sister; I was a contemporary of Ferdinand of Aragon and Isabelle of Castille, who sent Columbus's squadron to plunder and enslave the New World. And whom do you think they called in as the supreme arbiter in the first colonial disputes with Portugal? The uncorruptible, wise, and just Alexander VI!

I would like to remind you of one more of my contemporaries, albeit much younger: Niccolo Machiavelli. Here, too, history is mistaken—it was not Machiavelli who thought up Machiavellianism, so that generations of statesmen could be schooled in it. He simply observed the political life of our time up close, summarized it, and called things by their real names, justifying every crime and elevating baseness, hypocrisy, and treachery to the realm of theory.

Why am I telling you this, you ask? You already knew it all even without my denunciatory exposé. I am very happy to hear this. But then why would you, who know so much, reproach a dead man just like that, outside the context of his time, using some extrahistorical idea of justice as your jumping-off point?

At first, when I was summoned, I thought to keep silent—I have squared things up with my conscience and with God. If I were to speak, if I decide to speak any further, it is only because no one can remain impartial to history's judgment. I shall prove that I acted in the name of something, in someone's interest. There is no reason why I—the one whom the d'Aubusson clan considered their pride and joy—should go down in history as a stain on the family name.

First of all, do I really need to respond to your request: to say a few words about our Order, because—or so you claim—today few people know about it and its aims? This strikes me as strange, especially given that it is the only religious order that kept its own state down to your day, even though the name changed: the Order of the Knights of Malta. Today it rules Malta, a paltry little island in the Mediterranean, a fortress that seems forgotten amidst the waves.

It is true that our Order has had a rather rum history. Unlike the other knightly brotherhoods, which began as military forces and ended peacefully, feeding their monks thanks to the production of beverages, schools for children from good families, and so on, when it comes to the Order of the Hospital of St. John of Jerusalem (also known as the Knights Hospitaller),

VERA MUTAFCHIEVA

the opposite was the case: it languished for a long time after its birth, only to transform into a military rival to a series of Mediterranean states.

Its beginnings harken back to the eleventh century, when some Italian merchants built a monastery in Jerusalem near Christ's tomb. They called it St. John's in honor of the Baptist and handed it over to the Benedictine monks, an order very well-known in its day.

The tiny monastery with its hospital was on its deathbed under the Seljuks and had only recovered a bit when the knights of the Second Crusade seized the Holy Lands and founded their own states there. The city then became the center of the Kingdom of Jerusalem.

I am truly sorry you have only such a vague sense of life in the Holy Lands at that time—it is indeed one of the most entertaining pages in world history. Somewhere, at the very end of the earth, upon land populated by savages and brigands, our Lotharingian, Flemish, and Lombardian señors built the purest feudal society possible. Everything that in the West had been met with opposition from king, church, and people was here established in a few short hours—there was no one to oppose it, because the local people throughout all those hundred or so years simply had no interest in the fact that we existed and controlled the Levant. They lived out their nomadic, desert lives and really couldn't care less that they had been counted as subjects of such-and-such a count, duke, or even a king.

Incidentally, these tiny statelets—because everyone here hurried to found his own—were doomed to grievous poverty. The West's brave nobility had not stopped to think that the basis of their luxurious lives lay in their much-despised serfs. Here, in the Near East, those serfs were missing, and the knights, who seized the Holy Lands with such a great hew and cry—we must admit they captured it easily, because only a quarter century earlier Byzantium had destroyed the Seljuks and thus in those parts a carefree interregnum reigned, while the warlike Bedouins proved unsuited to subjugation under feudal law. And so in the end, there were a large number of kings and dukes, but no peasants.

Just imagine this scene, if you please. Our monsignors in the East built castles, organized tournaments, and added ever-newer titles to their old ones. But since there was no one to work the land and pay for their magnificence, they soon began eating bulgur with mutton and wearing their festive cloaks covered in patches. And worst of all—they stopped paying their mercenary battalions in full; the battalions dispersed and made their way back West, where the good serfs were still sweating away for their benefit. And thus, the Holy Lands were left defenseless. Quite a situation, no?

At one point, not even a full century after the Holy Sepulcher was captured, the local tribes decided they'd seen enough of this entertaining story and quickly swept the Westerners out of Jerusalem. But before that, one minor occurrence of great significance to our Order took place: namely, its founding.

At the beginning of the twelfth century, the head of the St. John monastery took it back from the Benedictines and created a special order: The Knights of the Hospital of Saint John of Jerusalem.

The Bedouins' first attacks forced the Order to take up military activities, still only defensive. The Holy Father in Rome blessed this change and transformed the hospital attendants into an order of warrior monks. They defended themselves unsuccessfully, and in the end had to leave their sacred nest, and the year 1187 marked the beginning of an odyssey that puts even the *Odyssey* itself to shame. And so, retreating along the shore toward Acre, which they found to be more or less a no-man's-land they conquered it in 1191 and declared it their own state.

Do I hear someone laughing? You can't get beyond the framework of your own time. You are astonished that a few hundred ragged soldiers could capture some city they had never even heard of and declare it their own—for us, this was completely within the normal order of things, just page through history and see.

And thus the "Knights of the Hospital of St. John" began a new life far from any hospital, monastery, or obligation to those in need, making ends meet by raiding the nearby villages. But the Order suffered a new blow in 1191 when the local population, driven to desperation, chased the knights out of Acre as well. They piled onto several ships, hopped over to Cyprus, captured the island, and so on. The history of the Order developed in precise iterations—once again several decades of rule over some entirely foreign, barely fertile island, once again followed by failure; in 1310 the Hospitallers left Cyprus, captured Rhodes, and established their state there.

I can tell you much about Rhodes. I personally spent the best part of my years there, thirty in all. I knew the fortress like the back of my hand, wrapped as it was in a half circle around the rocky bay, its narrow streets lined with tall, identical houses, the deep, cool colonnades arching over the flagstones. I knew every window and every person in the city. It was entirely made of stone—there was no place for greenery on that piece of land, where knights, local citizens, and foreigners mixed. The limestone mountains lavishly offered us soft, light stone, so Rhodes gleamed a blinding white under the southern sun like a skull that had long lain on the sandy soil.

The St. John's Cathedral loomed over everything in the city, oppressively enormous. It was never packed during services, because the local population of Rhodes remained Greek, adherents to that erroneous Eastern creed, and thus did not attend our services. The locals would leave the city to pray at the myriad impoverished and sheepish chapels perched on every outcropping of the island.

We left the Greeks to their wrongheaded prayers. Given our dismal experience, we did not want to irritate them. After all, they were producers and traders; they helped us during the numerous attacks on the island, and in the end, they were Christians, albeit unclean ones.

The other large building that lorded over the city was the grand master's palace. I lived there for decades and imagined I knew all of its hidden corners, and only far too late did I come to realize I'd been fooling myself. Every one of my predecessors had added new secret passageways to the old ones, and in this way every one of them had increased his own safety and his ability to eavesdrop, surprise, and punish. Afterward he had gone to his grave with the secret of these passageways, so it is no wonder that the next grand master, creating his own hidden doors, invisible peepholes, and staircases that began in a fireplace only to end in a cupboard, had no inkling of those that already existed.

Besides the palace, Rhodes had two more magnificent buildings—the hospital of the Knights of St. John and the Auberge de toutes les langues. The former was not strictly necessary—few of the pilgrims headed to the Holy Lands fell ill on Rhodes; the living conditions on the island were wonderful. Whereas the auberge was always packed to the rafters. Not with pilgrims, for which it had been intended, those were rare; merchants from the West and the Levant filled it. Because Rhodes was the acknowledged—inevitable crossroads for Levantine trade.

Gradually the warrior monks' task shifted. Their fight against the infidels—rulers of the Holy Sepulcher—was replaced by their struggle against Mediterranean corsairs. The Mediterranean Sea, in my opinion, is the cradle of that great movement. All kinds of would-be knights tossed out of the Holy Lands straight into the sea; all manner of outcasts from the ancient population of the Levant, whose lives had been made impossible by a series of invaders; all sorts of deserters from the sultan's army of Seljuks, Arabs, Ottomans—that whole desperate and extremely crafty riffraff of the East simply loaded itself onto a ship, raised full sails, and cruised with their impure intentions upon the most hospitable sea in the world.

But Italy and France's trade with the Levant and the Balkans passed through the Mediterranean Sea. It could've fed three times more corsairs than those already swarming those waters, but these traders were not at all amenable to supporting those already there with a third of their profits. For this reason, aid streamed toward Rhodes—the center of the fight against the corsairs—from Venice, Napoli, Genoa, and Marseille. Merchants fed the Order so their goods could travel safely; in short, they fed their own naval militia.

Don't think for a minute that we did not earn that gold with sweat, blood, and tears—fighting pirates is no easy job. But our knights had mastered it thoroughly—it was a question of practice.

So, you say you can imagine everything except the life of a warrior monk, whose everyday reality is the threat of corsairs. Here is the thing: in our times we took it as a given that a man lived with danger and difficulty, no matter whether he was a warrior, a merchant, or a monk. And we nearly found satisfaction in that—just imagine!

Even now, I feel pride when I recall Rhodes, our Rhodes, on holidays. Blindingly white, stern, and elegant, as if created to serve as the backdrop for the Knights of Rhodes. Some two thousand men—hard-baked warriors and cleric-scholars—in the uniform of the Order: black, with black cloaks that hung to the knee and a white cross over the heart. It always seemed to me—whenever I watched them from the palace as they moved through the streets—that their ranks were the shadows of the houses, the cathedral, and the palace, that they solidified the foundations of this ancient city.

Because Rhodes was truly ancient, it had known the rule of the Hellenes, the Persians, the Romans, the Byzantines, the Saracens, and other nameless splinter kingdoms. And we captured it in a dark time, just before the Ottoman expansion. But it would take a century and a half before the Ottoman fleet arrived on Rhodes. This is something I remember personally. What's more, history has dubbed me of all people the defender of Rhodes and the easternmost beachhead of Catholicism. I hope it does not strike you as immodest to recall: I, Pierre d'Aubusson, was the only person who forced Mehmed II to back down. Yes, even if a new hearing of Cem's case ends in an accusation against me, you will nevertheless not succeed in robbing me of my glory: with two thousand monks, I withstood the great Conqueror.

I will not tell you about the great siege of Rhodes in 1480, about the battles and our victory—they preceded the times of the Cem affair. I must merely underscore that our victory greatly elevated us in the eyes of the devout West. In all countries beholden to the papacy, dozens of tales or songs circulated, describing our feats, usually in exaggerated terms. We would have preferred that ardor to have a more material emanation, since the siege had sapped the Order's strength. Our treasury was empty; half of our ships had been sunk. For the past five or six years, Levantine trade had dried up; merchants were afraid to stop over at Rhodes, because Rhodes was at war, while their route from Genoa or Venice to the Levant was unthinkable without that stopover point for respite.

In a word, such warm praise was cold comfort to us. Thus, when we heard of the Conqueror's death, we saw the hand of God at work—the Almighty himself had cleared from our path the man who sooner or later would have put an end to Rhodes.

Soon after word of that death came other news, better still, about the internecine war between Bayezid and Cem. We didn't dare believe our ears. From the little I've told you, you're surely convinced we warrior monks were not used to gifts from fate.

Although hopeful, such news did not mean anything in particular to us. We did not have peace with the Empire yet, only a truce; Ottoman troops were still rallied under their banners, even if they were now occupied with Cem; Bayezid's sanjak-beys still seized our ships, imprisoned our sailors, or flat-out slaughtered them. Could we really hope Bayezid would not restart military operations against Rhodes once he'd taken care of his brother?

In my opinion, there was no basis for such hopes. We were only allowed to rest easy as long as Cem's rebellion lasted. Once Bayezid got rid of his brother, the subjugation of his troops would be absolute. And a quick victory would be especially desirable for the new sultan, whom the rebels accused of precisely lacking military acumen, and of being cowardly and peace loving.

Don't think that my line of reasoning is such because centuries have passed; that was my opinion even then. I was brought up by the Roman church and our Order. Have you ever wondered what Rome owes the unsurpassed endurance of its dominance to? Precisely to this: the ability to always soberly assess a situation and find the most suitable action or counteraction.

One of modern man's pleasant delusions is that only humanism could liberate human thought, freeing it from prejudice and replacing dogma with flexibility. A delusion, I'm telling you! Peruse the annals of the Roman church and you will be convinced that centuries before Machiavelli and various Renaissance scribblers and Protestant squawkers, we acted without prejudice; we recognized reality and took it into consideration; we operated within it. Perhaps we didn't confess it, we didn't preach it—therein lay our strength. There are things that are indecent to speak of; they go without saying.

Yes, I have gone on a tangent. I needed to explain to you that at the time, we understood events not very differently than you do now. Don't fool yourselves into thinking humanity, which has a million years of history behind it, drastically changed precisely in the last five hundred years. Incidentally, on the eve of July 9, 1482, I was absolutely clear on what we could expect from the end of Cem's rebellion.

SECOND TESTIMONY OF PIERRE D'AUBUSSON
ON THE EVENTS OF JULY 9–12, 1482

ON JULY 9, when dawn had not yet broken and I was preparing for holy mass, I was surprised to learn that a messenger had arrived from Ahmed Pasha. I had unpleasant memories of Ahmed Pasha: this overly competent general had recently captured Otranto, marking the start of the direct Turkish threat to the West.

I dressed quickly and went down to the receiving room, imagining along the way what awaited us if the truce were broken. Our defenses still needed to be rebuilt after coming under heavy fire from Mehmed's navy; a call to recruit Christian fighters from Italy, Spain, or France would take at least two months; refilling our treasury would take another kind of call—to all the believers in the West—which would require more than two months.

Candles burned in the receiving room. Dawn had still not quite broken, and I did not like to converse in the semidarkness —there was no reason for your opponent to hide his eyes.

The messenger was led in. He was not a Turk, I could tell that immediately. They had foisted these Christian apostates on me before, the ones who served the sultan better than any born Muslim, as they knew us far too well. More than one ambitious fellow from the enslaved countries or the West had found a welcome reception with the Conqueror. His palace feted hundreds of such traitors, while among them at least a dozen were only ostensibly turncoats—they did invaluable work for us. I am fully convinced that at least a dozen of the many Greeks, Levantines, and Dalmatians who had fled to Rhodes did similar invaluable service on the sultan's payroll. For this reason, we kept every refugee or repentant apostate who had again sought Christian shelter under close watch. We ostensibly followed their movements as well, but I would swear very little of what was decided even at the Order's Supreme Council remained a secret to the sultan. However, I consoled myself with the fact that we, too, were just as well-informed of Topkapi's secrets.

Ahmed's messenger struck me as more likely a Levantine than a Greek. As I expected, he announced that he did not speak our language and asked for a translator. A very cheap trick, which we regularly used with success at Topkapi, but which didn't fool us: the messenger would pretend not to know a given language so as to follow the conversation without anyone suspecting anything. But we were always suspicious.

And so the translator relayed to us Ahmed Pasha's offer. Through Ahmed Pasha, Bayezid insisted on nothing more and nothing less than transforming the wavering truce between us into lasting peace.

Well, well, well! We are no threat to the Empire whatsoever, so they have no need to offer peace without us even seeking it out, I thought to myself. *Therefore? Therefore, there are circumstances forcing Bayezid to make this disadvantageous offer.*

"We are particularly flattered by the benevolence of your great sovereign," I began slowly, trying to put my thoughts in order even as I spoke. "But we do not understand how we can speak of peace with the Sublime Porte when your master continues his unfriendly actions against us. Barely a week hence our ship the *Santa Marina* was captured, and we know nothing of the fate of her crew. Negotiations must begin with goodwill on both sides. We beg your master to free our brothers held by the Empire. Then we can negotiate in good faith."

"So this likely means"—the messenger had been prepared for such a turn—"that you will also free the captives taken during the siege of Rhodes."

"No. They were captured on our land. We want from you men who were caught in neutral waters."

The messenger was slow to reply. Clearly he was debating whether to accept such a humiliating, one-sided condition on the spot or to ask for permission from his superiors. Precisely the latter was my goal: let him sail back and forth for a whole two weeks! But quite suddenly the messenger announced:

"The *Santa Marina* was captured by the sanjak-bey of Lycia. He acted of his own accord and will pay for it. You shall receive both your ship and your men as soon as I return."

Come on, now, I thought. *This is really too much. Bayezid has authorized a simple messenger to accept our conditions. Something very serious threatens Bayezid.... Could it be Cem? Could we have underestimated him? It may be true that the army supports Cem.*

Despite my invitations, Ahmed Pasha's messenger did not rest before his return trip. He left us that very same afternoon of July 9 and with that further strengthened my suspicions that Bayezid was in dire straits. I refrained from sharing this with anyone whatsoever. Luckily the messenger had visited me very early, and no one, other than the translator, was present at our conversation. Thus I reported to the Council that Bayezid had offered us peace, and said no more. Why, you ask?

In our brotherhood, which numbered less than two thousand men, all the characteristics of a state were present: a court, factions, and struggles between them. Amidst the thirty or so members of the Grand Council and amidst the nine from the Sovereign Council, I knew there were champions of all the worldly powers. This was due to some extent to the very structure of the Order—it was split into eight languages, each of which had representatives on the Sovereign Council, and thus it was perfectly natural for those representatives to defend the interests of their sovereigns. I would have been ever so pleased if things had ended there. But they were much more complicated.

In the upper echelons of our ranks, you could find adherents of every tendency within the Vatican and Europe. Every cardinal, every grand master, every Western duke had his own paid man inside our Order. So I always felt like I was being watched from all sides—starting from the Holy Father himself and ending with the Duke of Burgundy, for example.

For this reason, I had adopted a certain type of behavior, which, I would argue, has been the fate of every ruler from the creation of the world down to the present day: I trusted only myself.

So I waited until the evening of July 9—one of many days during which my worries were solely my own, with no right to unburden myself, to seek advice or assistance. One of many days during which I prayed amidst a crowd of knights, debated the rebuilding of the fortress walls in the Council, ate roasted meat, and drank Cypriot wine; I read, I held discussions. And I tried to hide my alarm—effortlessly, because dissembling had already become part of my nature. But momentous events were on the horizon!

Nevertheless, the developments on July 10 surpassed all of my expectations. In the afternoon, they announced a messenger from Cem.

This time it was neither too early nor too late so as to give me an excuse, but I broke all the rules and received the messenger alone. I had no doubts that at least a dozen brothers would use the secret passageways in the walls, fireplaces, and chimneys to invisibly attend the meeting. But ten was still less than the Grand Council's thirty, and of one thing I was certain: no eavesdropper shared his findings with any other—it would have lowered the information's value.

The two brothers on duty led in the messenger.

I don't know whether I managed to hide my surprise—I, who hoped I could control every muscle of my face—when I saw whom I was to meet. Brother Bruno—and this man had the audacity to stand before me!

Four years ago, when our struggle with Mehmed Khan was only just beginning, I started receiving reports about Bruno acting strangely. Two or three times he refused to attend holy mass, without giving any explanation; he hinted to the brother sharing his cell that he had only now seen the truth and he still could not believe that which he had seen; once he had screamed—not drunkenly, he was simply off his head—that everything on Rhodes was rotten, stinking, revolting. In any case, I don't remember Brother Bruno's ravings exactly, but their general sentiment was more than clear to me, because he was not the first, and certainly not the last.

We'd had others like him before, men who had taken the tonsure in some trivial monastery in Bohemia or Bavaria and had served their long novitiate among a half dozen devout brothers feebleminded from fasting or mere simpleheartedness; thus they experienced a severe shock upon joining our Order. They were shocked by nothing more than the clash between their concept of a society of warrior monks and the reality of that society.

It is well-known that the truth is far richer in variety, coincidences, and repetitions than even the wildest imaginings. Spare me the details—I am not obliged to list off for you all the things that could shock a deeply devout provincial monk transplanted into the rich reality of Rhodes.

I had hoped that Brother Bruno would quickly sweat out the crisis of his revelations and would claim that which was his due—after all, the Order offered more than a few opportunities. If he still could not find the strength to overcome his crisis, we would have helped him. You can interpret that as you wish.

And it was just then that I found out Bruno had run away. But not before writing a letter to the brotherhood—addressed to all the brothers, what impudence!—in which he called upon them to destroy this nest of violence and depravity with their own hands and to scatter to the four corners of the globe. How does that strike you?

To us, the Grand Council, where we discussed his letter, it struck us as monstrous. Bruno was immediately not only excommunicated from the Order, but also from our Holy Church, and in the chapels of Rhodes an anathema against our prodigal brother was pronounced. In this way we cut all ties with him and very soon forgot him. No one knew where Bruno had pointed his sinful feet. To us, he was a dead man.

And now this dead man had dared to resurrect himself before my very eyes, and not even as a repentant sinner, but as the messenger of a prince.

With whatever swiftness my deep shock allowed, I decided for the moment it was best to pretend not to recognize him, as doing so would waste time unnecessarily. Plus I couldn't let the thorny but undecisive question of the apostasy of one of our rank-and-file knights distract me from what was incomparably more important.

I turned toward the window so as not to look upon that insolent face, transformed as it was by foreign garb yet nevertheless unpleasantly familiar; so as not to meet his mocking and challenging eyes.

"In the name of the Order, I greet Prince Cem in the person of his messenger," I uttered in some vague direction. "What news do you bring?"

Unlike Bayezid's man, Bruno did not ask for a translator. He spoke to me in pure Latin.

"My master sends you his respects. The vicissitudes of fate, which have still not had their final say in the dispute between Cem and his self-appointed brother, have forced my master to retreat to Lycia. Since he wishes to discuss further steps in his struggle with the wise brothers of the Order, Cem Sultan asks to be accepted in Rhodes with all the honors his birth demands. He believes that in answer to his request, the holy brothers will send ships to collect him and his men from the Asiatic shore. He also believes he will be given the freedom to enter and exit Rhodes as he wishes."

Bruno recited this speech with a bored, almost somnolent voice. Likely with this he meant to underscore how little he was impressed by his role as imperial messenger and by our holy reception.

I had to exert myself significantly—even though our spiritual training does not allow for extremes—so as to not curse aloud.

"The Order is flattered," I said instead, "that the son of the great Conqueror, cleansing his heart of the old animosity toward the brothers of St. John, has honored us with his attention. Once the Great Council examines the question, you shall be informed."

"I would only like to remind you that every moment is precious. While your Council is deciding, Cem Sultan may no longer be among the living."

"If you knew our Order better"—I could not help myself—"you would not accuse us of sluggishness."

Bruno withdrew with a deliberately casual gait—he wanted to annoy me.

VERA MUTAFCHIEVA

Forget Bruno! I wiped him from my thoughts. *Great God above! Could you really be gifting this opportunity to me, the third son of Count d'Aubusson, an impoverished knight from Creuse! An unfathomable opportunity. Only yesterday our Order was under threat from the Conqueror; only yesterday we sought funds in vain to repair our decimated walls so we could withstand a new attack. While today—two thousand knights, with me at their head! We will play a role in the fate of the world.*

At my invitation, the brothers gathered in the hall of the Great Council. It was majestic in its semidarkness mottled by the colorful stained-glass windows, with its walls dressed in cedar and Damascene brocade. Like a flock of old, wise birds, the monks flew in silently. "My eagles!"—I wanted to say to them, even though I knew half of them would give their souls and the world itself to push me out of their path—"Our hour has come!"

Our elders were already sitting around the long Council table. The dark marble of its surface gave a crooked reflection of thirty faces: woolly gray beards, holes for eyes, and no foreheads.

I informed them of Cem's request.

The hall stayed so quiet for so long that the sound of my fingernails tapping on the ebony could be heard. Every one of my fine brothers was now calculating what he would earn if he somehow sent word that very night to his unspoken master. I didn't care—that hadn't deprived me of my major bargaining chip. Cem would be in Rhodes before any of those masters could catch his breath. As you can see, our era, with its slow communications dependent on favorable winds, storms, and corsairs, had its advantages.

The first to break the silence was the Pilier of Castille, Don Álvaro de Zúñiga. If there is anything I envy you for, it is that you were not forced to endure the company of this individual; Don Álvaro was an exceptionally unpleasant man.

And this time he yet again explained in his pompous manner things that in any case had been clear from my first words. When he finally deigned to spare us further flowery speeches, I underscored how it was not the time for empty blather. Everyone supported me—the Council had never before seen such unanimity, I had never before seen the brothers so indecently excited. It was as if we were not a holy order, but an auction house, where expensive goods had suddenly dropped to a ridiculously low price, causing buyers to jostle and plunder.

Everything went unbelievably smoothly. I agreed without objection that Don Álvaro should set sail for Lycia—he, of course, had offered himself up for the job—at the head of a flotilla of seven ships, including the trireme *Treasure*, our flagship. For Cem and his suite, the trireme alone would have been enough, but we foresaw the possibility of battle.

When Bayezid's name was mentioned in that regard, I remembered that—swept away by the new news—I had forgotten his messenger from the day before. It was now crystal clear: Bayezid had learned of Cem's intentions before we did. He surely had learned them from a spy he had planted among Cem's troops. And so he had hurried to broker peace with the Order, so he could demand his brother a week later. During a mere truce, such a demand would be out of place.

I smiled at these thoughts; I imagined Bayezid when he realized he had missed his chance. Let him stew! Now we would have the upper hand, since we would be mediating between the two royal brothers.

VERA MUTAFCHIEVA

The only thing we had left to do was settle the bills for the celebrations. That business took more time—you never talk about money more than when you have none. Then we called in Cem's messenger to inform him of our decision. Inwardly on tenterhooks, I waited to see how the brothers would receive the erstwhile Bruno.

Their shock was difficult to describe; they sat as if thunder-struck; here and there I could hear whispers, exclamations. But these were monks schooled in fighting their own impulses, so their quiet murmurs soon died out.

That shameless apostate—he truly was the most cold-blooded monster I've ever met—walked all the way past the long table with a self-confidence that would have enraged even the angels. *God Almighty*, I thought. *Does Bruno really know so little of the Order that he feels himself safe from danger?*

"Our Great Council," I began when he stood before me, "discussed Prince Cem's request. It would be an honor for the Council to offer shelter and advice to such an eminent noble prince. Our flotilla will set sail immediately to collect him from the Asian shore."

"What portion of Cem Sultan's loyal troops will accompany him to Rhodes?" The messenger asked, his tone businesslike.

"For the purposes that lead Prince Cem to us, we do not see the need for troops. Our fortress is not so large, and feeding its inhabitants is already a challenge. It is of mutual benefit to not overburden Rhodes." Incidentally, whether he had five hundred soldiers or none, Prince Cem would continue his struggle from now on with the same chances of success; such numbers made no difference.

Bruno, standing with his face toward me alone and with his back to the Council, did not smile, but rather grinned like a guttersnipe, driving home that he suspected the real reason for our refusal.

"I recall to your attention," he said emphatically, "that my master has requested not only freedom to enter but also to depart from Rhodes, when he feels his work here is done. I did not hear your opinion on this matter."

"You shall hear it." And I read aloud the scroll they brought to me. "In recent days the excellent messenger Suleiman has come to us in the name of His Excellency Prince and Master Cem Sultan. Through the letter of said master, as well as verbally, the abovementioned messenger announced that Prince Cem Sultan desires to come to Rhodes to discuss with us various topics, upon which he shall receive and follow our advice as advice coming from friends who wish him well. In such a case, he demands that his person be protected according to the accepted laws.

"Furthermore, we, moved by the long-lasting friendship we feel toward him, and by the hope that his visit will be of mutual advantage, send to him via this bearer our agreement, through which he will receive a full, comprehensive, and universal guarantee for the safety of his person and the observance of all accepted laws. They apply both to His Royal Highness Prince Cem Sultan, as well as to those who follow him to Rhodes in their capacity as his royal court—Turks and Moors, or any other nationality. In full freedom and security, along with their possessions, valuables, and money, they will be able to live on Rhodes, to remain here as long as they like, and to leave of their own free will or upon the will of Prince Cem Sultan, without any obstacles or hindrances. As a certification of this, we place our lead seal below.

Promulgated in Rhodes. 12 July 1482."

The messenger heard me out, without the mocking expression ever leaving his face. He likely was thinking that even a dozen such certificates weren't worth a bag of grain. I personally had never heard a more exhaustive guarantee than this.

I sense that all of my oaths will fail to convince you that I speak the simple truth: we did not know how events would unfold, thus on July 12, we still had no unspoken intentions. It was enough for us that our interference would prolong the unrest that weakened our most fearsome enemy.

While Cem's messenger once again walked past them, the leading Hospitallers looked very triumphant. Even more so than the day when we had gathered in that very same hall to celebrate our victory over Mehmed the Conqueror.

SIXTH TESTIMONY OF THE POET SAADI ON THE EVENTS BETWEEN JULY 10 AND 27, 1482

WE NOTICED THE ships early in the morning.

We were not waiting for them on the shore; we were afraid. Over the past few days our little army had begun melting away like a snowdrift in the sun. Death had thinned our ranks, but fear much more so. The soldiers figured our cause had no future, and they didn't see why they should wait around for that future, baring their necks to Bayezid's blade. So every morning we woke up with 15 or so fewer men—our people were running away. And this meant that eventually, one of those runaways would find his way to Ahmed Pasha's camp by nightfall and, to save his own skin, would report that our messenger had set out for Rhodes. In short, we were afraid of being cut off from the sea as well.

Once again, Haydar saved the day. First, he convinced Cem it was pointless to wander farther through the sinister valleys of Lycia, and he asked Kasim Bey to secure us a ship. The bey took a whole night to give us his answer—surely he had a lot to think over that night—but in the morning he announced we would have a ship. Moreover, he declared he would send us to the shore with his Karamanians. He would outfit us with a letter making it clear that the last Karamanoglu was ready at any moment to step up and take Cem's side, but he himself would not board the ship with us.

Cem listened to his words, distracted. Our last experienced, old general was leaving us, and Cem accepted it as if he had long since taken leave of Kasim and his soldiers in his soul.

"Very well, Kasim Bey," he said simply. "Thank you for being the last to leave me."

"I'm not leaving you, my sultan!" Kasim blazed up. "In the future, too, you will be the master of my sword and my heart. Just one word from you..."

"Let us not hide the truth behind pretty words, Kasim Bey. We have fed ourselves on false hopes for too long."

"But my sultan, if you arrive at our western borders, if you set out for Rumelia with an allied army..."

"Yes, then things will be different. Not only you, but then many leaders will come over to my side. That's exactly what I need: an ally. I am going to look for one."

So ended the final conversation between Cem and Kasim Bey, even though the Karamanians led us for two more days. Cem was silent the whole time, lost in his thoughts; in those two days, Kasim did not speak to him either. Everything had been said.

I thought we must be dreaming when—between two jagged, crumbling cliffs, red as the whole of Lycia—the sea stretched before our eyes. We had grown so unused to other colors besides all shades of red, the sight of that calm, smooth, moist blueness took us aback—it seemed impossible. Then our troops, desiccated by the desert heat, charged toward the shore like madmen, wading right in along with their horses, splashing one another and laughing with an unnatural, long-forgotten laughter.

Water... I wanted to grasp it with closed eyes, to sense its nearness through the soft humidity, through the wonderful caress of the lapping waves. When I looked over, I saw Cem, too, had closed his eyes and thrown his head back, as if submitting to its caress. In this, as in many things, the two of us resonated in tandem.

Our second surprise was the ship. Off to the side, a ship with no flag was indeed rocking gently in a little bay. "A pirate ship," I shuddered, because Cem Sultan would be very precious booty indeed for any brigand; Cem, even if gaunt from hunger, ragged and weak at that moment, was still worth the weight of half of Bayezid's treasury.

"Pirates, hm?" Cem said without flinching. I think he could not have cared less whether he would fall into the hands of thieves or the devil himself.

"Even brigands have their price, my sultan," Kasim Bey explained, flustered. "And their heads can't reckon that my five bags of gold aren't the most they could get for saving some stranger, I swear to you!"

Now that's not something I would swear to, I thought. I doubted it was precisely fools who became pirates.

Cem received these assurances from Kasim Bey with indifference as well. We piled onto the unmarked ship, thirty or so men. Cem didn't pick and choose; we made the decision on our own. Barely thirty men wanted to accompany Cem into the unknown.

Perhaps it is not significant for you, but here I cannot keep silent: years later, I still recalled my movement as I pushed off from the shore, those hundred or so yards of water that changed me from citizen to refugee. A most ordinary movement—I had done it dozens of times before. A most ordinary strip of water—a hundred yards of calm, caressing sea.

Yes, it's true: there I again decided my own fate. Without realizing it was precisely what I was doing: defining my entire life. It was completely natural for me to follow Cem. Not only love bound me to him, a very deep love, devotion to the point of self-destruction; in my thoughts, Cem was everything worth living, fighting, and dying for.

It sounds unconvincing, but then I was convinced. I was convinced Cem was fated to embody the dreams of generations of thinkers and poets; Cem's victory would be the victory of wisdom over brute force; Cem's rule would free from prejudice, dogma, and vulgar idiocy the primordial law of beauty that had never been destroyed but which had never yet reigned.

I imagined Cem's rule as an unceasing triumph of progress. Is it just coincidence that precisely here in our lands for centuries heresies and new teachings had arisen? Is it just coincidence that precisely in our lands religious institutions—Christian and Muslim—had not managed to dull the striving toward profane poetry and positive knowledge? Is it just coincidence that here man had always lived as a seeker? *No*, I thought. *This centuries-old ferment of souls must one day lead to us, precisely to the East—some heretofore unseen and inimitable sovereign who will clear a path for this age-old thirst. Could Providence find a more brilliant weapon than the poet Cem?*

I had thought this for years and most of all throughout the year of our battles. It must have imperceptibly predetermined my choice to follow Cem, wherever his path might take him. Now Cem was setting off into exile, and I was obliged to accompany my master. I never thought twice about it.

Much later, as I told you, I recalled how we pushed off from the Asian shore. "Why, God," I said to myself, "why did something unusual not happen at that moment? A storm of red snow, bright green lightning, or a howl of wind like the horns of Jericho? Why did you not send us a fearsome sign, so as to stop us amidst the motion that decided our entire lives? Why must there be sin and after that atonement? Are you not a hard-hearted god who watches our suffering and sneers?"

Yes, God was likely watching me and laughing as our oars slapped softly between the shore and the ship. Watching and saying, "You must learn, my dear children, that every movement and word in your lives is a choice—you make choices in every single moment of your lives, but then cast the blame for your troubles on me. While I am simply watching you, my children, and waiting for you to pay the price for human experience."

I didn't hear the conversation between Kasim Bey and the sailors. Likely they were agreeing on when and how they would receive their payment. Then Kasim went over to our master and bowed as low as he could, to the very deck itself, and with reverence he grasped the faded hem of Cem's cloak and pressed his lips to it.

I thought Cem would start crying—if sadness had a face, it was Cem's face at that moment. Instead, the old warrior burst out sobbing. You do know that in our culture it was not undignified for a man to cry; sometimes decency even called for it, as long as there were no women present. And we rarely had women in our company. The words the two of them exchanged were the most ordinary words of parting. In such situations it is customary to speak of future meetings, even though often both parties know very well that there will be no such meeting.

I watched Kasim Bey's back as he climbed down the rope ladder from the boat—it was the broad but already slightly sagging back of an aged warrior. *If the day of Cem Sultan's triumph ever comes*, I thought to myself, *will you even live to see it, old man?*

For four whole days our ship sat at anchor near the shore. No one was chasing us, so there was no reason for us to leave the place where the knights would come looking for us. The Karamanians had set up their camp on the shore, and in the evening we could see slow shadows passing before their fires; Kasim Bey did not leave the shore, either, before he was certain the knights had accepted Cem.

In the late afternoon on the fourth day, we heard a din coming from the shore, we could see some kind of commotion. A yellowish-red dust cloud rose to the east of Kasim's camp. It crept tightly over the earth at the exact speed of cavalry.

Everything was clear without a word: Ahmet Pasha meant to cut off the rebels from the sea. He wanted to force them back into the hell that was Lycia.

Very cleverly, while they were searching for cover, our men moved the ship behind the rocks. And with our hearts in our throats, we watched the battle between Ahmet Pasha and Kasim. It wasn't even a battle—Kasim's forces defended themselves as they filed back into the mountains. Ahmed, for his part, did not follow them there. We saw how his troops stretched out, always keeping to the shore, and at night their fires would flare up, sometimes here and sometimes there. He was guarding the passes toward Lycia.

Whether Ahmed Pasha had not noticed our sorry bireme; whether he noticed it but did not have his own ships at hand; whether he figured that for him, Ahmed Pasha, even if Cem were onboard the ship, a further battle between the brothers would be especially advantageous—I don't know and I can't say. In any case, we remained close to the shore for another dozen days, and no one disturbed our peace. We did not sail out to sea, as we were waiting for our rendezvous; besides, we were afraid to meet others like ourselves: corsairs. We awaited this rendezvous with sinking hearts: Would they accept us in Rhodes? All day we paced back and forth along the narrow stern or bow of the bireme. Actually, only we were the ones pacing: from dawn till dusk Cem stood leaning his elbows on the railing, his eyes fixed on the Asian shore. I remembered the night—a year had already passed since then—when Cem had whispered to me feverishly, "I am afraid of the border, Saadi." Since then I had thought this fear of his had faded, but on that day the border was so visible, marked in yellowish red above the blue infinity, that Cem once again returned to his fear: the border!

I didn't try to cheer him up. In those days Cem seemed to have reached the very rock bottom of human anguish. I knew that inaction and uncertainty contributed to this: how were things unfolding in Anatolia, had Kasim managed to slip away, had the Porte and Rhodes already made peace? We knew nothing. Our ship rocked gently between the sky and the water; its oars jutted out, unmoving; flocks of birds rested in the rigging.

I have heard that sometimes poetry speaks of such ghost-ships, which shipwrecked men mistake for real ones. We resembled just such a ship.

Until we caught sight of the caravels on the morning of July 20. They were sailing headlong upon the morning's still-dozing, silvery waters, and the dawn transformed them into pink herons—Cem had kept such herons at his palace in Karamania, because he loved all beauty.

At the head of the flotilla, a large trireme plowed the waves, flying the flag of the Order: a white cross on a black background.

"They've come! Rhodes will take us in!" I wanted to rejoice, but my heart was still sinking; the flag immediately reminded me of Suleiman the Frank and his evil omens.

Cem had long been gazing at the little flotilla. It, too, probably seemed unreal to him, as everything did during those days. Only when his suite started scampering about did he say to me, "Saadi, get ready, get me ready as well. Let us not forget that I go to Rhodes not as a fugitive, but as the lawful ruler of an empire."

We dug through our trunks, which we hadn't even opened since Cairo—after all, we had spent the last half year always on marches or in battles. We took out Cem's ceremonial attire and dressed him in it; we wrapped a dozen ells of the finest silk around his head. Only then did I realize how gaunt my friend was—it was as if he had put on another man's clothes.

Yet he still looked magnificent. Over the past fifteen months since Mehmed Khan's death, Cem had grown up. I asked myself what gave this away and answered my own question: in the bitter sharpness that had broken Cem's carefree charm. Yes, that was it—perhaps a man grows up precisely when something in him is broken.

I followed my master onto the stern. All of us, his modest suite, lined up in a half circle behind Cem. Likely we were a cheerful sight in the oblique morning rays, a crowd of young men dressed in satin, brocade, and Morocco leather of every imaginable color.

The caravels had slackened their sails; their oars took aim at the sky. It was clear: the Order would not enter the coastal waters; they would abide by the law.

We saw a small boat break away from the large trireme and row quickly toward us. Cem did not take his eyes from the boat carrying his fate.

There were two of them; we could already make them out. One was a knight, dressed all in black. A moment later, we recognized the other man as well. Suleiman. Suleiman was alive!

Cem barely nodded at the knight—an aging, puffy man with colorless eyes. His voice was colorless as well when he extended a short greeting to Cem and even called him "prince." Suleiman translated his words, looking down on him with such disgust as if he were a louse—Suleiman could give such looks.

Without wasting any time, the messenger handed Cem the scroll. Suleiman began reading it—a lavish pile of words, from which the only thing we understood was that we would be welcomed to Rhodes and could leave whenever we wished.

I was already losing interest when something made me prick up my ears. In the very same voice, as if he were still reading, Suleiman turned to Cem.

"Master, only a half hour from now and it will already be too late. I swear to you, Cem Sultan, for the sake of all the goodness you have shown me: believe me, do not go to Rhodes!"

Cem's face went pale under his deep sunburn—Suleiman the Frank's boldness startled him. Then he realized that the man would not have warned him if the knight had known Turkish. Cem, too, tried to reply with indifference, as if he wanted additional news from Rhodes. "You have come back alive, Suleiman. That is no small thing."

"I am afraid I am the cheese that will draw the mouse into the trap, my sultan. I swear to you: you are in danger."

"Our lot has been cast, Suleiman," Cem concluded faintly. "Let us go!"

The Frank wanted to say something more, but Cem had already passed him by. Cem only paused for a moment, before tossing his leg over the ship's railing. He turned toward the sailors and their leader—the most motley crew I have ever laid eyes on—and said loudly, "Thank you, friends. For better or for worse, you have protected Cem Sultan!"

The corsairs crowded around the rail, shouting—each in his own language, and they were many. And these cries of thirty-odd brigands seemed to remind Cem of the welcome he had received from his troops; they recalled to him the voice of the crowd. Now Cem stood apart from the human crowd, because we were only his entourage—a handful of paid and fed servants.

Cem froze as he was, with one leg already on the rope ladder, his eyes sweeping over the corsairs—for the first time I read doom in his gaze. It was as if Cem wanted to hold on to that final moment in which he was the master of his own movements. And this impulse made him turn again to Suleiman—that living warning always attendant on our master.

"You stay, Suleiman," he said softly. "I will not have peace if you are with me on Rhodes."

"I shall follow you, my sultan. Nothing more can happen to me."

Then we climbed down the ladder. Ten or so of us at first, as many as could fit in the boat. It came back again and yet again to collect the whole suite along with our baggage.

We were received on the large trireme by Don Álvaro. It was a magnificent welcome. Expensive carpets covered the whole ship. They even hung off the edges of the ship, so that it glinted colorfully from afar like a water flower from a fairy tale. Against this wealth of color, the knights stood out like black stains. Sinister —I did not want to think this word even to myself, but it stuck in my head. Don Álvaro welcomed Cem with a very long speech. Suleiman translated it quite carelessly, or so it seemed to me since one short phrase of his corresponded to a torrent of words from Álvaro. Cem thanked him briefly and then retreated to the chambers assigned to him.

I will never forget our first evening among Christians. I later grew used to their customs and character, but then everything was still new to me. The knights thronged to the decks for dinner, out in the open. A colorful cloth had been stretched out above our heads. Dozens of candles in deep glass cups lit up the table, which was piled up so richly that it made my head spin.

After all, we had been surviving on hardtack and silty water for months already.

Actually, there were two tables, across from each other. The table on which the knights were to dine—a ridiculously high table —was much more poorly appointed than ours. They invited us to sit around a low table surrounded by pillows. As soon as we sat down—on our side we were only Cem's closest companions— Don Álvaro, following their custom, lifted his glass to our master's health. He likely assumed that we would not drink—that's what our faith demands, after all—because he was surprised when Cem also asked for a full glass and emptied it in a single gulp.

The men across from us hid their surprise and offered more wine. Their wine was very good, from Cyprus. Otherwise, the dinner passed almost completely in silence. Of all of us, only Suleiman spoke both languages, and he had given himself over to eating with such zeal that his mouth was never empty. We, too, acquitted ourselves well—Cem gobbled up the food with an abandon I had never before seen in him, like a wolf.

At one point I saw him staring at a knight who was serving him. Whenever he noticed that Cem reached for a new dish, the knight would slice off a bite of fish, foul, or game and instant- ly swallow it.

"Suleiman, what is this man doing?" Cem asked.

"Does His Royal Highness wish for something?" Don Álvaro stood up, which made me realize that he had been eavesdrop- ping the whole time.

"He asked," Suleiman replied, grinning rudely with his mouth full, "why this brother takes a bite of everything before he does."

"Explain to His Royal Highness!" Álvaro ordered him with an air of importance, and his arrogant command infuriated the Frank.

"Let me explain to you, Your Royal Highness," he said. "Among the Christians the following custom exists: if a ruler is present at the table, his food must be sampled in advance by an official taster."

"Oh, but this is wasted labor." Cem smiled broadly at Álvaro. "Your table is truly grand, you have excellent cooks, and your brother should not entertain any doubts about their work."

"It is not a question of refined taste, my sultan, but of poison." A laughing Suleiman dropped a baked duck in his lap. "You must know that after such feasts, often a guest or two does not wake up."

Cem stared at him, stunned. "But what's the point?" he murmured at last. "What poison could possibly fell the taster before I, too, had eaten from the same dish?"

"None, of course." Indifferent, Suleiman worked on the duck. "They are simply observing decorum, nothing more."

Cem had stopped eating. I even thought he would refuse entirely and never take another morsel from people for whom poison was such an ordinary thing, a common addition to a dish. But my master got ahold of himself. He stood up and again raised his glass; he gently pushed away the brother who tried to take the first sip from it and said, his gaze fixed on Álvaro, "It would be an insult to the Knights of St. John if I allowed them to taste my food and wine. Since I seek refuge with you, I have cast aside all suspicion. Please, Your Holiness, allow this man to sit with us and to share our table."

Suleiman looked as if he were choking as he emptied his mouth and translated Cem's words. Only with great difficulty can I describe the impression they made on those across from us. Those unblinking eyes were laughable to me, frozen as they were in endless astonishment above cheeks crammed full to bursting, above beards greasy with butter. Until Don Álvaro at last overcame his shock and replied, refusing to meet Cem's gaze.

"Nothing is more precious to us than a friend's trust. Thank you, Your Royal Highness. Thank you in the name of the Order and our Holy Church!"

Suleiman translated these words between mouthfuls. Then he added a few words of his own. "Remember well, master: they speak of trust!"

PART TWO

THIRD TESTIMONY OF PIERRE D'AUBUSSON
ON THE EVENTS OF JULY 29, 1482

IN FACT, I had already learned on the evening of July 28 from two brothers whom Don Álvaro had sent on ahead with a swift brigantine that our royal guest would arrive approximately a day after them. With this news, a tumult seized Rhodes, the likes of which I had not seen since the big siege. Throughout that whole night, the younger knights were busy decorating the fortress and preparing Cem's chambers. We had decided to put our guest up in the French auberge; I had insisted upon this, because I myself am a Frenchman.

First, I ordered them to bring out all our banners and carpets; we had quite a few, because the Christ-loving flock of the entire West as well as the Levantine merchants who were terrified of corsairs showered the Order with gifts. Hanging from the fortress walls, from the windows and terraces of Rhodes, they gave it the look of a village in Provence during its annual fair. In my opinion, we were almost insulting the stern majesty of Rhodes with this vulgar variegation, but it was fitting for our guest, the savage prince.

All this activity filled the hours until dawn, so only at daybreak did the porters carry to the auberge some of my personal belongings, meant to increase its splendor: a bed with a silk canopy, a small writing desk inlaid with mother-of-pearl and coral, several tiger skins, and countless satin pillows. We arranged them in the chambers designated for the king of France; our auberge had such chambers even though no French king had ever visited Rhodes, nor did any intend to visit it. Here I might note in passing—this is no longer significant, since neither Rhodes nor the French have been under our control for centuries now—that there were secret passages in two places behind the brocade upholstery on the walls of these royal chambers.

The rooms for Cem's suite were appointed without any splendor whatsoever. Despite our realization that an alliance with Cem would be of the greatest interest to the Order, I still could not shake off my disgust toward those savages—Turks, Saracens, and other such Levantine riffraff. I could not forget that only two short years ago, the fate of Rhodes was hanging by a thread because of them.

Day had fully broken when—as soon as I made sure the day would be cloudless, with no rain—I ordered them to spread carpets on the streets Cem Sultan would pass through as well. Such extravagance was foreign to Rhodes. Standing on the terrace in front of Cem's chambers, I contemplated St. Sebastian Square, also covered to its very edges as if it were not a town square but a large, brightly lit hall, in whose center rose a monument to the holy martyr—don't think for a minute that we servants of God are indifferent to earthly beauty.

All the brothers, dressed in their ceremonial garb, had already gone to the harbor. Our musicians—Rhodes also had numerous musicians, because not only monks, but merchants, mercenaries, and adventurists also stopped here—were lined up in eager anticipation of our guest, decked out in all the flowers the southern summer and Rhodes's tiny gardens afforded us. In a word, my efforts were rewarded—our island sparkled with color amidst the boundless blue of the sea.

I did not go to the harbor—my rank did not allow me to pay too much attention to a lay ruler. I remained beneath the silk awning stretched out before the monument, with the brothers who served as piliers of the seven Langues. The eighth had been authorized to meet Cem Sultan and lead him to the square. Thus, I was not witness to Cem's arrival. Only the exclamations of the local inhabitants of Rhodes reached me—loud, but rather thin, considering the population of the island barely numbered 3,000 people, including children. After the cries, music blared out; our musicians choked the July heat with rather eclectic performances. Clearly, they had understood their task quite simply: to make as much noise as possible.

From under my awning, I saw the lines of people stirring into motion. Cem Sultan was coming, the young man who had already managed to become a legend. I must admit that I felt the slight but natural envy of a fifty-year-old toward a twenty-year-old, the natural bitterness of the spiritual leader toward the secular ruler. Don't try to object that in my day the actual power of the Church was incomparably stronger than any earthly kingdom—I know it. In actuality, yes, this was true, but its power was limited in its external expression, in all those colors, horses, ribbons, and similarly pleasant foppery.

I will not deny that my first impressions of Cem Sultan were unexpected. He was riding toward me slowly to respond to this welcome, and he wasn't a savage in the least. Fair, just like our young men from Normandy and Alsace, perhaps a slightly lighter blond, with a more emphatic expression. Yes, this was precisely what struck me most: he had the expression of a thinking and feeling person, which did not correspond with my idea of the spiritual calm of Oriental man.

"Welcome to our Holy Order's lands, Your Highness." These were my first words to Cem. "Rhodes is happy to shelter the son of the great Conqueror. In this moment, let all hostility between our glorious armies cease once and for all. Let the dawn of your power be the beginning of an eternal peace between the Porte and the Order."

Our guest replied in his incomprehensible language, which in Brother Bruno's translation sounded rather insipid, along the lines that our happiness was mutual and Cem had full faith in the wisdom and piety of our Order.

I chuckled into my beard when they led our guest to his chambers. I, who was old enough to be his father, climbed the stairs without help, while he—a young man in the prime of his strength—was shoved and propped up by two pagans such that he almost stumbled. I later learned that this was their custom. Upstairs, in the chambers, Cem took a cursory glance around—his glance was not demanding, nor yet was it delighted. As if he had lived with such furnishings as ours his whole life.

"Rest from your journey, Your Highness," I said, "and ready yourself for the feast tonight in your honor. In the evening I will send my attendants to escort you to my palace."

Feast, attendants, palace—I purposely impressed my grandeur upon our guest, I underscored to him that Rhodes was no Karamania and that here with us life had forged other criteria, other conventions. Cem did not appear to notice my efforts; he listened to me distractedly, like a man eager to be alone. As a matter of fact, I, too, wanted the same thing myself.

This is because I spent the afternoon of July 29 laboring with more strain than Cem Sultan had surely expended in his year-long struggle. That afternoon, I struggled with all the world's powers, from Sultan Bayezid II to Our Holy Father.

I led the struggle from my office, or more precisely, from my writing desk. I wrote ten letters. Each of them was so different, it set events in such a different light and suggested such contradictory measures for their resolution that I felt as if I had changed not only my skin ten times, but also my entire interior and that I was embodying ten different rulers.

You astonish me: Why do you think only your modern world is torn apart by irreconcilable contradictions? Why, on every single day—despite its millennia-long experience—is mankind inclined to fool itself into thinking precisely that day is the high point in human history? Now see here: we—justifiably, I thought back then—had taken our era to be a "turning point in history." The Cinquecento, as you know, was a period ripe for clashes not only of opinion. It set the stage for the Thirty Years' War and other religious conflicts, as well as for the Inquisition, the Flanders Campaign, and St. Bartholomew's Night. So what, you'll try to convince me that your time, too, was even more fateful? Forgive me from deviating from my story again, but I insist you note something that has been obscured and passed over in the history of the Cinquecento: the end of the East as a European power.

For the preceding thousand years—this is half the life of the Christian world—the West had lost its primacy, it had turned barbarous. Ruling houses sprang up like mushrooms, forming short-lived statelets woven together in a complex dependence, fed by several thousand serfs each and defended by several hundred soldiers. The scope of the West had been subdivided to the point of triviality. The single, solitary thing that still held it together was Rome, the papacy. A cold comfort. While during this whole time the East got far out ahead. It was not barbarized by the barbarians; rather, it turned them into its subjects and satellites, raising them up to its level.

Byzantium! Do you have any idea, you, who are her heir, what Byzantium was to the Middle Ages? That which the Western fifteenth century trumpets as its great achievement—the discovery of the individual, the resurrection of antique knowledge, of positive science, if you will—all of that had lived on without interruption in Byzantium; she carried it forward from antiquity toward the newer time. Byzantium was a bridge between two civilizations, a brilliant bridge, I must underscore, even though I am a Westerner and a Catholic.

In the West a king was rarely literate, while not only in Byzantium, but even in its offshoots such as Bulgaria and Serbia, rulers were poets and men of letters. Why do you shove Luther and Lutheranism under my nose as the decisive spiritual turning point? Centuries before Luther, the East gave rise to heresies whose crumbs the Western peasantry used to feed their dissatisfaction; the East had an entire anticlerical body of writing that was passed on in secret, page by page, to the West.

It must seem strange to you, does it not, for a servant of Rome to disparage his own in this way; it is not in our nature, indeed. But we were obliged to know what Byzantium and the Balkans were, because they hindered us.

A hindrance, that is the precise word. Five centuries have passed and some truths can now be spoken aloud. We were hindered by the free thinking of the European East, where a king allowed himself to take a Jew or an actress for a wife, where the sovereigns themselves were often heretics, where all sorts of reborn pagan movements spread and society lived free from religious, class, and national prejudices; we were hindered by the fact that in the East the Church was subordinate to secular power and in this way set a bad example for our Western lords; we were hindered, at long last and perhaps most of all, by the fact that Byzantium and her satellites had a flair for producing and trading as never before. They held in their hands the roads between the East and West, they imposed prices and fees on us, they toyed with us—we, who had not yet mastered the secrets of glass, steel, Moroccan leather, and gold brocade. A thousand-year-old empire suffered all manner of blows from savages and barbarians, melting them away or twisting, growing, shrinking, falling, and springing back up again from the ashes.... Heirs to her legacy, doff your hats before Byzantium!

Then suddenly—the Conqueror. They called him "the great fear at the turning point in history." I find you ridiculous, begging your pardon. The Conqueror threatened Europe by complicating Levantine trade and destroying a few of our fortresses. But he did much more for us: the Conqueror got rid of Byzantium for us.

Haven't you ever stopped to think why exactly the fifteenth century marked a new era in the development of the West? Why was it exactly then that our cities grew rich and our citizenry thought of something more than bread, thus bringing the Reformation and all manner of revolutions down on our heads? Your answers are correct only to a certain point. I will tell you mine: in the fifteenth century, the West was liberated. Mehmed liberated it. The Conqueror—I am telling you the honest truth. And when I think about it, Rome to this day has still not built a monument to that short-legged, thick-necked Ottoman, my personal enemy.

Why such a tangent? Ah yes, I was explaining to you the complexity of the contradictions that our time had to cut a path through.

To put it as succinctly as possible, they came down to this: on the one hand, the Eastern rulers who still survived were prepared to make certain sacrifices so as to block the Ottoman advance and to push back the Turks, but not so far back so as to resurrect the state of some all-too-powerful neighbor in the process; they could be counted on the fingers of one hand—the Hungarian sovereign above all, but also the Polish and Russian kings. On the other hand, the West, which had just celebrated the death of Byzantium, had rushed in to snatch up its share when the world's bounties were being divvied up. Those dozen or so flourishing Western cities, whose stars were rising higher with every passing day, as well as their dozen petty yet already

VERA MUTAFCHIEVA

entrenched rulers, saw Turkey not only as a threat. To them, the Turk was the rich fool upon whom you could foist shiny, cheap wares at a good price; to them, the Turk was that affluent loafer who did not like to strain himself with work or trade and so left such base yet quite profitable activity to the Frank. As you know, the Muslims never tried to tell us apart—they called us by a common name, Franks—because for them in turn, we remained spiritually stunted people who poured unnecessary effort into labor and greed, while those very same Muslims used their time for something much more reasonable: gobbling up the legacy of Byzantium and the Balkans.

The papacy surely contributed in no small way to this knot of contradictions, so you must understand the difficulties it faced. Up until then, it had survived for obvious reasons: each of the numerous Western rulers needed the Church, because it blessed their sovereignty over the peasants and sanctified the law of serfdom. A ruler not blessed by the Holy Father could easily fall victim not to a conspiracy—conspiracies abounded and no one had anything against them—but to a peasants' revolt. The peasant was not sinning in God's eyes if he attacked an unsanctioned lord.

But this change to life in the West hit the papacy painfully hard. The cities grew rich. This meant new types of leaders—merchants, craftsmen—who did not seek out blessings for their power, which was sanctified by money. The owner did not force anyone to work for him—instead, they begged him for work. Because he paid.

And this little detail is all it took to upend life in the West and mark the start of a new era. Here you are completely correct in your reasoning: the simple act of paying a man who works changes everything. Rome felt uncertainty in the face of the future; Rome never fooled itself. For this reason, the Holy Fathers of my day did not make great names for themselves; they went down in history as petty intriguers, polygamists, or usurers—the old playing field for their power no longer existed. They tried to adapt themselves to the new order by taking part in the struggles between rulers and cities, by alternating between cruelty and universal absolution. They hoped to rise to the surface, above the judgment of time using time's own means; they put off the end of our rule. Rome was once against on the verge of victory over the barbarians. But now the barbarians came from inside. Or, more precisely: from below.

I don't believe it will be necessary for me to digress from my story any further; I believe this is so because I have to some extent introduced you to the essence of the Cinquecento. Thus, you can easily imagine what torture it was for me to write those ten letters to the rulers of the Old World.

I began, of course, with a missive to my direct commander: the Holy Father. I remember that letter as if I had written it just today: "It is now within the capabilities of Christianity to annihilate the hateful Mohammedan race. If we give Cem troops, his supporters will quickly rise up. His brother is without courage and will be deeply afraid; he has few capable generals at his disposal. The best of them, Ahmed Pasha, is only waiting for an opportune occasion to turn against him. He had written as much to Prince Cem, begging him not to despair of his fate and to temporarily retreat.[1] We have never had a more favorable chance to

---

1 Cem never received this letter. Our ship intercepted its bearer on his way to Rhodes [d'Aubusson's note].

take back the Peloponnese and part of the Archipelago—and what glory Your Holiness would win with that! To achieve this, the European rulers would not even have to make large sacrifices, because we will be helped in Europe by Cem's supporters, and in Asia by the Karamanoglu, who wish to reestablish their own power. Surrounded by enemies, Sultan Bayezid will not put up a fight.

"We don't know," I finished my letter, "what the success of our proposal will be. For now, we will watch over Prince Cem and keep his hopes up. If God wills this campaign to take place, we, on our part, will pour work and effort into it. Otherwise, keeping our word, we will act in the interests of Rhodes."

Do you find a judgmental hint in this letter of mine? I swear upon the Holy Trinity, I desired with my whole being for the campaign I proposed to happen, to link my name with Christianity's decisive blow against the infidels. But, I must admit immediately, I had very little faith in the success of my proposal, because I already knew all the prominent reasons Europe and the papacy had for refraining from such a strike. Thus, in closing I would underscore that I lay the blame for the failure of this campaign upon others and that I reserved my rights over Cem. At the end of the day, Cem was my hostage—or rather, my guest—and no one else's.

Several other letters—to the kings of England, France, Spain —were quite uniform. I appealed to the conscience of these rulers. I promised them glory and posthumous absolution in exchange for participation in this campaign, and I reminded them of the advantages a defeat of the Turks would have on Levantine trade.

The success of these letters was even more of a long shot—the fire was burning too far from Spanish and English lands. I had more faith in the Italian merchant cities—Venice, Genoa, Florence; goings-on in the Mediterranean mattered to them. But our dear Italian republics were tangled up in a fierce struggle among themselves; mercantile greed had overshadowed all their political sense to such an extent that it was difficult to foresee their answer.

The last letter I sent that afternoon was to the king of Hungary, Matthias Corvinus, son of John Hunyadi. This exonerates me before history; it proves I did not narrowly defend the West's interests in the case of Cem. Because Matthias Corvinus was directly threatened by the Ottomans and would gladly agree to my plan. Because a campaign by Corvinus against Turkey would resurrect Serbia, Bosnia, and likely even Bulgaria, if not Byzantium itself. I knew this, and still I offered him assistance.

I won't try to convince you that a man like me—a high-ranking cleric responsible for the fate of a remote island at risk—often took time to pay attention to nature, yet even to this day I remember the evening of July 29, 1482, very vividly.

Loud chatter, laughter, and music floated from inside, from the halls and chambers of my palace. There the Order and the leaders of Rhodes were paying their respects to Cem after our official conversation had ended. More than a few of them had had quite a bit to drink—various hints of excessive candor, of needless intimacy, of profligacy, even, crept into the voices of my guests. But here, in the open gallery before my chambers, where I had gone out to collect my thoughts and to order them into an intention, the July night reigned supreme.

Perhaps you have noticed what charm lies hidden in those late July nights—heavy, exhaustingly hot, inexplicably sorrowful. And above all, very, very tense. As if nature herself is taken aback by her summer extravagance and is afraid of its inevitable end—the exhaustion, the nearing autumn. Likely I haven't said it quite right; I have never been able to sense anything beyond man, let alone convey it. But on that night, some unnameable tensions truly did fill the air above Rhodes. If you ask me, that's how it is on nights when plans are being made for murder.

SEVENTH TESTIMONY OF THE POET SAADI

ON THE EVENTS OF JULY 30 AND 31, 1482

IN THE MORNING, we awoke with heads heavy from the previous night's feast—the brothers had not been stingy with the Cypriot wine. While we were freshening up, three of the more important brothers (back then we could not differentiate their ranks) were brought to us and told my master they had the honor of taking us around the island and showing him its landmarks. As far as I could tell, Cem did not seem particularly thrilled by this idea, but he never liked saying no; in general, he was afraid of offending anyone.

All day until late afternoon, our horses climbed up and down the various hills of Rhodes—they could not pass as mountains—while we listened to brother so-and-so's explanations. He described to us the events that had unfolded in these places and told us the names of the chapels, tumbledown pagan temples, bays, and cliffs. He did all this with exceptional diligence and was clearly in no hurry. We could not really figure out why. Cem, at whom his lavish lectures were aimed, could no longer contain his irritation and tried to cut the stories short with uniform, monosyllabic responses.

But brother so-and-so remained steadfast in his duty, and thus we returned exhausted late in the afternoon to have a quick bite before falling into our beds.

I was in Cem's room. I usually slept with him, lying across the foot of his bed. Ever since we had left Karamania, I had been dogged by the fear that Cem would be murdered in his sleep. The very thought that the killer would have to get past me gave me peace. And more importantly—it gave Cem peace. Since leaving Karamania, Cem had avoided being alone at night. He constantly sought companionship, someone to talk or listen to, sometimes to just be silent with, as long as he was silent with someone.

And so, on that afternoon, as soon as my master lay down to rest, I curled up at his feet on the tiger skins.

I could soon sense he was at least dozing off, if not actually asleep—back then when he was still young, Cem slept silently. I had sat up because I was afraid he had gone to sleep uncovered, when someone pounded at the door. Insistently, as if they would barge in without permission.

I quietly opened the door a crack. On the doorstep stood the Frank, who had caught a very young monk by the hand—but not as if holding hands, palm in palm, but grasping his wrist firmly.

The Frank's face immediately frightened me. I had thought before that he wore the most bitterly reserved, the most desperately bold face in the world. Only now did I realize his previous expressions were nothing compared to this; today Suleiman was shaken to the core—which was implausible, since he himself had stated hundreds of times that nothing

VERA MUTAFCHIEVA

more could shock him, he had nothing more to fear or to lose—and simply horrified.

Without uttering a word, Suleiman roughly pushed me out of the doorway with his shoulder and shoved the young monk inside. The boy did not have a white cross over his heart; I later learned that such unmarked robes were worn by the Order's novices. He looked as if he were about to faint—he was paralyzed by something, perhaps fear or anguish—I still didn't know what. The Frank kept his grasp on his wrist, as if afraid the boy would run away if he let go.

"Wake your master immediately," he hissed.

I obeyed that alarming whisper. "My sultan. Please, my sultan, listen."

Cem woke up slowly; he had just begun dreaming. He dragged a sleepy glance over me, the Frank, and the unfamiliar boy. And when he saw our alarm, he jumped as if bitten.

"What is it?"

"Master, my sultan, why did you not listen to me?" Suleiman raised his voice in despair, throwing all caution to the wind. "I was right. How I did not want to be right, my sultan!"

"About what?" Our dread had now infected Cem as well; it fused with his efforts to overcome his drowsiness, and my master went pale, looking tortured, almost pathetic.

"Today they showed you around all of Rhodes, didn't they, master? All morning and afternoon, didn't they drag you hither and thither, far from the fortress?"

"Yes. But what of it?"

"Do you know why, my sultan?"

The Frank was asking pointless questions.

"How should I know? Out with it!"

"So you wouldn't see them running into their thieves' cave, so you wouldn't find out that they were holding a council, deciding and acting, that's why!"

"Are you drunk or gone mad?" Cem said, shaking his head. "What cave and what thieves?"

"From morning until afternoon, the Grand Council met. They have decided your fate, my sultan."

"There is nothing more to say about my fate, I have already decided it. Last night the grand master and I agreed he would write to Hungary and the German lands. In a month at most— as soon as there is an answer from their kings—I will depart for Rumelia. Likely the grand master announced this today to his brothers."

"No, my sultan," Suleiman said emphatically. "You will not be departing for Rumelia. From morning until a short while ago, the Grand Council debated where you should be sent: to Rome or to France. Wherever they decide—because they have not yet decided—that is where you shall go, my sultan."

A terrible silence hung over the room, broken only by the vendors of Rhodes hawking their wares on St. Sebastian Square. While the four of us stood there as if around a fresh corpse.

"Suleiman," Cem whispered after a time that seemed endless to me, "are you sure?"

"That's why I've brought you a witness as well." The Frank shook the boy and said something to him in his language.

The boy nodded eagerly, as if he were mute. But his whole expression, his devoted gaze fixed on Suleiman, proved the Frank had spoken the simple truth.

"Brother Joachim slipped into a secret passageway near the Council Hall and heard from there," the Frank began cold-bloodedly. "He listened for six whole hours. The brothers wore themselves out with arguing. And they didn't reach any final decision, my sultan; we'll find that out tomorrow."

"Suleiman, I possess a letter from the Order, its written assurances." Cem was struggling against this news. "What ruler would have faith in d'Aubusson, if d'Aubusson lied to a ruler? No, he is not a madman, even if treacherous."

"Your conclusions are very wise, my sultan," Suleiman replied, "but they do not refute the simple truth: the Order will send you wherever it decides is appropriate."

"But that is captivity!" Cem shouted at him, as if the Frank was the one who had encroached upon his freedom. "The corsairs did not make their guest a prisoner, the corsairs! And you're trying to prove that the grand master..."

"I'm not trying to prove anything to you, master," the Frank interrupted him in a tired voice. "Fine, don't believe me." And he dropped the boy's wrist.

The boy didn't bow; he crawled out backward, and we could hear him going down the stairs, wildly, as if running from a fire.

"Who was that boy anyway?" Cem very much wanted to doubt the source of Suleiman's news.

"Does it matter?" The Frank shrugged. "He came to me on his own, I didn't go looking for him."

"Overly daring, don't you think?" Cem's smile was harsh; dread still froze his features. "Is your young brother not playing far too dangerous a game? Or some enemy of d'Aubusson, and d'Aubusson certainly has his enemies, has sent him to turn me against the Order?"

"A human life is far too high a wager for a game, master." Suleiman clearly meant not the young brother, but himself. "It's simply that the name Bruno means something on Rhodes; most probably some who think as I once did consider me a kindred soul. Without ever having seen me. Because of like-mindedness. Sometimes people are capable of much, thanks to like-mindedness."

I couldn't recall Suleiman ever using such a voice. The Frank was speaking softly, with a pride that was both sad and gentle. Yet, even though I was in no state to make observations, I could tell: the Frank—the outsider, close to no one, loved by no one, the Frank who belonged to no one—had finally found a cure for his pained soul. Bruno had his revenge; his name had become an example for two or three boys who also felt that which had driven their implacable, unknown, and kindred brother to us.

We should not be angry with Cem for not noticing the change in Suleiman; he was still stunned.

"Saadi," he said suddenly, "I am going to the grand master."

Suleiman gave a barking laugh. But he did it in his new way—bitterly, yet with a hint of tenderness; this tenderness had completely seeped through him, reconciling him with the world he only recently had fiercely hated.

"You'll ask the grand master whether I'm lying to you, is that it, my sultan?" he said without spite.

"I will ask him what the Council spent the whole day discussing."

Cem was flustered; he immediately heard how weak his words sounded.

"At the end of the day, I have the right to know what is being planned for me. Isn't that so?"

"As you wish." The Frank shrugged. "But for proof you'll have to call witnesses."

"And call them I will." Fear made Cem reckless.

"As you wish," Suleiman said again. "It is our obligation to sacrifice ourselves for the good of our master." And he added with uncharacteristic softness, "Too bad about the boy."

"How can you say such a thing? My first order of business will be to extract a promise from the grand master that he will spare that young monk. Besides, what all did he even tell us? Conjectures... empty words." Cem grew ever more perturbed under the Frank's gaze.

"A promise," Suleiman said between clenched teeth. "And you were promised that you would be able to leave Rhodes of your own free will."

"We'll see whether I don't leave!"

As I followed Cem down the stairs, I was thinking how much he reminded me of a child. Children's moods change just as quickly, with no transition and no rational reason; only children believe that something will happen simply because they really want it to; only children refuse to tolerate dark thoughts, they flee from despair.

Suleiman followed closely behind us—he was our translator, after all. I felt as if heat was pouring over me from the one side and cold from the other. The heat came from Cem; Suleiman gave off cold. Only a man who has discovered about the world everything one can discover over the course of a human life is that cold. It was the chill of death, because he who knows this dies even before his death.

D'Aubusson, for his part, also met us hot and cold at once. He melted with devotion upon seeing Cem Sultan and froze in affront when my master flung a torrent of disjointed questions in his face.

The Frank translated d'Aubusson's answer. "Your highness, it is beneath my dignity even to justify myself. Could Your Highness suspect that the Order would disregard your welfare for even a moment? It is our holy obligation to defend every traveler and sick man; just imagine how much more we are on our guard when a magnanimous, noble ruler is under threat?"

Here I could feel myself coming to a boil as well; unlike Cem, I had never doubted Suleiman's words. But Cem hesitated for only a short while, weighing to what extent he had the right to take advantage of someone's friendship.

Cem took a deep breath and shot at the master, "Someone present at the Council today, Your Holiness, is ready to confirm what I have said."

D'Aubusson leaned back on his throne, and his fingers dug into the smooth wood so strongly that they went white above the nails. I looked at them: they seemed to be sinking not into the wood, but into the neck of the young eavesdropper. D'Aubusson was silent. I knew what he was calculating: whether to admit it or to subject himself to a meeting with the unknown eavesdropper. And likely he decided that he need not expose himself as a petty liar, that it was too early for him to lose Cem's trust.

The grand master said solemnly, "Do not mention his name, Your Highness. This someone has hoped to break up our alliance, to blacken my name in your eyes—let him not succeed. Yes, we discussed which refuge would be safer for Prince Cem than Rhodes: Rome or France. Why should we be ashamed of our worthy concern? I not only had no intention of hiding our decision from you, but tomorrow—after we have suggested one or the other place and you make your choice—you will sign an agreement for us to take you to Europe under a trustworthy guard. If you do not wish to go, you will not sign, isn't that so?"

I could clearly see how Cem came to his senses in the face of the grand master's presence of mind. I, too, felt less sure in our accusations; the Council had not yet reached a final decision. Indeed, we did not have proof Cem would not have been informed of a decision that had not yet been made. So what were we accusing the Order of? That it had discussed questions concerning its guest in the absence of that guest.

"Is it not possible," Cem replied after a pause, "that I could be invited to your honorable Council tomorrow? In the end, I am not underage or incompetent such that you need to decide my fate without my input."

"Can't you see, Your Highness," the grand master replied, unflappable, "this would complicate things far too much? We would need a translator, and that is difficult when holding discussions and five or six people are talking over one another. I give you my word that you will learn of everything that concerns you as soon as we reach a final proposal."

Now this was not presence of mind, but sheer effrontery. As well as the grand master's desire to put an end to this unpleasant conversation immediately. But Cem once again showed his father's stubborn streak.

"Then please explain to me, Your Holiness: why must I be sent here and there? Had we not agreed that once I made a pact with you, I would sail to my Rumelian territories, or at the very least, to the king of Hungary? So why raise the issue of where to ship me off to? I don't understand."

I could tell Cem was struggling to hold back his shouts and tears. There was nothing easier than getting under his skin—his skin was too gentle, too sensitive.

"My lord," d'Aubusson answered him with morose dignity, "I did not want to cause you unnecessary alarm. But if you insist"—here the grand master visibly suppressed a sigh—"you are not safe in Rhodes, Your Highness."

"What? How?" Cem sputtered.

"Rhodes is essentially under siege. Turkish pirates are constantly roving nearby; the sultan is keeping a considerable force in Lycia and Cilicia. Who can guarantee that tomorrow Bayezid will not use every means at his disposal to capture our island or at least attempt a well-executed kidnapping? Must you really be here of all places, in the Order's riskiest holding, when you could wait for the right moment in one of the others?"

"Which other holdings do you speak of?"

"The numerous castles granted to the Hospitallers by noble patrons. Castles in Lotharingia, Savoy, and Dauphiné. I was personally in favor of such a proposal. Many brothers insisted on transferring you straight to Rome, under the protection of the Holy Father, whose involvement would force the rulers of the West to come running to help you and give you troops. But

I do not and will not support that. Such a move would be interpreted to your detriment. Cem Sultan in Rome… That doesn't sound good, does it?"

God Almighty, how the man toyed with us. How skillfully he switched from defense to offense; how he made us blush over our base suspicions and discuss with him questions that were my master's personal business.

Despite his laughable gullibility, I think even Cem realized how inappropriate our conversation was. "Thank you for your attention, Your Holiness," he said. "I will keep your advice in mind as I decide where to go when I leave Rhodes."

He bowed to the grand master; we bowed to him as well. Before I turned to leave, I caught sight of a rare mixture of emotions in d'Aubusson's eyes—yet all of them merely hinted at brutality, scorn, annoyance, tenacity.

Cursed be the moment we placed ourselves in your power, I thought. Cem must have been thinking the same thing as we went back to our auberge, because as soon as we got back, he asked me for his inkhorn and paper.

I could see he was not planning to jot down a few lines of verse; Cem did not look at all as he usually did when he sat down to his favorite pursuit. He sat for a long time over the white sheet of paper, his head propped in his hand, concentrating.

"Saadi," he said to me when night had already fallen outside, "do you know who I am planning to write to?"

"I have no idea, my sultan."

"To my brother," Cem replied, expressionless. "I shall write to Bayezid. He would not allow the infidels to make sport of a son of Mehmed, he would not allow them to pass me from hand to hand. Because we are brothers, despite everything, Saadi, and I have never wished for his death, nor for his whole territory. Yes," he went on, as if to himself, "Bayezid will not refuse to help me, since it is a matter of defending the honor of the Ottoman name."

"Oh, rest assured, my sultan," I cried, stunned by what I had heard. "Bayezid will toss you a rope to hang yourself with. What has been the point of all this if you intend to die?"

"There is no point, you are right." Cem's whole being emanated mortal exhaustion. "I was destined for an early death as soon as I was born—why did I resist it? Bayezid really will kill me, I know it. But that which these blackshirts are cooking up for me, is it not also death, just a slow, shameful one?"

"You can't possibly think Bayezid will kill you respectfully, with flowers and music?" I shouted; the events of the last few days had pushed me beyond my limits. "It will never be too late to die, master," I repeated like a tired old refrain.

"But perhaps it will become too late for dying as well!" Cem was now screaming back at me, even though such a thing had never happened before. "Don't you remember the Frank's words in Lycia: it will be too late!"

Cem shook his head impatiently. This was a sign to leave him alone. So I curled up next to his bed, silent. It was already dark; the black, suffocatingly opaque Rhodes night was advancing.

And Cem was writing. He didn't like to be watched while he wrote, so I did it surreptitiously. I could tell this letter cost him dearly; Cem changed color several times and wiped sweat from his brow. I must have dozed off, as I then felt his hand.

"Saadi," he said, shaking me awake, "look, read. I'm afraid it didn't turn out too well."

I took the paper, which was covered in writing. The first lines were of no import—standard greetings and well-wishes. Beneath them, I read: "Throwing myself at Your Majesty's feet, I beg you to grant my request and forgive my sins. Your supreme magnanimity would not refuse a wretch a small part of the blessing you shower upon the whole world, especially since this wretch now recognizes his guilt and humbly asks for forgiveness. Your Majesty would not allow me to be a hostage of the infidels, I, a true believer, who has spoken the sacred words: 'There is no God but Allah and Mohammed is his prophet.' My fate entirely depends on you, because I am a slave, my arms and legs in chains. The shroud of dishonor covers my face, my head lies beneath the blade, ready to receive the fateful blow. If such is your will, let God be praised—I will submit to it. But if your mercy and generosity rescue me from this terrible abyss of misfortunes, I swear to the all-seeing God that I will never again undertake anything without your sovereign will.

"Please, master, give succor to a luckless wretch who has no refuge besides the salvatory shadow of your benevolence. I permit myself to hope that religious rivalry and your sovereign magnanimity will lead you to such a decision and will earn your mercy for me."

You tell me that your scholars do not accept this letter of Cem's as authentic; it would be impossible, you say, for a man in his right mind to hurl himself from one extreme to the other, to hand himself over first to one enemy, then to another. Yet despite this, it is possible. Could it be that your deep scholarly pursuits, after much seeking, have not led you to the one absolute truth: everything is possible in the world we live in, nothing is impossible. Spare me your objections. So long as billions of people crowd this earth, there will be billions of actions, billions of decisions, billions of words, both true and false. Can you cite for me any other fact besides that number?

I admit: Cem's decision on the evening of July 30, 1482—his letter—was reckless, or simply foolish. But how can you accuse a poor animal who hears the cage snapping shut of a lack of common sense? Cem thrashed in his cage just so, as befits beasts deprived of their freedom; he bit himself, caused himself harm.

I was pondering all this as I read over his letter to Bayezid. It never reached its addressee, or else that addressee pretended not to have received it—we still don't know to this day.

"My sultan," I said. "What do you hope to achieve with this letter? I have often heard you say: there is no mercy for the fallen. Yet here you are showing that you are not only fallen, but downright trampled. Are you truly counting on brotherly mercy, Cem, my friend?"

He listened to me, his eyes closed.

"I'm not counting on anything, Saadi," he replied. "I no longer think about my life. It belongs to Brother d'Aubusson. I just want one thing—to justify myself before our people, before my father's memory, before posterity and history: I offered myself to Bayezid. Let him take me and kill me—he would be the one to kill me. Or let him leave me as a hostage of the Christians—this will be his doing."

Cem opened his eyes and, as if through the flowing stream of water in their depths, I saw hope.

"Why do we always assume people are evil, while goodness exists as well? Is it so impossible that a brother could be moved by the call of his blood? After all, Bayezid is fifteen years older than I am, I could be his son. How could Bayezid condemn me without the spirit of the Conqueror tormenting him?"

I'm going mad, I thought suddenly, because I truly did feel hundreds of ants swarming beneath my skull. There is no way out—a person cannot escape from the trap that is the world. Life is constructed such that your every word or action is either a crime or a humble prayer. The crime earns you a punishment, and the prayer gets you a blow. Blows rain down on a man from all sides, God, while he—weak and terribly short-lived man—must go on. Sometimes he is forced to run through the black forest of life, always keeping in mind that his every step is fateful, that everything, everything, everything is irrevocable as soon as it is done or said.

Who, whose heart and head, can stand this decades-long torture? Who are you angry with, God, for our sins? Are we to blame that your world is so large, so varied and confusing, such that not only we, but even you yourself cannot put it to rights, but instead heap injustice upon injustice? Merciful God, I hope I am not going mad; what would happen to Cem without me, God?

We sat in silence for a long time. The letter lay beneath the candle like a verdict or a last will and testament—in short, like one of those ostensibly meaningless scraps of paper that sometimes weigh more than a hundred-thousand-man battle, an earthquake, or a plague.

I don't know how we slept and for how long. That oppressive, nightmare- and apparition-filled July night was more terrifying than hell itself. We still had not arisen when someone knocked at the door.

It was Suleiman. Again, his appearance startled me, as it had the day before. After Lycia, Suleiman had lost his boldness as a man with nothing to lose. In the past few weeks, he had constantly looked upset and anxious, yet nevertheless charged with an active energy. But on that morning, the Frank looked like his old self, he had again found that bitter calm.

"What is it?" Cem sat up on his elbow.

"Let us have a moment of silence in memory of Brother Joachim, my sultan," the Frank said.

We stared at him, stunned.

"This morning, very early—here the fishermen go out before dawn—they found my young brother's body."

Suleiman said "my brother" as if he were truly speaking of a blood brother, and not a member of the same religious brotherhood.

"He was naked. They later found his clothes on the shore. He likely had gone down to bathe and swim a bit, or so they said.... Boys like to do that." Suleiman went on as if in a trance, his voice inhumanly flat. "Who knows why, but there was a large wound on his head, his skull had been smashed right in. Most probably the waves had thrown him against the rocks, or so they say."

"Who says that? What waves? Here in the morning the sea sleeps like a..." Cem began, but did not finish; the Frank signaled to him. He put one hand in front of his lips, with the other he traced a circle all around us. Suleiman was reminding us that the walls had ears.

Couldn't you see us on that ringing morning, which pressed into our room, bringing to life the colors of the pillows and carpets, playing on the cups and silver dishes? We sat across from one another in silence, trying to share our thoughts with glances and fingers; we wanted to stay close together, to feel less fear before the invisible, punishing hand of the Order. Three foreigners in the magnificent French auberge amidst the lovely island of Rhodes, which floated between the world's most cloudless sky and gentlest seas, through a wondrous, colorful July morning.

FOURTH TESTIMONY OF PIERRE D'AUBUSSON
ON THE EVENTS OF THE SUMMER OF 1482

PARDON ME, BUT I heard how Saadi regaled you with tales about the young brother's death and the subtle spiritual tribulations of his hero. On the whole—although it is none of my business—I get the feeling this Saadi never directly answers your questions; he wastes your time with childish contentions about days in which major world events were coming to a head. At that time, I, Pierre d'Aubusson, was still directing them.

In July, in strict secrecy from Cem and his men, I had sent two of our brothers to Adrianople, to Bayezid's residence. The new sultan was clearly avoiding Constantinople; there every stone recalled Mehmed's victories, and the crowd might be tempted to make unpleasant comparisons between the Conqueror and his enthroned son. I sent the brothers with a very blunt proposal for peace; it could even pass as a demand. It was time for us to pound our fists on the table—the future of the sultan himself was in our hands.

While awaiting their return, I had to get rid of Cem. Even if I had managed to begin my negotiations with Bayezid in secret, there was no way their outcome could be kept secret.

During those days, when I spent nearly every lunch and dinner with Cem, while I struggled to entertain him and at the same time to convince him that his life was in danger on Rhodes, I was exhausted from the burden of my task.

First of all, I was not quite lying to my guest when I claimed that he was in danger. Cem really did need to leave for Europe. But where to, exactly? There would have been nothing easier than sending him to Hungary; then the war between Corvinus and the Porte would be a matter of months. But would the Holy Father, the Venetian Republic, France, and Spain forgive me for such a war? At this very moment, when the Conqueror was gone and his son was handing out favors, and he was only just getting started, to Western merchants; when—in the absence of Byzantium—we were prepared to take up the leading role in trade with the East? No, I had no right to take such a step; here far more than the well-being of the Order and the Christian faith was at stake—the very primacy of the West hung in the balance, and I was not authorized to decide this question on my own. My job was to wait and keep Cem Sultan safe. And precisely therein lay the difficulty.

Only Rhodes was fully under our control. All our other holdings—a few castles in France and Italy, several monasteries dedicated to our Order—were in the middle of someone else's land. Some king, prince, or count. There, we were the ones subordinate to those sovereigns; we owed them our obedience. In a word, as soon as we sent Cem to Europe, he would be beyond our direct protection.

You have no idea how many anxious hours I weighed the abovementioned possibilities and possible dangers. And I kept coming to a conclusion that did little to comfort me: if Cem became what I imagined he would—the most prized/heaviest bargaining chip in international relations of our time—he could not remain the property of a petty power like the Order. Much more powerful players—the papacy, France, Venice, or Hungary—would do what needed to be done to get him for themselves. Then I, who had taken on all the inconveniences associated with Cem, would be left high and dry.

At times, during those weeks of deliberation, I cursed the hour in which that all-too-trusting and disarmingly charming young man had set foot on Rhodes. Why the devil, may God forgive me, did the refugee's footsteps lead him to Rhodes of all places? Why—since his fate would clearly offer an advantage to the papacy, France, or Venice—had he not taken up precisely in France or Venice?

These were defeatist thoughts. Nothing had yet been lost, because in the eyes of the world, I had taken Cem captive. Anyone who would wrest him away by force would essentially be inviting others to do the same to them.

With bitterness, I must admit that of all the holy commandments, a sovereign obeys only one strictly: "Do unto others as you would have them do unto you." Take a look at your world and you will notice that this golden rule is still in force when it comes to sovereigns; you will note that the world would be run quite differently if the powers that be did not tacitly observe this single, solitary, obligatory rule among themselves.

I knew that my messengers to the sultan would take about a month to return, even with favorable winds. Before their return I began receiving important letters: those whom I had informed of this unexpected divine mercy began to reply.

The first to respond was the king of Naples, Ferdinand I. How can I convince you I had foreseen his answer almost down to the letter? Ferdinand, of course, wrote that this chance, given to us by Providence, was singular; that now or never, Christianity had to hurl the Antichrist back into Asia. But Ferdinand could not take part in this notable campaign himself, because he was busy with a war against the papacy and Venice. In the event that I, d'Aubusson, might intercede before the Holy Father to affect a truce in the whole of Italy, he would not hesitate to lead every one of his troops, down to the last man, against the infidels.

As I told you, I fully expected such an answer and, indeed, such answers all around, yet this first letter nevertheless sent me into a fit of rage. So I, master of two thousand blackshirts, was supposed to pacify a pack of omnipotent, arrogant sovereigns so that our crusade could take place? Is that all you want from me, isn't there anything more? What, do you think Constantinople is my family fiefdom, and the salvation of Christianity is my personal prize, such that you would call upon me to carry out this impossible, absurd task?

And so, Ferdinand I of Naples had laughed in my face. I waited for the others, and they were not long in coming. It seems they had all copied from one and the same draft, so alike were they in their delight, in their gratefulness in this case, in their willingness to help. They were also alike in ending their missives with that insurmountable "but."

Matthias Corvinus's answer was different. The Hungarian king curtailed his delight and thanks. He announced in brief that he would make his entire army available to the alliance—as if such an alliance even existed, for Christ's sake—and that he would take up command of the land forces, while leaving the naval war against Turkey to the Italian states.

At first I thought Corvinus, too, was laughing at me, although the situation was not laughable in the least. Then I thought it over; what other suggestion could he make? Hungary had no outlet to the sea, while a good half of any war with the Ottomans had to be waged precisely on the sea.

"Poor Matthias," I said aloud, because I knew that our world would laugh in Corvinus's face as well as mine.

I had one final hope left: the pope.

As strange as it may sound, the Holy Father was in no hurry to rejoice over the grace God had rained down upon his flock. I had foreseen this to some extent as well. Years earlier, when I was still studying the divine sciences, I came to know very well the man who would later become Pope Sixtus IV and who would have rotted away outside all annals of history if not for his undignified squabbles with the Medicis and Ferdinand. Ah yes. He also paid for—with my money, along with the money of thousands of humble Christians—the construction of a small chapel in the Holy City. Some Michelangelo Buonarotti or other managed to win the commission for the frescoes, a shadowy figure, unreliable in every sense. Later—when both Sixtus and myself, as well as that Michelangelo, had gone to our eternal rest—artistic tastes degraded to such an extent that the artist's paintings not only became famous, but the chapel even continued to bear its patron's name: the Sistine Chapel. And with this, my erstwhile schoolmate went down in history. I do not speak so out of envy, believe me. But believe me as well when I say he was a completely unworthy man in every respect. Thus, I knew very well what Sixtus was capable of.

In that letter of his, he surpassed even himself in spinelessness. Can you imagine, the pope, under whose supreme power our Order lay, did not say so much as a word to indicate how relations between the Order and Cem should develop, or between the Order and the Porte, or between the Porte and Christianity. With a few brief words, Sixtus IV replied that he was satisfied with the turn of events, which was further proof of God's blessing, which, in turn, had resulted from particularly pious actions on the part of the Roman curate. (His phrasing was just as convoluted and arrogant as what you see here.) And that was that.

I recall that I laughed out loud at that stentorian missive, I laughed as my whole being twisted with rage. What could we hope for from the serf, from the weaver, the sailor, the monk, when God's representative here on earth was Sixtus IV? "To hell with it," I said. "Perhaps the whole Christian world is done for; perhaps it is high time it met its end under the hooves of the Antichrist, since it has grown so fat and stupid."

But I neither abandoned the Order's interests, nor my own.

Without a doubt, the papacy wanted me to take the lead in the case of Cem until the situation became clear and its advantages guaranteed. Only then would Sixtus IV recall that he alone governed the fortunes of Christianity, and he would remind us that Cem Sultan could not stay under the control of the Order, since that Order was subordinate to the pope. (In the interest of fairness, I must note that in his letter, Sixtus IV for the first time called the mess around Cem Sultan a "case," and with that, he showed he was not as hopeless as I had thought.)

I must admit to you that once I foresaw how things would unfold, I sincerely wished Cem would fall ill of plague or drown in his bath so as to upset the pope's schemes—I wished for my own harm, as long as it would harm Sixtus as well.

You're judging me, I can see; even without this last admission, I am still the most hateful figure in the case of Cem. But I believe—because for the first time someone is hearing me, Pierre d'Aubusson, out—you have already figured as much: I myself was a victim in this case. Others left me to dirty my hands so they could later reap the fruits of my sin. They knew from the beginning that I would act only as I did, and so they waited patiently; they waited for the crime to be committed so as to take advantage of it. With the right of the stronger.

I could sense their intentions across the seas and the mountains; I knew they would treat me just as I had treated Cem. What did you expect? It's the simplest picture of human society: every man lives off the evil he does to others, while suffering evil done by others in turn. Our only goal is to suffer less evil than we commit. I, too, did my best in this respect.

Cem himself helped me. One morning he asked me to send him away from Rhodes. He didn't feel his life and liberty were safe here, he said.

I offered to let him choose his new refuge. I told him about our castles and monasteries on the continent; I laid out their advantages and disadvantages. I purposely pointed him toward the holdings of the prince of Savoy. In Savoy, a battle for the throne was raging. Barely a year earlier it had swept the seventeen-year-old duke into the grave. There were various theories—that he was killed by his mother, by her lover, or by his dear uncle, that monster, the French king—and fourteen-year-old Charles had been installed in his place. His mother was the de facto ruler, but she was kept on a short leash by Louis XI. And so, without directly thrusting our precious guest into the king's clutches, we allowed him to intervene if he felt our guest was being threatened. I believe I have already made it clear: we considered only two possibilities dangerous to Cem—his death or his freedom.

Indeed, Cem chose Savoy, and preparations for his journey began. I was in a hurry because I was already expecting my messengers to return from Bayezid. And when everything was ready, I was left with the most difficult task of all: my final conversation with Cem.

I was convinced I had done right by my actions up until that day. I fought for the supremacy of Christianity over the Ishmaelites. The Conqueror had not shown any inhibitions when he put an end to Christian states in the East, when he launched his first attacks against the West. Any pangs of conscience I might have about the fate of his son were utterly unnecessary. This was not merely a belief—it was a very part of my being. Yet despite everything, that meeting strained me; I felt as if I had to face my victim.

As far as I recall, we met again in the morning, because some merciless light wounds my memory. Swimming out of that light toward me—across the whole great length of the Council Hall—came Cem. Dressed in white, such was their ceremonial garb.

The gold in his clothes and his hair shone so brightly that Cem looked as if he had a halo.

"I came to offer my final thanks to Your Holiness for your hospitality," he began.

Brother Bruno, alias Suleiman, translated.

"We only fulfilled our Christian obligation, Your Highness," I replied.

Cem did not intend to go on. He stood there, looking out the window. So I continued. "In my capacity as your adviser—after all, you yourself honored me with your royal confidence—I have several questions, Your Highness. I assume I am the one your brother will negotiate with about your fate. What shall I tell him?"

Cem's gaze returned from the street toward me, and he said harshly, "Does it make any difference, Your Holiness? How can I be sure my words will reach Bayezid, that they will not be replaced by others somewhere along the way, perhaps even in this room, if not on the ship or in the sultan's divan? If two people have reached the point of using an intermediary, only one has power anymore: the intermediary."

I knew that voice, those words, full of insolent despair; Brother Bruno was speaking through Cem. I had to blink so as not to strike Cem's translator dead with a glare—I was fully capable of it, believe me. *No, we do not need Bruno's grave on Rhodes. Not yet*, I thought to myself.

"Your Highness, you shall compose the message to your brother yourself. I will deliver it to him. There is no way I could possibly change it."

"You needn't try to convince me anything is impossible, Your Holiness. I am already convinced of the contrary."

I was preparing to break off our meeting. Like many others during that time, it would not bear fruit. Cem showered me with his aggrieved trust, without realizing that among statesmen, it was entirely inappropriate to hint at trust. So as I said, I was about to send him away, let him pour out his sorrows in his primitive poems, when he said, "Your Holiness, let them bring me two sheets of paper."

Oh ho, so Cem will abide by my request, after all. Indeed, Cem's actions were difficult to predict. They brought paper. While Cem was writing, I forced myself to look elsewhere—I wanted to emphasize that he was fully free in his choice of how to phrase his message. It was brief, since only a moment later Cem brought me the two sheets of paper: blank as before, except for a very complex, inimitable signature at the bottom.

"What does this mean, Your Highness?"

"I leave it to your translators to compose the letter to my brother. Arrange for everything as you see fit, in my name. I am sure you will not arrange for my murder, at least. Not because it would be ridiculous for my signature to stand below such a proposal, no. Because it is still not to the advantage of the Order."

"I would never agree to conditions that were... disadvantageous for you, Your Highness." This act of his was such madness that I lost control of myself. "Your whole stay on Rhodes is a guarantee of that."

"Yes," Cem said, with an expression on his face that I will not attempt to describe. "Precisely my stay on Rhodes."

While we exchanged these few words, I caught the Frank slipping a few of his own in. His translations were unnecessarily detailed; Brother Bruno was clearly trying to convince

Cem that he had done something irrevocable. But Cem did not change his expression, while his final sentence, because he left the room immediately after it, remained untranslated.

I know what Cem said, something very brief: "Isn't it all the same?"

Even if they had translated it for me, I wouldn't have disagreed.

EIGHTH TESTIMONY OF THE POET SAADI ON THE FALL AND WINTER OF THE YEAR 1482

IT WILL STRIKE you as unbelievable, my eighth testimony. Because of the seventh—that's how different they are. Just as different as our mood during the fall was from that of our summer weeks on Rhodes.

By autumn we were already in Savoy.

I report this to you colorlessly, even though here of all places I would call to assistance all my eloquence and poetic talent so as to describe my friend's meeting with the coast of Savoy. It was as if fated by the universe itself; to me, this inimitable strip of land seemed created for this one moment alone: its meeting with Cem.

We set sail from Rhodes in the first days of September. We set sail of Cem's free will. The beginning of our journey resembled nothing if not an escape—we departed under the cover of night and in strict secrecy. All too often after that pivotal conversation of ours with Brother d'Aubusson, he had told my master the Order had rooted out conspiracies or caught wind of negotiations. And all such plots had one and the same goal: to kidnap Cem Sultan and take him to Istanbul.

"If I were a man of words alone"—the grand master repeated this conclusion to us ad nauseum—"I would simply reaffirm the Order's promise: Your Highness is at home in Rhodes. But we are far too sober minded to be satisfied by words alone; we know that where the clang of iron does not ring out, but instead the clink of gold, power is powerless. Everywhere and at all times a man can be found who will give in. I have no way of recognizing him. My eyes cannot come to rest on some brother or other of ours and say: this one is likely to yield to temptation. Yet such a brother must exist; this is what reason and age-old human experience assure me."

Ever since—acting on the late Joachim's information—Cem had flown at d'Aubusson and accused him of making free with his fate, the grand master gave us no hint that he wished to send his guest away from Rhodes. He conscientiously kept Cem informed of every outed conspiracy, citing names and sometimes even quoting letters, which he would bring to be translated by Suleiman, without ever glancing at Suleiman himself.

At first, Cem took the grand master's dispassionate warnings with a grain of salt. But nothing conquers a man more easily and more rashly than fear. In less than a month, Cem was wholly convinced he was under threat. I believed it, too. Even today, if I must be honest, I will say again: on Rhodes, my master was not free from danger. And so, the day arrived when Cem himself requested to set sail for France. I read undisguised triumph in the grand master: he had gotten his way. Cem Sultan was no longer begging him for refuge—he was begging for protection.

The Council immediately arranged for the large trireme the *Treasure* to be readied for us; almost every day my sultan would be visited by or would visit the grand master—they had much to discuss, it seemed. After these visits—they were most often one-on-one, not counting Suleiman—Cem kept silent; he stubbornly began hiding his negotiations with d'Aubusson from me.

One evening I couldn't take it anymore.

"I am afraid, my lord," I said, "that in addition to all the evils that have befallen me, I must add yet another: the loss of your love. Why has your heart closed to me—am I nothing but the dust beneath your feet?"

"Stop, Saadi," he replied. "I have committed far too many thoughtless blunders before your eyes. I have heaped far too many worries on your shoulders. I have cried out so many remorseful sobs during our nights together. I think it is time I answer for my actions on my own."

"Fine, don't ask for advice or for help, but let me continue to be your wailing wall. Share your thoughts with me, Cem."

Cem let out a bitter laugh; his expression reminded me of d'Aubusson in his wise solitude. "There is something underhanded in merely sharing, Saadi. No living person is a wall. I really do want to decide my life on my own."

Again I was fearful. I was afraid of what Cem, left alone with the grand master, would get up to.

When they informed us that everything was ready and that we would set sail that night, I felt relief. It is understandable— in every departure, there is a shred of hope.

We left the French auberge under the cover of total darkness. A dozen servants were waiting to handle our luggage. Brother d'Aubusson was waiting for us, too. That night he was not wearing the insignia of his high rank; a simple black cloak hung from his shoulders, making him look like a conspirator, or a killer, who cannot tear himself away from the scene of the crime. The grand master clearly had no business being there. Everything to be discussed with Cem had already been discussed. His presence even got in the way of the servants loading our luggage. D'Aubusson likely sensed how inappropriate his being there was and thus tried to justify it with many well-wishes and assurances.

We quietly passed through the dead streets of Rhodes. It had started to rain—one of those rains that is almost summery, yet thick with melancholy. Cem rode at the head of our party. The grand master walked on foot next to his horse. At the pier, the trireme awaited us, its fires banked low and its sails unfurled; its silhouette softened in the sea mist, and the sailors leaning against the ship's railings resembled sad, wet condors.

One by one, boats loaded with our belongings and men pushed off from the pier. Cem continued to wait on the shore, completely elsewhere in his thoughts. D'Aubusson stood there, too. And so, from a rowboat, I saw them from below, with enormous heavy robes and tiny heads. Cem gleamed bright in the dusk, while next to him—like his shadow or his fate—the grand master loomed black.

From what I could tell, they parted without a word. Cem suddenly tore away from his shadow and jumped into the boat. D'Aubusson remained on the shore until we lost sight of him— until I lost sight of him, that is, since my master immediately went down into the hold and did not come out for many long days.

VERA MUTAFCHIEVA

It was a rough trip. The calm of early autumn had arrived, and the winds were at rest. For whole weeks, our trireme stood not on water but as if on dry land—without so much as even rocking gently. The warrior monks passed their time in whispered conversations, but as soon as we shut the door, we could hear dice rattling in a cup; they wore themselves out with gaming. And everything went on and on just like that—torpid, boring—until the wind finally caught up with us and pushed us toward Europe.

Then Cem, from whom I had heard all of a dozen words over the past weeks, livened up as well. As soon as dawn broke, he would go above deck and gaze north. I understood him: Cem was impatiently waiting for the world.

Because your homeland is not yet a world—it is your part of it, one very big house; you even know those nooks and crannies you have not seen—your knowledge of them comes from blood and milk. "Your own"—a heavy and significant phrase—everything is your own in your homeland. So how, in contrast, would I define the world, you ask? With difficulty... I cannot find enough ecstatic phrases. After all, every part of the world imprinted in our consciousness is our wealth—a priceless book we can page through in hours of contemplation, of pain, of captivity, and which we can carry with us unscathed until our final moment of darkness.... No, I refuse to define it, it is above words.

Nevertheless, there is something about the world that makes it so precious—this is precisely what you perceive: its uniqueness. Your every meeting with some city, island, or shore is unique, and the wonderful thing is that you know that it will never happen again. *Look, I am stepping on this shore for the first time*, you think, *for the first and last time; I have never gone down this street, and I never will again.* During such meetings, your senses work incredibly fully, as you never thought they could. You no longer have two small holes for eyes and two even smaller ones for ears; your whole self is a wide-open window, through which the world rushes in. It fills you to some extent, then afterward fills you to bursting; the world tears you to pieces and melts you. And for one brief moment—try not to miss it—you turn into that which you were at the dawn of time: a particle of the divine world.

I would not dwell on such speculations so far from your task at hand if I did not wish to explain Cem on that journey of ours. From Sicily onward we did not lose sight of the shore. We sailed along the coastline the whole way, and it changed by the hour. Cem changed, too—I have always been convinced that an inexplicable yet deep connection existed between Cem and the world. Feverishly desiccated in Lycia, exhausted in Rhodes, Cem seemed to ripen along the shores of Italy.

And what shores they were! They rose above the flaccid, dense sea, curved in a warm arc or suddenly sharp like a scream. Their white cliffs were dappled with bushes and strips of grass, while ivy and wild vines gushed from the crevices. I will not even speak about the trees and flowers on that coast—it seemed to me that the whole shore was created not by an unwitting power, but by someone who had surpassed the creator's ideas and taste and had mixed here palm trees with marine pines and cypresses, fencing them in with a wall of century plants; the bright yellow of the mimosas purposely called out amidst the swampy, olive-green, mossy ravines, and the painfully bright violet of the wisteria deliberately cried out amidst the gray rocky lichen.

Ah yes, and a golden belt of orange trees ran crosswise to it all, while above everything rose the edge of the olive trees in their muted tones: of pale gray, blue, and green, which seemed to join the horizon with the sky and make you feel as if inside an overarching temple.

That came out rather jumbled, forgive me, but my senses were intoxicated.

See? Every particle of my being exulted. *I am a citizen of this world, of such a world, I, the poet Saadi! Never mind that Iran is a month's journey away; never mind that I shall never see Karamania again. The poet does not serve like a soldier and does not toil for a salary—the poet is a citizen of the world.*

Now do you understand why Cem wrote his best poems along this coast? They do not speak of beauty; its name is mentioned only once in a very weak verse. Yet the poet Cem remained faithful to it; Cem kept his love for the world a secret. For this reason, his poems—even today they are treasured as gems of Eastern poetry—were not dedicated to beauty; they were part of beauty itself.

We did not speak of beauty among ourselves either. We kept silent all day, each of us gazing at our own forest, valley, peak. Sometimes, when the wind died down or we stopped for fresh water, Cem would strip naked and swim. He swam slowly, voluptuously—or so it seemed to my jealous eyes. I tried to return to my contemplation, yet I couldn't; I was jealous of the fragile blue light that my Cem caressed with his whole skin.

Don't assume that the rupture, which years later would part us, began then—these were merely its first messengers. I simply felt how Cem's love tore like a fishing net that had long lain in a heap. Now the waves were carrying it, pulling it, stretching it ever more widely.

You probably find it strange that during this brief interval between events Cem had given himself over to contemplating matters that had nothing to do with world history; and I had given myself over to the feelings that agitated every mortal. I can assure you that upon several planks bound together into decks—upon the great trireme the *Treasure*—a life somehow divorced from time existed. And one morning, in complete harmony with this, Villefranche—in all its unreality—drew close to our ship.

A small poem, that was Villefranche, the corsairs' harbor, not subjugated by any king or prince. On the sheer cliff, whose peaks swam like islands above the coastal fog, clung a hundred or so houses, framed by a wall. The bay itself cut very deeply into the land; I figured we had been sailing a whole hour as the long peninsulas that enclose the harbor rose on both sides of us.

Here reality asserted itself again: in pretty-as-a-poem Villefranche, the plague was raging. Our ship recoiled as if disgusted from the harborside street, empty, deserted, and dirty.

Then Brother Blanchefort—I will not describe him to you, because he resembled every other average, ordinary blackshirt—hurried to reassure me that everything had worked out for the best; Nice was to be preferred. Nice, he told me, was known for its beautiful women and wondrous gardens, and the wine was exceptional. Whether plague also awaited us in Nice, Brother Blanchefort did not say.

As far as I can recall, it is an hour's journey between Villefranche and Nice. Yet how different they are. While the sea at

Villefranche resembles the bottom of a well, the coast at Nice is wide-open, shallow, sandy. Mountains do not press down on Nice; they are its rounded and warm back. They call this place the Bay of Angels, and for good reason; surely such colors are found in paradise: the sleepy, silvery sea and the gently golden sands, greenery of every hue, from milky pale to buttery.

Before our meeting with the shore, Cem ordered us to dress him most magnificently. I left him to the servants and went up to the deck alone, thus I saw how our ship slowly neared the pier. They were waiting for us; Brother Blanchefort had surely sent a messenger ahead of us.

I could already see individual faces in the crowd. Most of them were townspeople, men—and women!—in marvelous costumes, bareheaded, noisy. Their cries reached us; they were cries of welcome—they were happy to see us. A group of people in markedly different dress immediately caught our eye. They stood out amidst the crowd like a tiny island of splendor. I realized it was the duke's suite. I also recognized him. He was standing on a covered platform, yet he still did not tower above his nobles, since he was a boy. During that time, our people also came to life aboard the ship. Cem came out of his chambers restlessly, and hurried toward the most anxiously awaited of all his meetings. He stood on the bow of the ship. I had never seen him looking so handsome. This was not because of his fragrance and his exquisite garb—every feature of Cem's face seemed radiant. Although as still as a sculpture, his whole being expressed ardor. The Bay of Angels could not have wished for a more passionate infatuate.

And in response to this passion, the bay lifted its face to him. It gleamed mother-of-pearl white beneath a spray of feathers, between the long, soft locks of hair that spilled over the shoulders of Duke Charles of Savoy. There was something touching and hungry and timid in those childish eyes. A boy was seeing how some Eastern fairy tale stowed the sails, how it dropped anchor, and this fairy tale's hero—mysterious, branded by ill fortune —was Cem.

We descended to the shore on stairs strewn with flowers. Cem walked far ahead of us. When he stopped and stood before the duke, I thought the boy would grab him and lift him up, so intensely did the two of them seem to be striving toward each other.

Down below, we exchanged greetings. The people shouted, women tossed flowers, musicians struggled to raise a racket, and all this celebratory fuss fit that celebratory shore perfectly.

The two sovereigns rode their horses and chatted with the help of the Frank. I watched them laughing with the same laughter, their conversation growing more animated, accompanied by those gestures between people who share no common language, yet who still wish to understand each other directly, without a translator. There truly was something very similar between these two princes who had grown up beneath different skies, between the poet and the child. Because the one was born to create, and the other to listen to, fairy tales. And so they set out side by side across the wide, wonderful field of the imagination.

For me, the months in Nice were... simply beyond compare. The coast looked even more captivating from land. We lived in the duke's palace; the boy was the king's nephew. Exceptionally esteemed and wealthy. But it is not his palace that etched itself on my memory, but its garden. The clusters of pomegranate, olive, and orange trees, the tall palms, the flowers scattered amidst a soft carpet of grass. The fountains. The quiet streams with singing beds. The deep sky and the heavy wine of Savoy.

And we drank and sang. Cem avoided any recollection of that skull-white island, of the black brothers and his own brother; Cem sank fully into that sweet scrap of the present; he gradually formulated a philosophy that there is nothing more unnecessary than memory or past experience, and there is nothing more precious than today. It was not difficult for a Muslim poet to cultivate such a worldview—just read our poets. They say one and the same thing: "We are powerless against fate—only the moment is ours."

In Nice, Cem composed much poetry. Between two glasses of wine, reclining beneath the palms and the mimosas, Cem would recite his new poems, and I would write them down, smoothing a scrap of paper over my tambur.

They expressed our mood at the time so well that I still remember some of them: *Raise this glass, oh Cem of Cemshid! Now we are in wondrous France and fate shall decide everything for us. Leave the crown to Bayezid, for my crown is the world. The whole world...*

Truly, not bad verses. Unfortunately, our fellow feasters could not understand them. No one there had an ear for Eastern poetry, let alone our references and puns, such as "Jamshid," the greatest mythological king of Persian folklore who is even credited for discovering wine. And if something tortured Cem during those wondrous hours, it was his poetic isolation: Cem had no listener besides me.

Incidentally, our days passed, split between songs and wine. The young duke sat amongst that company so unsuited to his age and got drunk on the presence of his fairy-tale hero. These were, according to history, our best days.

Cem, with his lightness, which I cannot call light-mindedness, grew ever more convinced our misadventures on Rhodes had been mere chance. Nothing around us implied any tension. No one spoke the names Bayezid, d'Aubusson, Qaitbay. Our fellow feasters looked terribly far removed from all intergovernmental embroilments; they didn't care a whit about the rivalry between some sultan's sons, the liberation of Eastern Christianity, or the glory of Rome. They drank wine and gazed at the sky, and there, in Savoy, both were of the highest quality. A cheerful young band of world citizens was taking pleasure in their empire—the world—and their only care was to have a few months more of the sweet life they were living.

NINTH TESTIMONY OF THE POET SAADI ON THE
SPRING OF THE YEAR 1483

THE BEGINNING OF spring found us at Nice, insofar as one may speak of a change of season in those parts, so invariable are both the greenery and the azure there. Nevertheless, in early February they redoubled their intensity: a quiver of alarm swept over the sea; a wild impatience welled up from the woods. It filled the whole space to such an extent that it even rushed into our dreams—our dreams grew thin, lightened by some unnamed alarm. Spring was coming.

Cem felt it, too; I have already mentioned there was a deep connection between him and the world. I have even thought Cem's blood must be green, as if he fed off earthly sap like the trees and grasses.

Cem's reaction to that spring was unusual; everything in Nice had convinced him he was no ordinary mortal. All of it: the young duke's adoration, the court singers' lavish praise; at least every other day they came to us with their new poems dedicated to Cem's beauty, misfortune, and valiance. Then they would disappear from our merry table. We knew: they had set off for the north, east, and west to spread their songs to other noble courts, to spread Cem's name and the story of his tragic fate.

In the span of a single winter, Cem had turned into the favorite hero of troubadour song, which seemingly had long been waiting for a foreign white-gold hero so rich in exploits and agonies.

Forgive me for digressing for a moment, but I must do so here, because for the first time in my story I have mentioned the troubadours.

I sense you do not know who turned Cem into a famous name, nor when and why. Indeed, history has seen far more misfortunate, heroic, dignified princes, to say nothing of more wondrous and talented poets—so you surely think, and with good reason. Yet it was precisely Cem who remained in the legends of several countries, with characteristics attributed to him that none of us—his closest companions—had ever noticed.

I hardly imagine I am revealing some unknown truth to you when I say that song did this. Song can do much, and therein lies the retribution that God gives to the poet for all the pains men suffer. The poet has more power than the king because he governs not human life, but human consciousness. With a single line—as long as it is sharp and elegant and hits its target—the poet can destroy what an earthly ruler has striven to build over decades; with a word, he can raise a monument, and that monument lasts through the centuries, floods, invasions and fires; he can build a monument to the most insignificant and unheeded peon of his time.

It is no accident that in my day, rulers held poets in contempt, yet indulged them. They paid them the full measure of their

VERA MUTAFCHIEVA

scorn only posthumously—they did not allow poets to rest in hallowed ground; beyond the cemetery walls, there you should seek the bones of hundreds of troubadours. But kings fed living poets from golden plates and poured them wine in golden cups. Don't think our kings were fools—they had to contend with the harsh law of the Middle Ages. And being clever, they flattered the poet, because they knew his strength. Permit me to offer you one piece of advice; after all, I have been observing for more than five centuries: do not insult poets; choose your enemies elsewhere.

As I was saying, in the winter of 1483, the troubadours discovered Cem. Their hungry imagination had long been languishing. The Crusades had come and gone; piracy was tied to plebeian names. The New World had not yet been discovered, nor had the Reformation's religious wars yet begun. The troubadours were bored. They rehashed various love stories in all manner of voices, and love, you must agree, is a topic with sadly limited possibilities: the lover either dies or is parted forever from his beloved or marries—I challenge you to think up a fourth option.

Cem was not merely new food—he was a bacchanalian feast for the troubadours. Cem came from a country the West knew nothing about, or even less than nothing. He was the son of horror incarnate and a princess who was a victim of that horror. He had passed through a series of misadventures only very vaguely known and thus alluringly mysterious.

The troubadours saw this before all their contemporaries: Cem was a sacrificial lamb.

Centuries later, you ask yourself: To what end was my young, promising friend sacrificed? You are looking down through the ages, so it is easy for you, and likely you will be able to name it after you hear us all out. But back then we could not fathom it; our hopes did not allow us to accept that Cem was doomed. The troubadours were the first to grasp this.

In a few short months—this is how legends are born—hundreds of songs sprang up around Cem. Only a small portion of them were created in Nice, at Charles's court. For the others, the opposite was true; they came to Nice from Eix, Grenoble, Breton, or the Netherlands. The West was amusing itself with a new hero, and what's more, with a new topic. Admit it—it is exceptionally rare for a new topic to arise, those sly dogs the Greeks had already exhausted them all way back when.

And here lies the key to understanding Cem's ostensibly light-minded intoxication in Nice: he believed the legends about him. I was next to him when the Frank translated some new song for him—of course, every troubadour who arrived in Nice wanted to be heard by his own hero, and not entirely without self-interest; despite all their flightiness, poets are strongly self-interested. Even if he had not been drinking, at such moments Cem looked drunk to me; Cem, conquered by the song, would take on the qualities imposed upon him one by one. It even seemed to me—and I myself was also a poet and have never placed a strict boundary between imagination and reality—that my friend grew more shapely and golden, exquisite in his misfortune. And so, song put the finishing touches on him, smoothed him out and perfected him. Cem soared somewhere between the sky and the sea of Nice, outfitted by foreign inspiration with wings and everything necessary for such a flight, in love with his own image.

For me, the spring in question was somewhat less inebriated. Because of the Frank.

The Frank turned up again, after a long period of avoiding our far-too-merry days and nights. I frequently saw him hovering about our master, and I was afraid Cem entrusted thoughts to him that he kept from me; ever since Rhodes, Cem seemed to be trying to establish some barrier between us, proud in his own newfound manhood, which (and this is what I was most afraid of) would likely express itself in a series of decisions. I consoled myself with the thought that, as far as practical decisions were concerned, the Frank would be a better adviser and agent than me; I consoled myself with Cem's tender intimacy, an intimacy almost without words. And yet, it presaged its own end; we feed ourselves with words to a lesser or greater extent. In silence, even a silence heavy with tenderness, every love comes to an end.

I was, if you can imagine, resigned. I knew nothing could last forever, not even Cem's love for a man who was his servant. Once, back in Karamania, we had been equals: fellow laborers in the fields of the word, and of the two of us, I was the more knowledgeable. Could I ever have imagined then that my Cem, my younger brother by the quill, would grow up to be the hero of legends?

It was none other than the Frank who snapped me out of my unhappy thoughts. One day he caught up with me in the gardens and with no preamble ordered me to start learning French. Had he gone off the deep end of late? In the past few days since Cem had drawn him close, Suleiman did not seem to have eaten or slept; the wrinkles between his brows and by his nostrils had grown deeper, he had become more impenetrable than ever.

"What, do you think I know too few languages, Suleiman?" I asked him.

"To hell with all your languages," he replied. "You won't be needing Persian poetry or Arabic philosophy anytime soon. You must learn French quickly and in secret."

"What about a teacher, books? Do those have to be in secret, too?"

"I'll help you. Precisely to keep it secret."

"So are you finally going to tell me why?"

"Because Cem Sultan will need a loyal translator when I am no longer around, Saadi."

For the first time, I heard my name on his lips. The Frank liked to speak without appellations. I broke out in a cold sweat. I recalled how the young novice had died because of a single word spoken against the will of the Order. Why, indeed, was Suleiman still alive?

"Do you suspect something?" I even grasped him by the shoulders, although this was foolish; they could be watching us. I could feel how emaciated Suleiman had become, wasted away.

"No," he replied sternly. "Nothing. But I know better than the lot of you that the brothers do not forgive. I only hope I can do enough damage to them before the end comes."

"They wouldn't dare, Suleiman. Cem would immediately see they'd done it as revenge—they're not crazy, after all."

"No, they're not. They're simply strong." And suddenly he screamed in my face, "Why do you think it still matters what Cem sees?"

After a moment, overcoming his outburst, the Frank asked again, practically pleading, "Promise me, Saadi, promise me you will learn French. We have no time. If they kill me tomorrow, every one of Cem's words will have to pass through their ears."

And so I buckled down to study, which was not at all in my nature. I worked at night, because during the day I made sure not to miss the lively celebrations. I worked with a heavy head, my whole being taut with fear; I was exhausted from wakefulness and effort. And if I achieved anything in that short time—enough to translate a simple conversation—I owe it not to my famous gift for languages; I owe it to the feeling that I was being pursued, and that I needed to reach my goal.

Sometimes during my nighttime vigils, the door would open and I knew: the Frank had come. Even more desiccated, almost translucent, with hair that had recently begun to go gray at his temples, with staring eyes, Suleiman reminded me of those apparitions that wandered the towers here at night—I had heard of them. Suleiman would take the book from my hands and quiz me as if I were a boy.

I'm telling you: never in my life have I been so diligent, never have I considered myself capable of such assiduous labor. I did it not so much for Cem and our shared future as for Suleiman. As you know, one might break one's promises to the living, but everyone keeps their oaths to the dead. Suleiman was already a dead man, that's how he felt to me. And the only thing I could do to soothe his soul was this: learn a foreign language. I studied it during our last weeks in Nice. I learned it on the road when they led us away—in every one of the castles whose names I will not even try to recall, they were too many.

Shortly before we departed, Cem was truly grieved. The young duke had left our company. They told us he had been urgently called to his uncle, the king, because Louis had suddenly felt ill and wanted to bless him. So the young duke had left without saying goodbye.

Cem saw only the hand of God in the whole business, even though he was sad about the boy, but I suspected there were other hands involved besides God's. Suleiman put these thoughts in my head when he hissed, "See, Saadi, they're starting."

Our departure was noisy. The numerous nobles of the Maritime Alps rushed to wish Cem well and to offer their hospitality at their castles. The springtime added a flood of light and colors, thus our journey resembled a triumphal march.

We climbed the steep incline to the road built in Roman times. It wound along the crest of the final ridge of mountains above the sea, its elevation allowing us to take leave of that unique region to our heart's content.

At the head of our train, amidst a suite of myriad languages, where I could see the raspberry, violet, and lemon cloaks of the provincial nobles and the stern cassocks of the brothers, rode Cem. In white and gold, of course. Cem tossed cheerful glances now to the left, where the mountains rose steeply, still snowy beneath the bright sun, and now to the right, where the Mediterranean Sea, with its cutaway coasts and islands, with its ships and fishing boats, gradually disappeared in the haze. *Does Cem realize he is leaving the kingdom of happiness?* I wondered.

Hardly. Cem was chatting—and here the Frank, concentrated and taut as a bowstring, helped him—with nobles and monks; Cem paid a lot of attention to some Roman monument, high, high columns atop a high peak, which commemorated Rome's victory over the mountain tribes and which held up the

Savoy sky to prevent it from fusing with the sea. Cem began his descent down the other side, beyond the ridge, without looking back. The hero of song does not look back—everything is ahead of him. The following weeks have remained in my memory like a handful of very colorful ladies' handkerchiefs that a merchant unfolds quickly to catch your eye and your money. We visited the estates of this baron and that count. We listened to singers, musicians, poets. We drank aged wines. We ate wild game, even in the morning for breakfast. We went hunting. Cem already looked completely estranged not only from me, but from all of us, our men. I observed him, to some extent with joy—let him rest, for who knows what awaits us in the future; and to some extent with pain—this was not how my master would win his throne.

But one day I got to thinking that Cem was playing at carelessness and that he had not given up his ambitious plans—Cem did not find it hard to pretend; it was in his blood. That day I did not see Ahmed Agha and Haydar, the peasant poet, among our ranks. As you know, we were not so numerous that someone's absence could go unnoticed, but the two of them had given themselves over to drunkenness during our most recent adventures to such an extent that I thought they were probably lying in the shade somewhere. They did not appear the following day either, nor when we set out for our next castle.

I went over to the Frank, because I rarely spoke to Cem in front of other people, and said, "Where are Ahmed and Haydar?"

"They left. We sent them to King Matthias."

"What were you thinking? The brothers will notice, if they haven't already."

"We didn't hide it from the brothers. Cem himself spoke to Blanchefort. He told him he wished to contact the Hungarians directly, without d'Aubusson."

"And Blanchefort agreed?"

"Yes. He even claimed it was fully in keeping with the order of things. But such easy agreement scares me.... Saadi, pray to God, pray to the Devil if you like, but our men must reach Hungary."

Yes, this new Suleiman is shocking, isn't he? In recent weeks the Frank had been cautiously drawing closer to me, he even sought me out. As if he were afraid of disappearing before handing over his job to me; he had chosen me as his replacement. And nothing in the world had ever flattered me as much as the faith of that harsh, renounced, and sacrificed man.

"Saadi," he went on, while pretending to tighten the straps on my saddle, "count the days. It'll take thirty or so days for our men on the way there, but King Matthias's messenger could arrive in less. If in two months' time we have no word from Ahmed Agha and Haydar, count them as lost. We'll start over from the beginning. Or rather you will, in my place."

"Perish the thought," I replied, as our peasant poet would have. What hardships could Haydar be facing? I had never held him in any particular esteem; I felt he profaned high art with his simple logic, but now I had gone soft with sorrow for Haydar.

While I ruminated over this news, while I wondered whether I should be offended that I was learning this only now, Suleiman kept talking, though I only caught the end of his words: "I'm terribly afraid, Saadi."

The poor, poor Frank. I could see with my own two eyes how fear of death can melt even iron, since it had melted the Frank;

it is excruciating to die of fear. I, too, already assumed his death was inevitable; I only hoped I would finally see the Frank at peace—every day was a torment to him.

And indeed, our men did not return. No messenger from King Matthias came either. I should have mentioned this later, but I note it now, so as not to forget. In fact, we became certain of Ahmed and Haydar's demise during our months at Rumilly, one of the Order's fortresses. I assume Brother d'Aubusson had reckoned that Cem was moving in far too mixed and uncertain circles, thus he hurried in early June to once again shelter us beneath his monastic wing.

A strange coincidence that our new refuge was called Rumilly. Cem laughed when they told us. "See, Saadi," he said, "we were aiming for Rumelia and now look, we've ended up there."

The castle was old and dilapidated; in recent decades, the Order had not been able to decently maintain its properties. Its long, dark corridors were overgrown with weeds; the beams in Cem's chambers were worm-eaten; the hastily hung curtains did nothing to stop either the wind or the damp—the latter crept up them and created a fantastical picture of dereliction. The Savoy summer did not enter into that stony dungeon with its narrow slits in place of windows, which gave you the feeling of being in a coffin.

Cem shuddered with cold when they led him to his so-called chambers. After the various noble castles of Savoy, which were more homes than fortresses, richly furnished, warm, inhabitable, Rumilly felt like a prison to him. The same thought crossed my mind as well, but neither of us said it aloud. So as to deter us from voicing the conclusion on all of our minds—it was not for our peace of mind, but rather for his; Cem hated to see his suite worried and crestfallen—he assured us this was exactly what he needed: a bit of rest after our rather too frequent diversions, and the proper conditions to devote himself fully to his statecraft.

The warrior monks paced outside the door. Recently I had noticed their numbers growing daily. Silent and decorous, they tried to give the appearance of an honor guard, rather than jailers. I found them inexplicably irritating—it was painful not to be able to go out through the corridor or into the enclosed courtyard, all covered in moss and tufts of weeds—without running into one of them. Clearly, the brothers had much work to do, and they did it with diligence.

Our days in Rumilly passed in a monotonous routine. Cem and Suleiman often sat together (they would compose messages whose replies never seemed to arrive), while during that time I would find something to keep me busy outside, such that I could eavesdrop around Cem's room. The knights seemed to disappear in my presence, yet I couldn't shake the feeling they were tightly surrounding me, in the very walls themselves.

The castle was isolated. Its village, scattered at the foot of the fortified hill, numbered some two hundred people. We saw them from up above in the morning, spilling out into the field until nightfall hid them. They worked without speaking or singing, as if the black shadow of the Order hung heavily over them as well.

The village was not on a main road, but once some Italian merchants who had lost their way stopped into it, so they even climbed the hill to our castle. They were selling silk and silver. Suleiman invited them in to see our master, where they tarried for some time before he saw them out, visibly angry—they had demanded an arm and a leg, he said, and expressed his great scorn for the merchant class as a whole.

Since there was not much entertainment in Rumilly, I stayed on the fortress wall while the merchants made their way down the hill in the evening dusk. It struck me that they had an unnecessarily large number of guards for a few dozen bolts of silk and a single trunk of silver, but I didn't share this observation with anyone. I had begun to see something premeditated in all of Suleiman's actions. Perhaps the Italian merchants, too, were not accidental visitors.

Their visit took place on a Wednesday, and on Friday morning we were awakened by an unusual racket. As you know, I slept at the foot of Cem's bed, since Cem did not like to be alone at night. The two of us jumped up at once and listened to the voices outside. The knight-monks were talking—none of our language could be heard. Yet amidst all the unfamiliar, repulsively coarse voices, I could make out one familiar one: the Frank was cursing and cursing in every language.

"See what's going on," Cem commanded me, his face pale.

Half-dressed, I threw open the door; someone pushed me aside and at least twenty brothers rushed inside. They looked like a pack of hunting hounds, well-rested, brawny, bloodthirsty animals. Three of them were holding on to the Frank practically with their teeth. Suleiman struggled for his life, while his face expressed such fury that it made him almost unrecognizable.

"Call in our translator," one of the brothers roared at another. The Frank was no longer a translator to them.

"Halt!" I stopped them with an audacity I never suspected I had in me. I spoke in their language for the first time, and this stunned them to no end; they almost lost their grip on Suleiman. "I will translate."

My tongue twisted in discomfort, my nose felt like it was stuffed up, and the foreign sounds tickled my palate in a ridiculous way. *Suleiman*, I thought, *my friend Suleiman. Had you hoped that in just such a moment you would reap the fruits of your diligent labor? Rest assured, my friend: I have been a good pupil to you.*

One of the brothers had stepped forward. He carried the little silver chest in which Cem locked his important documents since Karamania and Cairo.

"Tell your master"—the monk's eyes were shooting daggers at me—"that this morning we caught Suleiman sneaking his papers out of this room. Cem Sultan's mercy has fed the vilest of traitors. Suleiman has sold himself to an unknown master, but there is no doubt of his venality. And we will find out who his buyer is," he concluded fiercely and shot the Frank a glare that would have killed a rhinoceros.

My head was spinning as I translated, and the color drained from Cem's face to such an extent that I was afraid he would faint. He stubbornly refused to look at Suleiman. *What's wrong with him, why? Good God, just don't let Cem debase our friend with suspicion in his final hour,* I thought to myself, because Cem's outbursts were often illogical.

At that moment I decided, even though I was not sure, that among their pack there was no one who understood Turkish. But it was a question not only of something important, but of something sacred: he needed to see him off with gratitude, this man who was dying for his sake.

"My sultan," I added, "they are lying like carpets. It is all a setup. They want to take Suleiman from you. Don't believe them, Cem—save the Frank!"

"Be quiet, Saadi," Suleiman cut me off. His face was no longer twisted with hatred. "They will do whatever they have decided to do; we are in their hands, don't forget. Sacrifice me, my sultan!" He turned to Cem and something about the scene reminded me of our parting with the doomed young brother on Rhodes. "Sacrifice me quickly and with conviction so as to save everything else. I have long been a dead man in any case."

The monks stood there still as statues, the works of an inept sculptor.

Dirty, hereditary killers, I thought, as if with Suleiman's demise, his hatred had come to life within me. *Too bad for the God they serve; he surely will choke on the filth they splash before his altar.*

I averted my eyes from Cem—he was a terrible sight. He, the hero of legend, stood helpless before petty slander. They were separating him from his most-needed companion, and he couldn't even send him off with dignity. Because, of course, we had to pretend we believed them. *Not only will they kill us off one by one*, my thoughts tripped over themselves, *they will kill us in a shameful way and they will rob us before we die. Almighty God, why do you not leave us at least the illusion that we are human beings?*

While this silent scene lasted—and it lasted quite a while, since all its participants were out of their minds from horror or guilt—Cem was struggling like a drowning man. I also saw how he at last swam to the surface, with some superhuman effort, effort that takes years off one's life; Cem stepped forward and took the chest from the monk. He opened it (he always kept the key with him) and flipped through the documents.

"They are all here," he said in a choked voice. That was all he could do for the Frank.

"We didn't give him time to spirit them away," the monk cut in. "Even an hour later and they would've disappeared to who knows where. But you'll tell us everything." He glared at the Frank, yet the monk himself looked as if he was struggling to keep up his hostility.

"Your threats are unwarranted," Cem interrupted him grimly. "I can guess who might be interested in my letters."

Whether they were afraid Cem might say d'Aubusson's name and with that spoil their venal charade, or perhaps everything had been planned out in advance, but in any case the monk immediately added, "We have no intention of judging or torturing your servant, Your Highness; that right belongs to you. Suleiman shall fall under the blows of our justice only if you refuse to involve yourself."

"And what verdict am I permitted to pronounce?" Cem's voice shook. I was afraid some dam within him would burst and all would be lost.

"What permission does Your Highness speak of?" The monk feigned offended innocence. "You have the right to any judgment, even if it be the most indulgent. Exile, for example. I presume Your Highness would not retain a servant who has so basely betrayed him. The contrary would mean clemency, and the Order would not accept such mercy once its guest has been so affronted."

"Where shall I exile my servant to? Perhaps Rhodes, hm?"

"Oh no, Your Highness. Rhodes is holy land; a traitor's steps will weigh heavy upon it. A double traitor," the monk emphasized spitefully. "Simply exile him from Rumilly and let him choose for himself a hideaway to conceal his shame."

You would have had to have been blind not to notice how hope welled up within Cem; and with just such wild hope, he turned to Suleiman. "Go out into the world and seek refuge...." He didn't finish his sentence. As if he were trying with his final word to implore the Frank to run away and hide, to save himself from the Order somewhere at the ends of the earth.

Then something completely unexpected happened. Suleiman, who himself had ordered us to play their game, who had demanded we accept him as an enemy—Suleiman himself did not keep up the charade until the end. In a hollow voice, but with a force that frightened even his executioners, Suleiman commanded, "Let me say my farewells." And they let go of him.

The Frank knelt before Cem but did not bow his head; he did not kiss his master's robe, but touched it with his fingers. And that no longer young and not at all handsome man with his graying temples and torn shirt—they bared the necks of all convicts like so, to make it easier for the axe—was the picture of human loyalty incarnate.

Realizing the monks had already had enough and would allow him only a single gesture—because a word would have been too much—Cem bent down and hugged the Frank as if he would never let him go and pressed his cheek to the man's hair.

Two years ago, I had been by Cem's side when he took leave of his mother and son in Cairo. This parting was one hundred, no, countless times deeper than that one.

The monks observed decorum; they did not disturb this scene at all. Suleiman gradually, very carefully, as if not wanting to push away a child, removed Cem's arms from his shoulders and stood up. He walked over to me, but only held out his hand.

"You, Saadi," he said. I knew what he meant.

And he headed for the door.

I won't describe to you what Cem and I went through when we were left alone. We did not speak much—the fear that we were being listened to paralyzed us completely. Cem ordered me to go out onto the wall and to watch from there whether and when they would lead Suleiman out, and where he would go.

I did not budge from that wall the whole day, nor the next, nor the third, while at night we took turns with Mehmed Bey, another one of our men. The brothers often passed by us, and every time they nodded at us respectfully—they were honoring our grief. I tolerated them somehow; I was completely obsessed with not missing Suleiman.

In vain, because Suleiman the Frank never left Rumilly. And we lived as if sick with horror. We knew his corpse was buried under us, in the castle's dungeon, alongside who knows how many other such loyal, unconquered souls. We were living atop the bones of the Frank.

TESTIMONY OF HÜSEYIN BEY, BAYEZID KHAN'S ENVOY TO RHODES, ON THE EVENTS OF APRIL 1483

I AM HÜSEYIN Bey, son of Mustafa, the *kadi* of Dimetoka. When our glorious Sultan Bayezid II prevailed over his rebellious brother and took the throne once and for all, he removed all those who had inspired this rebelliousness or who had counted on it. Thus, a number of viziers and governor-generals left Istanbul, or the world, while others bid farewell to their lofty titles. Bayezid did not even allow them to remain as rank-and-file soldiers, because he never completely trusted our army. It is a well-known fact our sipahi were far too indebted to Mehmed Khan and hoped to see in the rule of his younger son a continuation of the cavalry's golden age. For this reason, Bayezid Khan seized the sipahi's land, gave it to our clerics, and gathered new advisers around his throne: the clergy and their descendants.

I was one of them. Not so long ago, when Sultan Bayezid was still only Şehzade Bayezid and governed Amasya, I was his teacher. As the son of an Islamic judge, I helped introduce the Şehzade to the theological sciences, especially astronomy. As an expression of his deep appreciation for me, Bayezid Khan did not make me either a vizier or a chief judge. He understood my essence: my soul's eyes were turned toward the heavens and I strove to decipher Allah's will and to dedicate myself to the triumph of Islam. For this reason, Bayezid Khan left me in the shadows, as far as court ranks were concerned; he kept me as his closest adviser.

I presume you will interrogate me about the peace negotiations in Edirne that took place in the fall of 1482. There is no point in describing them to you—they were like any other negotiations. Bayezid Khan did not receive the envoys from Rhodes personally so as to prevent one of the infidels, who have only the vaguest understanding of our refined natures, from insulting the sultan's hearing with a coarse word. Mesih Pasha heard them out.

Mesih Pasha did not give the Rhodian delegation a definitive answer; they only received such an answer in December, when our delegation visited Rhodes and signed the peace agreement. Bayezid Khan was obliged to maintain good relations with the infidel knights until his death. They, of course, were also so obliged, although we cannot consider it an obligation in their case—in fact, it was their most cherished dream.

Word around the court had it that our envoys had placed an article in the peace agreement, the contents of which would be composed later. By a special envoy. It was also known that this article had to do with Cem. We knew all of this from rumors—Bayezid Khan never uttered the name "Cem" in front of his subjects, court, or army. A sultan cannot afford to have a brother.

It was the spring of 1483. We had just received alarming news. There were informers everywhere. I suspect I will hardly shock

VERA MUTAFCHIEVA

you with this admission, since in our day a man cost very little: a purse full of ducats, for example, or a promise of a good position if they were ever unmasked. If they were unmasked, yet still managed to save their skin, that is.

The news was as follows: first of all, the infidel knights had moved Cem from Nice and even from Savoy entirely, sending him inland to French territory. We heard they changed Cem's place of refuge every month, and sometimes even every week. This showed they were anxious. Second, the rectors of the Venetian Republic had caught a man by the name of Nicholas of Nicosia in Modone with a letter from Cem to his mother in Cairo. The Venetians, so as not to spoil their relations with Qaitbay, let the intermediary in question go, but a copy of Cem's letter had been sent to us. This, in turn, showed Cem was keeping secrets from the knights. He realized the danger he was in and was looking to escape—that letter showed a lot of things.

Third, here and there in Europe, scholars and writers were appealing to Christian conscience, calling for quick action on behalf of the unfortunate prince. In Florence, Avignon, and Buda they spoke openly that the time had come for victory over Islam—the case of Cem was a divine portent in such an undertaking. There was nothing surprising in this; as clever as they may be, those involved in spiritual labor have never grasped the simplest thing—their insignificant role in affairs of state.

I knew my sovereign well, thus it was clear to me why he did not settle Cem's situation already in the autumn of 1482: Bayezid Khan was waiting for more favorable conditions. He believed events would undercut the cost of his highly overvalued brother. Prudent and experienced, Bayezid Khan knew the Ottomans owed their victories not so much to weapons as to the interrelations between world powers. Some of them truly did oppose our expansion into Europe, but another part of them secretly welcomed this expansion, because it spared them from having powerful rivals. We had seen enough to have grounds to hope that Cem—even if he were a prophet or a great military commander, which he was not—would not be able to unite the Christian East and the Christian West in his name. In fact, Bayezid Khan was waiting for this truth to become glaringly obvious so as to avoid the grand master's blackmail; he was waiting, even though every moment cost him much in terms of peace of mind. But my master—alongside all his other virtues— was also frugal. He was saving ducats with every passing day.

But now events forced him to hurry, because something new was involved, something that could not be reduced to a simple calculation: the sentiments of certain very zealous Christians or far-too-bold thinkers—the West suffered from them in our day. They were capable of arranging for Cem's escape and handing him over to Qaitbay or Corvinus. We could not allow this to happen.

Bayezid Khan did not grow flustered. He dragged things out, choosing the moment when it was neither too early nor too late. And so my mission to Rhodes was scheduled for the late spring of 1483. Before I left, Bayezid Khan saw me in his personal chambers to give me his instructions.

Some of those called here before me have spoken of our sultan's appearance. I must only add that power did not change him. Bayezid Khan did not grow fat as do most who feed on power, nor did he take on a majestic air. Moderate in eating, a foe of wine, Bayezid Khan remained as slight and dry as a dervish, and one did not feel anxious in his presence—one felt like an equal. If something unsettled me when I spoke to my sultan, it was his vigilant attention; Bayezid Khan lived somehow on guard during the whole of his long reign. He did not for a moment believe his power was indisputable, he did not believe in the love of his people and his army, he did not even believe in his own mind—even though he was as clever as three men put together.

I would explain his grimness with reasons clear to his contemporaries and to history—Bayezid had lived in the shadow of a very distinguished, very celebrated father; he had lived as his unfavored son, because Mehmed Khan did not hide his preferences and his scorn. Mehmed Khan claimed his blood had thinned to water when it passed to Bayezid, and I am quite sure—if death had not been in such a rush—the Conqueror would have done away with his firstborn son, so as to make Cem his heir. And since I, an observer of our ruling house, was so sure of this, Bayezid himself must have been that much more certain of his unenviable fate. The fact that he, despite the Conqueror's will, ended up as his heir, weighed on Bayezid. For this reason, his attitude toward Cem was double-edged—believe me. On the one hand, the sultan deeply hated his brother, who had fled death in defiance of the law and had turned into a banner to rally Bayezid's enemies. But on the other hand, he felt an unacknowledged guilt with respect to Cem—he was conscience-stricken before the memory of the Conqueror. He always lacked self-confidence, like a person sitting in someone else's place.

During that conversation of ours, the sultan saw me alone.

"I'm sending you to Rhodes, Hüseyin Bey," he began in his very even voice, "to settle the question of my brother's future. We know the enemy will bet heavily on Cem. In the coming years and decades, he will likely be our constant, open wound. We are not in a position to heal this wound—the Order will guard Cem like a rare treasure. Our every attempt to eliminate the criminal who has sown division in the House of Ottoman could bring us more harm than good. I do not wish to be thought of as a poisoner in a world of poisoners. If they ever decide to rid themselves of Cem, I will expose them—Cem is my blood, after all."

The sultan said all this without pause, as if he had long since composed it. And once again he confirmed what I already knew: Bayezid did not desire his brother's death, but rather feared it. I assure you, he had the chance to eliminate Cem many times and every time he froze up—thwarting the Conqueror's will unsettled his firstborn son.

Perhaps my words are going too far, but I am speaking about justice. Bayezid Khan was as devout as he was certain. He felt himself indebted to fate due to his unforeseen power and surely had made a vow—this was typical of him; he often haggled with Providence, honoring the clerics, trading for relics, freeing criminals. He must have secretly promised to keep Cem alive as some sort of talisman for his own supremacy. That's the only way I can explain how during a time of easy poisons and quick knives our most fearsome enemy remained safe.

"You shall not offer even the slightest hint, Hüseyin," the sultan continued, "that we desire his death. We would only be needlessly contributing to his fame. Besides, I want to show those people out there our moral superiority. Let the world observe how those compassionate Christians, so sensitive to human suffering, turn a guest into a hostage. Let us not forget that our era has two centers: Rome and Stambul. Thousands of eyes are watching us, Hüseyin Bey, watching us with fear, just as they watched my father's victories. Now we must show that besides our strength, we also come bearing a new morality."

This was the way Bayezid Khan usually asked for my advice: he would fix his gaze on my face and even forget to breathe until I answered. This time, I needed to think for a moment—my sovereign's words had startled me.

Without betraying my loyalties, it seems I must point out the only flaw I found in my master: Bayezid Khan was deeply and consistently moderate. He always observed himself from the outside, tailoring his appearance and behavior to that external gaze, always facing the world with a carefully cultivated image. Thus, when he mentioned the lack of hypocrisy as the foremost feature of our morality, I was at a loss for words. It is true that this differentiates Islam from Christianity. In a violent society, we do not deny that we use force, that we will continue to use force, that in our world everything happens through force.

And in the future, everything will happen through violence as well. Our means were the means of our time, but Christianity disavowed these means, even while cultivating them to perfection. Christianity accused us of preaching destruction, but we responded with a different reproach: Christianity sowed destruction, while preaching peace and love.

All of this is true, you know it as well as I do, but don't suppose that in this sense Bayezid Khan was any less our ruler. He introduced hypocrisy into the life of the empire. I'll tell you why.

Up until Bayezid Khan, our sultans were simple soldiers who didn't care what their enemy thought of them. There was no common language between Islam and Christianity. With Bayezid Khan, that changed, because Bayezid wanted to participate on equal footing in the international life of his time. We needed to find a language—we could no longer speak only with weapons. But since we were very inexperienced, only a few of us showed any talent for that language. But Bayezid Khan did. He quite skillfully crafted an emperor out of himself—not a soldier and not a fiery emir like Osman, Orhan, or Murad.

"A new morality," I echoed, as I didn't know what else to say. "And how am I to understand my task in Rhodes, my sultan?"

"It's difficult, Hüseyin Bey." Bayezid Khan got up, and I could no longer escape his gaze. "You will keep silent. They will make an offer."

"What am I permitted to accept?"

"Not a groat more than forty-five thousand ducats, that's what Cem is worth."

I jumped to my feet. Forty-five thousand gold ducats! That was half the income of our treasury for a whole year. How would we pay for the army, construction, weapons, and the salaries of the thousands of government officials with the remaining half?

"My sultan," I said, "my mind cannot fathom it."

Bayezid Khan smiled. I did not like his smile, because it sharpened Bayezid's already sharp features.

"Your mind cannot fathom it, Hüseyin Bey, because you think we are paying for a single person as much as we pay all our soldiers and servants. And therein lies your error: we are not paying Cem, nor paying for Cem. This gold, this heretofore unheard-of wealth, will do what even the Conqueror's victories could not: it will split the West apart. Everyone who has gotten a taste of our gold will become a mortal enemy of the rest; this gold will set kings against the Church; it will pay for much death and many defections. I have heard the counsel of the stars. We are making an advantageous deal, Hüseyin Bey; we are even getting off quite cheaply. You shall see," the sultan continued, no longer impassive, "my reign shall pass in advantageous agreements. You shall be there, Hüseyin Bey, when Christianity will help me against itself. Until now we were a threat that could unite the West to some extent. From now on we will become a more dangerous enemy, because we pay.

"I don't know if history will appreciate this, Hüseyin Bey, or whether I will go down as a ruler who failed to conquer any other states. Yes, the chronicle notes the conquerors, but does not stop to think that it is much harder to hold on to what has been won and to get the world to recognize it."

I long served Bayezid Khan, but I can assure you I had never heard him speak so openly. Customarily, he was sparing with his words. This conversation of ours was obviously very significant for the sultan, and he insisted on making certain I would act with conviction.

"You can count on me, my sultan," I replied.

"Your mission also has another purpose, Hüseyin Bey. Not only will you negotiate Cem's annual allowance with the Order, you will make a secret, written agreement with the master. I need d'Aubusson's signature on a document that would ruin him in the eyes of the world. With it, I will bind him better than any chain ever could."

"What if he refuses, my sultan? In the end, we are the ones asking, not them."

"He won't refuse—it's forty-five thousand. For that mountain of gold a man would sacrifice far more than his good name. So don't come back without an agreement, Hüseyin Bey."

That's how Bayezid Khan's commands sounded. He would say them just like that, in the course of conversation, but that did not make them any less obligatory. On the contrary, even.

"I would not say your task ends there, Hüseyin Bey," the sultan continued. "While still on Rhodes, you will request to leave for France, so as to make certain with your own eyes that Cem is alive and there is reason for us to pay. Let the monks not get used to receiving money on faith. You will give Cem my letter—you can read it; it is a complete repetition of the previous ones. But since we want to meet Cem, we have to have something to give him, don't we?"

I nodded silently. My task already looked very difficult indeed. God Almighty, how much work that headstrong boy had created for us. And what expenses! I sighed heavily at the insult and bitterness of it.

"Don't take it like that, Hüseyin Bey," Bayezid Khan said with a sour smile. "After my father's conquests, it was inevitable we'd have to make some contact with these Westerners who until yesterday did not even want to utter our name. And now, you see, God himself has given us an opportunity: today we and Christianity are negotiating, looking for a common language. Thanks be to God."

Bayezid Khan got on his knees and pressed his head down between his palms. In short, he sank into prayer. He often did this, and I often wondered whether it was an expression of deep faith, or whether this was my master's way of cutting off conversations, avoiding questions and annoyances.

What else could I do? I got down on my knees as well. This time I did not offer up prayers to God, because I was deeply worried. Fate had entrusted me, a judge's son, with the task of establishing first contact between the House of Osman and the West.

Gentle spring winds brought me quickly—in some ten days— from Stambul to Rhodes. I traveled accompanied by fifty or so sailors and clerics, and several sacks full of ducats that sat heavily in the bowels of the ship. No matter how I tried to reassure myself that my men were as loyal as can be and that our trip was a secret, I shuddered at the thought that loyalty had nothing to do with it but rather only pure idiots would let such a precious ship get away unscathed. And there were corsairs as well—these waters were swarming with them.

In any case, perhaps because I really was accompanied by pure idiots, or else the corsairs had incompetent spies on their payrolls in Stambul, we arrived in Rhodes without incident. We waited for nightfall in open waters and under the cover of darkness snuck into the harbor with our lights extinguished. Perhaps Rhodes was waiting for us, because in only half an hour the guards had come to escort us and settled us in some house. Its shutters were down in the front so no one would find out about our arrival. While we were still in the harbor, they had made me order my sailors to take the ship to another bay on the island.

The next morning, I was visited by two men dressed all in black with the faces of pickpockets. I felt if I turned my back, in an instant they would have rifled through my entire room, but I treated them as beneath my contempt, giving monosyllabic answers. They informed me the grand master would soon be coming.

How do you like that? I would not be welcomed by his grace in his ceremonial chambers, I would not be shown any honors. The grand master was underscoring that he negotiated his dark deals in the dark, and he himself would come to that inconspicuous house fit for a middling merchant.

I waited for him behind the drawn shutters and curtains, with a candle burning in broad daylight. I could sense the walls were watching me as soon as I set foot in Rhodes. I had to get used to that feeling.

The grand master entered, preceded only by a single monk, clearly a translator, who had inspected the room with a sharp glance. I wouldn't have been surprised if he had peered under the bed as well, but he saved me that indignity.

The grand master, an unusually gaunt and quite tall man, with heavily graying hair, was dressed in a simple cloak with a hood that had hidden his whole face in the streets. Clearly d'Aubusson was hiding our meeting. This offended me; I was the envoy of a great ruler, and if I had come to Rhodes with a less-than-honorable task, it was precisely d'Aubusson who was to blame—they owed me respect. I had the urge to raise the curtains, to throw open the thick shutters and shout, "Look, people of Rhodes, look upon your leader! See how he does not recoil from taking bags of gold in exchange for human suffering, as long as it is done in secret."

Of course, I did not do this—where would things end up if everyone gave in to their urges? His grace and I bowed to each other, but without shaking hands or exchanging a kiss.

"Your sultan's envoy has been slow in coming," d'Aubusson began. "A little longer and we might not have had anything to negotiate. Conspiracies are cropping up around Cem, did you know? Some rulers think his freedom would be a great boon for all of Christianity. Could our paltry forces really oppose them—the forces of one impoverished order?"

While d'Aubusson spoke, I nodded, emphasizing that, first, he was telling me things already well-known, and, second, these things were not a particular threat to us.

It was no accident—I noticed—that d'Aubusson finished his speech precisely with "impoverished order." It was obvious he was immediately hinting at money. He was getting to the point quickly, Mashallah!

"We were informed of these plots on time," I said through his translator. "Bayezid Khan does not see danger in them, and I will tell you why: Mehmed Khan's widow does not have much money at hand, and Sultan Qaitbay is loath to take it from her—Cem is too uncertain an undertaking, while what is absolutely certain is that having him will bring down on his possessor the rage of the all-powerful Bayezid Khan."

"As to whether Cem would be worth the money," d'Aubusson said, looking me straight in the eye with the expression of a wholesale trader, "we have yet to find out. After all, Cem is still young and has decades of battle before him. But is it really worth letting things come to that?"

Believe me, this is exactly how d'Aubusson spoke to me. He had thrown aside any pretense of politesse, thinking me the envoy of some savage ruler. He found all common courtesies unwarranted in a conversation with a Mohammedan. Who, I ask, gave this beast the right to consider us beasts?

I swallowed back my rage. "That is for you to decide. How many days do you need?"

I knew d'Aubusson needed the money quickly—our spies had told us Rhodes was all but destitute after all the outlays connected with Cem's visits, while the French king, whom we suspected of being the Order's partner in this whole business, was a notorious skinflint.

"We have already discussed it," he said, trying to force an air of dignity, even though that dignity did not square at all with the desperation of a common merchant who was sprinting so as not to be beaten out of a deal. "We discussed it and took counsel from the brothers, as well as from Rome, and here is what we decided: as long as Cem's situation remains unclear, and as long as Christianity is not threatened by a new attack from the Ottomans, we will care for this unhappy prince. We will provide him with a decent—no, make that an opulent life—and we will guard against attempts on his life or freedom by ill-intentioned persons. This, of course, will cost us—but the cause is great and requires sacrifice."

"Above all, Your Grace," I cut in, "let us understand what you mean by Cem's freedom."

"Above all, the impossibility of him being kidnapped," d'Aubusson answered. "We can guarantee this only if Cem is watched closely, if he is protected by a large number of guards, if he lives in one of our impenetrable fortresses."

A purely human horror gripped me at the thought of such freedom. Not very attractive, you must agree, but completely desirable for us. The poor wretch, he brought this upon himself.

VERA MUTAFCHIEVA

"And what guarantee will the Order give that it will protect Cem's freedom under the described conditions? Cem has a suite of nearly thirty people around him. Why couldn't one of them be his connection to Corvinus, the Duke of Savoy or Venice?"

"The guarantee?" D'Aubusson did not even blink an eye. "You shall suggest the guarantee. If the sum you pay to cover our expenses around Cem is sufficient, his guards will also be sufficient. As will our desire not to lose this sum."

You know, I had taken part—even though my clerical rank did not require it—in several of the Conqueror's campaigns. I had seen how the infidels, when the demise of their city or their village became imminent, would run with their women and children to their churches. There they sought their final hope: they would crowd around some priest or monk, begging him to ask their god for a miracle. I had also heard how those same people—once under our power—hid their books and collection plates, and took bread from their own mouths to feed their pastors. Only their faith consoled them against the force that we were.

Like every true believer, and a cleric at that, I felt scorn toward their faith as well as a great superiority over their pathetic priests. But a small part of me also envied those same priests, since they were fed by truly faithful followers. Would anyone feed us, the ruling clerics, like that? Or perhaps they followed us because it was very convenient, even advantageous, to be a true believer?

In that hour alone, I must admit, another thought dawned on me: I pitied my petty enemies, those thousands of infidels who in their suffering turned to the likes of d'Aubusson: hopelessly corrupted, hopelessly irreligious pastors.

You vermin! You rapacious reptile! I said to myself. After all, I had become a statesman only yesterday; before that—I was the poor son of a kadi.

"Forty-five thousand ducats," I spat fiercely. "And not a groat more."

D'Aubusson did not manage to hide his first reaction, which was his greedy delight. It flashed like lightning and was immediately suppressed, replaced by impassiveness.

"Only?" d'Aubusson said, tossing his head, his goatee bristling at me. "Is that the price Bayezid Khan places on his sultanship?"

Take it and scram, I would have screamed at that highwayman, to whom Cem was worth at most a fifth of that whole bribe. *Take it, because the others will beat you to it.*

Now I truly could not contain myself. "You forget, Bayezid Khan has no reason to pay for a throne he already holds. My sultan merely wishes to arrange a luxurious life for his brother. Every household has its price, Your Grace. Since Your Grace finds this price disadvantageous, we will seek another host for Cem. In recent days—perhaps even today, I have no way of knowing—our envoy offered the same amount in Venice. Only one of you can take it—it's either the Order or the Republic. You need to settle it amongst yourselves. That's your Christian business."

Those few words were my payback to d'Aubusson—I paid him back for not feigning at least a modicum of dignity before me. And no matter how hard he tried to control himself, d'Aubusson flinched visibly.

"Bayezid Khan has been hasty," he drawled, his expression ridiculous. "He has been hasty in his distrust of our Order, forgetting we were the ones who spared the House of Osman from vicious battles. Let God judge him; this time, too, we shall submit to God's will: we accept your conditions."

As if you would have refused, I thought, realizing that throughout his career, the statesman faces one very difficult task: not to burst out laughing.

"Both our and your conditions must be affirmed in an agreement," I continued. "Our relations will last some time. As you yourself said, Cem is young, and we wish him a long life. And so, let us sign."

Is this man really so base that he doesn't even blink an eye? I thought, because d'Aubusson was not upset in the least by our proposal. He even seemed satisfied, as if now he was preparing to deal a blow in our duel.

"The agreement has long since been ready, Your Grace," he said. "We need only note the amount."

The grand master pulled a document out from under his cloak, went over to the candle, and unrolled it. It was in our language—they had pulled out all the stops. The first thing that caught my eye was the signature: "Cem Sultan, son of Mehmed the Conqueror."

Indeed, d'Aubusson truly did deal me a blow I was long in recovering from. I fell silent, staring at Cem's tughra, clinging to a single hope: the calligraphic emblem must be forged.

"Does the signature of your unlucky prince surprise you, Your Grace?" D'Aubusson's voice was triumphant. "Bayezid Khan might think I am fooling him when I say Cem placed himself under my power. But Cem himself asked for protection from the Order; Cem is the body, whose soul I now am. See for yourself, he entrusted me with blank pages with his signature"—here d'Aubusson really did thrust a blank but signed sheet of paper under my nose—"so I could negotiate in his name. That's how unshakeable the prince's faith in me is. Your Grace, tell that to your sovereign. I think it would be good for Bayezid Khan to remember that."

It was more than my mind could fathom. I was choked by such rage and dared not make a sound. I rued the fact Cem had not died ten times over in Karamania, Lycia, or Cairo, so that now I would not have to take part, and not merely as a witness, but as an active participant, in the darkest deal of my time. I fiercely wanted—me, the cleric, the stargazer—to lift the heavy candlestick and bring it down with the full force of Islam on the head of this paid jailer. *To hell with you,* I consoled myself; hopefully my look would deprive d'Aubusson of his glee. *May God grant Cem dies soon and unties our hands for new outrages on Christian lands. We will stamp out the seed of the likes of you, your name will disappear.*

That's what I was telling myself, still scanning the document. I would be willing to bet the whole of this twisted and error-riddled scheme had come from the translator's quill. And d'Aubusson's mouth, of course.

I hope God forgives you, Şehzade, for subjecting the House of Osman to such humiliation, I thought as I filled in the blank space: forty-five thousand ducats a year. *I cannot forgive you.*

D'Aubusson took the paper and handed it to the translator— he clearly feared I had written five groats or some such thing. The translator nodded.

VERA MUTAFCHIEVA

"Let us create a copy," D'Aubusson suggested. He was suddenly magnanimous.

"We will make a copy," I replied, looking aside. "As is done in every sale."

Like I said, d'Aubusson held me in such contempt, he did not even continue our conversation a bit longer for the sake of appearances. He rolled up the agreement and stuck it under his cloak with the same movement highwaymen use to tuck away their spoils.

He will leave and I will never see him again, and yet I will not kill him. This crazy thought crossed my mind. You know in life there are moments when you feel as if you are missing out on so much, yet you stand there still as a stump. This is how I felt then: my whole life it would weigh on me that I had not killed d'Aubusson with a single blow from the silver candlestick. No matter what price I would have paid afterward, it would have been a low price indeed, and well worth it.

You have likely noticed: history only mentioned my name once. I was no longer involved in affairs of state; the stars and their impenetrable language remained mine. As unbelievable as it sounds, I myself withdrew from Bayezid Khan's court. This did not change the world, nor did it improve it. Nor—let us be frank—did it bring back my clean conscience.

TENTH TESTIMONY OF THE POET SAADI
ON THE SUMMER OF THE YEAR 1483

FORGIVE ME FOR breaking off my testimony, but the mere memory of the Frank costs me dearly. Never, while Suleiman lived with us, did I experience toward him the feeling that possessed me after his death. It was admiration and fondness at the same time; the Frank's final days left a mark on many of my years. From those days on, I—the poet, the Epicurean, who saw earthly delights as the only point of existence, whose only fear was death—became a close relative of death for a long time. To me, it became a cure, an almost desirable transition into the lush fields of immortality, where I would meet Suleiman.

Alongside this change, my role with Cem changed as well. I was no longer his tablemate at the feast of refinement and voluptuousness. An alienation crept into our relationship, as well as greater intimacy. I suppose this is how married couples live, who were once brought together by love, but who now share common children, common concerns, or common work. For them, too, passion is transformed—or deformed, if you will—into something both more and less than love.

This did not happen at Rumilly, exactly—it came about slowly, at first in shock waves of frenzied despair, which were replaced by a hostile resignation, and only later did our relations mellow into a deep and heavy, albeit not burning, devotion. During this time Cem needed me not only in times of ecstasy or drunkenness, but constantly. Like you need a piece of clothing or bread, or your mother. But no matter how significant this is, it is no longer love.

But why was I talking about this? Who cares about the poet Saadi's personal drama?

Ah yes, back to Cem.

It was precisely during those days after the Frank's disappearance that I noticed in Cem the first signs not of sickness, not yet, but unwellness. The transition from the world of songs, splendor, and self-confidence to this other world—it was still early to call it "prisonlike"—was too sudden. This change caused the first cracks in Cem's consciousness.

Back then, in Rumilly, Cem seemed to go missing for hours on end. No one had limited his physical freedom—they were constantly inviting my master to stroll through the vicinity or to organize a hunt, to listen to a new troubadour or to admit d'Aubusson's latest messenger. And d'Aubusson was drowning us in news. According to this news—I say this cautiously, since we no longer took anything from the Order at face value—Christianity was united in its resolve to interfere in the House of Osman's business. We were mere months away from a great alliance between the rulers who would help Cem claim his father's throne.

"Why then, instead of sending me to Hungary or Venice, are the brothers distancing me from them? Why is the Order finding ever-more-hidden places for me, cut off from the world?" Cem had spat this in the first messenger's face.

"Because the more direct a threat Your Highness becomes to his brother, the more the risk grows: Bayezid will spare no expense to get rid of you. Have faith in the monks' sympathy and help—they will protect you in the name of your ultimate victory."

No, we did not have faith. Ever since they had openly deceived us with the Frank, Cem had once again fallen into despair. Even back on Rhodes he had suspected d'Aubusson of playing secret games; in Nice, he had gotten up his hopes that the world would not support the grand master in those games and would wrest his victim away. But in Rumilly, in the Hospitallers' stronghold, under their guard, Cem once again retreated into his fear: we were being tricked.

The deeper he sank into such thoughts, the more Cem withdrew into himself. I have noticed this happens to particularly impetuous, trusting people. Since God has not given them the sense to discern the truth from lies, the first time their trust is utterly abused strips them of the ability to trust. Sometimes it comes back to them in fits and starts, but always in its entirety, without being selective and without resisting, only to disappear again, once more in its entirety.

After the Frank's death, Cem lost faith in everything and everyone. It crushed him. My master spent almost entire days in his damp and moldy chambers. Most often, Cem would sit on his wide bed in his robe, and when the dampness seeped into him thoroughly, he would pull up the covers over his shoulders. Cem was not yet subject to a prisoner's regime, since he could go outside at any time. His prison was still voluntary—the child was doing this to spite his guardian. Cem believed the Order would be alarmed by his pouting.

To a certain extent, his plan was successful. Our dear brothers, d'Aubusson's eyes and ears, surely reported to him that their guest was acting strangely, refusing meetings and visitors, and even sending away important messengers from Rhodes without hearing them out. How would d'Aubusson's comedy end if its main actor refused to play along?

Cem really did frighten the brothers with his morbid indifference and forced them to allow a series of meetings at Rumilly that could have caused them some headaches.

First and foremost—looking back now, I can't imagine this happened without the grand master's knowledge, even though I believed that was the case then—a merchants' caravan once again stopped in Rumilly. It was a different one from before, but one of the merchants had a red beard far too light for his dark eyebrows, while his gait was far too energetic for a trader. When he went in to see my master, Cem's face changed, and I led out the brother who had announced the visitors, leaving Cem to bargain on his own.

Late that evening the caravan set off again, without anyone searching it or stopping it, and Cem asked to stretch his legs outside. He felt ill from the constantly stuffy air, he said. The brothers politely let us out. We knew they were following us, but they couldn't do so from close enough to overhear our words. Cem purposely picked a path through the fields.

"Saadi," he said when we were in the open, "God has heard my prayers. Today I received an answer from my mother. I burned it immediately, so I cannot show it to you. She wrote she will pay the Order an enormous ransom for me. Do you believe it, Saadi?"

"And when did you write to her?" I couldn't restrain myself; Cem had been hiding his communications from me.

"Back when Suleiman was still with us. He got in touch with someone from Nicosia, a Greek. Remember those merchants back in April? Tell me, Saadi, do you believe it?"

"Of course. Why wouldn't your mother do everything in her power to free you?"

"No, not that. Do you believe the Order would let me go? What's more, I got to thinking, after I agreed to this and sent the merchant away: would it make sense? After all, we still haven't exhausted the possibilities of a true campaign against Bayezid in Rumelia. At this moment—if we believe the news—the world is ready to act. And suddenly I retreat to Cairo. I already know what to expect there: I become a private citizen, living out my old age with my mother, wife, and children. Where does that leave my struggle, Saadi? Why should I run away before Corvinus has given me his answer, before the pope has called upon all of Christendom? Do I have such a right?"

"You do. You are not only a ruler striving for power. You are also a human being. Perhaps this is more a question of your human freedom, if not of your life. You must try to save them. How could you not?"

"No, Saadi, this is exactly what I don't want. I have not yet come to that, and hopefully I won't anytime soon. I could not live if my hope for the throne were extinguished. Right now it is flickering—thwarted, betrayed, threatened—and it will go out completely as soon as I set foot on Egyptian soil, because I will have retreated on my own. Do you understand?" Cem leaned toward me. "Here I weigh upon their conscience, I force them to constantly think they are missing their big chance—a chance that only comes along once in history. This puts them at one another's throats and turns them against their own selves. They are torn between profitable schemes and glorious ambitious, between the thirst for easy money and the thirst for immortality. This is not an easy battle, Saadi, and we cannot foresee its outcome. I must wait it out, even if it costs me years."

Another one of his fits, I thought to myself. *Why must Cem make everything so frantic?* These jolts in his mood were beginning to wear on me, yet I nevertheless had to admit: he was right. Who—even the most stable person—would not wager their life for a throne?

"If only we had thought about it before we sent your agreement, my sultan," I said. "Now it's too late."

"No." Cem laughed, and his lonely laughter melted away into the night. "No, I sent Mehmed Bey off only an hour after the caravan. With an order: let my mother wait another half year. If by then she has received no sign the campaign is imminent, she should begin her bargaining with d'Aubusson. Clever, right? We won't need to send a second messenger."

"May God protect Mehmed Bey," I answered with a sinking heart. I was frightened with good reason: Why did our messengers never return?

"God shall protect him, Saadi," Cem concluded. "Mehmed Bey has already caught up with the caravan, they were only an hour ahead."

Mehmed Bey really did not return, but we could only suppose he had continued on with the caravan. That way he would arouse less suspicion than he would if he turned up again after a few days—he ran away from us, that's what we claimed. While the whole situation—the fact that Cem had thought it over and taken action after weeks of low spirits—seemed to erase the memory of Suleiman's death for him. We went back to hunting; troubadours again began to visit us now and then.

Ups and downs, I thought fearfully. *When will such an upswing finally not be followed by a downswing, I wonder?*

At the same time, we had a visit from a dear guest. Little Charles had broken away from his uncle's sickbed and had gone to Chambéry, his capital.

He arrived at Rumilly one very hot midday. When we heard the trumpets and horns from afar—their call carried unusually clearly in the heavy silence of the harvest season—we stood on the walls, and Cem ordered us to dress him in his ceremonial garb. Afterward—all on horseback—we went out of the fortress and met our guests on the hill. It was unimaginably colorful and cheerful. On his white horse amidst his suite, the boy Charles stood out in his red satin and black feathers, clean and neat, as if his mother had dressed him to go visiting. Cem's gray mare galloped toward him with its white and gold rider. The hunting horns sounded, a hundred horses snorted unrestrained, while our whole company stood out like a colorful, carefree stain against the grayish-yellow flank of the hill. Behind us the old walls of Rumilly jutted up, below us the fields glowed golden, scattered with reapers, over our heads that same satiny sky of Savoy unfolded, propped up by the snowy mountains.

The two young rulers jumped to the ground and embraced under the greetings of their companions, then walked up the hill toward the fortress. Later, a feast began that brought back memories of Nice, with the difference that it was sprinkled—and liberally, at that—with the brothers' black cassocks. The knight-monks did not annoy us, but their presence alone was enough; it is always annoying to drink amidst teetotalers. Cem tried not to look at them while the singers were singing.

For four days, we alternated between feasting and hunting. On the fifth day, Charles would leave us. And on that fourth hunt, Cem called me to him. The three of us were a bit apart from the shooting party, riding through sparse woods. The little duke—his cheeks girlishly red, hair tousled, and bare chested—looked more than ever like a child. He looked up at Cem with undisguised adoration, like a boy gazing upon his own much-dreamed-about future image.

"Saadi, actually the boy is the one who called you, not me." Cem let me bring my horse in between theirs. "Charles wants something. Be quick. They will catch up with us soon."

I turned to Charles. "At your service, Your Highness."

It was amusing how the excitement disappeared from his face, changing almost into sternness. But his eyes were still beaming—it was touching how he stretched his white, thin neck toward Cem.

"Tell my friend," Charles began quickly, "I shall not forget his struggle even for a moment. It is clear to me: the future of our world depends on Cem Sultan's victory. I will do everything I can to find allies and rescue Cem from the Order. I have friends, powerful relatives. I also have wealth. Tell my friend I will proudly dedicate my heart to this lofty goal: the rule of Cem Sultan. Ah?"

The boy uttered this final semiquestion like a sigh—he was exhausted from the excitement. He fixed his older friend with a searching gaze as I translated; he was anxiously tossing the reins from one hand to the other, straightening his horse blanket and smoothing down his springy curls.

My dear little knight—I wanted to pet him—*In our world, why do we only win sympathy from those who cannot help us, while the powerful refuse us? How much weight do the words of your thin little voice or the fist of your thin little arm hold, my boy?*

God forbid! Like a translucent vision, I saw before my eyes another young boy sitting on the blue princely saddle: the little monk. Their two faces fused for a moment, and I thought I glimpsed blood on Charles's soft sideburns, a dark spot of violence on his touchingly white neck. *Don't allow it, God*, I chased away the memory. *Must love for Cem only bring unhappiness?*

Upset, I had missed Cem's answer, but he repeated it impatiently; the shooting party was catching up to us, black with monks' cassocks.

"Let God," Cem had replied, "not mine, and not yours, but the one and only God reward you for your nobility, Charles, my friend. The only thing I can give you in return is my belief. I believe you, Charles. If we are allowed to offer up prayers to history, I beg of it: let you and I go down in history side by side. Let the world witness something heretofore unseen: friendship between two sovereigns."

When I report this to you now, I suppose it sounds ridiculous. The line between the touching and the ridiculous is very thin indeed, and Cem often stepped over it, because he lacked a sense of reality. Cem was a poet who had gotten inopportunely mixed up in history, and most of his actions, if not erroneous, were at the very least ridiculous.

And so, I was a witness—frozen with fear, because our wardens were already thundering near us and they would interpret the significance of the sight before them very accurately—when the two of them embraced, as if sealing an agreement. The sun was shattered into pieces, it ran in streams down hair and silk; the gray mare gently rubbed her neck against the white stallion; all around it smelled of warmed juniper, laurel, rosemary—in Savoy, even the stones have a scent, I swear. It was as wonderful and touching as a theater performance.

When the hunting party caught up with us, I could see how at least twenty pairs of eyes were studying Cem and noticing the dampness in his gaze. I felt as if I could hear twenty brains noting their highness's strange exultation and coming up with an explanation. It's as if I knew even then what would follow: the early death of Charles of Savoy, mourned by all of France. The nineteen-year-old duke was killed on the eve of a well-planned attack upon a road Cem would pass by on. They say he died of overeating, that he was a glutton.

But wait, why am I scrambling up my story? Charles was still alive during that fourth hunt, and he showed great skill at shooting. In the evening we once again feasted with him. He and Cem drank from the same cup and made the troubadour compose a new song about their friendship. They were deep in their cups, thus the next morning the duke's suite departed quite late. We saw them off to the road, and on the way back Cem was again downcast. During the past months, his whole life had been waiting or parting.

In Rumilly we had another, less pleasant visit, yet one with a wealth of consequences.

It was late July. The days in Rumilly again passed by listlessly after Charles's departure. Cem let me dress him and undress him, he went hunting, and in the evenings he barely read. He supposedly was hurrying to fall asleep, but I would hear him tossing and turning for a long time, suppressing his sighs, so as not to alarm me. That is how the days and nights passed—we were waiting for news from d'Aubusson, but the grand master had been reticent of late.

One evening—one of those glassy summer evenings when the sky is a ghostly green and stays that way for a long while—before the stars rose over Rumilly, we heard a commotion: a visitor had arrived. This was announced to Cem. We tried to eavesdrop, but they wouldn't tell us anything.

We hardly slept. As soon as day broke, a brother knocked on the door. He brought with him Rumilly's commander, an insignificant person whose name I cannot remember, and the commander informed us an envoy from Sultan Bayezid had arrived.

Cem jumped at the sound of his brother's name—he was unable to preserve his self-control. He hurriedly got himself dressed on his own—something absolutely undignified—then suddenly snapped to his senses and froze.

"Whom exactly... am I to receive shortly?"

"Hüseyin Bey, a close companion of Bayezid Khan."

"Yes, just a moment..."

The brother had not yet shut the door when Cem turned to me; I could see he was not in his right mind.

"Wait, wait! What Hüseyin Bey, what Bayezid Khan? How can I accept an envoy from that imposter? What does Bayezid think to do, negotiate with me? I already suggested that to him two or three times and always got the same answer: the empire is a bride who must choose one bridegroom, there is no brotherhood among rulers. I will not bargain with the man who took what is mine—that would mean I acknowledge him and acknowledge my dependence on him. How could I lead the campaign against Rumelia tomorrow if I have negotiated and peaceably settled my quarrels with Bayezid? No, Saadi, this must not be. Tell those monks."

"My sultan, think it over carefully. Perhaps Bayezid has changed his mind."

"You don't know Bayezid. He is so narrow-minded, it's a miracle he was able to make a single decision, and now you're hoping he'll make a second. No, I am on the right path: as long as I refuse to acknowledge Bayezid's power, I will be a pillar in the fight against Bayezid. Even let me fall as a victim of that battle, Saadi, but I won't be party to a deal."

"Your Grace, tell the envoy Cem Sultan refuses to see him," I called outside.

And that was that. The brothers did not try to convince us; in Rumilly, we were being watched, listen to, searched, but to our faces they kept up appearances, and so no one foisted Hüseyin Bey on us.

After midday, Cem and I went out. The brothers conscientiously followed us at a distance of a few hundred feet. I could have sworn when I turned around, a stranger in Turkish dress was standing on Rumilly's walls, looking down. *Probably Hüseyin Bey*, I thought. But I didn't mention it to Cem. Why upset him? Toward evening we again heard noise; the brothers were sending Bayezid's man away. Cem seemed to sense the absence. He suddenly relaxed, grew talkative—that's how he always was once he had made a decision or taken action—livened up.

We were already getting ready for bed when there was another knock at the door. This time the commander had come alone.

"Your Highness," he began in his unpleasant, creaking voice, "since you refused to see Hüseyin Bey, it falls to me to give you his letter from Sultan Bayezid."

We read it by candlelight, together. At first, I thought Cem had been right: Bayezid for the third time stated he would not allow any division of power. Bayezid reminded Cem he had chosen his own fate, thrust himself into the infidels' hands, and, in so doing, brought indelible shame down on the House of Osman. But, this was the new part; Bayezid Khan in his piety did not want his brother—light-minded though he was—to suffer deprivations. Thus, Bayezid Khan would pay the hosts his brother had chosen for himself forty-five thousand ducats a year—let him live in luxury with this money and remember their father in his prayers.

Cem seemed to skip over these lines with indifference—he always considered Bayezid mediocre and was repelled by his clichéd phrases. Only when we came to the number forty-five thousand did he whistle through his teeth, as I hadn't heard him do in years.

"Hey, how can you not be touched," he exclaimed. "Despite Bayezid's well-known tightfistedness... I'm simply shocked."

And then he went on reading as if it were nothing.

But I had stopped. Did Cem truly not understand what had happened? Did he really not see that at this moment, an enormous golden padlock hung on our cage? How nicely everything had been arranged.

"Cem." I do not recall losing my grip on myself to that extent ever in my life. I screamed frantically, "Cem!"

"What is it, Saadi?" He looked at me over the letter with eyes that truly did not understand.

"Cem, they've struck a bargain for us."

"So what of it? D'Aubusson will get the money until the campaign starts. Then the allies will demand me from the Order; that's clear, since the fight against Bayezid is pointless without me. What are you afraid of, Saadi?"

"I am afraid such a pile of gold is unheard-of. People kill for two gold pieces—just imagine what they'll do for forty-five thousand a year."

"True, it is a lot," Cem agreed. "But do you believe it would definitively tip the scales against what is good for an entire world, the Christian world?

"This is the only thing that weighs on my mind." He followed his train of thought aloud. "I am forced to bet on the goodness of their world. Undignified for a true believer. But once I am on my father's throne, I will resurrect the Conqueror and will wash away this brief retreat with victories."

I listened to him, stared at him. He irritated me to no end. At the end of the day, Cem, too, was an inhabitant of this earth; he should know its laws. *Better you don't realize the truth, my friend,* I decided. *I hope you live a long time yet in your imagined world,*

VERA MUTAFCHIEVA

where people like you and little Charles ride through green fields and cheerful woods, while sun-dappled gold rains down upon their hair.

That night Cem fell asleep easily, without tossing and turning. There was not only something childish, but also something womanish in Cem. He fell into fits of rage when faced with another's calm, and vice versa: he would sink into blissful silence when someone around him was out of their mind. That's how my fit of terror affected him.

But perhaps it was something else as well—ah, human vanity! Cem was likely flattered his brother and enemy had valued him so highly, even setting aside half the income of his empire. You know, a man's main concern is that he will turn out to be small, insignificant, anonymous. Now Cem slept calmly like a child recovering from illness, rocked in his dreams by the proud fact that he was the costliest, most highly valued person in the world.

It didn't last long, this upswing of satisfaction—such hours grew ever shorter for us. Only a week later—during which time we again hunted, took walks, and filled our hours with all sorts of nonsense—the commander once again brought us news. In recent days nothing unusual had happened at Rumilly, unless you count the appearance of thirty new brothers. This did not surprise us—they were likely planning to move us to a new fortress, thus they were doubling the guard. We had gotten very used to these frequent journeys, and besides, Rumilly had not predisposed us to miss it in the least, so we were happy: we would finally get out of this sinister citadel. We associated it with the Frank's death and Hüseyin Bey's visit, with mold, rats, and centipedes. The commander was likely coming to announce our departure, so we received him without any anxiousness. The monks who accompanied him were in their knightly armor, complete with weapons—that's how they escorted us on the road.

"Your Highness," the commander said with exaggerated diction, as if he were reading aloud. "Today I received a message from Brother d'Aubusson. It concerns you and your safety, your imperiled safety. In his desire to rid himself of a debt to the Order—a debt he willingly took on—Bayezid Khan is plotting your kidnapping. We have reliable evidence of this. All manner of means has been put into action—money, force, promises. Bayezid Khan has expressed certainty this kidnapping will succeed. When it will take place and by whom, we do not know. But at least we managed to learn the kidnapper is not one of our brothers."

"And why has the investigation taken place without my knowledge?" Cem interrupted him. "I am tired of being protected like an invalid. I am not taking part in what should be every person's first concern—their own self-preservation. Do I not have the right to wonder whether the danger is invented? You already sacrificed the Frank—who will be next?"

He yelled, yes, he yelled, "Who will be next?" I saw this moment had added a new fear, the worst fear of all, to his old ones: the fear of loneliness.

"We will present you with documents that tell the truth, Your Highness," the commander replied, unruffled. "The investigation continues. Yet we must not put off even for a moment new measures for your security. I presume you can imagine your fate, were Bayezid to succeed?"

"What, pray tell, shall these new measures consist of?"

VERA MUTAFCHIEVA

I could sense this time Cem would not back down, they would not persuade him. The brothers had already lied to us far too shamelessly, so even the gullible Cem could back down no longer. He took a step toward the commander. The man drew back almost imperceptibly, as if expecting a blow, but kept up his open insolence—I cannot call it anything else.

"Brother d'Aubusson has commanded your entire suite be removed from Rumilly, Your Highness," the commander said firmly, "until we discover who among your people is the traitor."

All the blood drained from Cem's cheeks; he stood mute and stunned, simply frightful in his helpless rage. The business with the Frank had been nothing at all; the Frank had been one of twenty-five—today, twenty-five men were to disappear all at once.

Silence. With the Frank, the silence had been filled with unexpressed tenderness, while the silence now was different, weighted down with despair and hatred. The charade was over— this was open battle. Our only choice was to fight a powerful enemy, as pathetically small and pathetically weak as we were.

"What if I oppose this order?" Cem asked in a voice that made my hair stand on end.

Is today the day the end will come? I thought. My knees went weak with horror; after all, everyone imagines their own death as something far in the future.

"If I do not agree to be deprived of my people? What will happen then?"

Forgetting himself, Cem grabbed the commander by his black collar and shook him like a cat. Strangely, the others did not step in. It was clear they had been warned: only if the commander ordered it.

"I ask Your Highness to unhand me," the commander said with beastly cold-bloodedness, his eyes flashing a span from Cem's. "I am carrying out an order and I will carry it out in full. Brother d'Aubusson has given his word to keep Your Highness safe at any price. If Your Highness does not agree, I will remove his suite even without consent."

So, the truth is finally out.

I closed my eyes so as not to see what happened. I waited for my death, our shared death—strangely, almost without fear. After all, what would our life be after the words we had heard? They no longer counted us as people: they forced and coerced us, without even keeping up polite appearances. Don't tell me appearances are a small thing, what's important is the essence. Doesn't politesse allow you to fool yourself, and where would we be without self-deception?

From the dark prison of my eyelids, I could hear only labored breathing. Air noisily escaped Cem's constricted throat; it was almost the wheeze of a wounded animal. How many times had a new lock clicked shut behind him, yet he always managed to forget it, only to fall into a new, completely fresh horror when faced with the next trap?

"Fine"—his words reached my hearing as if out of an abyss— "very fine indeed... Well then, I do not consent."

"I am sincerely sorry, Your Highness. But for me your life is more precious than your goodwill."

I opened my eyes. Cem was no longer holding on to the commander. He had retreated toward a crack in the thick wall and through it—as if it were the only outlet to the world—he did not cry, but roared, "Violence! Rise up, all true believers!"

There are such moments. Such moments are so frightening that you start convulsing with laughter, hysterically. Something like a smile passed over the black-robed brothers, and I expected to hear crackling, so stiff were their faces with tension. Cem had forgotten them. He was all ears, listening at the crack, waiting to hear the footsteps of soldiers, the clang of weapons, the thundering of horses—this is what followed a sultan's order.

Silence. And as it grew, Cem shrank beneath it, buckled, lost. He stepped back but did not fall. He remained on his feet, leaning against a column.

"Thanks to our foresight, Your Highness," the commander continued, as if nothing had happened between his last words and these, "we foresaw that in your anger—the result of fine motives, inarguably—you would cause unnecessary bloodshed. And we insist not only on protecting your life, but also that of your companions. They were disarmed a short while ago. They did not resist. They have a clearer notion of things."

"It is beneath my dignity to speak to you," Cem began after some time; some dull senselessness had completely overtaken him, making me fear for his reason. "But I speak to you because it does not concern me. If you take this one from me"—he did not indicate me with his hand or his gaze, but I knew he meant me—"I will find a way to die."

There are some statements so mad you can believe in them only in very, very rare moments. Now was one of them—both the statement, and the moment. The commander realized the Order's entire future was truly in the hands of a stunned man willing to go to extremes.

"Your distress is unwarranted, Your Highness," he said quickly. "We have never suspected Saadi. He stays."

Cem's expression did not change; it was as if the news of his victory over loneliness did not reach his mind.

"Tell them to get out of here, Saadi," he asked me quietly.

They did not allow us to say farewell to our men. Two whole days—while they were preparing for the journey—they let us out only into the corridor and onto part of the wall. Thirty-odd feet of wall, just enough to keep you from going mad from lack of movement. Once again, just as I had hoped to catch a glimpse of the Frank, I met the morning and saw off the evening between its jagged teeth. In the late afternoon of the second day, they led our men out. I counted them, I recognized their faces. Our men were riding, but they carried no weapons. They were very silent, very dignified. On all four sides, the blue-yellow-white patch was edged with black; the knights were leading away the last of Cem's men toward the sea.

I had told Cem; both of us were standing up above. Again it shocked me that Cem seemed devoid of expression. The thought crossed my mind: *A living doll.*

"Call out—they might hear you, there is no wind," I said. It seemed terrible to let them be sent away without a farewell. Cem shook his head.

I led him away like an invalid. Cem stumbled, leaned heavily on me, then collapsed.

TESTIMONY OF JOHN KENDALL,
TURCOPOLIER OF THE ORDER OF THE HOSPITAL
OF ST. JOHN IN JERUSALEM, ON THE EVENTS
FROM MAY 1483 TO MAY 1485

SO YOU FINALLY got around to me. I was expecting it. After all, I was turcopolier. Likely Brother d'Aubusson's testimony no longer inspired sufficient confidence, so you'd like to double-check his version through another witness. At the risk of sounding immodest, I salute your choice—who, if not the Order's turcopolier, commander of our Eastern mercenaries and officer in charge of the coastal defense of Rhodes, would be wholly informed about the details around all things Turkish?

I hardly need to dwell at length on my personal history. The fourth son of a noble family, I was obliged to dedicate myself to the Church, despite my proclivity for the military life. I satisfied both callings by joining an order of knight monks. I preferred the Hospitallers because they were the final Western outpost against the great threat of our time: the Ottomans.

I counted on military glory so I could go down as at least a footnote in history. I was successful in this to some extent; I distinguished myself during the great siege of 1480, but there is nothing glorious in a siege, even in one that heroically held out. So it was entirely unexpected even to me that I made my name in connection with the most significant international affair of the fifteenth century: the case of Cem.

You've likely noticed that until Cem's departure from Rhodes, I had no hand in his fate. Representing the Order was left to others. Only when the first complications arose around the case and it entered the dark, back corridors of international relations did I, John Kendall, start to play a role in it.

The grand master involved me when it became such a heavy load of work that one person could not possibly manage it alone. Brother d'Aubusson informed the Council of his business around Cem only in the most general of terms; from the start, he managed the case in his own name and even at his own expense, I would say, since the d'Aubusson family reaped significant advantages from the strange gift of fate.

Thus, on one spring day in 1483, the grand master called me into his study and announced that from then on, I would be his assistant in the case of Cem. I know, my age—I was a whole 15 years younger than the grand master—made me an unsuitable adviser. But d'Aubusson was perspicacious, and how. He knew that a person who fully shared his views and temperament would only reproduce his own thoughts. D'Aubusson clearly preferred that I oppose him, and thus through our arguments more easily discover the weak points in his plans.

My introduction to the case of Cem coincided with the departure of the Turkish envoy. Brother d'Aubusson had just informed the Council that Bayezid would pay a considerable annual allowance for his brother, for which he had won great

VERA MUTAFCHIEVA

praise. And rightly so; our pathetic income and empty coffers were a grave concern to the Order. Setting aside such praise, the grand master was worried: Cem Sultan was such big game that he could not remain the property of such a petty player. Our goal was to relinquish Cem to a stronger master, as late as possible, under maximally advantageous conditions. It was our duty to win time and friends, and to choose from among them the one who would pay the most.

"The major danger now comes from the French court," d'Aubusson said, laying out his predictions for me. "Even though we are holding Cem at the Order's various fortresses, with our commanders as his hosts and our brothers as his guards, these castles are on French land; their rulers are the king's vassals. The command needs only be issued, and they would be obliged to hand their guest over to the king—their oath of fealty binds them."

"If you are certain of this, Your Eminence, I don't see any hope for us. Louis XI is a sly dog."

"Our hope lies precisely in the fact that Louis XI is a sly dog. I'm willing to bet Louis will claim before the world that Cem is a guest of the Holy Church, represented by the Order. In this way, the king will block the aspirations of other rulers with respect to Cem."

And so, reassuring me and himself in this way, Brother d'Aubusson ordered Cem not be held for too long in any one fortress; he also ordered that he be watched as closely as possible. He insisted to Louis XI that little Charles be removed from the equation, at least temporarily—it was well-known that the boy was impressed with and particularly sympathetic to Cem. A wide network of informants—for lack of a better choice, we used papal agents as well, as we did not have enough of our own—also kept watch on Sultan Qaitbay's court, where Cem's family lived, as well as Nice and Villefranche, where any secret emissary of Cem's would depart from. And Venice—we feared Venice above all as a major player in the Mediterranean. This cost us much labor: we sifted through dozens of reports, investigated suspicious characters who had been caught, and sent many instructions of our own.

You may be curious to know that the Cem-related documents possessed by the Order toward the end of this case constituted an impressive sight, to say nothing of what had accumulated in France, Venice, Hungary, or Rome. My task was to keep them in order, because with them Brother d'Aubusson repeatedly proved his right to primacy over Cem Sultan, unmasking one sovereign's dark dealings or blackmailing another for considerable gains. This enormous pile of paper was d'Aubusson's wealth when he was alive, as well as his posthumous estate.

And so, our informants, sent to Venice to find out whether the Senate would accept Bayezid's offers, were delayed by months—thank your lucky stars you are not informants in Venice. There state secrets were held in such strict confidence—every senator paid with his head and his entire estate for a single leaked word—that our spies sank for long stretches into the coastal damp and still came back empty-handed, when they came back at all. Yet this time, we were in luck: they reported Venice had rejected Bayezid's generosity, deciding not to meddle in the case of Cem. At least for now.

Surprising, yes? In all times and eras, that golden republic has been known for what it in truth was: a many-armed,

VERA MUTAFCHIEVA

many-eyed monster that kills and plunders. So why, you ask, would Venice remain passive in the face of such a tempting scenario? The only possible answer: because it would reap advantage from doing so. If Venice got its hands on Cem Sultan—as unlikely as that was—it would immediately be saddled with the task now crushing us: defending Cem against other states. Remember, Venice couldn't count on anyone's affection—it had even been anathemized by the pope, despite his general cautiousness with rich masons. So, with good reason, Venice feared a serious alliance against it, were it to take up Cem. In short, by promising Bayezid it would abstain from meddling in this dispute, Venice sold its abstention at a good price: it received a peace and trade treaty with the new sultan, who gave the republic exclusive rights in the Levant. Note that the case of Cem brought gold not only to those directly involved, but to others as well, for simply being clever spectators.

On the whole, the year 1483 was continually punctuated by important events. Just imagine how the two of us needed to rise to meet and hold our ground against them. In August news reached us that Louis XI had died. His contemporaries always spoke ill about that unworthy individual and great statesman. Even his nearest and dearest were hoping for his death, but it was untimely for the Order: we were afraid his heirs—his sister, a quite flighty woman even for a regent, ruled in place of the underage Charles VIII—would not have the same sense as the late king and would want to possess Cem directly. So he needed to be moved again, now to regions more weakly tied to the French crown; defenders for Cem needed to be found inside France itself—people who, in hopes of getting their hands on

Cem, would protect him from the king. A terribly delicate business and very difficult to orchestrate from afar.

The first thing we managed to arrange was to send Cem to the northeast. But before that—on the grand master's command—he was deprived of his suite. We already had plenty of information about the devotion of those thirty-odd Saracens to their master—incidentally, Sultan Bayezid also insisted on this measure, too, in one of his messages to the Order. This command also included Saadi, who is well-known to you. So as not to send Cem into extreme despair, we had decided to get rid of his only remaining close companion later, by instigating an unfortunate accident. We reconsidered the question of Saadi over and over again in connection with Cem's illness. Cem turned out to be unstable when subjected to emotional upheaval, thus we were forced to spare him. In other words, this means Saadi survived.

Don't think we were unjustly cruel to Cem's Saracens—they would have treated us no better over in Turkey. Besides, they truly refused to behave. You know, for example, that Cem—this time without our permission, secretly—had sent several of them to the Hungarian king. They were easy to catch; they didn't speak the local language and didn't look like Christians, even in Christian clothes. We transferred them to Rhodes, where Brother d'Aubusson did what he could to make them talk, but they preferred a pointless death, keeping a secret we had long since known: they had been sent to Matthias Corvinus. In his royal fury, Matthias Corvinus had told us this himself.

Brother d'Aubusson told you Corvinus, in his very first response to the Order, had expressed his readiness to arm and lead a massive campaign against the Ottomans as soon as we released Cem to him. The king explained that given the strong dislike of Sultan Bayezid in Rumelia, there was fertile ground for revolt among the Turks themselves. Strengthened, of course, by the rebellions of those peoples who had lost their freedom quite recently, he would surely break Rumelia away from Constantinople. In such a case, the campaign's success was child's play, King Matthias was more or less arguing. As unbelievable as it sounds, he was right; we knew it even without his detailed explanations. That was exactly why we delayed our answer.

Without waiting for it, Corvinus wrote us again, and after that simply flooded us with paper. He was clearly losing his self-control.

At first, Corvinus—in his letters, Cem was always "sultan" —humbly insisted on receiving Cem Sultan; he laid out the advantages. Later he began making promises, yet they were sincere promises and thus not extravagant; Hungary was broke after long wars on two sides—against the Ottomans and against the German king. Finally, losing patience with Brother d'Aubusson's noncommittal responses, Matthias Corvinus unleashed on the Order a tide of indignation. He blamed us, saying it was our fault the people of southeastern Europe had slept through a whole year—the most opportune time for a war against an empire that had not yet recovered from an internecine struggle; he charged us with being greedy merchants, haggling when an entire future was at stake; he thrust upon us the responsibility for everything that would follow (and you will soon find out what followed), and in conclusion declared: we had missed an unprecedented, unbelievable chance for Christianity to free itself from a scourge.

In that final letter, King Matthias mentioned knowing about the disappearance of the messengers Cem had sent—he had included it among his numerous accusations. While we, for our part, immediately deduced someone from Cem's erstwhile suite had passed that news on to Matthias. After which the remnants of the suite—it had dwindled as it passed through the insalubrious regions along the mouth of the Rhone, where there are mosquitoes and fever—were moved to the even deeper reaches of the dungeons beneath the Rhodes citadel, so such accidental voices would not reach King Matthias and Lord knows who else.

Brother d'Aubusson was rather distraught over his correspondence with Matthias. To me, he complained the Hungarians had always been less than zealous Christians, doing things their own way without coordinating with the Holy See and its orders, and they didn't understand the spirit of the West—not rushing, that was the spirit of the West. But when alone with his conscience, Brother d'Aubusson likely recognized another reason for his distress: King Matthias had voiced the same qualms the grand master himself harbored.

I shall digress here for a bit, because I have noticed the very course of your investigation has gone awry with respect to this Corvinus, who has been so praised by the witnesses. He was the only one, they say, who recognized the uniqueness of the moment; he was the only one willing to risk everything to get Cem and to put him at the head of a campaign against Bayezid. Because we hindered King Matthias, they say, Eastern Christianity's cause was lost. Fine. But then how to explain the agreement signed between this same King Matthias with that same Bayezid during the autumn of 1484? Shouldn't the king—even without Cem, if Rumelia really had been so ready to rebel, as Matthias thought it was—have tried to launch a major campaign? Isn't Corvinus attributing wondrous power to Cem so as to justify his own hesitations?

Well, yes. Corvinus signed with Bayezid not a peace treaty, but a five-year truce; Matthias Corvinus hoped to have gotten Cem by that time. But after those five years, wouldn't Rumelia have been more subdued under Bayezid's rule than after one? Even if by then Bayezid had not undertaken any actions—not waged war against the West beyond Rumelia, for example. Because that's exactly what happened, I must remind you. Reassured with respect to Hungary, the sultan pounced on Herzegovina, and on Poland a year later. During that same time, King Matthias was settling old debts with Emperor Friedrich III, sieging Vienna and capturing it, while only a week's journey away from an ever-moving border with his most dangerous enemy, the Ottomans. In short, King Matthias took an active part in the endless wars between the Christian rulers. So much for King Matthias.

May God forgive me, I put too much fire in those last words of mine. I allowed myself this liberty because I can see how you are falling into delusion—King Matthias is not the hero in the case of Cem. I beg you to grasp this in the very depths of your souls: no contemporary of mine was up to the task his time demanded of him, no one rose above his own petty arithmetic so as to use the case of Cem in a truly historic way. Not even Matthias Corvinus. This is all I'm trying to say.

While the rulers were involved in various wrangles, Brother d'Aubusson and I suffered through dark days. Three times in three years, from 1483 to 1486, we found out Sultan Bayezid was readying his ships for battle. We were convinced his aim was not Rhodes; Sultan Bayezid had nothing to gain from destroying his relations with Cem's jailers. Yet perhaps Bayezid had started to understand Cem was no longer completely ours? Did he know the extent to which this whole process had changed? Had the time come for Cem to be wrested from the Order's clutches and transferred to the control of other powers? Who could name the powers in question? What was their goal? Did Bayezid even know?

Now, I presume, you can imagine our situation. It was incredibly tense and simply frightful. Every time we received news from Constantinople of Bayezid's naval preparations, other messengers would arrive on Rhodes from the opposite direction—from the pope, from the Neapolitan king. They knew we held the key to peace with Bayezid and asked us insistently, not without gifts or threats, "Hint to Sultan Bayezid that Cem will set out for Rumelia at the head of 200,000 men." And d'Aubusson would drop hints, if they can even be called hints at all: he would send the sultan a letter via some brother, and the letter would say our agreement demanded the Turkish navy not leave the Straights. If it did, the Order would consider the agreement breached and would no longer keep Cem Sultan as its guest.

Implausible, yet true. Sultan Bayezid backed down in the face of this blackmail—he backed down once, twice, three times: in 1483, 1484, and 1485. I have heard that at a certain point some began arguing the case of Cem was overinflated and dismissed it as unimportant. But judge for yourself: three times, the Turkish sultan called off his campaign, his inevitable victory—for there was no one to oppose him, since Christianity was fighting amongst itself, as I already told you. You see, he feared Cem's reappearance. It's true, as unbelievable as it sounds: Cem was a legend not only here in the West, where the troubadours had prettified him. Cem was also a legend in the East. Matthias sincerely believed that standing shoulder to shoulder with Cem, he would win a quick victory; Bayezid very sincerely believed his troops would fall apart facing Cem and his fortresses would open their gates to his brother. To say nothing of the peoples there—no one can ever be sure what the people will do—but we had evidence they would have rushed to embrace any rebel against the Porte, even if he was Mehmed Khan's younger, kinder, blonder son.

Each of those three times when we sent a messenger to Bayezid with the brazen demand that the sultan call off his campaign, we awaited his response on eggshells. Would Bayezid back down, or would he reply tersely via one of his own men, as he would have slaughtered ours: "Venerable sirs, I would like to see the troops you would give to Cem. Where will you get those troops, which you so desperately need for battles throughout Ferrara, Florence, Napoli, Vienna, and wherever the hell else? Where will you take Cem from, so as to put him at the head of this army—from France, Rhodes, or Rome? How will you forgo, most venerable sirs, your thousands of gold ducats a year—do you really intend to sacrifice them in a war I will win?"

This is precisely the answer we expected from Bayezid, and the very, very surprising thing is we never received it. From this, we drew one conclusion, or rather, two: either Bayezid was an idiot, or Cem really was worth the money he cost his brother.

No, we came to a third conclusion as well, which, thankfully, Bayezid did not suspect—that we were the idiots. And in this, and this alone, do I see divine Providence, which protected the West in those years of great danger. Even Bayezid, whom we described as a savage—a description not proved out by history—would not stoop to fight such idiots when he could pay them off instead. The West would truly let an unprecedented historical opportunity slip away for the sake of forty-five thousand gold ducats, for a few trade agreements, for the exultation of its greed.

When Brother d'Aubusson had made his first moves in the case of Cem, when he had written upon the blank page signed with Cem's tughra, and when he blackmailed both the pope and the French king, as well as the sultan of Egypt—despite all of this, which I know because I witnessed it—Brother d'Aubusson had trembled before the censure of his world. He was afraid he would be accused—just as Corvinus clumsily and unconvincingly did—of perfidiousness. It was time for us Hospitallers to overcome our fear. Our possible accusers very quickly found our perfidy petty by comparison and surpassed us with great ease.

This, I think, happened in the hour when Sixtus IV died.

These were days of interregnum for our Holy Church—the time it took to choose a new pope. I am sorry I did not happen to be in Rome then; they say one cannot imagine anything more complicated, more breathless, more filled with unexpected twists and spectacles, more costly than the election of a new pope. We from Rhodes had no say in the matter, as we had no cardinal among our brothers. The grand master quietly gnashed his teeth as we debated the question. "How is it possible," he would say, "that an Order with such a glorious past, with such a major and recent victory over the Conqueror himself, does not count at least one cardinal among its ranks? And why not? Because that very same fight has exhausted our treasury to such an extent that we have not been able to buy ourselves a cardinal's rank. This is the sole reason."

So we waited for the end of the selection as spectators. Brother d'Aubusson kept saying he would have voted for Innocent, because he was a man of action and vision. I knew why the grand master found Innocent sympathetic. The cardinal was a native of Rhodes, even if not a Hospitaller, so he and d'Aubusson were old friends. And, as it happened, I found out the name of the new pope before d'Aubusson and told him: Innocent VIII. I also saw something extremely rare—the grand master laughing in delight. He doubtlessly saw himself as very close to the pinnacle of church power and was already calculating what would come out of it. Quite a lot: it is always more advantageous to be a ruler's favorite than to be a ruler yourself.

In accordance with church law, every new pope must accept oaths from his spiritual flock. So in the spring of 1485, delegations from the various orders and bishoprics streamed into Rome. I had been sent from Rhodes along with Brother Kaursen, the Order's vice chancellor. My task in my speech was to paint a picture of our service against the Turkish threat and express the hope that a native son of Rhodes would not remain blind to the knights of Rhodes's needs.

"If the issue of Cem arises"—this was the last thing d'Aubusson told us—"you will claim you are not authorized to discuss this question. Let his Holiness lay out his demands. We will give him our answer later."

We set sail for Italy in mid-April and met no corsairs on our journey. We arrived in Rome toward the end of the month. Rome was still celebrating the new pope's election: all the streets were decorated, in the evenings torchlit processions crossed the city, and almost every other day there was a pilgrimage to someone's grave, worship of someone's relics. Innocent VIII used these processions to appear before the people, giving out small coins and blessings. It was noisy, exhausting, and tedious.

Every morning we, the delegates from the monastic orders and bishoprics, would witness several oaths. The emissaries would read their speeches—they were almost identical and only the very experienced ear could pick out those small but crucial places where a given attitude toward Rome was expressed. The rest was always the same: every speaker was equally indignant about the constant wars between sovereigns, insisted on the swift pacification of Italy and Central Europe, and expressed apprehension about the still nebulous but clearly growing restlessness amidst the populace. And above all, they called for unified, decisive action against the Turkish threat.

"What do you know about it?" I would have asked with relish, even though it wasn't my place to do so. Because out of all the Catholic rulers, only the Polish and the Hungarian kings had directly experienced the Ottomans' power. They also devoted the most words to the necessity of a swift crusade against Istanbul. Here, of course, Cem's name was uttered, as Matthias Corvinus's delegate expressed his master's bitterness over our Order's actions.

I must have made some unwitting movement at these words —the Hungarians had chosen the moment poorly, and I meant to show them that. But then I met Innocent VIII's gaze, which was accompanied by a subtle gesture: *Keep quiet*, he was saying. I obeyed.

Something strange followed that very night: I was visited by one of the pope's marquises, who invited me to see His Holiness. Innocent VIII wished to speak to me before our oath. It was absolutely in violation of the rules, I assure you, to accept your subjects as a new pope before they had sworn their vows. This means Innocent would be speaking to me in his capacity as a private citizen.

I followed the marquis—he was picturesque in his violet and green clothes, with his long white socks and golden baubles—and walked between two Swiss guards, who were also rather picturesque, but in yellow and red. We moved through the torchlights lining the palace's endless labyrinthine corridors until the marquis led me into a smallish, simply furnished room and withdrew. I stood there for quite a while before a curtain was thrown aside, and Innocent sailed smoothly into the room. He had taken off his vestments and was wearing a simple white cassock.

During this meeting, as at our later ones, Innocent VIII made a deep impression on me. He was a figure to be reckoned with—at least that is indisputable. Not overly tall, not overly thin, but very wiry in appearance; not haggard, but also not pale. As he neared fifty, Innocent had the look of a man who had lived a decidedly nonmonkish life—he resembled any middling trader or sailor from Rhodes. What set him apart was his sharp gaze, at once both exacting and understanding. As he came in, the soon-to-be pope gave me a good looking over—no longer or shorter than necessary to gather an impression. He did not give me his hand to kiss—I had not yet sworn my oath.

He invited me to sit. "I think the papacy needs to settle some questions with the Order, which we cannot discuss tomorrow at the oath," Innocent began without taking his eyes from me. "You have already noticed that all our spiritual brethren expressed, through their emissaries, their readiness for a swift crusade to the East. You must understand that for a pope, there is no holier duty than this: to tie his name to a crusade. The Holy Fathers who have managed to reconcile the hostilities within Christendom and to lead it into battle for a godly cause can be counted on the fingers of one hand. I am telling you this because I personally blame my predecessor—I would not delay or hinder such a great deed. What's more, I would dedicate my life to it."

I listened to him with perfect composure; I knew what I would hear. Brother d'Aubusson had guessed correctly: negotiations over Cem could not wait even until the next morning. Innocent likely feared we would make a deal with Matthias's delegates or with the French and hurried to place his most holy interdiction on our precious goods.

"To you, as soldiers against and victors over the Turks, it is clear what difficulties such a crusade entails. There is still not peace in Italy; the kings of Germany and Hungary fight to the death. I will do everything for the peace of my papacy—may God aid and succor me. But in one thing we must not wait, as danger lurks: we must not hold Cem Sultan far from Rome. His presence here would be a sign the crusade is truly imminent. And it would deprive our enemies of any chance to kidnap or betray him."

In his excitement, Innocent got up and began pacing around the room.

"I am simply amazed the late Sixtus allowed for such negligence," he continued. "Let us thank the Almighty for protecting Cem to this very day, yet the Almighty alone cannot protect the negligent. Incidentally"—Innocent stopped in front of me, so as to better watch my expression—"I have commanded Ancona and its surroundings, one of our holdings, be made available to Cem Sultan. There, papal and Hospitaller guards shall protect him. I have appointed their leaders, I have provided for their upkeep, I have distributed the corresponding ranks to the suite that will surround our guest. How could we place at the head of an army a person we keep like the lowliest beggar out among the provincial towers of France, whom we have deprived of his proper magnificence and milieu? That is not the way to make kings and princes join our crusade, not at all, Brother Kendall. Surely this must be obvious to your master?"

For some time, I could not get ahold of myself—His Holiness had stunned me. He spoke as if the papacy itself, and not we, were the masters, or rather, hosts of Cem, as if an agreement between Rome and Rhodes was already in place, rather than in store.

"I have not been authorized to speak on the case of Cem." This was all I could come up with.

"Would such authorization even be necessary?" the pope asked me, astonished. "Could it be Brother d'Aubusson considers the Order something separate from our Holy Church? Is not what is ours also yours?"

"Not exactly. Your Holiness, if I dare." And I did dare, because things were getting so far out of hand that it frightened me. "When Rhodes was under siege, only the Order's soldiers defended it. When we need to repair our crumbling fortifications, to improve them—since that menace still hangs over us—we do it ourselves."

"Not exactly, brother," the pope corrected me gently. "I looked over our ledgers. Rhodes received from us two thousand ducats after the siege."

Now that is truly clever, I thought. At the time, our losses amounted to at least twenty thousand, so those two thousand felt like a mockery. And now, on top of everything, you are throwing them back in our faces. You demand our golden Cem in exchange for them.

"I am not authorized to speak," I said again.

"And no authorization is needed," Innocent repeated. "I only ask you to tell Brother d'Aubusson that Ancona is ready to welcome our guest. Cem's splendor will cost us dearly, but the papacy will ask of your Order—Bayezid pays for his upkeep, does he not?—only thirty thousand a year. The rest you can keep for yourselves. We recognize the exceptional service of the Hospitallers, who welcomed and protected Cem Sultan, and such service shall be rewarded. Tell your grand master the following: Giscard d'Aubusson, our humble brother, has been made a cardinal."

Carefully but not sharply, Innocent watched the effect of his words on me. To be frank, he astonished me. In our three centuries of existence and service to Rome, the Hospitallers had never gotten a cardinal in the conclave. It took some insanely unlucky barbarian prince to earn us this grace from the papacy.

You truly do work in mysterious ways, God, I thought, delighted by Innocent's quick mind. The pope was bestowing this

honor not on Pierre d'Aubusson—the quid pro quo would have
been all too obvious. He was making a cardinal of his brother—
that mediocre, unambitious, and easily-led old man to whom
nobody on Rhodes even gave a second thought, and who, up
until now, had been firmly led by our own Pierre. Thus, the
deal would constitute an enormous advantage for Pierre, while
still leaving him with something more to strive for: becoming
a cardinal himself.

The papacy certainly won't wither away with you leading it, I
concluded. Innocent VIII's very first steps already indicated
a new turn.

"Tell my brother Pierre d'Aubusson"—the pope had waited
for me to collect myself before going on—"I value even more
highly his personal service in the case of Cem. As soon as our
guest arrives in Ancona, Pierre d'Aubusson will be declared a
cardinal deacon."

May the Lord have mercy on me. I clutched at my chair. I felt
as if I were falling. In this short amount of time Cem's price had
grown beyond measure. Cardinal deacon! Do you even know
what that is? And this whole flood of earthly blessings would
pour out onto Pierre d'Aubusson—leader of two thousand ragged monks on an island condemned to ruin.

Truly your ways are mysterious, I repeated silently, thinking
I would die of impatience while waiting to see how my news
would be received by Brother d'Aubusson.

"The certificate of appointment is ready." Innocent unrolled
the certificate in front of me. "It will come into effect on the
day I mentioned. Now, Brother Kendall, I will ask you to come
with me to the chapel. Tomorrow you shall offer the Order's

oath before my Holy See. But this evening you shall swear upon your life—we mustn't mix God and his martyrs up in earthly business—no one besides Brother d'Aubusson will learn of our conversation."

The chapel was dark, lit only by the candle Innocent carried. I knelt before the simple crucifixion—the place where many of our popes had prayed, and thus the place where God meets his earthly deputy—and swore. Upon my life. I wouldn't call it an oath, exactly. I simply had to make clear my understanding that my life truly did depend on my tongue. But Innocent seemed to think I would need more time for this, thus he mercifully suggested, "Read your evening prayers as well, brother. Few rank-and-file members of our church have knelt here."

Later, I told Brother Kaursen His Holiness had simply wanted to discuss the particulars of the next day's ceremony. The vice chancellor kept silent. I never did find out whether he was bound by a similar oath.

The next morning, I read aloud our congratulatory address; Kaursen and I knelt before the Holy See, swore an oath, and received blessings, and on the following day we departed. We loaded the ship near Ostia. Before we left someone very casually caught up with us and said he was from the Neapolitan delegation. He urged us to stop by Naples on our way back to Rhodes. It would be of great benefit to our Order, he insisted. The decision was in my hands. Kaursen avoided my gaze, refused to give me counsel. And I didn't decide until the very hour we set sail under a heavy black cloud of smoke from Vesuvius.

I suspected there was at least one sailor gilded by papal gold on the ship. Or perhaps even three. How might they interpret

VERA MUTAFCHIEVA

my visit to Naples? But what of it? I had sworn to keep the pope's proposal a secret, but no one had forbidden me from stopping here and there.

We sailed along the coast, yet I did not see that coast at all; I was blind with worry and thoughts. I was not amazed by the welcome we received, which Brother Kaursen would later describe as royal, nor by the suspiciously lavish gifts King Ferrandino showered upon us. The whole time I was expecting a conversation with the king and when it happened, it was almost an exact repetition of the one in Rome, but with slightly different words: King Ferrandino emphasized he had a right to Cem precisely because Neapolitan lands and especially Sicily were directly under threat from the Turks. The king made promises without measure—he promised us land and money, troops to defend Rhodes. But he could not promise a cardinal's rank to Brother d'Aubusson, and so he would lose. I even felt a bit guilty as they loaded our ship with gifts from Naples—they were a pure waste for King Ferrandino. *A fool and his money are soon parted*, I thought in consolation. Indeed, Ferrandino must not have been a particularly clever king, since he didn't realize he was not the first to make such an offer, and since he did not grasp that Cem was now worth far more than even a king could pay.

This last phrase was uttered by Brother d'Aubusson after my return, when he told me Sultan Qaitbay had offered the Order one hundred twenty thousand ducats for Cem. Part of this sum—twenty thousand—had already been delivered to our treasury. The Conqueror's widow, Cem's mother, had sent the gold with some of her people; she had hurried to shower upon us all her wealth—a sultaness in exile could hardly be expected to have much more than that—in hopes of getting ahead of our likely hesitation, in hopes of making us feel obliged.

Everything we had so far received for Cem—it was already a lot, you have likely been counting—did not alarm me like those twenty thousand gold pieces. And they were alarming, were they not? There are things a person finds hard to pass up. A prisoner's mother, for example.

"May God be my witness," d'Aubusson said, as if peering into my conscience. "One day I will return that money."

And so he did. You can check: this was the only money given for Cem that we ever gave back. Not out of goodwill—let's be honest. D'Aubusson was forced to do so.

Contrary to my expectations, the grand master listened to Innocent VIII's proposal not only without delight, he was downright morose.

"Your Eminence"—I tried to help him process it—"this is far more than we had even dreamed of. Cem's price is growing by the hour."

"Precisely," d'Aubusson said through gritted teeth. And again with emphasis, "Precisely. They infuriate me in their mad attempts to outbid one another. They constantly show me what else I could stand to gain if I possessed Cem."

"But Your Eminence, what are you saying? Cem is ours. Did we not take all possible measures..."

"What measures?" I now saw Brother d'Aubusson, too, was capable of pure human spite. "Cem is on French territory. You don't think the king will let us whisk such a treasure out of his holdings without interference? Good God, just because we have been idiots, we shouldn't assume others will be, too."

"Your Eminence, what choice did we have? Since Cem is really worth his weight in the gold they pay for him, here on Rhodes he certainly would have been kidnapped. This way we at least get a cut of the profits from Cem."

"A cut," d'Aubusson echoed angrily. He looked like a bankrupt moneylender. "Can you possibly fail to understand, Brother Kendall, how cruel it is to possess only a cut, when the whole used to be yours? Besides, you still do not know everything, Kendall. While you were away, Bayezid invaded Syria and executed Kasim Bey, the Karamanian leader, for his part in the case of Cem. Qaitbay is next. A month ago, Bayezid demanded Cem's mother and wife from him: Qaitbay refused. By the new year we'll have a war. In the Mediterranean. Now that the battles have begun on land, I cannot simply order Bayezid to keep his ships in the Straights. Now Bayezid will reply that he is fighting in Egypt and needs those ships there. And what will stop him, once he's in our waters, from turning his canons on Rhodes? What, I'm asking you, Kendall?"

"What do you mean, what, Your Eminence? Christendom, of course. When I think of Pope Innocent's decisiveness, of many rulers' desire to get their hands on Cem and to rush into a campaign—an attack on Rhodes would be exactly the thing to start a war between the cross and the crescent."

"Your cheerful prognoses delight me, Brother Kendall," the grand master hissed. "As far as I am concerned, I see only one true ally: Sultan Qaitbay. All the rest"—his voice was sharp with loathing—"would prefer to see the end of Rhodes. So they can snatch up the cut d'Aubusson is still receiving. That's the truth."

This made my hair stand on end. And the worst thing was it looked as if the grand master was right. At least judging from our experience so far. I was just going to ask what measures he thought to undertake, so as not to leave ourselves at the mercy of such events, when d'Aubusson started in again.

"Whatever happens, we can rely only on Innocent. He would show certain restraint. You will travel again to Rome, Brother Kendall, to relay my acceptance of his offer. We will hand Cem over to the papacy in exchange for everything he has listed. Let Innocent worry about how to get Cem—it is already out of our hands. And we mustn't fall completely into despair. The contract for Cem's upkeep is between me and Bayezid. The sultan might not be willing to sign a new one—with the pope, for example. The river of gold will still flow through Rhodes, right?" D'Aubusson let out an agonized laugh, like a man who has just lived through anguish. Then his laughter died out, thanks to a very sudden conclusion. "Who knows whether it is for the best. When Bayezid finds out Cem is being transferred to Italy, he will think the crusade is imminent. And he'll hardly concentrate the bulk of his forces in the Mediterranean Sea."

ELEVENTH TESTIMONY OF
THE POET SAADI ON THE PERIOD
FROM OCTOBER 1483 TO JUNE 1484

AS FAR AS I can remember, my previous testimony ended with Rumilly—the Order's stronghold in Savoy. I had spoken to you of Rumilly with loathing, yet when I look back at the entirety of our exile, Rumilly was not so objectionable. In Rumilly we still had hope.

Our stay there ended suddenly in the autumn of 1483. Immediately after Cem's illness and, in fact, before my master was fully recovered. I have already mentioned Cem had his first fainting fit when our men were sent away. That night I somehow dragged him to his bed and tucked him under the covers. Cem lay there deathly pale; even unconscious, he had not lost his expression of suffering and pain. *Cem, my dear friend*, I thought, *where have the days gone when you would be waiting for us in the morning, already warmed from riding, flushed and tan, lively and joyful for no reason? You yourself were like the dawning day, so wondrously well did we greet the day with you.*

I had dampened his temples and unbuttoned his robe. I was afraid to call one of the knights, even though they surely had already noticed Cem's unwellness. I was afraid of the cup they would bring to their guest. We no longer had anything of our own within the walls of Rumilly. We had to stumble along, clutching onto each other like the blind man and the deaf man from that old fable.

I did not sleep for a whole week, passing my nights in some kind of light dozing. In the darkness, the curtains seemed to ripple with human movement, while the wind's howl was warm with human breath. Everything around us breathed an all-pervading hostility, and we were completely alone, completely defenseless in the face of it.

No matter how I describe it, you will not be able to imagine: two young men, Eastern poets, untested by the world, far from their homeland, sitting locked up within unknown walls, surrounded by incomprehensible warriors—a fully foreign world.

No, you are once again sidestepping the core of our drama. You are inclined to pity us because of the imprisonment our own trust led us to fall into. But that was not the main problem. What oppressed us most, what truly made Cem ill, was the clash not between two deeply different ways of life, but ways of thinking.

I'll have you know, your modern viewpoint places Oriental man in an untrue light—you judge him according to a much later image. This image offends me, an Eastern thinker from the fifteenth century. Because during the Middle Ages, which were on their way out at that time, the East was something mighty. It did not know nations made up of a single people; in its boundless empires dozens of languages were spoken and several faiths professed, alongside quite a few heresies. There, no one had erased the legacy of antiquity; there, soldiers became emperors, while many emperors died in exile. In the East then—and this is the most important thing—no one at any time ever managed to truly get the better of man, naked man, born with a right to happiness, seeking and acting man.

Throughout the whole Middle Ages, light had shone from the East, and it was not without reason that we Orientals considered Western man a barbarian. He had only recently settled into his land, just a millennium or so ago; he had immediately given up his freedom to a heap of petty masters, while he surrendered his mind and conscience to the one and only Church. Over ten centuries, Western man did not even learn to bathe, letting hundreds of exquisite Roman bathhouses fall slowly into ruin—the newcomers didn't know what a bath was for.

During those same ten centuries, we had been selling the West perfumes, silk, spices, books, and heresies, until finally—sometime around my day—we taught the West to reason as well. Precisely then did Western man take up our heritage; he took it up with the death of Byzantium. Like every nouveau riche, he got too big for his britches: he brought about what no one would have ever imagined. I'm not talking about the case of Cem, that was just a ripple in the self-awareness and growing self-confidence of the West.

We had been brought up differently. I am not trying to defend my faith or my nationality—believe me, an Oriental during my day was above all a citizen of the world, he had been taught to think about the world as a whole and about man as its crowning jewel. Read our poetry—our imams railed against it, but not a single poet of ours was burned at the stake or locked up because of a poem. Even our faith accepted the fact that a person had the right to earthly happiness and that such happiness was an end in itself, and all higher considerations must give way before this.

I am not wasting your time with nonsense—I want to explain the discrepancy between the two ways of thinking that appeared in especially sharp relief in the case of Cem. Even today—if you sit down with books written by generations of monks describing and justifying this case, if you sit down with the countless saccharine novels about Zizim that flooded the West during the sixteenth and seventeenth centuries—it will remain unclear to you how and why Cem had to go through everything he went through. His light-mindedness remains inexplicable, his trustingness looks childish, while his suffering seems deliberately sought out. Yet all of that was the inevitable result of our way of thinking, of our entire worldview. It has no room for Brother d'Aubusson, nor for the blackshirted knights; in our world there are no palaces that double as prisons or any double-edged messages. It excludes the possibility of writing a person's death sentence when his own signature stands just beneath it; it cannot conceive of taking away from a condemned man his sole remaining possession—thirty-odd unarmed friends. This was precisely the clash between Cem and the West that lay at the heart of his illness.

There is something expedient in the structure of the human mind. If it gets to the point where at the next moment it will go stark raving mad, it switches itself off, a heavy curtain falls between it and reality; it continues along in fits and starts somehow of its own accord, without seeking sustenance in the real world. This happened to Cem. From that day forward, Cem broke with basic logic, he wandered off into some world of his own filled with wild thoughts of escape, with groundless hopes of aid coming from unknown quarters, and with memories, so many memories. Cem raved deliriously about crusades led by a Muslim prince or about brutal revenge visited on the blackshirts by Bayezid's conquerors. Even though made up of actual people, possibilities, and events, Cem's phantasmagorias stunned me—they paid no heed to reality whatsoever.

Don't consider Cem crazy, not in the least. He walked, talked, and thought like every other person, but between his mind and the world hung that heavy curtain. I myself did not dare lift it, I did not try to prove to Cem that he was raving. Why not? Because I knew it was the only way he would survive. Physically, at least.

And at that time Cem really did lie in bed unconscious for endless days and nights, and I was terribly afraid for his life. He did not eat for a dozen days, sunk into his stupor. Every morning he looked more translucent, more emaciated beneath the covers, while his features disappeared amidst layers of golden hair—I had thought only dead men's beards could grow so fast, rough, and thick.

Shortly thereafter this stupor was replaced by a feverish tossing and turning and muttering. Cem spoke in fits and starts, unbelievably loudly or in a conspiratorial whisper. Cem called out to the Frank—to him above all—to Mehmed, Haydar, or Hüseyin Bey; Cem gave orders to attack or to flee, he argued boldly with d'Aubusson, negotiated with Matthias Corvinus.

Cem had other voices in those days as well—he sobbed over the Conqueror's corpse and gently complained to his mother; Cem swore the little duke to a vow of eternal friendship, he sang his poems about the nights in Karamania, and, most amusingly, he sought simple words while speaking to his son. Not once did Cem mention me, he did not call out to me. It was as if in his dreams he could sense that I alone was there, that I would always be there—to Cem, I was a part of his very self.

Terrible days and nights wore on for me, one after the other. Especially the nights. Behind the curtains of the high-ceilinged room, its dome disappearing above the candles, enemies darted, and as the floor creaked with mousy teeth and woodworms the room would fill up. All those whom Cem called in his sleep passed through it. Our poets arrived on light feet—a crowd of fresh-faced boys, extravagantly joyous and radiant—we had left them in Konya; the Karamanians passed through, led by Kasim Bey, stern and loyal, blood seeping through their hemp shirts— we left them scattered throughout Syria, Lycia, and Cilicia; the little duke would arrive, on horseback no less, and the nocturnal shadows would age him—wherever could the little duke be now? And almost every night d'Aubusson would come—he did not pass through, did not enter, he was simply there, he was present in the darkness of the corner and breathed with the wind.

The astonishing thing is that I did not go mad, locked up as I was with a babbling madman, left alone with everything Cem ran away from into his illness so as to save himself. Most likely the caretaking saved me; my care for Cem may have been useless and absurd, but I clung like a drowning man to the task I had set for myself.

VERA MUTAFCHIEVA

I didn't count the days, but on one of them—late in the afternoon—Cem slept for a long time without any fits. I, too, drifted off as well, as hours of quiet had become a rarity for me. And suddenly I heard: "Saadi, is it day or night?"

The sound of his voice left no room for doubt: Cem had returned. I leaned over him, over the face I could hardly recognize. Cem was studying it as well; he ran a very dry, very white hand over his brow to his temples, and from there down to his chin.

"I've grown as hairy as a dervish, Saadi," he said. "Was I sick a long time?"

I clasped him to my shoulder, as I didn't want him to see I was crying. He was scrawny, yet strangely heavy. I felt as if the sea had washed up into my embrace a drowning man for whom I had long been searching.

"Cem," I said. "We have passed through this as well, Cem...."

This did not mean, however, that more did not await us. A week later the brothers announced we were leaving. We no longer bothered to ask why: the answer would have been "it is necessary for your safety." Only after some time did we find out this move was connected to Louis's death and the Order's fear of Charles of Savoy.

When they led us out of Rumilly and brought us our horses, my hair stood on end. No, this journey did not resemble our previous trips. Our colorful, gold-brocaded suite was gone; Cem would not be riding amidst his guards, under the shouts and music of our Turkish virtuosos. Only months before, these journeys had gathered the nobility of Savoy—back then, Cem gave rise to songs and poems at every step.

But on that autumn morning, a sad procession slipped out of Rumilly. Two foreigners, dressed in bright colors, sat in silence on their horses. Both of them looked newly recovered from a long illness. They squinted painfully in the light and sat unsteadily in their saddles. While all around them—front, back, and sides—rode the black brothers.

Cem did not speak during the whole three-day journey. We were still riding through Savoy, and my heart was sinking at the thought of leaving it. I had grown used to its white cliffs and low, sharp shrubs, its sparse woods tormented by the mistral, its clean sky. Here we were still to some extent ourselves—we caught the scent of the Mediterranean, and on its far shore lay our home.... The hills here slightly resembled Bursa's. Our journey to the northwest tormented me—we were getting ever farther away from our world.

No one had seen us off and we met no one during the journey. The brothers were clearly keeping us hidden. On the third day we reached some castle, after several weeks we traded it for another, then another. I made a study of the Dauphiné, as if I planned to draw up a map. That's a joke. Of course, I can make no such map. It is not roads, castles, woods, or valleys I have preserved in my memories of that time. For me, that period remains tied to a single face, animated in turn by impatient rage, resigned annoyance, brief lucid moments, and the most miserable, miserable despair—Cem's face. Surely I looked no different, but there was no one to describe me. Cem was always concerned only with himself, while the Dauphiné's nobles did not spare much attention for a sultan's servant.

Everywhere the Order offered us one and the same entertainments: hunting, troubadours, gluttony, and drunkenness. In our own way, the two of us broke the monotony with quiet nighttime conversations, since fear of the brotherhood had become part of our everyday existence. At night we immersed ourselves in whatever news reached us, which was very scant indeed, and perhaps manipulated. We hypothesized about what Bayezid was up to or what Corvinus's intentions were, what steps the Holy Father was taking before Christendom, where our thirty comrades had been taken—these and countless other puzzles filled up our impatience.

Don't ask me why we were impatient above all, this should be obvious even without words. As they distracted us with celebrations, we well knew that we were being toyed with. In the beginning, in Nice, this seemed natural: a Turkish ruler was visiting France, they welcomed him, honored him—all fine and good. But no welcome should have lasted so long; in that time any other foreign ruler would have had at least one high-level meeting, signed at least some paper—a contract, agreement, commitment. While for seven whole years in France, Cem had not been received by a single lord with a relatively impressive title; the local lordlings spoke to him of nothing but wine and hunting; he received no letters, none, not one.

Once a year, no matter where we were in April, we would receive a visit from Bayezid's emissary. The same one who had brought Cem's allowance to Rhodes. With the Order's assistance, he verified whether Şehzade Cem was still among the living. These were dark days for us; we felt them coming weeks in advance. Bayezid had become more demanding as well; his emissary was no longer satisfied to see Cem from afar, as Hüseyin Bey had done. We were forced to appear so that he could examine us up close.

During those years Cem still took those hours deeply to heart. After all, Bayezid's man was the only Turk—hence the only one of Cem's future subjects—whom we saw. Cem seemed to be trying to stun and conquer him with his appearance alone; he never uttered a word in front of him. Cem made me spend much time and effort dressing him before each such meeting; normally careless about his exterior, he selected his adornments with exactitude, changing them several times until finally deciding on the most suitable ones. He stared at the mirror, eyes narrowed, to discern whether everything about his appearance was harmonious, whether in the necessary combination between colors, hues, and materials some aesthetic balance had not been lost—in these hours Cem readied himself as if for a portrait painter, and not for some sultan's bey.

After that, my master would evaluate me as well—dressed as if I were the grand vizier. In the end—those moments were very strange, I cannot help but mention it—Cem would begin the most difficult part of all: pulling together and ordering the features of his face, erasing from it any human emotion, until he arrived at an immaculate, majestic indifference. He truly looked like an idol and not a living person in those hours, which repeated themselves every year.

The monks always irritated Cem, but on such days he demanded their presence. They lined both sides of his entire route, in full armor, their faces also frozen. We set off between them. Often the staircase in the fortress would be small, no one had ever foreseen it would be needed for a ruler's official reception, and so our gold-threaded robes would rub against much chain mail; often the flagstones were quite worn here and there, such that Cem's steps were uneven, as if he were riding; often the doors of the so-called reception hall were too narrow for Cem Sultan's advance guard to pass through in formation, and they would jostle together awkwardly, giving off a metallic sound. But always and everywhere in those provincial fortresses, Cem himself looked invariably magnificent.

I would walk behind him with my humblest expression, as befits a sultan's vizier, walking as if I were following the sun. Cem would go up several steps and stand in front of the just-cobbled-together throne. He would not sit down. He would stand for a bit, unbelievably handsome, unbelievably splendid and expressionless. A living picture of sovereign power would present himself to the subject who had chosen the wrong master.

It was amusing to watch that subject—incidentally, they were different every year. I saw how Cem instantly dazzled him. I'm sure Cem would have simply bowled him over if the emissary had not been on his guard. And not only because Cem was a legend; Cem's infamous charm had still not begun to fade, it continued to captivate and rule. Despite the miserable food these foreign fortresses inhabited by hound masters, squires, and, at most, petty barons could offer him, despite the isolation and uncertainty, I think the most enduring part of Cem was his charm.

For several moments my master would revel in the admiration of his only subject for that year. He would take that admiration back with him, through the corridors, tunnels, and chambers; he would tuck it under his pillow so as to enjoy it at night; he would sneak it along on hunts and feasts. I am absolutely certain that at some feast, when Cem would suddenly be off in his thoughts with a distant smile, he had taken that homage out of his memories, he was intoxicated by the thought of his still-potent charm.

A sorry consolation, you will say. And you are right. But do you know what ravenous vanity rages inside a twenty-five-year-old wealthy, healthy, and spoiled pretender to a throne? It is stronger than any sense of lack—you cannot compare it to thirst in the desert, to unrequited passion, even with starvation. Burning and all-consuming, this hunger turned Cem into a firebrand of impatience. "When"—sometimes every one of Cem's cells would shout, howling—"when will I finally lead the invasion, when will I be victorious, when will I enter Topkapi as a sultan? When?"

Oh, how well I understood him. I, whose own freedom would bring neither a victory nor a throne, who strove toward freedom as a simple mortal, not seeing it as anything more than just freedom. My own striving was already enough to fill my every thought, fantasy, and dream—I suspect it had already changed my very movements, such that I felt everyone around would ask, "Are you still here, Saadi? How can freedom exist without you?"

It could... Everywhere besides Rumilly, the Château de Vaux-le-Vicomte, Rochechinard, and various castles around the Dauphiné, men of my age lived—they made war, deals, houses, debts, and children—while I rode amidst polite jailers and noblemen dolled up on command. I shot rabbits, in the evening I listened to maudlin songs about young maids deceived in love or evildoers punished by God, and I drank—I drank watered-down French wine. How enormous the barrel must have been, such that it never ran dry in all those years,

VERA MUTAFCHIEVA

that barely reddened water they served to me, a connoisseur of Cypriot and Shiraz wines, thick as the blood of a Bedouin dead of drought.

Ah yes, I have gone off on a tangent again. But what events can I use to mark days that passed for us uneventfully? How can I describe to you all the devils that leapt out at us, shoving us hither and thither, forcing us to take steps you will call pointless and perhaps even ridiculous?

And so, we were at Rochechinard. I will spare you a description of the middling castle, why should I describe every one of our refuges? They were way stations along our life's journey, since at each one of them we left something of ours until we found ourselves as naked as the day we were born, not stripped physically, but spiritually. And Rochechinard was no different than the others. Its ruler was the commander of Avignon—we continued to drag ourselves from Hospitaller to Hospitaller.

At Rochechinard, of course, guests immediately began visiting us, they set to work organizing diversions for us—I could no longer imagine a day without such filler; I had started to think they would be doing me a good turn if some morning they started beating me and did not leave off till the evening—what wonderful variety that would be! In vain I asked the same questions of the Dauphiné nobility. I asked about Charles, as always. They gave me evasive answers: he was either in Chambéry or in Lyon with his relatives.

I could sense how these responses hit Cem's impatience like boiling oil on a wound. We nursed two hopes: Charles and Corvinus. Charles hadn't managed to do anything over an entire year, but what about Matthias? Why did all our messengers to Hungary, both secret and official, seem to get swallowed up by the earth itself? Why did the Order never mention Corvinus in its news?

"Reckless as it may be, we need to ask about him," Cem decided. "The brothers will feed us lies, I know. But what if you asked one of these lordlings or their squires?"

This was Cem's new attitude. He thought it was time for us to act—we had left things to the world powers for too long. These arguments of Cem's bolstered his impatience until he was trembling with nerves. But they were still more tolerable than his self-pity during his fits of painful despair. All day and all night—but mainly at night—Cem cooked up impossible schemes and told them to me in great detail. I am not sure whether this was due to his illness—I no longer ever looked upon him as a fully healthy person—or whether it was a natural response to everything we had experienced and which our future promised. But in any case, Cem began living with the thought of escape.

"We must only make it to Chambéry, to Charles," Cem would whisper to me at night, while everyone was supposedly asleep, but we knew they were eavesdropping on us. "Charles will outfit us with a messenger to Hungary. It's not impossible, Saadi."

"It is indeed impossible. The grand master and the king have at least a dozen spies at Chambéry. Within two days, both of them will learn you are there. They could force Charles to put you under a guard loyal to them. An escape to Savoy solves nothing."

"Then our only choice is to make a run for Hungary. Don't try to talk me out of it, Saadi. What if they take away even this option from us tomorrow? What would we have to lose with an attempt, Saadi? Their trust?"

"The illusion of our freedom, Cem. You have not lost it sufficiently. We could land ourselves in prison. An average, ordinary, harsh prison. With no hope. Now at least we have that...."

"No, no, no!" Cem exploded with such fury I was afraid he would spill everything aloud. "Time is passing, we don't know whether Corvinus will give up on his war against Bayezid a few months from now. Every moment is precious, Saadi. First thing tomorrow morning we need to..."

Our conversations had various endings. Cem would either order me to study the routes between the Dauphiné and Hungary, or to find out what Corvinus was up to at the moment, how the king of France was treating Charles, and so on. The very same night I would concoct my conversations for the coming day. Good thing I am a writer and singer rolled into one—I had gotten used to performing for listeners and immediately weaving any mistake into my act. Whether I was riding or feasting amidst the signors of the Dauphiné, I never dropped the threads of the charade. I was most often successful with the simplest of bait—I pretended to be drunk; after all, it is common knowledge that poets are rarely sober. Then I would drown my conversation partner in a flood of words—not always pronounced properly, I could tell because they would snicker up their sleeves at me. I would bare my soul and dreams to them and thus provoke them to let some paltry bit of truth slip. Of course, I never asked about the roads to Hungary, because such behavior on my part would have been far too obvious. I hoped if we did run away—although I never really believed we would succeed—we would make our way by the stars. And so I nevertheless managed to gather some fragments of news about events in Europe.

Cem met each one of them in the same way. "See, we mustn't wait. We have nothing to lose. D'Aubusson is not going to kill me, because I bring him gold. Think of something, do something, Saadi!"

I began to work in earnest in the spring of 1484. By then we had become fixtures in Rochechinard: the local nobles were our regular guests, I knew their suites and their singers.

I set my sights on a singer. He won my trust likely because we served the same God. He was young, but already famous; his song about Richard the Lionheart in prison is positively the best thing I have heard about Richard. The master of the Château de Vaux-le-Vicomte—d'Aubusson's brother—brought him to us.

As soon as he started to sing, he very much reminded me of our village poet, Haydar. He clearly had not been born among the nobility, nor even among their servants; the young man lacked any refinement. Yet in his song there was something sincere: inspiration. Awkward while they introduced him, Renier—that was his name—could not relax, yet he seemed to fly away as soon as he started to sing. I could see he was not there with us. Wholly given over to his creative work, I could sense him perfecting it; those tiny strokes of luck, surprising even to him, in a certain word, in a certain new image, carried him ever higher above a world that was not his.

I watched Renier—I was no longer listening to him—sunk in bitter memories: once upon a time, before Cem discovered me, I had sung like that, begging your pardon. Once—the first time I stood before Cem—I had sung like that and made him favor me before all other singers he had ever heard. And that favor—call it love, if you like—had killed me as a singer. I realized this in the hour I listened to Renier. My thoughts and my heart could no longer fly away, and this was exactly the problem; for years I had not known moments sublime with suffering and bliss, that simultaneous effort and ease that is inspiration itself. I was chained to the earth, because on earth there lived and suffered someone I loved. I was his possession.

Yes, I watched Renier and saw he had gotten the upper hand on our dunderheads from the Dauphiné. *You don't need to understand art,* I thought, *few grow to be truly worthy it. But sincerity can be felt by an unnamed sense. Once you've risked sincerity, you have already gotten the upper hand....*

And just imagine to what depths I had fallen, I, the poet Saadi, since—as soon as Renier finished and withdrew—I followed him. I did not start speaking to him in our shared language, I did not regale him with my bitterness as a dead poet, but very shallowly, yet very characteristically for the person I had become—a clumsy statesman—I immediately tried to awaken his sympathy for Cem.

"Your song moved me to tears, Renier." I uttered this trite phrase while the poet in me truly wept for shame.

The singer looked at me, sizing me up. "I'm glad," he said. "I am very glad I have made you cry."

This did not perturb the statesman I had become, not at all.

"You clearly seek out tragic heroes for inspiration. Perhaps you also have a song about Cem. Why don't you sing it for us?"

"Because I don't have one. I am surely the first troubadour to sing for Cem not about Cem. You know—you are Saadi, are you not?—I believe a man should avoid intimacy with that which he has praised. It's better that way."

We crossed the courtyard as we spoke. Renier was going to take his supper amidst the hound masters and falconers. And I accompanied him, which was completely beneath the dignity of a near-sultan's highest lord.

Renier noticed my mistake. He stopped in front of the kitchen door and stared at me intently for some time.

"I know," he said suddenly and quietly enough so no one could hear. "I know how much you have cried and what kind of songs you need. On the whole, I think I know far more than you do, Saadi. Because I am on the outside. The whole Old World is discussing Cem's freedom or imprisonment. They'll discuss it and then forget it, just as it was with Richard the Lionheart, no?"

I realized: Renier was not waiting for me to catch up with him, he himself was running toward me. I gathered all my courage, I could not let such an opportunity slip away. "Why should we wait for them to forget, Renier?"

"Ohooo!" he drawled with a laugh. "And what if the brothers have paid me off?"

"They have not," I said in despair; such conversations would mean death for me. "You would not have appeared before Cem with a song about the Lionheart, you would not have sung it like that."

Of course, I was talking nonsense. But at that moment, Renier stopped smiling.

"I agree, my lord. Tomorrow morning I will greet Cem Sultan as he awakes with a song from Alsace. I will also sing for him while he hunts. I know many nice hunting songs."

In short, the next morning during the hunt I spoke man-to-man with Renier. Don't imagine that the singer was a conspirator, that someone had sent him. He simply loved that demichild of a duke; all the troubadours of France loved Charles and wanted to make him happy. Beyond that, I sensed in Renier some hostility toward the brotherhood. It slipped out in his words. I never found out whether there was some other reason for it, or whether it was simply born of that age-old hatred between poets and monks.

Renier promised us two horses waiting at the little bridge in the woods and a set of clothes on each saddle, and he pointed out our best escape routes in general terms.

"It would be foolish to ride for Chambéry, but even more foolish still to head east. Go straight to the sea, but not in Savoy. Make for the mouth of the Rhone. Or Mauritania, if your strength holds out. And look for a ship to take you across."

"To Cairo?" I asked, astonished. We had not thought of fleeing to Egypt.

"Qaitbay is at war with Bayezid. While Corvinus made peace with him months ago."

"Peace between Bayezid and Corvinus?" This news all but struck me dead on the spot.

"Yes, my dear friend. Don't pin your hopes on the Hungarian king. He is hatching other plans."

Renier then walked away, after warning us not to make our attempt until he had slipped away from Rochechinard—and in this, too, he reminded me of Haydar; he liked to make a thorough job of things. And I stood there, unable to pull myself together—all our expectations, our routes, our prospects for success had changed. Why indeed had we waited for peace with Hungary, and would it not be followed by yet another—between Turkey and Egypt?

Merciful God, let them beat us to death tomorrow night if we do not succeed. It was becoming ever more intolerable to be alone with Cem in the middle of a game being played between two entire worlds. *Hopefully it will all end tomorrow, one way or another....* In a whisper I told Cem about my negotiations and the singer's promises. In the darkness—we were pretending to sleep—I felt Cem's fingers on my brow.

"Thank you, Saadi," he whispered back. "I knew you would do something."

We decided to sneak out as the feast was winding down, when the sober were dozing off and the drunk were going wild and no one would figure out who was going off to their beds and who was wandering outside to see to their needs. Of course this is the most obvious time for an escape, but we were naive and so we chose it.

We embraced it with all the excitement of novices. During the dinner Cem looked both drunker and rowdier than he had ever been, while I made a show of inexplicable drowsiness. We thought we were convincing, or at least no one made any hints to the contrary. When it was finally late enough, we slipped out separate doors, met in the courtyard, and crossed it in the bluest shadows. We hoped it would not be inconceivable we should pass through the kitchens to avoid the castle gate—there Cem, putting on a show of complete drunkenness, poured a dipper of water on my head, to wake me up, he explained to the servants, and after that we "mistook" the exit.

VERA MUTAFCHIEVA

Outside the night was pitch-black—this part of our escape was as it should be, too. Rochechinard casts a thick shadow, it passes through an almost-sheer river valley, which leads in turn through a forest.

We stumbled along, huffing quietly, slipping in puddles and sinking into the creek. To the bridge. There two horses really were waiting for us. With a bundle of clothes on each saddle.

"We'll change clothes at daybreak," Cem whispered. "Saadi, I beg you, hurry!"

Even without being begged, I was hurrying along feverishly. I knew the pathways through the forest; we had galloped down them on every hunt. I led the horses quietly, shuddering at every sound, figuring the shortest way to the field.

Thank you, God—you who did not will our escape to succeed—for giving us that hour's ride through the open field. It suddenly gleamed before us, despite the night, after the forest's double darkness—to us, it was an incarnation of our long-forgotten sense of spaciousness. We let our horses run through it. Cem urged them on with a triumphant cry, if I can call a slightly louder whisper a "cry." I pressed my face to my horse's neck—a quite small, cheap horse—and I was moved to tears. I could see Cem just ahead of me, again limber, again jubilant. Cem's stance was slightly odd; he was not bending forward, but rather seemed to want to scoop up more wind and nocturnal chill with his shoulders. We were lost in the moment. I don't know how long we rode willy-nilly.

Then Cem stopped. "Saadi, lead us by the stars! Which way is Chambéry, Saadi?"

I stopped, too. In all the rush, I had not even told Cem that while we had been feasting in the Dauphiné, the world's power structure as it related to our circumstances had shifted and we needed to ride for Cairo, not Savoy. Before I replied, for a moment all was quiet—our horses' tramping did not fill the night. And in that silence I caught the sound of other horses approaching. More than eight hooves, more than two riders. No, it was not an echo. They were not only chasing us—they had caught us.

Cem's face seemed very terrible to me then; that must be how sleepwalkers look when someone suddenly startles them awake. Strained, dead—empty. As our pursuers surrounded us, I thought I heard not the horses' sinister snorting, but rather the brothers snorting in their beards. This ridicule showed their disdain as well as their satisfaction and superiority. It was with such disdain that Brother Antoine d'Aubusson turned to Cem and spat, "Your Highness has gotten lost on his nighttime stroll. Rochechinard Castle lies far to the left."

That was our first attempt. Others followed—I don't recall how many—more sophisticated, more cunning. But none of them managed to outwit the Order.

TESTIMONY OF BATTISTA SPINOLA, WITH NO SPECIFIC OCCUPATION, ABOUT THE AUTUMN OF 1484

THAT PART ABOUT no specific occupation isn't true. Everyone figured that I, too, had my profession, how could I not? But I see you will observe the rules of propriety, I suspected as much. The world hasn't changed a bit since my day. It hasn't budged an iota. Anyway.

I, Battista Spinola, was born in Genoa. Most of the Genoese in my day were sailors. And when I say sailors, that doesn't mean they were all the same—there were rich fat cats as well as the smallest fry struggling to makes ends meet. The worst off were the ones who fell somewhere in the middle. Like Christopher Columbus, for example, who later got famous, even though he was never my better.

My dad, may he rest in peace, left me with nothing more than the clothes on my back. But I didn't feel like breaking my back as a sailor from Genoa to Cairo, Marseille, or Malta for half a ducat a year. So I set out to remedy my situation in ways I won't list here. In short, by 1480 or so I suppose I'd gotten

pretty wealthy, and some first-class folks used my services—
our successful merchants, petty noblemen, and others. What
were those services you'll ask, but I won't answer, because most
of them weren't meant for polite company, plus I don't want to
dig up stuff I've already been paid double for: once to do it, and
again to keep my mouth shut. As you well know, the bigwigs always need the likes of yours truly, Battista Spinola—we do the
dirty work, while they skim the cream off the top.

Incidentally, in 1484—I was in Marseille then, selling a
Bavarian prince's serfs for Egyptian gold; Sultan Qaitbay preferred blond boys for guards—a stranger introduced himself to
me in Marseille. He told me he was speaking for Duke Ercole
of Ferrara; he showed me his seal as proof. As far as Ercole, in
case you're asking, even in the underworld there was no bandit
like him. True, in our day there wasn't much difference between bandits and rulers, or at least I couldn't see one. But in
Italy some outright bandits had cropped up amidst the rulers,
because those constant wars left them so broke they had to
cover their expenses somehow and so turned to highway robbery. Let's take Boccolino—nobody knew where Boccolino had
come from, but he sieged Osimo near Ancona—while Ancona
itself belonged to the Holy See—captured it, and in that very
same year of 1484 he was looking high and low for a buyer. He
was selling the harbor for cash, with God as my witness. Or take
Medici, I'm talking Lorenzo, the ruler of Florence; now he was
an esteemed and very respected man, despite his wars against
the Holy Father. Another Medici, a corsair by profession, captured Chios, which supposedly belonged to the sultan, and
collected taxes and ruled it with an iron fist. What I'm trying

to say is that in my day there was no clear line between corsairs, bandits, and princes—they were one and the same. Now you say there is. Fine.

Anyway, Duke Ercole was a bandit of the highest order. Anytime anyone wanted to get up to no good in Italy—start a war, hire mercenaries, seize some village or mountain pass—they always turned to the Duke of Ferrara. And he never said no. And he did these deeds most often with help, from men the likes of me. Since his man had come all the way to Marseille to find me, I was sure we were talking big money—after all, he'd dropped the name Ercole of Ferrara.

The guy warned me this business was absolutely hush-hush. Of course, he threatened me, saying they would rub me out if I so much as said a peep about it. This was unnecessary—the likes of me know how to keep our mouths shut. And he made me go see Ercole, with him. The duke wanted to talk to me in person.

I left my partner, also a Genoese, to sell the Bavarians and set off. When we got to Ferrara they saw me right away. The duke, that is. Unlike other bigwigs, Ercole always negotiated these deals face-to-face, which is why he succeeded in whatever he set his mind to.

As for the duke, what can I tell you? A man like any other. Except he was very blunt in his speech, as if he was about to start throwing punches; he wanted you to catch his drift from half a word. So Ercole very curtly explained that I needed to arrange for the kidnapping of the sultan everybody was talking about.

I hadn't expected anything that heavy. Everyone was saying the brothers from some sacred order were guarding the sultan with their lives. So how did Duke Ercole see this happening?

That's exactly what I asked him: How do you see this happening?

"If I could see it happening, why would I have contacted you, idiot?" I'm not exaggerating, that's the way he talked. "I don't want your answer today, not even tomorrow. Think about it, talk to your people. But if you take this job, you've got to finish it. Is that clear? Otherwise, you'll have to answer to someone far more serious than Genoese merchants or Bavarian princelings."

"Is the Doge of Venice paying?" I wanted to pry something out of him. Back in our day in Italy, the biggest deals of this kind were always bankrolled by the Venetians. And they were nobody to mess around with, that's the truth.

"The doge, ha!" Ercole hissed. That's all I got out of him. "Go back to Marseille, arrange everything, and name the price."

I suddenly grew bold. Since Ercole had sought me out, that means he'd struck out elsewhere. And this wasn't just any job. Everyone knew the sultan was the biggest deal of our time, who could imagine a bigger one? So what? I'm expected to put my neck in the noose without Ercole even telling me who was paying, is that it? Just because we work in the shadows doesn't mean we don't have questions. Like hell we don't!

"I want to know who's paying," I said, surprising even myself. Ercole stopped—because he had been pacing during our whole conversation—and looked as if he would crush me. Then he laughed.

"You want to know, huh? Fine, know! They'll rub you out before you can let it slip in any case. There's two of them paying:

King Matthias and the little duke. Hm? You're a fool—otherwise you would've preferred not to know. I hope you don't lose your head."

"I can keep quiet, Your Highness," I said with dignity. "And when will the two gentlemen in question pay?"

"When payment is due. For a job well done."

"Ah, yes, I know that trick. You get a knife in the back instead of payment. I don't start the job until in some Roman or Florentine bank—your choice—one hundred thousand ducats are deposited in the name Battista Spinola. Only then."

"And how will you finish the job?" The duke laughed again; he was enjoying himself.

"We'll calculate it. Our expenses and our profits. We'll get the difference when we hand over the sultan. I won't ask for more than ten thousand for profit, with God as my witness."

"You and your witnesses," Ercole spat. "Are you aware Sultan Bayezid collects one hundred thousand ducats annually from his whole empire? And you'll earn that much for a single night."

"No, I won't earn that much, I'll pay that much," I corrected him. "Has Your Highness thought about my expenses? I'll have to work with at least thirty expendable men."

"Expendable men are cheap."

The duke calculated in his head. I can tell you what he was calculating: he would have to ask those two kings for two hundred thousand—two times the annual income of the largest empire in the world so something would be left over for both him and me.

"Won't I hear a more reasonable offer?"

"You won't, Your Highness. Ask others, that's the price for the sultan. Don't worry, they'll pay and earn it back in triple."

"All right, go," Ercole of Ferrara said. "I'll tell them how much you want."

I set out for Marseille again. On the way I thought about who to tap for this job. I ended up deciding on my partner—it was no coincidence I'd taken him on as partner. The kid had really been around the block. I'd picked him up off the street and kept him in line by knowing a few things that would get him broken on the wheel if I ever decided to talk.

When I found him in Marseille, he'd already loaded up the Bavarians for Cairo and counted out the money for me— his accounts always came out right. I told him about this business, and in one night he was ready to go. Because we'd decided he should head north and find out which fortress they were holding the sultan in—it wasn't hard, these things got around. Then somehow he needed to get to the sultan's people and tell them the Hungarian king had arranged for his escape. He'd let them arrange things there, and he'd come back. Then we'd tell Duke Ercole everything was set, we'd check whether the king had deposited the money, and, God willing, we'd do the deed.

In the whole story, my role was not decisive. Through me— because I had a name in the underworld—Ercole was really giving the job to Giovanni, my partner. For this reason, even though I made a show of bargaining with Giovanni, I must admit he didn't ask for much: thirty-five thousand, that's what we agreed on. I knew while he was on the job it'd grow to at least fifty, that's how he was; he had a knack for wheedling and insisting—he'd tell me every morning what new expenses had cropped up. But even fifty wasn't much.

In short, at the end of September, Giovanni set out north with three packhorses loaded with books—they said the sultan bought books, plus Giovanni needed to look harmless. I waited for Giovanni and worried about him quite a bit, because it was well-known the brothers of any order were no patsies, nor did they forgive. During that time I got news from two separate sources. One was named Cesar Valentine, and he didn't know our language well. He said he'd been sent by the Hungarian king and asked how things were shaping up. I only managed to squeeze a bit out of him—you'll get your money at the end, he kept saying. But I realized the king was very impatient, and this made me glad, because once I stole away that little sultan, then the real bargaining would begin. If we managed to hide him in the meantime, of course.

The second person who came to me was Pietro the Martyr from Mantua. I'd known him a long time. He'd gotten his nickname because after a major robbery he'd hung on the wheel for two days, and then was cut up, burned, and flayed, but he survived, so they turned around and pardoned him. Anyway, the Martyr came in the name of Charles of Savoy. *It's clear Charles is still wet behind the ears,* I thought. *Otherwise why would he trust this business to the Martyr, who would sell his own mother and sleep with his own sister?* As you well know, even among rogues like us there are honorable men and complete cads.

The Martyr asked me lots of questions about how things were going, saying the little duke hardly ate or slept from anguish over his beloved friend, and that's how it would be until he saw him set free. But I noticed Pietro asked for just a few too many details about where, when, and how. I figured he might be up to something: trying to organize the sultan's escape himself, to hide him away as a bargaining chip. So I hurried to send him away however I could, but he still wrenched two ducats from me, saying he didn't have money for the return trip to Savoy.

I had already started to fear Giovanni had walked into a trap and I'd need to find a new partner when—at the end of December—he came back. At that time of year the weather in Marseille is truly miserable; the wind doesn't just blow, the mistral is downright deadly, and for whole days at a time the harbor is empty—people hide in their cellars so as not to be driven mad by the howl of the wind. So I, too, was hunkered down for shelter when I heard Giovanni's voice. I was overjoyed to see him—until then I had thought nothing would come of this business in the end.

Giovanni was unrecognizable. He was wearing a wolfskin coat, while his clothes—trust me, I know about these things— were of the finest Flanders wool. He had grown an enormous beard, and he was wearing gloves and even a ring.

"Well, well, well," I said, after we'd gotten greetings out of the way. "You've really let loose your purse strings. You're not eating up Hungarian ducats on credit now, are you?"

"No," Giovanni replied. "I've been eating up cash. Cem Sultan's money."

"Did you manage to talk to him?"

"That would've been stupid."

I've noticed Giovanni had the terrible tendency to put on airs, street scamp that he was.

"But I talked to Saadi. Please!" He offered me his hand. "This hand has been kissed by Saadi, Cem sultan's closest adviser."

"And what did you agree on?"

"First let's eat, my dear partner," Giovanni interrupted me, peeling off his fur coat. "First pour me a drink, then we'll talk."

That wasn't a bad idea. Giovanni might play the big merchant or even the prince, but the minute he was drunk, his tongue loosened up and he spilled his guts. So we sat down to drink, and Giovanni spat it out.

"Well, Battista, our days as poor men are done. You'll buy not just one ship, but five, Battista, while I might buy twenty. We'll go back home to Genoa dressed like royalty and watch the Genoese choke with envy."

"Come on now," I said, "don't get ahead of yourself."

"What's to get ahead of? Everything is ready. I don't even want to go into how I snuck into Bois-Lamy, which is where they've recently moved the sultan. I passed for a book merchant, and three monks peered with four eyes each at the books I took out of my trunk. That time I didn't do anything, I just pretended to feel sick and stayed in the village. Then I paid a boy to help me meet Saadi—he's the only Turk left with the sultan. We met when Saadi came down to the village, supposedly to get some herbs, and I told him everything we'd talked about. I mentioned the Hungarian king and Charles, I said we had thirty loyal men who'd sworn on the holy cross to free the sultan from captivity. Saadi rushed to kiss my hands—I guess that's their tradition—and I ordered him to ask his master when and where. Saadi said he'd hardly get a second chance to slip out of the fortress unnoticed, so we'd better decide right there and then. So we decided. The next day I 'recovered' and set off. And that's all, Battista."

It didn't escape my notice that Giovanni had left out the most important thing: what they had decided on. Perhaps he wanted to take my place in negotiations with Duke Ercole.

"What did you agree on?" I asked, realizing Giovanni was not anywhere near as drunk as he seemed.

He winked at me and put a lordly hand on my shoulder. "Knowing too much makes you grow old before your time, Battista. When the time comes, you'll find out."

I pushed his hand off my shoulder. This street rat was acting all high and mighty with me. Who gave him his daily bread?

"Don't forget, little brother, the money has been deposited in my name. Nobody has ever heard of any Giovanni."

"You can't take a joke," he said, clearly taking my words to heart. "Since you don't, then listen up: in Bois-Lamy there's an underground tunnel that leads to the river, where it's low. The entrance is hidden. They used to use it during sieges. Saadi told me a servant who really loved the sultan—that's how Saadi put it, but it was probably actually a question of money—showed them the tunnel. But the two of them, the Turks, they didn't dare sneak away because they'd tried to escape a few times already but always failed. They didn't have anyone waiting for them to help them get away. And they decided it wouldn't happen without outside help. That's why he kissed my hands—they had been waiting a long time for someone to come looking for the sultan. Saadi explained the tunnel to me. That's where I'll meet them with our men on the tenth of February, during the night."

"Where does the tunnel come out?" I didn't let him dance around the most important thing.

"Do you really need to know that, Battista? I'm the one who'll be there, not you, right? If you were up for the trip, why didn't you go to Bois-Lamy, hm?"

I sighed. Giovanni was twenty-odd years my junior, and a whole head taller. I was in no shape for fighting, nor for kidnapping sultans in the dead of winter. *Never mind,* I consoled myself, *he'll have the sultan, but I'll have the money. We'll come to an agreement somehow.*

The next morning, I led out my horse under the mistral—I led him by the halter because I didn't want to risk being blown out of my saddle—and I set out for Ferrara. I thought about how many people would lose out on so much if I were attacked on the road by bandits—real bandits, not those like Duke Ercole or Giovanni. But no one attacked me. I passed through Cassis, La Ciotat, and Nice—three years ago, I recalled, all the pomp around the sultan's arrival had played out exactly here. Then I headed inland and in only three days I had arrived in Ferrara.

This time I had to wait for hours in Duke Ercole of Ferrara's antechamber. They finally brought me in to see him toward evening, so we spoke by candlelight. Duke Ercole was in a thick robe that made him as wide as he was tall, and once again he paced around the room like a caged beast.

"Ha! Signor Battista, is it?" The duke burst out laughing as soon as I stepped through his doorway. "How are we, signor?"

"Very well, I daresay. Your Highness, everything is ready. Besides the money, we must ask King Matthias for four changes of horses, three mounts each."

"Why three?"

"For the two Turks and my man."

"And why four changes of horses?"

"That's what we've figured for the road from Bois-Lamy to Ferrara."

"And when will it happen?"

"On February 10, I daresay. If I can confirm the hundred thousand have been deposited by then."

"Signor Battista," the duke began, once he was convinced I was not lying, "a little obstacle has arisen. King Matthias refuses to pay for such a costly escape. He thinks such business cannot be completely certain, and with good reason."

"We will hand over the sultan in exchange for the money," I said, my hair standing on end. "No one is asking him to pay in advance."

"Yes, this is what I told Cesar Valentine as well. But the question of the price remains."

"Is King Matthias trying to bargain, Your Highness, or is someone else?" My temper flared. The likes of me don't always stand on ceremony—at the end of the day, the bigwigs need us, not the other way around. "This whole business has passed through so many hands, lots of middlemen have gotten involved."

"It is none other than King Matthias who is bargaining," the duke said with spiteful emphasis; he loved playing with people, may he rest in peace. "You could light a votive candle for him in church if he were only haggling. But King Matthias has simply refused."

"What?" I couldn't believe my ears; we had worked like dogs, risking our lives. Or at least Giovanni had.

"Just that. He refused. He had hoped, he told us, the whole business would cost him around ten thousand ducats."

"Let him steal the sultan for ten thousand!" I had forgotten myself at this point. Then another thought cut me to the quick. "When did you learn this, Your Highness?"

"In October. The middle of October. Why do you ask, signor?"

"Because you could've let us know somehow, Your Highness."

"I didn't think to do so. Plus, I knew you would come back."

I have no memory of how I made my way out of his palace. I noticed a middling-sized pouch in my hand and recalled that at our parting, Ercole had said to me, "For your silence." It was not for our silence, don't believe it for a minute. The duke simply realized he might need me again and didn't want to part on bad terms—the likes of me hold grudges, that's a well-known fact.

I walked through the dark streets of Ferrara, wanting to cry. I even felt sorry for Giovanni, who had imagined himself rich and powerful, whose hands had been kissed by some Saadi or other; most of all, I felt sorry for myself for having gotten my hopes up about those ships, my chance to sail away from the underworld of Genoa and Marseille.

Did I feel sorry for Cem Sultan? No.

SECOND TESTIMONY OF JOHN KENDALL,
TURCOPOLIER OF THE ORDER OF
THE HOSPITAL OF ST. JOHN IN JERUSALEM,
ON THE YEARS 1485 TO 1487

AROUND 1485 THE case of Cem got so tangled up that it was not
only difficult to lead it, but even to follow it. Brother d'Aubusson had guessed rightly back in 1482 that Cem was the ultimate
bargaining chip in international relations. In short, in the years
noted above, the wretched pretender's price rose so high I don't
believe anything similar has ever happened elsewhere. We, the
ostensible owners of the living treasure in question, were sitting in Rhodes, receiving reports brought by our spies in Napoli,
Venice, Île-de-France, and Constantinople. We organized this
information, calculated our profits or losses in the case of Cem,
and tried—ever less successfully—to influence it. The case itself
was already moving in spheres high above us. Very high above us.

The most difficult thing for us about international life between 1485 and 1487 was the Turks' meddling in that life. Up
until the Conqueror, the Ottomans had been newcomers whom
no one had had anything to do with, nor had they wanted to.
The case of Cem changed that. Part of the West was now in

negotiations with the sultan, who had taken on obligations to one or another Western power to guarantee his brother's imprisonment—they had discovered certain mutual advantages. And a competition had begun immediately in that respect.

During the period in question, the major European rulers negotiated on the one hand with the pope about a crusade against Bayezid, while on the other hand, they maintained ties with the very same Bayezid; they informed him of papal intentions, assuring him they would not allow such a crusade. God only knows where the rulers of the world were being more honest: in their desire to neutralize the Turkish threat or in their desire to live with the Turks in mutually beneficial relations.

Perhaps in those years only the papacy and Matthias Corvinus were not playing both sides—they were the only ones who stood to gain nothing from peaceful coexistence with the Turks. For this reason, however, neither the pope nor Corvinus had any interest in coordinated efforts—each of them insisted on fully leading the crusade, refusing to concede any fame or spoils to the other.

If I have to describe those two years in the most general of terms, they were filled by Innocent VIII and Matthias Corvinus struggling to obtain Cem for themselves. The other states' constant negotiations with the Turks' enemies as well as the Turks themselves provided the wider backdrop for their actions.

Just as we had expected, the case of Cem heated up the atmosphere over the Old Continent; unheard-of machinations were put into play and enormous interests were at stake. Cem as a person—in fact, few knew what this person looked like, and no one thought of him as a living human being with a fate, will, and intentions of his own—had already tacitly become a common possession of sorts.

I had told you earlier we had agreed to let Innocent VIII take Cem, since his conditions were satisfactory. The pope sent a request to Charles VIII, or rather to the Royal Council, which ruled France until he reached his majority. The Council's reply to this request was vague: it would not be desirable for Cem, whom so many states and most of all Bayezid wanted to kidnap, to make a journey. The Council hinted an enormous amount of money would be needed to guarantee the safety of such an undertaking. At which point the papacy temporarily fell silent, since this was the most unsuitable moment to raise the question of money. Thus, Innocent VIII withdrew from the game, and perhaps it would have died down entirely if Matthias Corvinus had not thrown himself into the fray with desperate measures. I personally was present as one of the Order's observers in this exhausting story, and I can recount it for you in detail.

It began in the spring of 1486. We learned that Matthias Corvinus, taking advantage of his truce with Bayezid, had decided to gain possession of Cem. This news was unbelievable, yet we dutifully reported it to Rome and Venice. Above all, we wanted to warn Corvinus's rivals. Despite the indifference with which they replied to us, we could sense their panic. The pope was afraid Corvinus would steal away Cem and, in so doing, sully the authority of the Holy See, while Venice was gripped with a much more understandable fear: a war would have very negative repercussions for Levantine trade. And so, without committing outright betrayal, we knew that Sultan Bayezid, too, had already been warned.

Matthias, for his part, answered our underhanded actions with an open offensive that will long be remembered: he sent a delegation nearly a thousand strong to France. Have you ever heard of such a thing? Along the way, they were to stop in Milan, where they would arrange the engagement of Matthias's son to Bianca Sforza. A clever plan: in this way King Matthias, in attracting the Duke of Milan as an ally, drove a wedge between the Italian states. In short, he made the papacy's already difficult position in the case of Cem even more complicated.

After we learned of the king's masterful move, I had no choice but to set out for Italy to catch up with the Hungarians and to appear alongside them at the French court. Even though my mission was obvious, they could not possibly drive me away. After all, I was a member of the clergy.

When I arrived in Milan, the engagement celebrations were in full swing. The Sforzas' enormous palace, the size of a whole village, was simultaneously the most impenetrable of fortresses and the coziest of homes I have ever seen: it was richly decorated to the very top of its crenellated walls. In the evenings, there was feasting and dancing in its spacious inner courtyards, where I met several prominent Italian nobles. They were still a far cry from a full assembly, because Italy continued to be riven by wars. These lavish betrothal celebrations seemed indecent upon the ruined, stripped body of the Peninsula. But like the Medici in Florence, the Sforzas were arbiters of Italian affairs. Bianca's wedding to John Corvinus brought their house yet further prestige.

On one of the numerous evenings in the palace, I was introduced to Duke Gaetano. He lived up to the image I had created of him—slightly clumsy, but good-natured, far removed from those restless, impoverished, and stop-at-nothing Italian rulers so numerous during my era. But Duke Gaetano was not my aim—I hurried to make the acquaintance of Matthias's ambassador; incredible rumors had been circulating about János Pruisz, the Bishop of Varad, today a town in Romania known to you as Oradea. They say he was very wealthy, erudite, and clever—one of the best diplomats in Europe, if not the best.

The first thing that struck me when we were introduced was his almost unnatural beauty. Pruisz was likely my age, still a young man, athletic, with a head as I have seen only in the sculptures of antiquity. As soon as he started toward me—without dropping my gaze; it seems he, too, had very much been looking forward to this meeting—Pruisz reminded me of a military commander, even a hand-to-hand combat champion, and involuntarily, even though I considered him an adversary, I was filled with pride. Look, such men serve our church. You know nothing about the so-called clergy of my time.

We started chatting. Even from our first few words it was clear to me I was up against a very dangerous opponent. The exquisite charm of this physically and spiritually endowed man was dangerous; his undisputable perfection was dangerous, as was the fact he was fully aware of it and used it as a weapon, lure, and prize. Believe me, I met every last one of the participants in the case of Cem; not a single one of them compares to Pruisz. This explains to some extent the difficulty of my task—without suffering from low self-esteem, I nevertheless had to acknowledge Pruisz's absolute superiority.

We were standing apart from the guests, and this was to be expected: two men of God have their own, nonworldly business.

To an outside observer we surely resembled combatants before a tournament; we were studying each other, getting to know each other; we quite simply liked each other, even though we had been pitted against each other. When a man has a healthy self-respect, the one thing that truly flatters him is a worthy opponent.

We talked about the most ordinary things. Pruisz asked me about the siege of Rhodes and my part in it; he expressed great admiration and regret that he had missed it—at the same time the Hungarians had been fighting their own battles, he said, against the same enemy. But the siege of an island—that was something different and very entertaining; this was a new staging entirely and a wholly new dramaturgy, much condensed—that was exactly how he put it. I could not help but notice that in front of me stood a true artiste in his chosen field; beneath the cassock I sensed a man who lived not only with joy, not even with gusto, but rather with voluptuousness. Unwittingly I strove for mutual recognition; I tried to charm Pruisz, to be his equal. I doubt I succeeded—I don't know what would impress such a perfect man. He delighted in his own voice and movements as we spoke; with one and the same relish, he demonstrated his eloquence and strength, self-control and flexibility. Like a Croesus of sorts, he graciously allowed me to enjoy his treasures. And I felt deep jealousy, not so much of such perfection itself, but rather of the consciousness of it, of his masterful control and use of it.

We had been speaking for around an hour when János Pruisz himself suggested, "Since we are on the same route and have the same destination, brother, why don't we travel together?"

Yes, Pruisz could afford this: offering a hand to his opponent, that's how confident he was. I accepted. We set out a full

VERA MUTAFCHIEVA

month later, after the end of the betrothal celebrations. Pruisz used this month to dazzle and win over the Italian nobility. As well as to become a living idol for his fellow feasters and hosts and to make sure rumors about him had already reached Île-de-France, so we could follow the path they had cleared for him.

Even if the case of Cem had caused me three times the worries, I would nevertheless consider myself well rewarded—thanks to my journey with Pruisz in France, thanks to that half year during which that extraordinary man and I stalked and delighted in each other, battled and smiled. I know the pleasures of earthly life have long since been counted, but I don't know whether one amongst them has been emphasized in particular: the great game.

We left Milan in a strange procession—unique, I would say. It truly represented Matthias Corvinus to the fullest, that half-Eastern and at the same time very Renaissance ruler who wanted to dazzle the West. Three hundred young men from the noblest houses in Hungary made up the core of our suite. They were so alike in age and appearance to the point of absurdity. Three hundred exceptionally blond youth dressed in crimson with pearly-white wreaths and gold necklaces rode their three hundred snow-white horses, while their squires, in orange, led their raven-black change of horses.

János Pruisz watched me when I encountered that spectacle for the first time. Laughter flared up in his wondrously expressive, velvety, warm eyes. I did not know whether he was laughing at my amazement or at the cause of it, but I suspect a man like Pruisz indeed found good King Matthias's grand gesture ridiculous. Once I got over my astonishment, I started thinking it through: even if Hungary had three hundred noble families, which it didn't, and even if every one of them had a twenty-year-old son, and that would be hard to believe, how is it that they all happened to be blond? This means King Matthias searched his quite reduced lands to round up three hundred identical, handsome lads, hence at least half of them had to be peasant boys, scrubbed clean and dressed up.

I will not describe the Hungarian baggage train—more than five hundred loaded horses. *Like a traveling theater,* I thought. *King Matthias could not have found a more irresistible main character than János Pruisz.* As I watched their one and only performance, Cem slipped ever farther from my mind—what significance could a barbarian poet and failed pretender to a throne have amidst a reality such as ours?

We traveled for more than twenty days. During all those days I never saw a sweat stain upon the blond boys' crimson cloaks, nor dust on their boots. The procession wound its way through the passes of Northern Italy and the hills of Southern France, every bit as colorful and impeccably magnificent as it had begun. Shortly past Lyon we were met by Admiral de Graville.

You might ask what an admiral was doing on dry land, because you are ignorant: Admiral de Graville represented the much-talked-about regent Anne de Beaujeu. Her infinite greed was well-known, as was the fact that to achieve her ends, she was willing to risk everything, including the crown's honor. We knew she even lied in her confessions, according to her confessor, who could compare confessions with facts and inform us of both. As for the admiral, he governed France in that most common of capacities—as the regent's lover. More gullible types hinted he had come to power via her bed, but we were not fooled: the lady had brought him to her bed because she found him the most promising among the French leaders at hand. And given her enemies—the Duke of Bourbon, her dear brother-in-law, alone was enough—having a strong back and two clever hands was more than crucial.

The fact that de Graville himself met us was very significant: France was paying high honors to King Matthias. With me, the admiral acted quite reserved; surely I looked very pale indeed compared to Pruisz.

Since the young king and his sister, the regent in question, were spending the summer at the Château d'Ancenis, they led us there. A spectacle worthy of the gods: that was our entrance into Ancenis. Too bad Matthias Corvinus was not with us— what food for his vanity it was! Our procession, the likes of which no one had ever seen, streamed into the chateau's deep-set entrance for half an hour. It screamed with every color in the soft grayness of that northern summer, until dark-gray Ancenis resembled a deep, antique cup splashing, sparkling, and overflowing with crimson-orange wine.

They all came out onto the steps to meet us: Charles VIII, a sickly child grown old before his time, and his Council, along with Madame de Beaujeu, a rather dry, ash-colored woman of a dangerous age. They all struggled to keep their composure when faced with this sight, but their last drops of dignity evaporated when János Pruisz dismounted from his horse, climbed the stairs with his innate, perfectly controlled ardor, and gave a slight bow to their majesties, highnesses, and excellencies.

A purebred—that's what Pruisz was. He stood like an Arabian stallion amidst ponies scrawny beneath their expensive blankets and immediately attracted all eyes. I almost laughed aloud at the lady. She was sizing up her guest with undisguised avarice—women have such eyes when they have but little time left for sin—and a mix of desire, delight, and hatred.

In the evening, once the guests had rested, I was present at an Eastern spectacle: János Pruisz presenting King Matthias's gifts. Some of this show took place outside—there, the Hungarians led out the horses. They were of three kinds, twenty-five each. The remaining gifts clearly anticipated Madame de Beaujeu's taste for extreme luxury. One after the other, the Hungarians brought into the hall several trunks full of dishes made of the laciest porcelain, clothes spun of pure gold thread, jewelry so encrusted with gems that it burned the eyes. And, finally, as the coup de grace: a bedroom set case of pure gold, or at least thickly gilded.

I found something almost laughable in all that magnificence, which looked as if meant for Attila or Tamerlane. But the French court, and above all the regent, did not share my opinion. I noticed that King Matthias's generosity stunned her, especially in combination with the exceptional charm of his ambassador. Madame de Beaujeu's heart melted to such an extent that she, in turn, was equally extravagant in her feasts, dances, and entertainments. Thus I came to realize: we needed to act immediately; every minute Pruisz spent at Ancenis was a pure loss for us.

On the third morning after our arrival, I secretly sent a messenger to Brother d'Aubusson. In my letter I insisted two of Cem's men—the most trustworthy ones, of course—immediately be sent to France to ready him for the plan we had long since hatched. Additionally, one of our men needed to leave for Venice right away and warn the Republic that Cem would very likely be handed over to King Matthias. We knew all of Venice's reckonings and its close ties with Bayezid—Venice would do everything in its power to prevent Matthias Corvinus's success. In such a case, Venice would be working to the papacy's advantage, albeit unintentionally.

After carrying out this duty, I stood by and witnessed Pruisz's further endeavors in high spirits. And they were indeed inexhaustible. János Pruisz truly invested all his charm and talent in dazzling France. His eloquence won over everyone he spoke to; his wide-ranging knowledge, wealth, and generosity made the court see in Hungary some elevated, flourishing country, Lord only knows how. Pruisz spared no expense. He did not even spare himself, to achieve his ends.

Strangely, he did not succeed within the first ten days; the Royal Council benevolently heard out his arguments and accepted his gifts, yet dragged things out. And this is why: entangled in a war with the English, the French were afraid of the Holy Roman Empire, or in other words, Germany. Things were as muddled there as always; various factions struggled against one another, while the claimant to the throne, Archduke Maximilian, was a die-hard enemy of France and, in his capacity as the ruler of Flanders, was doing them daily mischief.

In short, the court was looking for a power beyond Germany to threaten its flank, while France itself settled its business with the British. And that power was none other than Hungary.

What interest would the king of France have in handing over Cem? Indeed, an alliance between France and Hungary would then not only be possible, but assured. But Corvinus, having gotten ahold of Cem, would throw himself into a war with the Turks, leaving the Germans at peace, while France would find itself between two fires. And if the Council refused to hand over Cem, the break with Hungary would be complete. So, the French court did the only thing it could to protect its interests: it dragged its heels. And during that time—a whole six months— János Pruisz scattered his gold and his charm all around, from Ancenis to Paris and back to Ancenis again, burning with impatience, and later with fury as well, smiling at the lady and her lover, the bloodless little king and his ministers. He invariably treated me well, as if our shared misfortunes around Cem made us brothers.

Incidentally, from August 1487, it was no longer just two of us, a third had arrived: the Venetian ambassador. In Ancenis we looked upon him as an interloper; he had joined our competition late and could not play on equal footing. But we also sensed he held an advantage: he alone out of the three of us did not want Cem for his master, but rather constantly advised the Council to keep Cem for France.

By September we—Pruisz and I—were convinced this is precisely what would happen. A frostiness crept into the Council's attitude toward us. The lady no longer tossed hungry glances at Pruisz, while the admiral took his leave with restraint and headed to the battlefield in Brittany—they had suddenly begun to feel his absence keenly. It was only now that Pruisz lost patience: the court had gone too far. The Bishop of Varad started to go off on his own, hunting and traveling; in the evenings he sat in society not at all the cheerful charmer he had once been, and from his hints he made it known Hungary would seek an alliance with Germany.

No one had any right to be angry—not with him, even less so with King Matthias, who in September ordered the delegation's return. Hungary's largest and most expensive attempt to win Cem had ended unsuccessfully. Despite this order, Pruisz made one last entirely desperate attempt. He appeared before the Royal Council with a speech so masterful that Cicero himself would have envied it, in which he spelled out the consequences of France's shortsightedness: it would leave Bayezid's hands free to launch victorious wars in Italy and Central Europe; it would deal a heavy blow to Levantine trade, leaving the Old Continent exposed to horrors not seen since Attila's invasion. It was not merely oratorical mastery; Pruisz's speech held sincere conviction, a prophetic fire that made even me, his rival, shudder. Thus I was disconcerted by the terse retort. The Archbishop of Bourdeaux, the other de Graville, the admiral's brother, said, "Don't forget, Your Grace, it was the French who stopped Attila."

"Because he squandered his strength on an overly long journey, my brother." Pruisz was unperturbed.

"Sultan Bayezid will also squander his strength."

Insolence should have some limits, should it not? When the French refused to save Eastern Europe, they at least could have done it more elegantly. Why underscore that France had always been sheltered from barbarian invasions? Why make a point to emphasize that France didn't care at all about the European East's misfortunes?

At that same moment, I saw how János Pruisz could embody not only radiant goodwill; he took de Graville's words to heart just as any of those villagers whose home and land had been razed would have taken them, just as every soldier maimed in the battle against the Turks would have taken them. Harsh hatred transformed the beautiful face I so admired, and Pruisz's reply hissed like the crack of a whip.

"If, Your Grace, you were on your knees when asking for help, faced with an enemy three times your strength, likely you, too, would remember our first Christian command, 'Love thy neighbor as thyself.'"

"I don't recall, Your Grace," de Graville quickly returned the blow, "anyone helping us when we stood against the Saracens. And they were a no-less-powerful enemy."

It was more than clear: we no longer needed to fear an alliance between France and Hungary; we no longer even needed to worry about civility. King Matthias would never forgive such an insult.

János Pruisz left Ancenis during the first days of October. The court loaded him down with gifts—everyone knew they barely amounted to 300 silver marks, while Corvinus had spent at least a hundred thousand in gold on his envoy. Pruisz left the West, heading back through Lyon and Milan to lead Bianca away to her new homeland. Personally, I, who had worked to assure he failed, who had even reveled in it, felt a vague sense of guilt, the same as when Brother d'Aubusson told me he had taken money from Cem's mother. After all, we had accepted to our own great advantage countless sums and fanned countless hopes from those who were suffering in exchange for the imprisonment of one suffering even more greatly. Surely men of God think about divine retribution more rarely than any others, but at that time I definitely felt fear.

I thought to depart immediately after Pruisz, since his failure marked the end of my mission. But a letter from Brother d'Aubusson kept me for another half year in Paris. The grand master insisted I stay for many reasons; he believed I would again manage in such praiseworthy fashion when facing the next difficulties. Above all, I needed to continue watching the Venetian ambassador; Venice's behavior would change once the alliance with Hungary had failed. Besides, d'Aubusson reported that Cem had already sought an alliance with opponents of the de Gravilles, the Duke of Bourbon and his supporters. I needed to keep in mind these attempts. Finally, Brother d'Aubusson tasked me with helping in the negotiations between the papacy and France. They would begin soon; Innocent VIII had already sent his legates.

While waiting for the papal legates to arrive, I received more news from Rhodes. First, they reported Venice had already told Bayezid not to worry about Hungary; second, Ferrandino of Naples had promised Bayezid he would kidnap Cem on the road to Rome and send him to Constantinople—this was to be entirely financed by Naples, since it would deal a harsh blow to the papacy; third, Lorenzo de'Medici, France's one and only friend in Italy, was taking an active interest in the case of Cem. This last bit of news scared me—Lorenzo was a figure to be reckoned with, while his connections to the French court made his likelihood for success quite possible. In short, I did not rest even between the two major delegations' visits to Paris. Thus, when in December I set out alongside the representatives of the Royal Council to meet the papal legates, I was truly glad—I was receiving reinforcements.

The Holy Father had paid the same attention to his delegation as had Corvinus. Alas, he did not have on hand a man with Pruisz's perfections, but the two monks, Antonello Chieregato and Antonio Flores, were among the most enlightened minds in the Vatican, experienced diplomats and orators. Clearly, due to a lack of funds, the pope was accentuating the oratorical side of the matter. The legates were received with all the honors due the pope's men, very high honors, I mean to say. They immediately informed the Council that Sultan Qaitbay was ready to pay an unbelievable sum for Cem. Realizing international relations would not allow for Cem's transfer to Egypt, the sultan demanded he be sent to Rome, Florence, Venice, or Hungary. That is, as close to Turkish territory as possible. Qaitbay cleverly underscored, through the papal legates, that the West's actions up until that point had reassured Bayezid his brother would never lead an invasion because he was being used for other ends. This certainty on Bayezid's part would cost other Eastern countries dearly, including Egypt.

I was present at the Council meeting when Cardinal Flores laid out this viewpoint. I wouldn't say the French found it very convincing. The Council remained completely calm even when Flores named the sum Qaitbay offered: one hundred thousand gold ducats. The French crown had recently grown used to such enormous gifts out of nowhere, such that it no longer connected them to the case of Cem; it simply believed it deserved such riches.

"Our belief," Admiral de Graville replied, "is that the Christian world will see negotiations between the papacy and a Muslim power, Qaitbay, as unseemly. Even for two times one hundred

VERA MUTAFCHIEVA

thousand ducats we should not undermine the authority of the Holy See. This is what the Royal Council thinks."

But for ten times one hundred thousand it would think otherwise, I mused, even though it was well-known there was no country in our day that could have gathered such a sum.

De Graville's answer flustered the legates. It confirmed the suspicion that France would release Cem only in exchange for unheard-of amounts of money, and the papacy did not have such funds. Innocent VIII was using the last of his cash to win back Osimo, that small harbor near Ancona whose ruler, Boccolino, had struck a bargain with Bayezid. All of Christianity was revolted by these base negotiations—they were a pure betrayal of Italy and the West as a whole—and for that reason, Innocent had decided to begin the battle against the Turks by taking back Osimo. But the papacy's poverty did not allow even for such a petty campaign, and Roman mercenaries had already been slogging for five months beneath the walls of Osimo without any success. Incidentally, France was clearly taking advantage of this.

Then, instead of Flores, Cardinal Chieregato cut in. A great scholar, he was known as one of the most skilled orators of our time. His speech to the Royal Council confirmed this opinion beyond a shadow of a doubt.

"We are honored," he said, "to stand before the king of France. Since time immemorial, the kings of France have been famed for their laudable piety, for their responsiveness to the woes befalling united Christendom. The popes inspired your predecessors to win back the Holy Land from the infidels and to tear the Eastern Christian provinces from their grasp. French crusaders were the flower of European knighthood. Fear of God lived in people's hearts. At that time, the threat was distant, yet your kings did not strive to increase their own lands. Their only goal was to affirm the name of Christ and to win over thousands of misguided souls for the true faith. In their religious fervor, they created armies and navies, they gave everything—their sons and brothers, even their very selves—to win glory not here, but in heaven. Those warriors, those heroes of our faith, live eternally and their names are passed on through the generations. Glory, eternal glory!"

Even though I am reporting his speech word for word, you cannot imagine how Brother Chieregato uttered it. The impression he made was so strong that it held the Council spellbound. Our glorious crusaders truly paraded before our eyes—long-forgotten kings and knights from a long-forgotten time—heading with exhilaration toward their eternal life.

But suddenly Cardinal Chieregato dropped the hand raised in blessing. His whole being expressed bottomless anguish. "Today our faith has perished," he continued. "Our raptures have died. The Holy Roman Catholic Church has not sent us to you because of Jerusalem, Asia, or Greece. We are speaking of Italy itself. Things are going from bad to worse. If not for the Conqueror's death and the struggles between his sons, the fire would have long since spread to our own lands. Can't you see, you before whom we fall to our knees and beg, can't you see how quickly the Turkish threat spread from Asia to Italy? Yet there are Italians who are shortsighted enough to call in the Turk himself and sic him on the Holy See. If not for the Holy Father, Boccolino would have led Bayezid into Osimo a month ago, launching his victory over Italy. But Italy is not strong enough to deal with the danger; for this reason the Holy Father turns to united Christendom. How can Christendom fight when it is torn apart by wars between kings and city-states, between neighbors who share a common faith?

"The Holy Father has sent us so that we, too, might help you to bring peace to your Majesty's lands as well. Once the hostilities die down, France will have fulfilled its Christian duty of turning all its efforts toward the war against the Turks. A crucial figure assures us victory in this fight: the sultan's brother. We invite you to hand him over to us. Because as soon as the pope possesses Cem, Bayezid will not undertake his sinister attacks on Italy. The Holy Father is certain you will not refuse to help your spiritual mother. She is begging and pleading with you. What's more, Pierre d'Aubusson, who made Cem his prisoner, has added his prayers to ours, and the prisoner himself supports them. Your father—may the memory of his greatness reign eternal—promised Cem to the Holy See. The papacy is now asking you, Your Highness, and awaits your answer."

When Brother Chieregato fell silent, I noticed that more than one royal councilman discretely blew his nose; the young king's eyes glistened with tears. Only Madame de Beaujeu was not moved to tears, but in all fairness, even she showed signs of agitation. No matter how deeply secular depravity had seeped into our times, the memory of the triumph of our faith, the reproach that she lacked warriors, did its job—the French royals were ashamed of their own baseness.

But it is a well-known fact that feelings come and go quickly; and indeed, that flash of goodwill lasted all too briefly. Even though the admiral promised to hand over Cem after that memorable speech, on the very next day he once again started talking about the dangers of such a journey, pointing to Venetian intelligence.

We again came to the question of the price—again the price of Cem. The French did not offer any clear indications in that direction. They simply recalled history had never before seen a personage of such importance for the Old Continent's future. From this general train of thought, I concluded France was determined to keep Cem for itself for a long time yet—it was leverage for all its foreign relations and it only made sense to wait for its price to rise even higher. At the end of the day, the French had no reason to hurry.

Admiral de Graville, casually in passing during a conversation, mentioned that his own brother, the Archbishop of Bourdeaux, a man with so many good qualities, deserved a cardinal's rank. I hurried to report this to Innocent VIII, begging him to consider de Graville's wish. I did not expect His Holiness to reply so harshly. *How could you have thought*, he wrote, *the papacy would ordain yet another Frenchman; wasn't it enough that the French didn't care a whit about the Holy See, while the legates were still in Paris, and with their presence essentially sanctifying the actions of the Council? That was more than they deserved already. Let them not hope for more; de Graville and his whole family were usurpers and tyrants.*

Aha, what news His Holiness has given me, I could say, as if I hadn't already known the de Gravilles were highway robbers. Wasn't that exactly the reason we had to win them over?

I really would have liked to have seen His Holiness's face when I sent him the following request from the Council, as it truly went above and beyond all limits: the French wanted the pope to refuse to confirm Maximilian's selection as emperor of Germany. Because, as I noted earlier, even back in our day the French were afraid of German violence, and Maximilian looked very promising in that regard. But even if he had wanted to, Innocent VIII had no way of doing such a thing. Indeed, Maximilian's forefathers had lain in the dust before Canossa until they received the pope's blessing, but those were different times, for God's sake. Now an interdict would only enrage Maximilian, who needed but little encouragement to fly into a rage, and it would show Germany could be governed—and completely successfully at that—without the pope's blessing.

Perhaps my request not to send such harsh messages to Paris, since no real sanctions stood behind them, inspired Innocent to reply that he would defuse Maximilian without pronouncing an anathema against him. The pope simply issued a decree announcing that in Flanders and Lotharingia—the German territories bordering on France—all deals, such as buying, selling, contracts, and inheritances, would henceforth be invalid, while all sentencing of criminals would be illegal. The courts and notary publics there lost their right to swear binding oaths and to hand down sentences.

Why are you laughing? This time Innocent showed he was wise. Without mentioning Maximilian's name, the pope made his life impossible. Can you imagine a state where there are no valid laws? The Flemish had no choice but to rise up in rebellion and throw off Maximilian's rule.

I get the sense I am now going into details that have no bearing on your work. But at least I hope they demonstrate how complicated and difficult my time was. I hope you at least understand how many contradictory interests were interwoven in the case of Cem, turning it into the true question of questions during the fifteenth century.

The papal legates remained in Paris until the spring of 1487, even though their chances of getting Cem decreased by the day. Madame de Beaujeu swore to her confessor that she desired the eternal bliss of handing Cem over to the pope, but the Council impeded her; the Council depicted de Graville as a godless tyrant, while de Graville assured us a kidnapping attempt on Cem would almost surely succeed if we were to undertake it.

Thus, in April 1487, it became clear that the Royal Council was playing with us—the Holy Church—as far as Cem Sultan was concerned. Brother d'Aubusson wrote that my stay in Paris had become superfluous; Chieregato and Flores would continue their wrangling without me, and without any prospects of success, the grand master noted. While Brother d'Aubusson had need of me to help him think through an idea of his: using brute force in the case of Cem. Because we had no time, and Cem's price was rising with every passing day.

You will likely be shocked when I tell you the brute-force weapon we used was a woman.

VERA MUTAFCHIEVA

PART THREE

TWELFTH TESTIMONY OF THE POET SAADI
ON THE YEARS 1485 TO 1487

HER NAME WAS Hélène, Philippine-Hélène more precisely. Actually, this testimony will take you back a bit further with respect to Monsignor Kendall's words, because my previous story ended with our first escape attempt. While the world was experiencing the events the monsignor described, we spent our days and nights, whole months, in Bois-Lamy, the Order's fortress in the Dauphiné.

I have already mentioned the brothers arranged daily entertainment for us. Of course, the Dauphiné nobles were tight-lipped about the questions that keenly interested us, yet I nevertheless managed to interpret words that slipped out here and there. My conclusion, derived from such slips, smiles, and our fellow feasters' excessive respect, was that Cem's significance had not waned. This was also clear from our guards' behavior—they followed our every move and searched and interrogated every newcomer arriving at Bois-Lamy.

For Cem, the Order's increasing scrutiny grew ever more unbearable, because it epitomized the "respect" that surrounded him in its most precise sense—that of surveillance. He became extremely irritable, lashing out at my gentlest remarks or ignoring with annoyance my attempts to soothe him. The brothers' mocking attitude toward our escape attempt infuriated him; Cem would have preferred they lock him up and take away his inkhorn and paper—then at least he could feel as if he had done something that had threatened the Order. While, in fact, everything continued as before: they entertained us and tried to lull us to sleep.

Likely because we could sense this attempt of theirs, we resisted it; we eavesdropped, we sought contact with the world beyond Bois-Lamy, we struggled to understand the ways of the West, since we needed to reckon with them. During the time between 1485 and 1487, we had still not given up. I suspect this made things difficult for our jailers to some extent, but let us not exaggerate their challenges—despite all our efforts, we remained amateurs among hardened professionals.

Philippine-Hélène came into our lives exactly at that time. I would not say she was the first woman allowed into our company, but she was not the hundredth either, believe me. As a rule, we rarely saw women. They were either the wives of the noblemen who took us in for a night, a week, or a month, or the innkeepers along our journey. We were the guests of a monastic order. Dancing girls were out of the question. Incidentally, we had heard that in the West they were still a rarity; men normally provided society's entertainment. Once in a while we might catch a glimpse of a lady on our hunts, again some signor's wife or his daughter. What made an impression on us was the men's attitude toward them.

You will find it strange that during those years of stress and suffering we discussed something with so little bearing on our fate as the West's attitude toward women. True, but it imposed itself upon us, shocked us, and seemed the most striking difference between everyday life in our homeland and here.

I recall the first time I noticed it. We were hunting in Savoy. Madame So-and-So was riding with us, some husband's wife. She rode lightly, despite her age and weight, and with every step of the horse's hooves her breasts—revealed in a plunging décolleté—bounced beneath the gazes of thirty or so men. Madame was sitting sidesaddle and one hem of her skirts was tucked into her belt, such that we could see not only her ankles but even her calf, ending in a pretty, rounded knee.

At the beginning of the hunt, Madame rode by her husband, but no one found it indecent that she later mixed with the hunting party, trading jokes with this one and that one, laughing loudly, her cheeks flushed by the various challenges of hunting. Cem was staring at her, not entranced by her charms, but in astonishment. The spectacle reached its peak when we returned to the castle and Madame went to dismount her horse. A young man stepped toward her—he was nothing to her, that much was clear—and let her lean on him bodily. The lady first stepped on his shoulder, then on his outstretched palm and then—as he bent down to set her on the ground— she simply clung to him with all her skirts, petticoats, and sweaty proximity, laughing with an open throat.

I thought something terrible would happen: the young man's face was only a span away from her bare breasts, while her husband was busy with his horse only a few steps away—such an outrage could not go unpunished. Yet the lady calmly let down her skirts and without a word headed into the castle alongside the men.

Cem stood by the horses, thunderstruck. "Saadi," he said, "did you see that? How's that for morals, hm? What shamelessness! These people will need centuries to catch up with us. They have not yet developed even the most fundamental human trait: decorum."

Later both Cem and I grew used to the West's oddities. We even began to think what a powerful thing habit is—indeed, with respect to women, here, too, one can observe a sort of decorum, even a complex, almost ritualistic attitude. We saw how our fellow feasters would leap to their feet as soon as a lady entered the hall, how they would immediately relinquish the most prominent place to her and fall all over themselves to be of service to her. We heard how they would often shower even the plainest of women with compliments, bowing and taking them by the hand. We even heard songs praising female beauty, if you can believe it! These people truly did not blush to shine broad daylight on the most sweet and sacred thing in their lives. We simply could not imagine how they were capable of delight, since they squandered it by making a public show of it—like allowing hundreds to peer into your bed.

Incidentally, this only further strengthened our conviction that only as many women dined at our table as had desired to do so. It was obvious: no one had deliberately selected or rejected them. We were forced to admit our company likely did not attract the ladies of Savoy and the Dauphiné. We surmised this from brief comments here and there. They revealed that our customs—or rather, their idea of our customs—provoked here the same disgusted bewilderment as we felt about theirs. The West was full of offensive fabrications about our behavior toward our women. After all, it is not true, is it, that we despise or torment women? We simply believe each one is such a precious part of every man's life that she should not be put on display, as if on offer.

I think precisely such false beliefs about the East caused local noblemen to bar their wives and daughters from our company—they were afraid we would disrespect them. Those who did come near us did so out of curiosity. We could read it in their wide eyes, in the exclamations that accompanied Cem's every move, in their smiles—either haughty or mocking. Those few daring women were observing a rare Eastern animal, and I could sense they were struggling to contain their impressions until out of our earshot; once safely away from us, I imagine tales were being told that did little to flatter us.

We were surprised when Baron de Sassenage, a neighboring nobleman, visited us at Bois-Lamy along with his daughter. The baron was a husky, gray-haired man, with a clearly difficult temperament, reticent, yet sharp-tongued when he did speak. From his suite it was clear he was not rich. How he treated his daughter—the Hélène in question—did not quite follow the rules: it was contradictory. On the one hand, the baron often cut her off with cruel contempt as she spoke or laughed. Yet on the other hand, immediately thereafter he would give her a look filled with pained guilt, trying, indeed trying too hard, to elevate her in the eyes of others. To us, both one and the other were in bad taste—foisting such complicated parental emotions on society was unwarranted.

What can I tell you about Hélène herself? Our opinions about women surely differ quite a bit from yours. I personally did not find Hélène beautiful. We prefer more striking women. Everything about her—her eyes, nose, mouth, neck—had clean outlines, but was not at all notable. Indeed, Hélène's misfortune lay in her body; in our lands it would be difficult to marry off a daughter with such a figure. Madame de Sassenage was quite simply flat—this was clear even beneath her stiff, excessively pleated clothing; it was clear from her too-thin wrists and ankles. Despite this, what I found attractive about her—and not in a womanly way, but rather in a simply curiosity-piquing way—was impossible to define. She gave you the feeling she was a person like you, that thoughts and doubts passed behind her smooth forehead, that her little mouth was making an effort to stay silent. Precisely some kind of forced reticence set her apart from all other women I had met and caused me to suspect Hélène had either weighty memories or weighty premonitions—in short, too much weight for such a frail woman. Yet at the same time I could see this fragility was an illusion—at times Hélène's looks and movements recalled her father. Not his words; most often she sat in oppressed and oppressive silence, as if those around her were unbearably irritating.

Cem noticed Hélène during our very first meeting with de Sassenage. Throughout the dinner he openly studied her, but without a hint of admiration; he was amused by the presence of a young woman. While I was amused by the looks she shot back at him: very calm looks, above all, as if Hélène spoke with Turkish sultans every day—they expressed neither curiosity nor sympathy. The other strange thing was Hélène did not play games with her eyes. She put nothing unsaid or mysterious in her gaze to ensnare you, nor anything arrogant to set up a barrier.

"Saadi," Cem asked me when we got back after the dinner, "what kind of bird is de Sassenage's daughter?"

"A plain one," I replied. "And besides, she seems beyond the decent age for a nobleman's unmarried daughter."

"You're right. Surely she must be twenty-five."

The next morning and for several mornings thereafter, Hélène took part in our hunts. I was struck by the fact that she loved to ride not amidst the hunting party, but off to the side. She rode with a fury, as if the galloping, and not the hunt itself, allowed her to open up and free herself.

"Hélène!" The baron would call out to her at such times with nothing but concern. "Easy now, Hélène!"

She did not hear him, or pretended not to hear him, and when she again returned to the hunters, her expression would be more distant than ever.

On the third hunt, I did not fail to notice how Cem sought to be near her. He kept his horse slightly ahead of or behind hers and shot her amused glances—that was all he could do without a translator.

It is well-known that any woman is flattered by any man's attention—this means nothing in and of itself. Yet Hélène did not seem to obey this rule. Perhaps precisely because she accepted Cem's attention, both naturally and indifferently, he was driven to her. One day, as we were returning to Bois-Lamy, I saw my master leap from his saddle and head over to Hélène's horse. He offered up his shoulder and palm to help her down. Cem blushed from the awkwardness, but Hélène smiled for the first time, a crooked smile, not the kind a woman uses to mark her conquest.

The others were staring at them. They were already laughing out loud, very happy they had turned the Turk to their own shameful lack of morals, they were laughing in encouragement, but also with a nasty tone, it seemed to me. This snapped Cem back to his dignity, and he was silent during the dinner. That evening he sat close to Hélène, and I discovered something shared in their silence—the shared insult, I believe. Don't imagine a pair of lovers always shares everything: tastes, desires, judgments. Every person is made so differently it is an absolute miracle if he finds even a bit of common ground with another at all. That evening I sensed it vaguely, while later I came to know it: that shared insult had bonded Cem and Hélène.

At the dinner, Baron de Sassenage was unusually agitated. It was as if he were catching our fellow feasters' knowing glances, as if he were afraid of again hearing their posthunt laughter. I don't think I'm overestimating my own abilities, but I've always had a sense for others' feelings; I noticed then the elderly petty nobleman was horrified of human laughter. Or human mockery—I still wasn't sure.

The next morning the baron left, taking his daughter with him. That was as it should be, usually guests visited us for only so long: a week. But I kept thinking something had made the baron hurry away. We saw them out into the courtyard, as was expected. Cem did not speak to them. He nodded in response to de Sassenage's bow and remained standing upright, somehow foolishly, when the nobleman's daughter curtsied.

Several days passed. Life at Bois-Lamy went on as before. Yet I found Cem changed. His mood had become unstable, he swung between dreamy stupors and outbursts, as if he were trying to convince me of his illness. That most ancient of illnesses, well-known since time immemorial: he had fallen in love.

He did not speak of this to me, and I could guess why. Everyone knows human affection is fleeting. But no one, when they fall out of love, admits the same law applies to the opposite party as well; everyone thinks the other continues to love him as before, and this has been the cause of many sad misunderstandings. Thus, a person tries to hide the end of his own love from the other—he is afraid of killing the once beloved, while the other side is doing the exact same thing. This is what Cem was experiencing; he hid his new love, which had come to replace ours, for fear of destroying me. So I brought it up: "I wonder if Madame de Sassenage is home yet?"

Cem looked at me, stunned. Funny how we think we are unreadable.

"What made you think of her?"

He tried to dodge the topic, but his selfish desire to talk about Hélène immediately won out. I could sense slight disappointment in Cem: this change in his affections had not killed me, I had not even taken it too hard.

"Could you have understood everything, Saadi? You're not angry with me, are you? You would have the right to be, you and I used to think the same about women. About our women"—my newfound admirer of women corrected himself—"they are different here, Saadi, aren't they? Every woman is somehow separate, unique."

"Who knows?" I could not resist a bit of revenge. "Perhaps our women, too, were separate and unique, but we simply saw them too generally."

"No, but Hélène..."

I knew what would follow; I had been the confidant of more than one besotted lover. Cem would now try to convince me for hours of how singular Madame de Sassenage was, that's what I had to look forward to.

I must admit, Cem did not bore me too much over the following months at Bois-Lamy. Even if lacking a sense of reality and completely in thrall of his imagination, he realized his sudden love for Hélène had no future. They didn't even allow him to have his own servants, let alone a woman. I was afraid he would take it very badly—after all, even animals were not deprived of their females; now Cem would be truly undone—he would be eaten up by his new, male hunger.

This did not happen, thank God! For a week or two Cem spoke to me constantly about Madame de Sassenage, he found either too much or too little joy in life. He was snapped out of his sweet suffering by the rumor that Matthias's envoy had arrived in France to demand Cem from the king. And so this as-of-yet-unblossomed love was nipped in the bud, without catastrophes.

Imagine what this news meant to us, what anticipation, fear, and impatience it sent us into! Now or never, we would escape from captivity—God, please let it be now and not never.

We could not learn anything more through our eavesdropping. After all, the Order did everything it could to make it difficult for news to reach us in Bois-Lamy. We spent some exceptionally feverish months, a half year.

By the late summer of 1486, Pruisz had not achieved anything, or at least not anything we knew of. I don't know how he took this failure, but we took it terribly hard—Cem literally stopped eating and sleeping. With cajoling I forced him to choke down a bite or two under the brothers' watchful eyes; they observed us very carefully during the following months, yet without showing any outward concern.

One morning, when we saw two dozen horsemen enter Bois-Lamy, we lost all semblance of calm: Had Pruisz finally succeeded? No, and no again—most of the riders were Hospitallers. I had begun to think they were half the world's population, since we only ever saw black cloaks with a white cross on the left breast. But amidst the Hospitallers arriving at Bois-Lamy, there were two others who looked vaguely familiar, dressed like Turks.

"Saadi!" Cem clutched at my sleeve, as if he were about to faint. "I can't believe my eyes. It's... it's Sinan and Ayas!"

It really was them. Our loyal friends whom the brothers had dragged away three years earlier. For three years we hadn't known whether they were alive or dead—we had long since stopped believing the Order's assurances. And now we had lived to see them again. I stood still, fearing it was a dream. Cem ran toward his men, showering them with incoherent questions, hugging them, almost sobbing from happy excitement. I then drew closer. Ayas and Sinan greeted me with reserve—or so it seemed to me—and I must admit they were very, very changed.

True, they were older than we were, near forty, but a man of forty is not yet old, while in front of me stood old men. With identical waxy pale skin, with identical gray hair—they radiated a kind of guilty resignation.

This is not a good sign—the thought jolted me. The resurrection of one you'd given up for dead and remembered with love and affection is never a good sign. The gap between death and resurrection has already made many insurmountable changes to both you and the resurrected one. Cem did not seem to notice this, which shocked me; he kept hugging Ayas and Sinan in ecstasy as he led them toward his chambers. His bedroom was suddenly full to bursting—for years it had only been the two of us, while now two times two felt like a crowd.

Our guests sat cross-legged on the pillows on the floor. They started talking about their long journey. They had come from Rhodes, where all our men, or at least those who had survived, had been taken. Ayas Bey was telling us all this. A soft, happy smile settled onto Cem's face; he was glad to hear our language from someone besides me, he was glad fate had returned some of his own to him. Yet all of a sudden—I did not miss this, since Cem's thoughts mirrored my own—Cem snapped out of his reverie. His suspicions had been awakened; our life in recent years had been only suspicion and fear. Cem started listening distractedly, as if preparing for one of the Order's endless games.

Ayas was telling us about our men on Rhodes. They hadn't treated them too badly, they wanted for nothing—Brother d'Aubusson personally made sure of that. But Ayas did not look us in the eye as he spoke, while Sinan Bey was absorbed in beating the dust out of the skirts of his robe. Cem lost his patience at that point.

"Ayas Bey," he began with a difficulty that made him go from pale to flushed, "why do I get the feeling the two of you didn't live so well on Rhodes? In three years you've caught up with your father. Perhaps this is due to d'Aubusson's care?"

Ayas not only did not look up, he bowed his head further and gave a hollow reply. "I assure you, my sultan, our men live well on Rhodes. We want for nothing."

"But why are you still on Rhodes? Why couldn't they return you home?"

"It was our choice, my sultan. In Turkey, Bayezid would kill us."

"Then why not Hungary? Matthias Corvinus would gladly take in my men."

"We did not want to go to Hungary, my sultan. We did not want to."

Here Ayas Bey gave Cem such a despairing, pleading look. *Why are you tormenting me?* his eyes said. *What more do you need, isn't it clear?* Cem fell silent. For a long time no one dared speak, any word would have been merciless.

"It's cruel," Cem finally said, somehow gathering his strength. "It is cruel they have taken this, too, away from me: trust in my own men. Understand me well, Ayas Bey. Both you and I have suffered enough to speak man-to-man. I cannot believe you, and I will not believe you. I can only imagine what your loyalty to me has cost you, and I do not blame you for not holding out. The ones who remained loyal—I will never see them again, just as I have not seen them since our parting. You can stay silent; I know they are dead. I didn't learn this from you, Ayas Bey."

Cem went over to the aged, drained man who had once been Ayas and put his hands on the man's shoulders. This was absolution and at the same time, a rueful plea for forgiveness.

"Believe me, Ayas Bey, I am deeply glad to see you both. But I will speak to you as d'Aubusson's messengers, I will sense behind your every word lies and blackmail. They've changed your language, and perhaps your thoughts as well, my friends. I have now learned what fear is and what it can lead to. But I dare to hope they have not changed your hearts: while we try to fool one another, you will love me as I love you. Not everything is controlled by fear, is it, Saadi?"

Cem turned to me. It had been a long time since I had seen him as that once-bright Cem from Karamania. These emotions seemed to have purified him.

Cem relaxed and smiled, and, slightly amused, asked Ayas Bey, "What does Brother d'Aubusson want from me?"

Stunned, Ayas did not reply immediately. He seemed to realize his master had not suffered any less than he had since he took their defection so lightly.

"I find you changed as well, my sultan," he said, apropos of nothing.

"Come on, do what you were sent to do, Ayas Bey," Cem replied.

And Ayas did it. Very dispassionately; another was speaking through him, after all. He informed Cem that Pruisz's envoy had failed—everyone had allied against Hungary, even the papacy had joined with Venice and the Medici to hinder any campaign that would help the Balkans. But even if this hadn't been the case, Pruisz still wouldn't have succeeded; France refused to let Cem go—due to purely self-interested reasons, Ayas made sure to underscore.

"Oh yes! While the papacy wants me for purely noble reasons," Cem said.

"Master." Ayas spoke with more feeling now. "Please understand that now it would be best for you to go to Italy. The Hungarians will not receive you in any case. The West will never allow the rebirth of Serbia, Byzantium, and Bulgaria, and a victory by Corvinus would mean exactly that. Your only choice is between France and the papacy. Unlike France, Italy is directly threatened; it will very soon be at war with Bayezid, and then your moment to lead will come. Here, they will keep you your whole life, like the hen that lays the golden eggs. You don't believe me? Fine. But believe Qaitbay and your mother!"

Ayas handed Cem several scrolls and fell silent as Cem hungrily read them, forgetting the rest of us. His reading seemed to go on too long. Suddenly, letting the papers slide from his hands, he squeezed his temples with both hands and did not say, but rather groaned, "I can't even trust my mother, Saadi! Leave me, get out of here, get the hell out of here!"

To hell with your get the hell out of here! Ayas Bey had been sent to do a job his life depended on. I can't say whether he was truly moved by Cem's suffering or merely tormented by fear of the black brotherhood, but Ayas Bey found the only words needed at that moment.

"Think of us, my sultan. Fifteen of our living, breathing men are still in their hands."

Slowly, very slowly Cem awoke. *God Almighty*, I told myself. *How long will they keep demanding more and more from him. How* long will they force him to take part in his own punishment? Is there no end to human methods for torturing another human being?

There is no end, I answered myself. *If he is truly a human being, they will blackmail him with everything they can, by threatening him not with his own death, but with torture of his loved ones. Thus, he will even take part in his own well-planned, well-organized murder.*

"What does Brother d'Aubusson want from me?" Cem asked again. Feeble, resigned, once again indifferent.

"To answer your mother and Qaitbay, my sultan. More precisely, to give me two more blank pages with your signature. And then, most importantly: don't resist when they kidnap you."

"What? The brothers foiled four of my escape attempts. Who will kidnap me? Duke Charles, Corvinus, who?"

"No, my sultan. The brothers themselves will kidnap you. You have no idea—the Order is no longer your jailer. Tell me, my sultan, have you not noticed any changes?"

"No," Cem replied with an empty gaze.

"Have you not had unusual meetings during hunts, in the nearby forests or on the roads?"

"Is this an interrogation, Ayas?"

"You misunderstand me, my sultan. But I did not think the new circumstances in Bois-Lamy would remain so well hidden. The area around the castle is swarming with the king's troops. They are quartered both in the village down below, as well as in the more distant villages, sometimes in disguise. The woods you hunt in are full of ambushes. In any direction a few days' ride from Bois-Lamy, large bands of guards keep watch every night over the paths, the bridges, and the passes. The royals no longer want you to be the Order's possession, my sultan."

"Possession!" Cem burst out, jumping up and pacing around his chambers. "Possession... For the first time someone has said it to my face. Thank God it was you, Ayas, because I'd sworn to strangle the first who dared. It would be foolish... it would be terribly petty. There is no revenge for turning a living person into a possession."

"That is exactly why the Order will take revenge on the king, as long as you don't hinder them from kidnapping you, my sultan," Ayas said after some time, having waited for Cem to cool down. "You still have no idea of true imprisonment. I don't want to scare you. The king would lock you up behind bars; after all, he doesn't need your cooperation, only Bayezid's money...."

"Be silent, Ayas, be silent," Cem interrupted him weakly. He was again on one of his downswings. "The Order will take revenge for me! The Order will free me! All human existence is a mockery, Ayas...."

"Still, my sultan"—Ayas was now drenched in cold sweat—"I must return with your answer."

"The only thing allowed to us"—Cem had not heard Ayas's plea—"is this: to refuse to agree. I know my refusal changes nothing of the mockery that has been made of me, of my mother, of the fate of thousands of people—even if I am not written in the annals of any country—but I will still be a human being as long as I refuse to agree.... Give them this answer, Ayas Bey: do what you want, but Cem Sultan does not agree."

He was now speaking with his forehead pressed to the wall, his back to us, as if turning his back on all of existence. "I will not be surprised if tomorrow Cem Sultan leads a campaign, not against the threatened Southeast, but simply a crusade against the Turks.... What a wonderful sight that would be! The son of the man who lived to impose the crescent upon the cross now rides beneath Christian banners and psalms.... He could even wear a cloak with a cross over his heart...."

Now, breaking his silence, Sinan Bey cut in. "God is one, and there is no other," he said, refusing to meet our gaze. "Since that is the case, both we and they serve Him. Just under different signs, isn't that right?"

"I hope they plated the Conqueror's coffin thickly enough with lead, I hope they buried him deeply enough," Cem was now speaking to himself, "so he will not see what I have come to."

The next morning Sinan and Ayas, dressed as Christians— that's how the brothers outfitted them—headed north. Despite Cem's refusal, they would seek out the Duke of Bourbon, the king's most powerful enemy, to offer him the chance to join Innocent VIII's side in the case of Cem.

VERA MUTAFCHIEVA

TESTIMONY OF PHILIPPINE-HÉLÈNE DE SASSENAGE,
WHO TOOK THE VEIL UNDER THE NAME MAGDALENE,
ON THE EVENTS OF THE SUMMER OF 1486

I SEE MY fate has dogged me even down through the centuries. It is not customary for a true lady to be entangled in legal inquests, but, apparently, you have found out: there is no need to stand on ceremony with me. Indeed, no one stood on ceremony with me even when I was alive. Need I explain why? Because of Gerard. No, no, do not apologize for taking me back to memories that might be painful. I was forced to repeat the story, to offer justifications and repent for Gerard so many times it no longer pains me. In every person, suffering has its limits, beyond which it turns to pure spite. My limit was not so large, it seems.

Anyway. At the age of twenty-one, I, the daughter of the Baron de Sassenage, entered into a criminal liaison with his squire. A criminal liaison—I heard this characterization so many times that in my head it has replaced the original description: love. I don't know whether I would have abandoned myself to it had I known what it would cost me. But everything around me convinced me I was not doing anything out of the ordinary. My time, my milieu, and my family were not particularly chaste.

Pardon? It is not proper for a woman to make such statements? Just what kind of woman am I? Woman—this is what I thought during those long years in which I was left to my thoughts alone—is a creature just like man, yet one whom everyone requires to play some kind of role. And women play this role at a very high price. Fine, in my case, this necessity fell away; I had mistaken my role from the very beginning and had no way of ever making up for the bad impression once made.

I repeat: our life was not a shining example of chastity. The masters of the household—fathers, husbands, brothers—would disappear for months, if not years, swept up in their manly duties; their place was not in the home. Women remained at home, surrounded—so as to be protected and served—by a gaggle of boys, immature, not so much in terms of age, as in terms of provenance, for the aforementioned deeds. There was a tacit understanding that noblewomen did not occupy themselves solely with embroidering velvet while their husbands were away. Our life presented us with quite varied temptations, as well as quite certain comforts during those months of solitude. The ladies' only concern was for secrecy. This was not difficult. In the domestic world there was an unspoken alliance against those who were out seeing the world. It likely was grounded in envy and dependence, yet it was unshakeable.

Our house was not wealthy and thus meager in terms of servants. For his whole life, my father, the second son of the House of Sassenage, had to be satisfied with his wife's, my mother's, castle, and put up with her brother, his wife, and his children.

He avoided them—we rarely saw Baron de Sassenage among us, thus it is no wonder his sons, my two brothers, also left to see the world. One died young in Naples's war against the papacy, while the last news we had of the other was that he had entered into service with King Matthias. Thus, I was left as the sole heiress of the castle. I emphasize this, because it, to some extent, explains why my sin remained unforgiven amidst thousands of equally egregious sins.

I would prefer not to speak of what happened with Gerard—it does not bear on the case of Cem, and I insist on keeping at least a bit of my life for myself alone. Gerard was a squire. Even to this day I am not sure whether I desired him truly with love, since he was so immeasurably far below me. But he was young and handsome, and our three months together have remained simply as sense memories.

But they caught us. Or rather, my uncle did. My father was again somewhere far away. Back then I didn't understand why my uncle made such a large fuss about the whole story, why he so loudly declared it a disgrace for our entire family. I accept the fact he killed Gerard; it was only fitting, but his murder could have been explained a hundred different ways, if there was any need to explain the death of a servant at all. Yet my uncle seemed to go out of his way to complain of his deep shame before ever-more people, which drove my mother into a frenzy. Around the clock she harped for me to take the nun's veil before my father returned to avoid an even worse end. Since I couldn't imagine anything worse than my current suffering, I insisted my father alone should decide my fate. In a word, I refused the nunnery. Incidentally, even my agreement would not have meant much. No noblewoman simply entered a nunnery; she needed money, lots of money—the dowry for a bride of Christ. Where would we get the money?

I lived through terrible weeks. Everyone in Sassenage—my family, the servants, the neighbors, even the peasants—looked upon me as a monster. Some blamed me, I knew, for sullying the nobility, while others because one of their own had died on my account. This double guilt scorched me so cruelly that at night I did not dare blow out the candle—Gerard always came out of the darkness immediately, as I remembered him during our last time together: passionate and satisfied, proud in his manliness. That's how he looked only an hour before my uncle took him out to the courtyard and didn't allow him a weapon—how could he fight a servant on equal terms?—and ran him through. In the groin, so it would take him longer to die. Gerard indeed howled for hours, crawling around as if drawing a nightmarish picture with his blood on the flagstones in the empty courtyard—everyone had hidden away. And in my visions his fatal wound gaped open everywhere—the whole of Gerard became a wound upon my conscience. And this was for the best. Otherwise, I would have killed myself out of self-pity.

I no longer cried. I had moved beyond the limits of pain. I felt a cold malice. I didn't burst into tears even when I stood before my father and told him word for word when, with whom, and how. My uncle was there, to make sure I didn't lie. My father, pale, with a clenched jaw, looked truly murderous, thus I expected the worst; after all, everyone had been drumming this into me for weeks. But I had only just begun, calling the saints to my aid, when Baron de Sassenage roared, "Enough! I

VERA MUTAFCHIEVA

can imagine it even without your help." He jumped up. I said my final prayer and even though I had found it hard to live these past weeks, I felt anguish I would live no longer. But my father passed me by, and behind my back I heard, before I could even turn around, the blows of his heavy fist. The baron was beating his brother-in-law with the bitterness all patient people feel when their patience has come to an end. My uncle was not at all prepared for this, but I don't think he would have resisted in any case—he wasn't a brave man. "You hyena," I heard my father sobbing. "You slithering vermin! Get out of my sight!"

When my uncle slipped out, never to be seen again, my father and I were left alone. My father suddenly collapsed, hiding his face in his hands, while I wondered whether he was really crying. He was not. Only then did I realize the extent to which everything within me had been scorched, because I felt neither pity nor contrition.

"Hélène," he said after a short while, "you know very well what you have done to me. De Sassenage has no wealth or power, a has-been soldier living in his wife's house, that's what de Sassenage was. I believed I had at least kept my good name...."

He didn't say it: "But you have stained it."

"You might tell me you are not the first or the only one. I know the people we live among, and I know that to them, the only criminal is the criminal who gets caught; you should have kept this in mind. You should have remembered that in our house lurks someone for whom it is advantageous for de Sassenage to be left without an heir. But I will not allow it! I will not send you to a nunnery, Hélène. The two of us shall right the wrong the two of us have done."

That's the kind of man my father was, may he rest in peace. I hope you can appreciate him, because all of the Dauphiné mocked him. Everyone thought he should punish his daughter and disown her so as to preserve his own good name to some extent. My father did the opposite: he started taking me with him on all the hunts, tournaments, and festivals around the Dauphiné. I was not blind. Suffering had sharpened my senses. I could tell Baron de Sassenage was foisting me upon the local nobility, showing off my charms in the hopes of finding me a husband. I felt incredibly humiliated. For his sake—believe me, I had long since gotten over such feelings on my own account. I could see how in society he tried to strike a delicate balance, both showing he condemned his daughter, yet without allowing them the same liberty with respect to me. I could sense how he bristled at any laughter, as if afraid it was directed at the two of us. I sank into pity for my father—on top of everything, he lived in constant fear: What if he were to find me hanged some morning? I tried to convince him I was having a relatively pleasant time—it would have infuriated him if I had felt true joy—and that I appreciated his forgiveness. God alone knows how easy that was for me.

Despite all my father's efforts, or perhaps because of them, he did not find me a bridegroom. Men were particularly kind to me, kinder than was proper, but only when we were alone. I had no illusions—they thought me available. While in society I sensed emptiness and coldness all around me. No one wanted to take up the role of the third clown alongside the Baron de Sassenage and his daughter.

And so, four years passed. I would have traded them for four years of hard labor. With each passing year, my father lost

VERA MUTAFCHIEVA

patience; he grew suspicious, short-tempered, spiteful. It was already too late for the nunnery. Besides, how could he explain it? He'd forgiven me publicly—hadn't he shown he was not ashamed of me? There was no other solution: we went around to the neighboring castles, sometimes invited, sometimes not, and I displayed my new dresses and my riding skills like no other lady in the Dauphiné.

When we learned the Turkish sultan everyone was talking about had been moved to Bois-Lamy, my father saw this as a great opportunity: Bois-Lamy would become a hub for the nobility from the Dauphiné and Savoy, all the foreigners would come pouring in here. Likely my father hoped to unload me onto one of them, the foreigners who did not know who I was. I could tell he was ready to sacrifice me even to a singer. We arrived at Bois-Lamy along with other petty noblemen from the region. The castle was full to the rafters with Hospitallers, troubadours, and guests. The next morning they geared up for a hunt.

I saw the sultan for the first time that morning. We were already on horseback when he came out, accompanied by another Turk. I had heard so much about him that I studied him carefully. Cem Sultan was almost young, around thirty, unexpectedly fair for a Saracen. I wouldn't call him handsome; his features were inharmonious and rather large, like a person of low birth. I found his companion rather different. He was quite a bit smaller, not swarthy, but very dark eyed and dark haired, with something delicate, exquisite not only in his face, but also in his expression, in his comportment. Looking at them side by side, one might unwittingly conclude Saadi was the prince, while Cem was his squire.

Don't read too much into this judgment of mine; I had suffered under the fist-waving, loud-voiced callousness and violence of male coarseness to such an extent I had likely lost my sense of the more general concept of masculinity. But one thing is certain: Cem did not behave nobly. He spoke unnecessarily loudly, from his throat, helping every word with his hands, as if he were not chatting but rowing—in short, grandeur was foreign to him. My first impression of Cem Sultan was unflattering. It took a few days for this to change. I glimpsed something touching and disarming in this person: his naturalness. Don't imagine our nobles from the Dauphiné were overly refined; a very thin veneer of good manners disguised yesterday's soldier in them, and if they sat down to drink and let themselves go, they were intolerable. Yes, I was wrong about Cem.

Cem's charm lay not in his naturalness, but rather in the fact that being natural, he did not display any baseness. Precisely when he was drunk, Cem sharply rose above our men; he acted like a person for whom drunkenness was a common state of the soul.

No matter what a damaged woman I was, with womanly intuition I immediately noticed I had caught Cem's attention. It was no more than curiosity, devoid of the lewd ambiguity in the gaze of all the others; to Cem, I was unusual not because I had slept with a squire. On the third evening, his curiosity was now tinged with something more: delight. I did not notice desire.

I did not realize my eyes were answering him—isn't that what Saadi claimed?—I was already dead to everything essentially female. Most likely I was simply pleased someone did not know me and had no way of finding out, since he didn't speak our language.

When we went out hunting, I liked to distance myself from the hunters—a few minutes of freedom from their leers. While riding, as long as I kept galloping ahead, I had the feeling I would reach an unknown land, and I would be unknown in that land. I was happy when Cem began following me in my lonely gallops —I would have taken him there with me, since neither of us belonged to the Dauphiné.

In Bois-Lamy, we did not exchange so much as a word, thus I was surprised when after a hunt Cem offered me his shoulder. He did so awkwardly, and I had to grasp him firmly so as not to fall. For a moment I felt his heat, I saw his eyes very close to mine. Now this was desire. I admit, it came from both sides very strongly—most likely due to the fact that both he and I had been awakened to love, yet had long lived without it.

As if from afar I heard—after all, the two of us were standing for a moment upon that unknown land I told you about—the Dauphiné nobility laughing. It was enough to bring me back to my fear: What would my father say?

Indeed, he was gloomy that evening. I could sense the coming storm; they had been frequent of late. And this was precisely the reason I accepted Cem's smiles, and returned them. In the end, if a person must pay a high price, let it at least be worth it. That's what I thought then, and I thought the same later as well.

"Hélène," my father started in on me after dinner, "I can't take any more. Four years I have pretended not to notice how they look at you, but at least they were people who have the right to do so—you have sinned according to their laws, our laws, and you will be judged by our God. But what happened today was too much for me, Hélène. An animal, one of those who keep several wives, dared to desire my daughter! What's worse, I don't see you upset; you are not insulted. Could you possibly have lost your sense of human decency?"

As you know, back when everyone heaped shame upon me, and I had to explain to everyone how things had been with Gerard, I had put up with it. Why was I now gripped by fury, by the desire to defend myself? Was it because I no longer felt entirely alone? Cem had my back. What am I talking about? He and I had not even exchanged a word. Just imagine how they had broken me down if even a stranger's fleeting sympathy gave me courage.

"I can't take it anymore either," I cried. "Do you think you're the only one suffering? The only reason I am still crawling on the face of this earth is because of you, Papa. Hell sounds like the promised land to me. And who are you calling an animal?" I continued furiously, as if screaming out my four years of pain. "Who here does not have several women? Women who in turn have several men of their own? Why are only Cem and I a stain on good morals? Don't you realize the moment we came together, he would be my only man, while I would be his only woman? What does before and after matter?"

Repeating these words now, I am not ashamed, but I do realize they are ridiculous—look where long-repressed pain leads a person. But my father did not laugh. He again clutched his temples and fought back tears.

"Merciful God," he said, "take me home so as not to see or hear this."

Don't imagine he gave in. We left Bois-Lamy the next morning. At our parting, the sultan stared at me intently. I did not read pain in his gaze, but rather the question: Why? Yes, why indeed. But had they answered me, so I could answer him in turn? I forgot him quickly; every new experience sank into the dead end of my days.

Brother Blanchefort visited us in the spring of the following year. We were not used to visits from honored guests at Sassenage; moreover, our family did not have anyone in the Order of St. John, while the brother in question was their commander in Avignon. Nevertheless, my father accepted him with all the dignity we could muster. After lunch, Blanchefort withdrew for a private conversation with my father, which puzzled us—Baron de Sassenage was not a personage with whom private conversations were held.

Cem. The thought flashed through my mind as we wondered. Wasn't Cem the Hospitallers' prisoner? This had to have something to do with Cem. I thought this with fear. What, do you think I cared about Cem's fate? No. I simply recalled with gratitude that there was someone somewhere who had not insulted me.

Toward evening—my father and Brother Blanchefort had spent the whole afternoon talking—they called me in. I found my father agitated—but agitated in a good way, it seemed. He endorsed the monk's words with exclamations of approval; he did everything he could to make me consent to a game that would finally free him—my father—from the constant humiliation, and, more precisely, from me. Everything comes to an end in this world—why not a parent's love as well?

"When your task is finished, madame," Brother Blanchefort concluded that evening, "you will receive the Church's deep gratitude and the Holy Father's personal appreciation. And his support. You will choose the most refined nunnery in France or Italy, but that is not the most important thing. You shall receive complete absolution, Hélène. The people who have received complete absolution from the pope himself can be counted on the fingers of one hand."

"Have you ever dreamed of such a thing, daughter?" My father embraced me, and now he really was crying.

"No," I said. Now I was no longer simply hardened, I felt wooden. "I have never dreamed of such a thing."

THIRTEENTH TESTIMONY OF THE POET SAADI
ON THE SPRING OF 1487

FOR US, IT was a very sad spring. From the brothers—who now acted as if they were our coconspirators—we learned the papal legates had done only marginally better than Pruisz. The Royal Council gave them to understand it would hand over Cem only in exchange for piles of gold and another cardinal's seat for France. Innocent did not have the first and was very afraid of the second. Thus, this attempt to bring Cem closer to territories threatened by his brother also looked doomed to fail.

Cem received this news with undisguised delight, as he was still not over Pruisz's failure—we couldn't care less about the haggling between France and the pope.

I must admit, however, perhaps we were wrong. Cem never rationally considered the advantages Rome offered him. He did not want to take part in anything involving monks and priests, he would always say he had seen their true face, he knew their tricks. Thus, Sinan and Ayas's mission to convince us to ally with the papacy not only failed to achieve its goal, but even had the opposite effect: Cem saw in it new proof of the brothers' hypocrisy.

Indeed, Cem's hatred of the Order and the Holy Father was growing ever deeper. As you know, when much is taken from you—let us not yet say "everything"—the only thing left to you is love of something: love of your work, of pleasures, or, in extreme cases, of some person. Cem lost them one after the other, these loves, replacing them with something equally powerful: hatred. Now he passionately hated everyone dressed in black, from Innocent VIII, even though he, being the pope, wore white, to the rank-and-file Hospitallers, who blackened our everyday life. Cem dedicated hours to expressing this hatred, with the same satisfaction with which he had once sought exquisite words to pour out his love of beauty. He now sought the most vulgar, repulsive, and offensive epithets for the brothers. I wondered where he found the strength to curse them more fiercely every day. I didn't try to stop him, as I knew hatred, like love, must be vented.

In a word, as soon as he found out the papacy wanted him as an ally against France, Cem let loose a venom toward our hosts he had heretofore not expressed. While they, for their part, had never been more attentive to us; the monks, to put it lightly, were fawning over us. They told us news we had not asked for; they assured us our boredom—had they only noticed it now?—would end if the pope managed to get the best of the Royal Council; they recounted the delights of the Eternal City to us in quite unmonkish terms.

"Hm," was Cem's unfailing response to these all-too-transparent arguments, while the brothers tore their hair out over his indifference.

VERA MUTAFCHIEVA

I will not enumerate the kidnapping attempts organized by Charles of Savoy or the papacy in the meantime. We learned this news from the brothers, thus it may not be true. Or it may be highly abbreviated or overly inflated. I'll mention just one such attempt, since it changed life at Bois-Lamy—and after all, our world began and ended with Bois-Lamy.

The Duke of Lotharingia, an ally of Bourbon and an enemy of Lady Beaujeu, hence particularly devoted to the papacy, had contacted Charles of Savoy to ask him for men he could trust completely. I suspect the plot was exposed already at this first step, but no matter; Charles outfitted him with two such men who were considered extremely skilled in such endeavors: Geoffroy de Bassompierre and Jacob de Germigny. The Lotharingian duke's aid was limited to sending thirty desperate men. They were supposed to reach Savoy, and from there, along with the two noblemen and Charles's soldiers, they would attack Bois-Lamy and kidnap Cem. I cannot fathom how they imagined this happening; it is well-known that during this period, castles regularly withstood thousand-man sieges for months at a time. But Charles likely imagined something particularly knightly and heroic. As for the duke, we were convinced he simply wanted to demonstrate his loyalty to his more powerful allies—the pope and Bourbon—with this half-hearted help.

Thirty-odd thugs from Lotharingia were captured somewhere in Burgundy by the royal guards, and without even being tortured—they had been dragged en masse before the Council—they confessed the aim of their late-winter journey. I presume this news was a heavier blow to Charles than to us. We had already grown used to practically identical, failed, half-hearted efforts to liberate us. The brothers were particularly irritated by these attempts.

"Isn't it nice, Saadi?" Cem would say. "You sit down at the feast table, you go on a hunt, and you know someone else is losing instead of you. Splendid!" But he couldn't fool me—he didn't look like a person having a splendid time.

Meanwhile, all around Bois-Lamy spring was raging. The damp green hills looked as if lit up from the inside as the warm, gray, sunless sky hung over them. Actually, there may have been sun—in the north I simply could never tell whether it was shining or not. There, everything slumbers in a grayish light of various hues. There, spring is not marked by the brightest, dazzlingly light colors. The northern spring to me was simply very juicy, very fragile and young in its greenness. Forgive me for saying so, but I was sorry I was not a cow, one of the many white or golden cows we observed from Bois-Lamy. Because if you ask me, there, it is mainly the cows that taste the wonder of spring.

Indeed, jokes are unwarranted, as I must inform you of something important, a change in the case of Cem. It happened in April 1487: the royal guard arrived at Bois-Lamy Castle. They got what was coming to them. The brothers, that is. Now they likely understood what we had felt when their numbers were constantly growing around us, as we had said in dismay: more and more jailers.

The royal knights rode up the hill in solemn silence, if we don't count the rattling of their iron mail and the clopping of hooves. The brothers watched them from above, mute from shock, as if thunderstruck. The newcomers looked like they meant business. Once in the courtyard, they leapt from their horses with ever-more-joyous rattling and took up formation six abreast with their banner before them, and only then did their drums start to thunder. Bois-Lamy echoed like a stone bell as the brothers came down from the walls.

A battle, you ask? No, it didn't come to a battle—Bois-Lamy was an island held by the Order amidst sprawling French lands. Out of the crowd of Hospitallers, Brother Blanchefort, who had followed us to the Dauphiné stronghold as well, simply stepped forward and asked the royal guard, without any pleasantries, the purpose of their presence.

I could've answered that. I had long been waiting for the king's meddling in the case of Cem to take a more visible form. Very coldly, the royal guard's commander explained to Blanchefort that the most recent attempt to attack Bois-Lamy had forced the king to consider our security. The Order, with its meager resources, could not protect Cem on its own. In short, the royal guard had arrived to reinforce our defenses. Now Cem really could say with good reason, "Splendid. Haven't you been repeating over and over for seven years that you've stayed close at my heels for my own security? Now it's your turn. Let them protect you a bit as well. Now you can experience how sweet it is for someone to watch over your sleep and your drunkenness."

For days on end, the expression with which the brothers tolerated this outside imposition, the abject fear and confusion written upon their bearded faces, was the subject of our discussions. Yet more proof we are not animals: for a person, schadenfreude is a greater pleasure than one's own triumph. Of course, we, too, soon tired of it, especially because the soldiers added to the already gloomy surveillance over us. Our hunts were now accompanied by two sets of guards, the Order's and the king's; when we ate, our fellow feasters split into two groups: monks and royal guards. They split quite literally, because they always kept apart, going so far as to leave empty space between them and trading glances I would not call polite. I felt as if Bois-Lamy were giving off sparks, so heated was the air around it. And all of this would have been funny if it hadn't been insanely depressing.

Spring helped us cope with that tension, to some extent. Cem never did get used to the frigid weather and he complained night and day about the wind and the damp. So at least we had been freed from the cold's watch. My master came back to the castle only as evening fell, with new ideas for walks, hunts, and guests. Not once during that spring did he ask about Baron de Sassenage and his daughter and he did not ask for them to be invited to Bois-Lamy.

But I knew him too well to think he had forgotten them. Later, I suspected his memory of Hélène was so dear to him he was afraid a new meeting might ruin it. Until one day, to our immense amazement, the two de Sassenages showed up uninvited.

They came directly for lunch, without having been announced. When Cem entered the hall—he always came in last, as befits a ruler—I could see he was stunned, and it was not at all difficult to conclude that during the long months of silence and ostensible forgetting, Hélène had occupied his thoughts. Getting ahold of himself, Cem strode straight to the feast table, glowing, as if there were no living being in sight except him and Hélène. He gave her a French bow, which she returned with an even lower curtsy, spreading a dozen layers of skirts and petticoats around her.

Since this scene was all too clear to me, I tried during that time to keep a sharp eye on our tablemates, our hosts or guards, call them what you will. We had already long since figured out that nothing happened around us without it meaning something. I wanted to find out who exactly had caused the de Sassenages' reappearance, which of our two jailers had called them in. But my efforts were in vain; the French knights stood ramrod straight, with the most respectful of expressions, while the Hospitallers looked stone-faced, as always. Only Brother Blanchefort, d'Aubusson's nephew, observed those present as closely as I did, albeit more skillfully than I did. I concluded either Blanchefort had arranged this business or it was being done to his detriment. In other words, I concluded nothing.

We finished off the game meat, then the immoderate drinking began. Until then Cem and Hélène had only traded glances and half smiles. I was struck by the impression that this time, the father's and daughter's roles had been reversed. Hélène was more dispirited, more gloomily concentrated, while the old man shone with a new self-confidence, a sense of importance, and heightened attention toward his pretty daughter. She passed him by distractedly, often answering his questions only when he repeated them, and somehow with disdain, at that. And this disdain did not seem aimed only at her father—she showered it over the whole table, making conversations strained.

Cem noticed nothing of these tangled relationships. He gazed at Hélène with radiant eyes, pushing cups and platters toward her—he was acting openly ridiculous, in short. Yet I was happy he would have a few days of respite amidst a life always full of the same thoughts and fears.

After lunch we were finally alone, but I kept silent, leaving Cem to his pleasant feelings, until he spoke up.

"Saadi, please be there when I'm with Hélène."

"You need a translator?" I managed not to laugh out loud. "You can count on me."

Even though I was with him at all times, even though that afternoon, and the next, and the one after that, Hélène not only did not avoid him but even encouraged him with her constant presence, Cem nevertheless continued speaking to her with his eyes alone, as if words frightened him.

Finally on the third evening, when our company was thoroughly tipsy, and even Hélène herself did not appear tediously sober, but rather downright sick with irritation, Cem caught me by the elbow and—leaning toward her over the table—asked the question it clearly had taken him three whole days to compose: "What can I do to dispel your boredom, madame?"

Something like mockery crept across the lady's forehead, but did not lighten her scowl. She replied to Cem's question with a question of her own, slightly out of place, if you ask me. "How is your health, Your Highness?"

"Fine," Cem said, puzzled. "Fine... Why?"

"Because our air is surely harmful to you. I always imagine you must suffer from the cold here."

These words meant nothing. Hélène was clearly not attempting to put Cem at ease, but rather to prove to some third party that she had come out of her shell. Cem, as sensitive as always, grasped this; he regretted having spoken and having disturbed an intimacy that was beyond words. He took a deep breath like a diver and said, "Let me invite you on a short hunt tomorrow morning, madame. It will be just the three of us. Please do not refuse me, I beg you."

Hélène stared stubbornly at her ring. Her expression showed offended anger. But here the old Baron de Sassenage cut in—we had been fools to think he was drunk.

"That would be an honor for my daughter, Your Highness. She will be waiting for you tomorrow morning."

Hélène shot him a sideways glance, bowed, and left the room. Brother Blanchefort escorted her out with a worried look.

"Saadi, I have offended her," Cem whispered to me, quite upset. "Perhaps we do not know their customs. What should I do, Saadi?"

"Give her some of your poems," I said, "or some piece of jewelry.... How should I know? I don't know which is more fitting for a lady. Back home they are simply women."

"True," Cem said, and for the remainder of the evening I could sense he was pondering how to behave the next day.

In the morning, I dressed him not as if he were going hunting, but rather presenting himself before a king. Cem made me change this piece of clothing or that, he found fault with everything—I had never seen him so concerned about his appearance. When he was finally ready, he was unbelievable—he shone like Harun al-Rashid at his first wedding.

My comparison must have slipped out with a smile, because Cem grew angry, stripped off all those rags—those were his own words—and put on his everyday hunting clothes. They were unusually tight by our standards—little by little our clothes had come to conform to the local standards—thus they beautifully emphasized Cem's shapely legs, as well as his slim hips and flat stomach, while leaving his shoulders free. Cem had very handsome shoulders, like a swimmer.

Which of our men, so long dead or more recently deceased, or locked away in Bayezid's dungeons or on Rhodes, would recognize our master in this blond Frank? Actually, what was Cem to us—a tragic amalgam of East and West, an incestuous infusion of Christianity and Islam, a mistaken mix of the Epicurean and the Stoic—a lovely combination of blond and swarthy? Was his whole life not proof that a half blood never belongs to anyone—he himself never manages to smooth the rough edge where his two halves meet; why should he expect our own or others to fully accept him?

Cem was already on his way outside; he took the steps two at a time, his whole being emanated careless determination, which only very young, very handsome men can indulge. We found the lady in the courtyard, not yet in her saddle. Her skirts were tucked into her belt of golden rings; her petticoats—white, stiff, and edged—were slightly shorter, leaving her calves in their tight, soft boots exposed. She was pretty despite her scrawniness. This was exactly what made Hélène not of the flesh and hence allowed her to act so strongly upon the imagination. Cem helped her onto her horse, she leaned on his shoulder only with her fingers, as if the softness of her palm would be too intimate and naked. Cem struggled to catch her eye, but she deliberately looked away.

We set out through the spring meadows, the guards following us at a distance. As unwelcoming as I found the Dauphiné, spring had beautified it; the grasses bloomed with hundreds of hues and even gave off a light, tangy scent. Translucent clouds chased one another around the radiant sky.

VERA MUTAFCHIEVA

The two of them rode ahead of me. I tried to keep to the side, so as not to disturb their silent conversation, but Cem once again needed words.

"Saadi," he called to me. "Why have you left us alone? Ask the lady if she slept well."

I asked her. Hélène ignored his question, just as she had the night before. Women really do possess a maternal pity: they take upon themselves the first difficult steps in a decisive conversation.

"I have thought of you often, prince"—that's what she called him, not "Your Highness"—"throughout the whole winter...."

"I likely thought of you more often, madame," he replied, "in my terrible loneliness."

It is generally assumed that a man, in his striving to impress the object of his affections, performs great feats in his chosen field. He shows off the strength of his legs and his shoulders if he is an athlete; he unfurls a carpet of beautiful words if he is a poet; he scatters a thick layer of diamonds and pearls if he is a ruler. But that comes later, I'm telling you—we use such things in our struggles not to win over, but to keep a woman. But the first blow we strike—a sure, unfailing blow—is to awaken her pity; nothing conquers a woman like pity.

This was Cem's aim as well; he had barely spoken before he mentioned his loneliness, even though I would not have called him isolated during that time.

Hélène turned, no longer averting her eyes. They understood Cem. "How do you bear the loneliness, prince?"

"I'm sure you can imagine." Here Cem followed his instincts and did not offer any description, knowing that without his words, Hélène would imagine something far more terrible. "Have you ever been immolated by loneliness, rejected, forgotten, insulted?"

The woman fell silent, as if trying to overcome some internal struggle. I sensed how her closed nature, which had allowed her to cope precisely with loneliness and insults, struggled against the primordial need to open up and share, in hopes of receiving sympathy. I knew the latter would win out; Cem was betting on a sure thing.

"I have," Hélène replied in a voice that came from deep inside her; I heard her voice for the first time. "I feel as if everything you are experiencing has already happened to me long ago.... Perhaps in a more cruel and hopeless way."

"Hélène." Cem turned his horse with one of those gestures from his younger years and placed his hand upon hers.

I looked at their hands, two hands, male and female, upon the horse's damp neck. Cem's stroked hers almost imperceptibly; Hélène's was perfectly still, not as if dead, but rather stunned. I have noticed this among very impetuous, passionate people, who—once they let go—have difficulty stopping halfway.

"Trust me," Cem began, with that most common of lovers' vows, clearly not knowing how to continue.

But Hélène pulled her hand away sharply, tossed back her head, and looked at Cem with a despairing urgency, as if she wished to cut straight through him.

"You should not trust me, prince. Don't trust me."

And she glanced around furtively, as if fearing she had been followed and overheard. Cem was stunned.

"Hélène," he said, "don't ask the impossible of me. To me, you are another me, a better and surely longer-suffering self. Nothing you do could be bad, otherwise it would upset the harmony of the world. I trust you like I trust myself, Hélène."

Madame de Sassenage untangled her reins as irritation gathered between her brows. It was the same look children have when you deny them something.

"I warned you, prince," she said.

Now I remember this conversation of theirs, which passed through me. I am glad I recall it because it exonerates Hélène. Many claim that in love, one treacherous and cold lover fools the other. A pure lie! In love a person always fools himself, insistently, with no regard for the truth—and I don't mean just its hints, but its frank confessions. And this is likely the most beautiful thing about love: it allows you to fully forget the truth.

I shall not relate to you their conversation after that point; it completely resembles all such confidences, in which love is simply an excuse to talk about oneself in detail in front of one's most longed-for listener. Have you noticed people rarely hear you when you describe yourself? In principle this only happens in declarations of love.

I took up their words and tossed them back to them. The two of them no longer sensed me as a separate person—I was their living echo. It was funny how Hélène or Cem would sit for a moment with a frozen smile, while one of them uttered heated moans—at that moment, the other did not yet know their meaning. Only after my intrusion would their face light up when the words reached them. It was a wonder indeed, that intimate love talk between the three of us.

On our way back, they galloped so fast I could hardly keep up, but I don't think they missed me by then. I could see them in front of me, young and light in their saddles, carried by one and the same wind: a premonition of pleasure and pain, hope, belief, fear. I followed them, thinking one must be very naive to envy those who are in love—I felt sorry for them.

During the following days, the fear of them taking her away from him paralyzed Cem. But no, this time the brothers' wakefulness had fallen asleep as right under their noses Cem gained a beloved, the flesh of his flesh, as the Bible says. This was suspicious.

"Does it not surprise you, my sultan, that the brothers are suddenly acting as pimps?"

"I don't want to hear that word in reference to her," Cem shouted, thus demonstrating that his flight from reality was in full swing.

"Don't be afraid of words, but of what they signify," I insisted. "For six years now the brothers have not let anyone you love live."

"Are you saying she is in danger?"

"No," I snapped. "Why would they serve you up Hélène, unless it was to their advantage? God Almighty, Cem!" Now I was shouting, too; we were outside, so I dared raise my voice. "You are not an imbecile—think it through yourself. Who else have the brothers allowed to sympathize with you, to be alone with you without supervision? Something is fishy here, Cem."

"It is, it is." He shook his head impatiently. "But let it be, do you hear me? You are my friend, Saadi." Cem's voice was now that of an overindulged child, as I remembered him from Karamania. "How can my friend not understand I am running away? These weeks are the only thing truly mine amidst years of mistrust, estrangement, and fear. Why are you waking me up, Saadi?"

How strange, Cem was almost always wrong when he followed his reason and almost always right when he opposed it. Truly, I had no answer to such a question: "Why are you waking me up?"

And so, my suspicions fell silent, but did not die. I quit warning him. My conscience was clear: the only thing we take from this world are a few sweet weeks of self-delusion.

As a necessary third wheel, I took part in all their subsequent conversations. With every passing day I realized the two of them were heading toward the moment when they would no longer need a translator. I myself awaited it with impatience, as if their passion, passing as it was through me, had swept me away. But Cem and Hélène talked a lot then, having smashed the cage of silence and isolation that had oppressed each of them separately for many long years. Now they were making up for lost time.

Cem poured out his six years of suffering to Hélène, his transformation from an army's idol and a nation's hope into the property of the Hospitallers; Cem complained to Hélène about his despair and his helpless rage, his doubts about humanity. Cem never spoke so much to anyone before or after that. Don't think this was inspired by some exceptional qualities on Hélène's part. When it comes to the degree or strength of love, its object is not important. What is important is merely the moment, your own maturity or decline, your hopelessness or faith. In short, only your own self is important. In those days, Cem was on the edge—the edge of human spiritual endurance. For six years he had been fighting against something inevitable: his transformation from a person into an empty name. Cem struggled bravely, but everything was stacked against him in this fight. It would end the moment Cem gave in to the countless, endlessly more powerful outside forces. But between the two—between Cem's struggle and his defeat—there needed to be a boundary. He could not give up his six years of resistance lightly.

I did not consider all this at the time, I came to this conclusion much later. Far later did I realize Cem threw himself blindly into that love not because of Hélène's charms, and not because of a trust she pretended to offer him, since from her first words, Hélène left no room for trust between the two of them. Cem likely sensed his strength was flagging, thus he himself was striving toward some grandiose shock wave that would either allow him to swim to the surface or drown him completely. Cem sought justification for his defeat. And what better excuse than a false, damnable love?

I'm not saying Cem planned for this love affair to end unhappily—God forbid. It was subconscious. I have always wondered just how subtly Cem led his second life, the one invisible to others and without any significance to world affairs. In this other life, everything was masterfully thought out, yet I can testify Cem never thought so far as his next move, let alone any moves far in the future. Because he possessed something given only to women and poets: insight.

In the days I am telling you about, we had no reason to complain. The brothers were conciliatory and amenable, and the only function of the Order's guards who accompanied us on our outings with Hélène seemed to be to balance out the royal guards. I knew they would be more than happy to skirmish amongst themselves, even though I did not know who would have the upper hand in such a fight. I personally found the French knights' feathers, ribbons, and gold-plated weapons a weaker expression of manliness than the Rhodian warriors' heavy, threatening blackness.

And so we rode beneath the May skies of the Dauphiné, the northern sun deepened Cem's tan, and he began to remind me of our days in Karamania with all of their groundless gaiety, when I would fall asleep anticipating the wholly fleshly pleasures of the following day.

Yet Hélène somehow remained aloof to our happiness. Every morning she would come down into the courtyard, where we would be waiting for her to go hunting or on a walk, with the same expression of withdrawn affront she always wore. Only after an hour would she change; Cem would drag her along with him. A remnant of jealousy gnawed at me whenever I saw them galloping together: they were full of a wild desire, which our blood pulls us toward when it is excited by some physical exertion, in this case riding. I assumed after precisely such a gallop, breathless, exhausted, they would reach the moment of no longer needing a translator.

I also felt a bit of envy. You know that in Cem's court, not only did we not find relationships between men unseemly, on the contrary: we were proud of them, we elevated them above plebeian dependence on women. Only now did I see Cem was expressing precisely that love so untypical for us. Most likely because Hélène was so different from him, thus he needed a long time to describe himself and his world to her in detail.

But you are on the right track, since you haven't paid much heed to Hélène's assessment of Cem. To a woman, a man appears not as he is, but as he would like to be—Cem lied to her an awful lot in those sweet weeks. If you excuse him by saying he was a poet, you are unjust; I have even heard dockworkers do this.

I don't know whether Hélène believed him; I did not see in her little Charles's ecstasy. This made me conclude she was not a virgin—women always believe the first time. Something else also led me to the same conclusion: Hélène's hunger was obvious. One would never suspect it behind such a smooth, coldly open forehead, but sometimes I caught Hélène's gaze. Without curiosity or fear, yet with a certain knowing, her gaze ranged like a warm hand from Cem's dark-blond head to his shoulders, then wound firmly around his waist. Women look at men like that only from behind, thus men have no idea such a look even exists.

I noticed something else as well, but perhaps it was part of local customs: Hélène did not avoid being alone with Cem. In the evening she often stopped by our chambers. During such visits I worked late into the night, as Cem would not shut up. If madame had come seeking only conversation, I could not tell; she did not seem either spellbound by Cem's eloquence or disappointed he did not go beyond words. Cem chalked up her visits to tender sympathy, yet I knew of the hunger I had glimpsed in her eyes. Both one and the other demanded a response.

One evening, as I sat across from my lovebirds, I sensed they wanted me to leave. Cem had been distracted, as if his whole room was clogged with anxious impatience; it even weighed on the candles' flames. Their light convulsed on the two faces before them. Lost in their thoughts, each sunk into themselves; Cem and Hélène looked completely estranged, as people are before a long and unknown journey. Yet I hesitated about whether to leave—I was haunted by the feeling I would be allowing evil in, that it shouldn't happen, and that stopping it was within my power. Cem glared at me almost with hatred; I could tell, in just another instant, he would grow ruthless, he would say words to me I would carry to the grave.

I didn't even make an excuse, I headed for the door. He didn't stop me.

In the hallway, on my way out to the wall, I passed two Hospitallers and a royal baronet. I could've sworn they were smiling —everyone looked like a pimp that night.

I went out to the fortress walls and spent hours there. I shivered in the night's dampness as I measured time in steps. I tried to think about something else. When I got back after midnight, Cem was already fast asleep, his covers in disarray. He was as naked as a Christian martyr.

After that I frequently spent my nights on the wall. I no longer shivered, but made sure to take a coat. Cem began spending not only the nights without me; during the day as well he preferred to hunt only with Madame de Sassenage, certain he could speak to her sufficiently and convincingly without a translator. But the lady was of another mind. *Are the subtleties of language really so necessary to her?* I wondered when she asked me to accompany them one morning.

As we set out, I felt more superfluous than ever. I rode far behind them, trying to look at least slightly less ridiculous. They stopped in a small meadow, and it didn't seem to be the first time they had stopped there. Cem spread out his cloak, while Hélène, with purely female adroitness, laid out food.

"Join us, Saadi," she said.

This was far too much attention for a mere servant. No matter, we sat down. Through the sparse trees we could see the guardsmen walking their horses. Not close—they kept their distance.

Cem was bareheaded and his shirt hung open, as always when he hunted. He leaned on Hélène's knee with that serene and pathetic feeling of ownership men who have recently begun sleeping with a woman have. Hélène did not pull away, despite my presence. Was her intimacy with Cem not only obvious, but even demonstrative? And why, God damn it, did this intimacy not alarm anyone at Bois-Lamy? Why not even her father, who only a few months earlier had whisked her away after Cem touched her with the tips of his fingers? Why did Cem not suspect anything, why did he not make me ask who Hélène was and what she wanted from us? That's what I was thinking when Hélène turned to me.

"Saadi, I must speak to your master about something important."

Half-reclining, leaning as he was on her knee, Cem looked up at her.

"Your Highness," she began, wiping her brow and breathing unevenly, "I can no longer bear your suffering. I can no longer ride with you under the watchful eyes of dozens of jailers. I can't bear to meet armed guards before your door at night, Your Highness."

Here she stopped, as if the words, so well rehearsed in advance, ended there.

"Hélène," Cem replied without sitting up, his hand sweeping lightly over her hair, "why are you speaking to me so formally?"

"I don't want you to suffer any longer, Cem," she said in despair —and I don't think this despair was inspired solely by Cem's suffering. "It must end," she said.

Of all human emotions, Cem wore bewilderment best. Now he expressed it in full force. Incidentally, he had every reason to be puzzled: nothing in their relationship had prepared him for such a conversation.

"Cem, I beg you," Hélène continued quickly. "We must leave here."

He needed time to digest her words. Then Cem laughed, condescending and bitter at the same time.

"Except I don't want to go," he replied. "I am terribly glad to huddle here in Bois-Lamy under the crossed gazes of the Hospitallers and the baronets."

"How can you even joke about it? What are you waiting for, what are you counting on?"

"The sky," Cem replied.

I could tell he really wanted her to shut up.

"I'm asking you truly, Cem, do I mean so little to you that you would hide yourself from me? Who would desire your freedom, if not me?"

Here I recalled the Frank; I remembered how, when he sensed a threat to Cem, he would translate someone's words very thoroughly, mixing in his own warnings. But, tell me, had Suleiman ever been in the spot I was now?

I translated Hélène's moaning. I was completely numb. Not from fear—thank God, Cem had no secrets to confess. From foreboding.

"I swear to you, Hélène"—Cem took her hand—"if I knew anything, you would learn about it by evening. I honestly am not counting on anyone. I have lost all hope of escaping captivity.... And that is for the best—otherwise I wouldn't have met you, Hélène. Why are you telling me all this? Are things really so terrible for us here?"

Hélène should have agreed; in fact, it was obligatory. But she did no such thing. *Either she is the basest weapon in someone's hands*, I thought, *or she really does love him*. Believe me, it was only then that I even considered the latter.

"Cem, I have long waited for you to speak, to ask for my help. Yet you have kept silent for four weeks. You entrust concerns about your freedom to others. Or have you given up on your freedom, Cem?"

"Good God, my freedom!"

He said it in such a tone, as if during the last six years he had not been striving for it, as if he would never budge from his place near Hélène's knee because of some freedom or other.

"Never mind, so be it," Hélène said solemnly. "Despite your obstinance, I will do what I can. A woman can do many things, Cem. I just beg this of you: trust me."

"What a strange plea, Hélène," he replied. "Would I have offered you my shoulder to dismount your horse one long year ago if I didn't trust you?"

Honest to God, Cem said this, exactly this, and worse yet, he even thought it. This from the one who had felt so devastated that he had declared, "I don't even trust my mother anymore."

SECOND TESTIMONY OF
PHILIPPINE-HÉLÈNE DE SASSENAGE
ABOUT THE SAME PERIOD

AFTER SAADI'S TESTIMONY you surely think me a monster. This is the typical accusation against a woman who uses her charms for premeditated ends.

I won't justify myself, I did too much of that when I was alive; I was penitence and atonement incarnate, until both one and the other became intolerable, and I let myself get drawn into the case of Cem. My participation was the price I had to pay to finally find peace. You find my role base, but I swear, I would play a role even twice as base to escape a life that was an agony every waking day. I know you will not believe it if I—the woman used as bait—try to claim that in the game laid out for me, I did not participate merely as an actor, superficially. I truly gave myself over to my role; it became a part, indeed the most essential part, of my being. Thus it was all the more awful when they forced me back to precisely such a role; those who promised me peace in exchange for baseness saw me as nothing more than a weapon.

My task seemed difficult even when they first explained it to me. I had to seduce—what a word, the one Brother Blanchefort used—the Turk, to win his trust and to discover his secret connections with the outside world, and then convince him I would help him escape. The brothers would arrange for his escape down to the last detail so as to wrest Cem out of the French guards' hands and deliver him to the pope. The Order had already realized this was their only remaining option. And since Cem did not wish to be handed over to the pope under any circumstances, he couldn't know the Order was organizing the escape.

A difficult task, right? Above all, was Cem really as trusting as they tried to convince me he was? And if I won his trust, would I find the strength to deceive him?

I'll find it, I thought. *What choice do I have? My father is in their power; they can arrange or refuse my acceptance into a nunnery. What would I do if they refuse to let me take vows? I would be dragged around by my father not for four, but for ten more years under the local aristocracy's mocking laughter, looking for a husband. I would be reproached and cursed by my loved ones. Or I'd be sold to some extremely desperate knight and would have to listen till the end of my days to how much he had had to swallow by deigning to honor me with his name. Good God, death would be better!*

And so, having decided to make one final effort to win the right to withdraw from the world, I set out for Bois-Lamy with my father.

I will not repeat what Saadi said about my first meeting with Cem. Saadi in large part noticed what I was going through: I was struggling with contradictory feelings. Sometimes I strove to get close to Cem and win his confidence with the clear intention of carrying out my task, while other times for whole days I would give myself over to being truly loved, truly adored and desired.

The brothers had been mistaken in their choice of weapon—even the most experienced, coldest readers of people often make mistakes. Why did they think Hélène de Sassenage was the most suitable woman for this case? Hélène has been disgraced, they thought, she has nothing to lose; she is under pressure from all sides and has no will of her own. But didn't they realize the person who has nothing to lose is so incredibly desperate that they can permit themselves the impermissible? And isn't it clear that precisely a woman who has known love and been rejected and isolated would let herself be tempted, even by a crippled love?

No, I don't want to imply Cem's love was crippled. I don't believe any of the pure ladies of Savoy or the Dauphiné have ever received in one short month as much and as undeservedly as I did then. *Perhaps*, I thought later, after they had left me alone, *there is divine justice after all: after everything I suffered as a woman, I had the greatest womanly revenge of all.*

But those weeks were terrifying for me. I had achieved more than the brothers had dared to hope: Cem submitted to me without a fight, as if he had long been waiting for me of all people; he gave me access to his hopes. Saadi was not correct: Cem did not listen to my plea to let me help him with indifference; he simply found it unexpected. His love was so far beyond all everyday considerations that Cem had not mixed it even with his burning desire for freedom. But from the moment I planted this thought in his head, I noticed he loved me all the more—he would not only escape through me, but also with me.

I had to promise him we would not be parted once we escaped. Never. I knew between lovers there was no more obligatory lie than "never," yet I still burned with misery. I could not tell him we would be split up at the very first change of horses; I would return to Sassenage, only to go from there to some nunnery for aristocratic ladies while he, Cem, would be taken to Rome.

Here is how the days of my double life passed. In the morning, I would go outside the walls of Bois-Lamy with Cem and spend hours immersed in a joy I had never before experienced. It didn't feel like with Gerard, as if I were committing a crime— everyone around us was helping my intimacy with Cem. We would gallop through the meadows of the Dauphiné. I tossed aside all fear and guilt; I gave myself over to the happy fact that for a few hours, it was just the two of us, and we loved each other. The wind bathed us, the sun washed us clean, and the whole of spring spread before us. Words pale against the joy two prisoners feel when let free for a short while—I would not compare it to anything.

For me, I don't know why, those days are fixed in my memory in color. Pale pastels and bright, rich hues. Spring over the Dauphiné was pale with its grayish sky and fragile green, against which Cem's white mare, the rider's rust-colored clothes, and his dark-gold hair stood out. Cem's room at night was also rich with color—from Cem I learned the language of Eastern dyes. Crimson had never seemed so bloody to me as the scarlet covers of his bed; indigo had never been so night-dark as the pillows tossed about upon a riot of tiger and leopard skins. The candles' light sank into the ebony of the chairs and bounced off the emerald of Cem's robe, off the gold embroidery that whispered here and there out of the semidarkness, while velvet quietly called attention to itself with opalesque folds.

In the evening, Cem did not wear his rust-colored hunting garb. He waited for me in one of his robes, which would have stunned even the most renowned Lyon master silk weaver; he was exquisite, as if he had just stepped out of an Arabian fairy tale. Once I asked him to dress as he did only one day a year—the day when Bayezid Khan's envoy came to see whether Cem was alive. I had heard the brothers then showed off Cem in his full glory —and thus justified the enormous expenses for his upkeep.

"I hate those clothes," Cem replied. "More than anything they remind me I am a puppet."

Yet I insisted. I must admit I was attracted not only by Cem's heat, his undisguised passion; Cem also stroked my imagination. With Cem, I was overwhelmed by the whole charm of the East—that fairy-tale magnificence and mysterious strength. And so, I insisted.

The next night I found Cem so transformed I let out a frightened cry. He went beyond my wildest imaginings. All in white and gold, before me stood a Saracen sultan twice as large and twice as old as Cem. My lover was so unrecognizable I thought that they had already split us apart, that Cem had been taken from me—the thought alone was terrible. It forced me to really think about the horror that awaited me: the end. How precious our every remaining moment together was.

"Please take it off," I told him with a gesture.

He laughed—again he was Cem. He pulled me toward him as he blew out the candle.

In the greenish night that slipped in through a crack, the only bit of gold remaining still glowed—it shone from the floor, from the discarded sultan's robes, as if gleaming with its own light. Afterward all colors faded. The only thing left was a very large warmth that was all mine.

I left before dawn. Only once did I wait for the sun with Cem—what an inimitable sun that was. Only fools associate love with the night; there is nothing sweeter than waking up in the morning next to your lover and going out into the sunshine together. I wanted to experience that with Cem and paid dearly for it—that very same morning Brother Blanchefort threatened that the Order was now in a position to carry out the rest of this business without me unless I fulfilled their commands down to the letter.

Incidentally, in addition to all the strings—or rather chains—they pulled to control me, another unexpected and impermissible one was added: my attachment to Cem. Now they blackmailed me with our impending parting as well.

After every hunt, after every night together, I had to pass through the chapel to get back to my room; as the most senior Hospitaller in the castle, Blanchefort spent most of his time there. I could only imagine to what lengths he had gone to check all the walls of that chapel, because he spoke there without fear. My visits passed under the guise of confessions—after all, I was a sinner and penitent, thus in need of spiritual guidance.

At first our conversations went well—I had nothing yet to confess. But with every passing day they grew ever more intolerable. Blanchefort did not like beating around the bush. He would even quiz me about the expression on Cem's face when I said some word or another. "Would you swear he was not lying to you, daughter?" he would ask, while I tried to convince him Cem harbored no hopes of his mother, Corvinus, or Charles of Savoy organizing his escape. I would swear, of course. I swore on all the saints and the Virgin Mary, and I came to hate all the saints and the Virgin Mary. How could she permit the vileness in which I lived? What posthumous peace could the Hospitaller commander promise me? If hell existed, it would be far too small to contain me. Was it possible for a sin a dozen times worse to atone for a far more minor one?

After such thoughts, I began lying under oath; I lied deliberately, ever more skillfully. Every one of my lies was meant to save Cem a moment of suffering. Blanchefort saw through me without ever saying straight out that he did not believe me; he hinted I was letting myself be deluded; he talked about Cem's extreme depravity when it came to women—he had three hundred women in Turkey, that's what he would tell me, but I didn't bat an eye. In Bois-Lamy I was Cem's woman and couldn't care less about any intrigues. For four years my face had been a stiff mask, but only during my confessions to Blanchefort did I finally feel impenetrable. The commander noticed this as well. One night, just before dawn, Blanchefort suddenly stood up with his back toward me, as if wanting to hide how much I infuriated him, and uttered emphatically, "Do you think you're very clever, madame?"

I froze, as I had never fully believed I could fool a man like Blanchefort. *Now they'll drive me away from Bois-Lamy; I'll bring a heap of trouble down on Sassenage; now there is nothing left for me but death*—such thoughts ran through my head.

"Be so good as to realize, madame," Blanchefort continued, dispassionate, "your every dodge does nothing to help the Turk. I hope you are sufficiently sober minded not to imagine"—here Blanchefort turned and looked at me with indescribable scorn— "you could kidnap Cem for your own purposes or for your own pleasure. Let's be frank. What would happen then? He would either stay here, under the king's guards, who will likely sell him to his brother, or else Bayezid will finally manage to poison him via some baronet desperate for cash. Is that what you want for Cem?"

Blanchefort fell silent, and I could not find the strength to refute the merciless truth of his words.

"You could have let us know, madame," he went on, "if you found your task distasteful. Yet you accepted it. Could you have been lying to the Holy Church even then? Think about the consequences your unworthy sympathy will bring down upon your home and the Turk himself. I leave you to your prayers, madame. Tomorrow at lunch—you shall not leave your room before then— you will inform me of your intentions. This time without any beating around the bush. By the end of the month, we either will have succeeded, or all will be lost. Your romance with the Turk is finished, madame."

It was the first morning since I had been at Bois-Lamy that I did not go hunting with Cem. Outside an almost summery sun was shining and from my window I could see the woods, the hills, the meadows where Cem and I had ridden so many mornings. Finished... Indeed, my warm dream was coming to an end.

Blanchefort visited me at lunchtime. I told him I was committed to bringing things to a successful conclusion. My stubbornness had not helped at all, and besides I would have done anything for

VERA MUTAFCHIEVA

a final meeting with Cem. For a farewell, which I would utter inwardly, not aloud—Cem would not know it was our final meeting.

Blanchefort drily informed me the kidnapping had been entrusted to the Duke of Bourbon; the duke was happy to meddle in any business that hurt the Lady Beaujeu, the admiral, and the little king. A large group of his knights would ambush Cem on his hunt Friday morning. There would certainly be a battle, but the Bourbons would likely prevail, thanks to their numbers. Of course, the Hospitaller guards would pretend to help the royal forces, since the Order insisted on appearing uninvolved in the incident.

Then Blanchefort explained my part in the kidnapping: I needed to convince Cem that it was to our mutual advantage to run away together to Savoy, to Charles. I needed to secure not only Cem's nonresistance, but his cooperation; the battle could get drawn out or the Bourbons could be defeated. For this reason, while the battle was still raging, Cem, Saadi, and I, along with two of the duke's men, needed to break away and take the shortest route toward Villefranche. There a papal ship would be waiting for us under a false flag.

That very night, I repeated Blanchefort's instructions to Cem word for word. I noticed Saadi was listening far closer. Cem was uneasy. The fact that I had been gone all morning, that for the first time in weeks he had gone riding without me, upset him, which was completely understandable. Cem also sensed the threat hanging over us and suffered at the thought of our parting.

"Why are you speaking to me like this, Hélène?" he asked me, his voice pleading, as if the mere thought of a new effort wearied him. "The important thing is that you are still here. I was already convinced I would not see you again."

"Let's escape before they tear us apart, Cem," I unconvincingly tried to convince him. "Today is Wednesday. On Friday they will be waiting for us by the fork in the woods. While they are fighting, we will ride south to fool them. As soon as we reach La Rotonde, other conspirators will meet us and take us to Charles in Savoy."

I recited this like a lesson, while Cem's expression told me everything was decided. We would do it, of course, but for now let us not count too much on luck, let us think about ourselves and what we had at Bois-Lamy. Then Saadi cut in—until that moment he had never spoken to me in his own name. I hoped I had won him over as well—Saadi was unsurpassable as a companion, a true echo of Cem.

Now Saadi suddenly became an independent will. "Madame, wouldn't Charles have sent us a sign? He did it in all his previous attempts."

I was surprised, because Cem never would have asked me for proof.

"Is that necessary, Saadi?" I replied, flustered. "I contacted Charles through a series of people; perhaps he was afraid of leaving clues, of betrayal."

"I am afraid as well, madame," Saadi said, staring at me. "After every one of our failed escapes, our freedoms, if they can be called that, have been further restricted. I beg you, I plead with you for my master's sake, madame: do not do this unless you are very, very sure we will succeed."

Now here, this was the height of my agonies with Cem. I could not bear to meet Saadi's gaze; I wanted to scream at the top of my lungs, *I can't take any more, I don't want this!* But I kept silent under Saadi's quiet reproach, realizing he likely had long since known who I was and what I was after in his master's bed. Saadi had not tried to stop me earlier, in hopes Cem might steal a few weeks of happiness. Now Saadi was stopping me—after all, our romance, as Blanchefort had called it, was over, wasn't it?

"I pity you, madame," he said very quietly.

I was on the verge of bursting into tears. All the penitence they had drilled into me for so many years, all the scolding and sermons had not affected me. People no better than me had been disgusted by me. To those same people, the Oriental was not even a human being: a Saracen, a Moor, a Turk, or a Greek— we lumped them under the same label and the same scorn; they were the manure upon which our strength, trade, and culture flourished. Yet I met two true human beings during my life-time—please write that down, I insist! One fell in love with me without asking who I was, and the other forgave me without reproach for the worst baseness a woman is capable of.

At that moment I felt as if an unknown power swelled within me—surely this is how slaves feel when they head toward death; surely every humiliated person rebels like this just once. I was prepared to reveal the entirety of my disgrace, I swear to you. *Enough*, I thought, nearly out of my mind, *enough!*

Cem prevented me from doing so, if you can believe it. He began to speak, and Saadi translated. "My master is unhappy we are speaking amongst ourselves, without him. He agrees to your plan, madame."

He said this, got up, and walked out. Cem watched him go in bewilderment—he suspected nothing.

That night, I regretted fighting Blanchefort to win a final meeting with Cem. It was unbearably difficult. As I lay next to Cem with my head on his shoulder, listening to his heart beating deeply as a bell, I kept thinking how fine it would be if a person could choose their own moment of death—I would have chosen that moment. Nothing existed beyond it.

Most likely, if we had shared a common language, Cem would have found out everything about me that night, with nothing held back. Because I really did talk and talk; my fingers passed over Cem's skin, seeking not to hold him, but to remember; my tears gathered in that familiar dip between his collarbone and his shoulder. It was a true leave-taking. One-sided. He took it simply as a deep fit of affection and stroked my hair, twisting it into curls. From time to time he spoke in his unintelligible, barbarian language. I think he was comforting me, his words caressed me. Actually, why am I so sure that Cem, too, was not also taking his leave?

I left before dawn. I didn't want the sun to surprise me with this face. I needed to somehow put my features in order and hold them thus until Friday morning. After that... there would be nothing after that. We parted like every other time. I didn't dare leave my arms twined around his neck any longer—let it be like every other time. I slipped out quietly into the darkness. So I was startled when at the end of the corridor I ran into Blanchefort.

"Keep quiet," he whispered. "Follow me."

We did not go to the chapel, but rather to the commander's office. He had never before showed such recklessness. There all the candles were burning. It was clear Blanchefort had not slept at all.

"Madame," he turned to me without offering me a seat or sitting down himself, "we have been found out. I don't know how I will face Brother d'Aubusson. I don't see any further hope for the Holy Father, since now the king has every reason to triple our guards or else he will simply shut away the Turk in some royal fortress. We fumbled our final chance, madame."

"I swear to you, father," I said, trying to note everything that flooded into me with his words—horror, above all. "I swear to you I did everything within my power."

"I believe you," he cut me off. "If I did not believe you, things would go very hard for you, madame. Yet the denunciation was specifically against you. You have upset someone's reckonings, which means you've done your job well. Good Christ, who would have thought."

Why and how was none of my business. My only thought was Cem surely knew everything now. I imagined his bewilderment, which sharpened into revulsion, which in turn became desperate hatred. *No, Cem is not Saadi. Cem will not forgive, because he once loved me. Once... just an hour ago.*

"I do not wish to wait until morning in Bois-Lamy, father," I said. "Please make the arrangements."

A week later, I was accepted into Saint Mary's Abbey in Arles. The last layman I saw was Baron de Sassenage. Father was watching as they led me away under the long colonnade. He was deeply moved and happy. Without my death, shame had been washed from the House of Sassenage.

FOURTEENTH TESTIMONY OF THE POET SAADI ON THE
MONTHS OF JUNE 1487 TO SEPTEMBER 1487

INDEED, NOTHING IN my previous testimonies has given you even the slightest hint that I, Saadi, hand and voice of my master, would meddle of my own volition in the case of Cem, has it? Poets are not known for taking action, true. But I made my decision, because since time immemorial we have assumed the worst things always come from a woman. From the day Hélène appeared in our midst I felt constant uneasiness. As defenseless against the world as he might be, until now Cem had always demonstrated at least a few crumbs of common sense, yet as soon as Madame de Sassenage entered his life, he went blind and deaf. Thus, I felt wholly responsible for his fate.

During their very first conversation, when Hélène abandoned the topics of the weather, health, and hunting and sobbed over Cem's suffering, my hair stood on end. Hélène was working toward a goal. Taken together with the brothers' benevolent nonintervention in the love story unfolding before their eyes, this conversation convinced me they had arranged for Hélène to be there. Then I second-guessed myself—my explanation was too simple. Wasn't it possible the brothers only knew Hélène was someone's agent—perhaps they even suspected or knew with certainty who had planted her there—and for that reason they were watching her, letting her play out her game so they could catch her accomplices as well? I found the complexity of this interpretation satisfying. I was beginning to understand the West.

I've already mentioned I had given up on waking Cem from his dream. *Sleep, my dear boy,* I thought, being the older, wiser one. *I will not let them bind you in your sleep.*

And then came the night Hélène just spoke of so heart-wrenchingly. I say this without mockery; she was truly distressed, the poor thing. I saw with my own eyes she was planning precisely to bind Cem in his sleep. He was so upset by the likelihood of being parted from her that he took all her advice. He was capable of all manner of madness if it meant a few more days of love. I knew he had never taken too seriously her dreams of his freedom, but surely during their amorous nights he had imagined himself with her outside in the open, under the stars, without that hateful band of brothers and knights at his heels.

That night I noticed Hélène was also upset, but she went too far in her sympathy for Cem, which led me to conclude they had reined her in. That's how it is with women, as you know—they can simultaneously and sincerely experience emotions that reason considers mutually exclusive. I found nothing monstrous about the fact Hélène wove the rope for Cem, whom she loved desperately; history and books have given us plenty of examples in this regard.

VERA MUTAFCHIEVA

I was observing not just the two lovers, but also the third person between them: I was observing myself from the outside. Why on earth did you write in the title of these testimonies of mine "the poet Saadi"? I was no longer "the poet," you see. For far too long, I had carried out the functions of vizier, treasurer, prisoner, wet nurse, babysitter, and pimp for Cem. I was one half the Frank and one half d'Aubusson. Otherwise where would this merciless attitude toward living, breathing people come from, these suspicions that were almost as dark as reality itself? Almost, I say, because despite everything, my ideas about life never fully coincided with life itself—within me, the magnanimity of the East, if not burned, at least still smoldered, along with its love of beauty: such love hinders you from fathoming the world to its very depths, but instead helps you bear it. And in the end, it seems that between the two of us, d'Aubusson and myself, the grand master was the one to be pitied: if I looked upon life as he did, so precisely and certainly, I would drown myself in the deep blue sea off Rhodes.

Forgive me, I digress, but I must draw your attention to my observations of the third party in the game, the formerly renowned poet Saadi.

Incidentally, that evening I clearly saw Hélène was being forced to carry out her duties under a tight deadline. Someone had found out she had become overly convincing when it came to the amorous aspect of her role. And so, Hélène would have to be unscrupulous. Why, you ask? I could come up with two answers. The first: out of depravity, and depravity explains many inexplicable actions; the second: because they had something on her, something dire. Personally, I preferred the latter explanation, for the reason I mentioned above: for love of beauty. And also because Hélène was simply sick with remorse before my eyes. Baseness, it seems, was not innate to her character, and like a fragment in a healed wound, it at least caused her discomfort. I still didn't know who was using Hélène in the case of Cem, but I mentally cursed them and pitied her (she recounted my feelings toward her very accurately). It was unconscionable to force her to drudge along between her fear and her love—either one alone would have been enough for a little partridge like her.

I left them to their heartrending night and took up my place on the fortress wall. I remembered Haydar, who had met his end somewhere on the roads to Hungary, without ever having learned a word of the local language; I remembered the Frank, who lay buried under Rumilly, the bitter Frank who belonged to none, the skeptic who had died of loyalty; I remembered Kasim Bey, killed by Bayezid, who preferred the sultan's revenge over Cem's fate as an exile; I remembered Sinan and Ayas Bey, reworked in the dungeons of Rhodes and sent out into the world as heralds of Rhodes.... No, I no longer felt any pity for that partridge, installed here with us by Lord knows who—many men far more worthy than Hélène de Sassenage had fallen victim in the case of Cem.

"Forgive me, madame," I said out loud, and in French, no less. "You shall not get your way."

And with that, my decision was made. Now all I had to do was carry it out. But how? This was not the first time I had asked myself this question—as those two made love, I had been thinking up answers.

It struck me as wrongheaded to inform the brothers that Hélène had talked Cem into escaping: I wasn't sure they were not precisely the ones behind the plot. Yet informing the royal knights also did not strike me as much more promising; it was entirely possible none other than the king was planning a move that would free him from the Order's irritating, albeit ephemeral, ownership over Cem. So what to do? Turn to Matthias Corvinus? Only everyone in Bois-Lamy who was not a Hospitaller was a royal knight.

Aha, the thought suddenly struck me. I was so happy I ran through the dark corridors of the fortress like a madman. What a fine thing a decision is! I could sense how a single word from Saadi could upend the plans of the pope, the king, and many others.

The guards stopped me outside the commander's room. "Wake him up!" I shouted, needing to make as much noise as possible, or else they would have quietly done me in. "I have made a terrible discovery."

The guards thought for a moment, then one went in while the other kept an eye on me. A short while later the commander came out in his shirtsleeves. He hadn't managed to tuck his shirt in and had his saber in his hand.

"Sir," I began, my voice again needlessly loud, "I beg you to come with me to see His Grace Brother Blanchefort. You will hear something most unbelievable."

The commander toddled along behind me, practically sleepwalking. I raised the same ruckus in front of Blanchefort's door, but he had not been asleep and burst out as soon as I started shouting.

"I want to make a disclosure," I said, somehow managing not to laugh out loud.

"Now? In the middle of the night?" the monk asked me very coldly, yet he had gone pale, which immediately convinced me he had been Hélène's puppet master. The poor dear!

With a lightness I had not felt since Karamania, I swept past the monk and slipped into his room uninvited. The commander followed me. They were standing there staring at me, but their facial expressions were quite different: the royal commander was struggling to wake up, hoping my important disclosure would offer him a chance to shine before his betters, while Blanchefort struggled in vain to master his fears.

I was brief. "Sent by an unknown conspirator, Madame de Sassenage tonight convinced my master to run away, Your Grace, Your Honor," I said. "In this vile game she used all the means available to her, she spared no efforts. I am happy to be able to reveal her secret ambitions to you, my master's lawful guardians."

That was it.

The commander was now fully awake. So much so that he could read Blanchefort's expression—the royal guard gave him a triumphant look; he, like me, had realized my news had crushed the monk.

"Thank you, Saadi," he said before emphasizing the next word. "*We*, Brother Blanchefort and I, will see to our guest's safety."

I walked back to the fortress wall not entirely at ease, wondering whether the brothers would try anything. I placed my hopes in the royal guards; they would have to prevent it. As I made my way down the corridor, I realized I had done Hélène a good turn: I had described her as more diligent in her task than she actually had been. *Never mind*, I told myself. *Why shouldn't at least one person involved in this mess live to see another day?*

You say I have relayed the events of the night of May 29, 1487, far too cheerfully? There was nothing cheerful about them. You know I was once a writer, and a skilled one at that; a terrifying story should never be told in a single, terrifying tone. Only when the human mood can play does it perceive events in their full measure. What's more—I truly was in good cheer that night. We had already lived among enemies for years, yet only then did I realize the upside of our drama: whatever you do, you do it to the detriment of your enemy, and never to the detriment of your friend. Because you have no friends.

Yet despite all my storytelling mastery, I never could finesse my tale to fit that which followed: the final point of turning Cem into a captive. For you this point has surely long been obvious: you have considered Cem a captive since Rhodes. But this is not how he experienced things; his day-to-day life changed frequently—the brothers alternately tightened Cem's handcuffs with the death of one or the other of his companions, with our forced journeys from fortress to fortress, while at other times they created an almost bright atmosphere around him. Turn back the pages and you will notice: until the summer of 1487, we were practically guests in French territory; they feted us, entertained us, protected us from Bayezid. This last bit—the protection—took a form that could be interpreted both as simply overzealous or as a violent imposition; we were not sure to what extent the Order was fending off a real danger and to what extent it was inventing such a threat.

Moreover, despite Cem's helpless rage over being kept under surveillance and not being allowed to travel to Hungary, despite all our suspicions and fears, until the summer of 1487 we lived passably well. At the time I didn't realize the extent to which we had a hand in this. Cem still gave no indication he had given up his fight, he tried to influence every step in our fateful journey. And so the brothers were forced to reckon with us.

Yet as I already told you, I was too close to Cem to notice that his strength, his hopes, his whole vitality were nearing some kind of limit. I was afraid to imagine what lay beyond this border; Cem had always been unpredictable, thus one could never foresee how he would look in his complete abdication. So, despite myself, I was happy about Hélène, about every new thing that delayed that moment. But then Hélène disappeared. She literally disappeared—we didn't know when she left Bois-Lamy. In the morning after my decisive involvement, Cem went down to wait for her in the courtyard, as was his habit, but he was not too worried when she did not appear—after all, she had not showed up the previous morning.

"They are starting to play games with her as well," he said.

The two of us went out hunting. Cem was mostly silent, yet I did not sense any anxiousness in him, as I had before our early escape attempts—this time Cem did not truly believe in his freedom, because he did not particularly want it.

At midday I saw how Cem's alarm suddenly soared—Hélène had not appeared at lunch either. The brothers and the royal guards were more cautious than ever. Cem did not touch his food, he was in a hurry to retreat to his chambers. Under the watchful gazes of our fellow feasters, we excused ourselves and retired.

Cem ran up the stairs. "Saadi, they've kidnapped her," he whispered in horror when we reached the top and leaned against the door from inside, as if fearing an attack. "Oh, I knew it, I foresaw this. Who knows what terrible fate awaits her? They will stop at nothing. Saadi, how can we at least save her life? I don't want her for myself, understand? I only bring misfortune, and I want Hélène to live a happy life. Hélène! The only thing I have possessed in this cruel foreign land."

Cem sobbed as if in verse—this is how deeply one's craft makes an impression on a person. And have you noticed, as soon as you catch a whiff of craft, you immediately exclude sincerity? This holds true even for me, who knows how often a bard not only does not make things up, but only reveals a tiny portion of his true suffering. Or perhaps at that moment I was looking to justify the blow I would deal.

"Cem, do not torment yourself needlessly. It was not love that brought Hélène to you, but instructions: she was supposed to kidnap you for the papacy. She didn't succeed; they found her out and tossed her aside like every used-up weapon. And thank God. Hélène changes nothing in your life, not for better or for worse."

I said all this in a single breath, expecting a terrible storm; Cem couldn't stand interpretations of reality that differed from his own. But yet, as I spoke, I could see there would be no storm. Leaning his shoulder against the door, Cem hung his head lower and lower, as if something enormous pressed down on him with its weight. He did not lose control of himself, as he had during many more minor misfortunes; he also did not fall into the stupor with which his illness had begun. My words had merely confirmed the suspicion Cem had carried through his whole love affair with Hélène. So this meant only Saadi was a shabby poet, since the poet Cem could still love even with the dregs of doubt in his heart.

"So you say she didn't come to me out of love," Cem said at one point. He had moved away from the door and was sitting on his bed, with his head in his hands, hiding his gaze from me. "You're probably right. It crossed my mind as well.... But she left with love, Saadi. No one can convince me otherwise. I can feel it. And the fact that she failed, that we did not escape, is no coincidence. Hélène herself refused to go through with it."

"They did not succeed!" Cem started speaking with the feverish, abrupt inspiration of a high priest of human love. "They failed to degrade absolutely everything. Something remained beyond the grasp of their will: something as weak, malleable, and frightened as only a woman can be. Saadi, much has been taken from me, but God has also given me much: true love."

He went on speaking in this vein for some time. I stopped listening. I had so unexpectedly received aid from Providence that I was paralyzed by gratitude: Cem had found solace in the misery from which I feared he would not emerge of sound mind. Cem did not wish to know how Hélène's plan had failed, and this spared me from lying or making a painful confession. This time, too, Cem seemed to remain within the borders of his hopes. *Merciful God, please let it be so*, I prayed.

Yet during the night I heard him crying. Quiet, muffled sobs—I could see he had pressed his face into the pillows. Had he only been pretending to find consolation for my benefit? Or would he feel the pain of Hélène's absence only gradually?

Indeed, I have noticed the first days after a parting are easy, almost joyful: you are left to feel your love fully, without the shadow of its visible countenance, which sometimes exposes all your dreams as empty. The agony comes later—with the hunger of your blood and skin, with the coolness of the wide bed, with the silence in the room. With all that very physical loneliness, because a person is still alone in spirit, even when in the throes of the most passionate love.

Cem cried more than one night; his grief was not manly, it was that of an animal or a child. He did not curse those responsible for their parting. It was as if he had been sure from the very beginning that it was inevitable; Cem did not take it as a parting from a woman—they had parted him from human intimacy, had robbed him of every last thing.

Strangely, he did not speak of this to me; instead, every evening I sensed he was impatient for night to fall so he could leave the feast table—he was hurrying to visit his memories. This was no longer his illness from Rochechinard, although it did return later in a series of fits; it was a resigned, sweet suffering. I was terribly afraid he would come to love this suffering itself and abandon himself to it—a man is done for the moment he falls in love with his own suffering.

I struggled to amuse Cem. During those days I thought up all manner of escape schemes and delightful surprises. Cem did not lose patience with my awkward attempts. He showed me the quiet sort of gratefulness the terminally ill have for their caretakers, nothing more. While at night I could hear his uneven breathing, his crying. This meek misery was terribly hard for me to bear. I remembered the time when Cem had thrashed about and moaned, hurling curses and threats, railing again his fate. Why does such raging wear itself out and simply cool into sorrow? You can be sorrowful your whole life long—it does not tire you, you grow used to it. I would have given anything to find a cure for Cem.

One day he found it on his own.

"Saadi," he said without looking at me, "don't you have any hashish?"

We had hashish, of course. Back in Karamania, most of our men smoked hashish. I had even tried it myself. We never managed to convince Cem—he believed hashish was harmful to a man who meant to long remain a man; hashish made you soft, he said, it made you flabby, it ate away at you. Some of our men tried to tempt him with the beauty of hashish-inspired dreams, but Cem would always answer, "Is there any dream more beautiful than life, my friends? Live instead of dreaming!"

He wasn't exactly right about that—everyone has the need for dreams. And if Cem had no need for hashish, it was only because he was able to dream while wide awake. That's why my heart ached when he made his timid request. Cem could no longer dream without help. Something surely had been killed off for good within Cem.

"I shall look and see, my friend," I said.

I found some for him. A little bit left over amidst the belongings of our men who had been led away in 1484. I recognized the pouch—it had belonged to the Karamanian Latif.

Remnants, only remnants, I thought. Back then we'd all had a present, as well as a future. And now we wandered like the dead through the memories of Karamania, Lycia, Nice, dried flowers from Hélène—Cem did not allow me to throw them out—Latif's pouch, Haydar's books. I brought him the hashish.

"Do you know how to do it, Saadi?" Cem asked me when I brought him the hashish, without lifting his gaze.

I knew. I cut off a bit of grayish dust and stuffed it into the pipe. I worked slowly, as if putting something off for as long as possible.

"Cem," I said hesitantly, "you must preserve your strength. You have heard what hashish does.…Your struggle is still ahead of you. Go into it strong."

"A man preserves his strength for the future if he can get through the present day without hashish," he replied. "While I have the feeling every hour I live consciously is killing me. I have gone beyond the borders of my strength, Saadi."

There is something irresistible about an outstretched, open human palm. Cem reached his out toward me. I sat down in front of his bed. Cem was begging me: *Help me bear many more days of life. Do not deny me my dreams. Let me return with them to my homeland, to my youth—let me return to myself. Let me go back to the other side of the border.…*

I would have placed not hashish in his hand, but rather would have liked to fill it with my life; but Cem needed much more than that, more than the hundreds of lives cut short due to Cem's rebellion: he needed oblivion.

"Don't smoke until the ashes have cooled," I said. "It's stronger then."

"Thank you, Saadi. You will leave me alone, won't you?"

After his hours on hashish, I found him dazed—as he should be. Yet shame crept into his daze, like a man who has allowed himself to be disarmed and taken alive. Latif's pouch was soon empty, and I was forced to ask the brothers for hashish.

"Hashish, you say?" Antoine d'Aubusson asked me; Blanchefort had been replaced only three days after Hélène's failure.

"I'll give orders to have some delivered. They sell it on the streets in Marseille. After all, we are obliged to satisfy our guest's every whim. His every whim."

If by his every whim, you mean hashish, I answered him silently, and he guessed my thoughts.

"By the way," he said, "we have finished building the Turkish bath the Order has prepared specially for your master. Inform the prince."

"Where?" I asked, puzzled. "We did not see it being built."

"In Bourganeuf. Some Saracens built it. We Europeans know nothing of such things, while His Highness clearly suffers without a bath."

"Yes, just imagine, we bathe. Perhaps that is why in the East only the dervishes have lice."

I slammed the door hard. The brothers' fits of politeness always put me on my guard. Why they would mercifully allow Cem to smoke hashish was as clear as day. There is no surer enemy to human action and will than hashish. Cem himself offered the brothers a jailer they could only dream of. Was it pure coincidence Cem had arrived at the thought of anesthesia?

I thought back, searching my memory: several times, even before Hélène's appearance, why had I seen our fellow feasters and Cem very strangely, happily sleepy? Why did I recall that, as a rule, you never smoke hashish for the first time alone? After all, a person would not fiercely crave a food they had never before tasted.

Damn it all to hell, I concluded. *I no longer know what is good and what is evil. If sobriety drives you to madness, what is the point of being sober?*

This left the second mystery: the Turkish bath. What was Brother d'Aubusson, albeit not Pierre, trying to say with this? For years Cem had been irked by this enforced filth, while the West shamelessly scratched itself wherever the lice bit. It was difficult for us Easterners, who had been bathing since birth. Up until Nice we at least had the sea, but the north's waters are cold and murky. Since we had been left just the two of us, I had to explain to every brother individually that we needed warm water, a lot of it, a full tub, and every week at that, and the brother in question was always amazed. "We are bathing," I would explain to every one of them, and these ridiculous baths of ours in Cem's enormous domed room soon became a subject of gossip all around the Dauphiné.

In short, we had somehow been living dirty for years—what caused the brothers to suddenly pamper us now?

It was July, late July. Nothing had changed in Bois-Lamy besides the absence of Blanchefort and Cem's ever-more-frequent retreats into the land of hashish. During those hours I wandered alone through the castle, with nothing to do, and without any guards even. A heavy boredom weighed upon Bois-Lamy; it reminded me of something already well settled in and which would only settle further into place. I did not sense the earlier tension between the monks and the knights, as if the two halves of Cem's jailers had realized this was how things stood and had made peace with it. I sometimes saw them playing dice together in the kitchens. Their calm was not a good sign.

Right at the end of September, Antoine d'Aubusson told us we were setting out for Bourganeuf, on the river. They led us there like captives, with no suite of our own, and with no pomp.

I had hoped Cem would want to say farewell to the places where he had galloped with Hélène, where he had laid his head upon her lap.

"Why add more memories, Saadi?" he replied. "I have too many as it is."

We traveled for a week, always to the northwest.

Once this had driven Cem mad—we were getting farther away from Rumelia, from the fight. Now he was quiet and very distracted. Since he had gone out only very infrequently of late, he was sickly pale despite the summer. He looked at the woods and fields along the road with indifference. What could Cem Sultan have in common with the Dauphiné, with Auvergne?

"At least we'll have a change of scenery." I struggled to wake him up. "I was sick to death of those three scrubby hills in Bois-Lamy."

A grunt was Cem's only reply.

"Whatever the case, we are citizens of the world, and thus of Auvergne as well. Why should Auvergne be worse for us than Bois-Lamy?" I prattled on.

"There are no citizens of the world." Cem suddenly livened up, or rather, he grew irritated; he had become peevish.

"There are: poets."

"Have your thoughts really not grown up over all these years, Saadi? If a poet has no homeland, then why doesn't he sing here? You speak their language, don't you? Yet you can't sing in it. Because it is not your mother tongue, my dear citizen of the world."

"Yet you wrote a lot in Nice, Cem. So that means…"

"Sure I wrote!… But for whom? For whom, I ask you? A poet cannot exist without listeners, just as a sultan cannot exist without an army. When I parted from our people—whether they be listeners or soldiers—I ceased to be both a poet and a sultan, Saadi.

"Listen." Cem drew his horse up very close to mine, yet he was not whispering, he was practically shouting, as if feverish. "Remember what I tell you now, because in a month or a year I will no longer say it, and I might not even think it then, I might not be thinking anything at all: I am no longer Cem Sultan, inspiration to the poets of Karamania and leader of the sipahi. Where is that court full of poets, where are Mehmed Khan's cavalrymen? They are gone, gone! So Cem, too, is gone, Cem is dead.

"You know what a person is, Saadi?" he asked me, still shouting as if giving a speech to an invisible multitude. "Beauty, talent, strength, dozens of qualities—this is still only possibility. This potential becomes a person only when someone's love delights in his beauty, when there is a crowd to cry over his songs, or an army to carry out his conquests. Many people are needed to transform the potential person into the actual person. My people are gone, Saadi. And Cem Sultan will go down in history as an unfulfilled promise...."

Alarmed by Cem's agitation, by his inexplicable outburst, I glanced around—what would the brothers think? They appeared dispassionate, even though they kept a close eye on us. Likely they figured the Turk was having yet another fit of rage, despair—he was rabid, in short. But I wanted to make sense of it for myself—since Hélène had appeared, Cem had not spoken to me like this. He seemed to be steadily replacing the whole world with hashish, bit by bit and hour by hour. And this overwrought, uncalled-for speech was the spasm of a dying man, a lucid insight, a brief return toward oneself on the threshold of darkness.

"Why are you telling me this, Cem?"

"Because I have a bad feeling, my dear citizen of the world, and I am afraid of dying with no last will and testament."

"What nonsense! What do you mean by last will and testament?"

"Please, Saadi," he replied, "I'm begging you, write it down. First write down what I told you now. Let it be known that Cem knew, and his life was not naked self-deception. It was that only to a certain extent, until now. Then write about the other things."

"What other things, Cem?"

"Of that which will happen when I am gone."

"But you still have more than half a life before you, Cem. You are healthy, thank God, and young."

"I'm not saying I'll die, my friend. But whatever happens from this point on *will happen without me*."

PART FOUR

1487

Our journey ended two weeks ago—our final journey, I'm afraid.
Our new refuge—our final one, I'm afraid—is called Bourganeuf.

So here we are at Bourganeuf. This time I'll describe it, since
we'll be staying here; Bourganeuf is not simply another stop
along our unfathomable wanderings.

Approaching the castle, you pass through the city gates to
enter the settlement, which I would even call a "town," part
of Brother Blanchefort's domain. The inhabitants are subjugated to the commander in both the mundane and spiritual
sense; they consider our man Blanchefort, thoroughly oppressive character that he is, second only to God himself. This is
important for our purposes, since as extremely loyal subjects,
they are our additional, unpaid jailers; we will find no sympathy among them.

Bourganeuf consists of 150 practically identical houses,
each very tidy, and shops. I wonder who does the buying in
Bourganeuf, since every single person is selling. Its streets are

narrow, paved, and as clean as if indoors. And empty, I might add—here the whole population works from morning till night, nary a human voice is heard, only the sounds of labor. In the evening even those sounds fall silent, and in every house a single window is lit up: the family dinner. Then they sleep. A night of deep sleep after a fifteen- or sixteen-hour workday, the eve of another equally long workday.

A hill rises in the center of Bourganeuf, the houses are pressed between its slopes and the old city walls. At the foot of this hill there used to be a moat, which has since turned into a bog—thankfully there are at least frogs to break the silence. The hill is bare, but upon its crest the castle juts up—that's what they call the ring of tall buildings whose outer walls are an impregnable fortress. Inside this ring stands the church, built two centuries ago and freshly renovated, with no frescoes. Instead, a clay statue of John the Baptist stands inside, covered in a hemp robe.

As we made our way up the hill toward our new refuge, I could see two rather large towers. This surprised me to some extent; here the castles usually only had one. I noticed something else as well: the larger one was brand-new, gleaming white as if the stone had been quarried only yesterday. Later I read the inscription above the door, which said: "In the year 1484, work on the large tower and renovations on the church in the fortress Bourganeuf began, financed by the religious community with three thousand five hundred gold ducats, thanks to Brother Guy de Blanchefort, Grand Prior of Auvergne, commander of Cyprus and Bourganeuf, nephew of the widely respected and powerful monsignor, the Grand Master of Rhodes, Pierre d'Aubusson."

This means three years ago, as we went from castle to castle under the troubadours' serenade, the Holy Order was already building us a personalized prison: while Matthias and Qaitbay fought for Cem, and while Cem himself believed every day brought him closer to his victorious campaign, in Bourganeuf stone upon stone was being laid to raise the tower known as "La Tour Zizim"—a prison designed with all the comforts of our time.

A cruel truth. Our companions left us to digest it in silence. I translated the inscription for Cem, but he did not deign to reply. He had halted his horse between the church and the tower in question, looking bored.

Evening had almost fallen. A monk led the way with a torch. The winding staircase smelled of fresh wood and creaked irritatingly beneath the brother's feet. We followed after him and were struck immediately by the dampness—the mortar had not yet dried.

First, we climbed the old tower and from there passed along the fortress wall before descending four stories into the new tower. The ceilings were low. Pitch darkness. The monk illuminated a small space with brick benches and a cauldron. "His Highness's bath," he whispered, as if letting us in on a secret. Of course. This bath was the supposed reason we'd suffered this weeklong journey.

We went upstairs. On the first floor our guide pointed at the wall. "That is the ground floor. The stables," he again explained in a whisper. Would we, too, need to whisper in this mysterious abode? On the second floor, a large round room: "The kitchen." On the third level, several smaller, very simple rooms with rough-hewn floors and fireplaces: "Rooms for the royal guard." Here, too, was the door out to the fortress walls. There was no other way out of the tower, unless we count the entrance to the stables, which are not connected to the upper floors. The fourth floor was meant to dazzle us with its magnificence. It was divided in two, into a large and small room. The large room featured a fireplace lined with colorful stone. Next to it stood a canopied bed, a heavy table, two chairs, a rug, and several trunks. The only light filtered into the room through something like a funnel. High, high up, the ceiling's dome came together in a round window. "When it rains or is winter, we shut it"—now I realized the monk was whispering out of a certain discomfiture—"This is His Majesty's room." A little door led to the neighboring room: mine. Only a bed and a trunk. A narrow slit instead of a window.

We climbed up to the fifth, sixth, and seventh floors with difficulty. Our legs, throats, voices ached. My heart cried with its every beat: "Prison, prison!" Finally, events had arrived at where they had inevitably been heading. I didn't look at the cells intended for Cem's suite—Hospitallers and knights, that was his suite.

We went out onto the roof, a circular space with a crenellated balustrade. "This is where the guards will stand, here and in front of the doors to the third floor," the monk explained. "Finally in Bourganeuf, you will be certain your life is not in danger, Your Highness."

Cem was already running down the creaking stairs, knocking into the still-wet walls. I could hear his steps below—uneven, faltering, stumbling. The sounds of a person running away from something worse than death.

I went after him, feeling my way down; the torchbearer did not follow me.

I looked for Cem in his so-called chambers—they were empty. Another floor down—the wall. Cem was there. He had stuffed himself through an embrasure and hung over the courtyard, looking dazed. I touched him gently, and he turned as if stung.

"Saadi, have they locked us up?"

I couldn't see his eyes in the darkness, but I could imagine them very well.

"Calm down, Cem. This is nothing new, we have been prisoners since Rhodes."

I led him away like a sick man. A fire was already burning in his chambers, yet it did nothing to warm the tower's tomb-like dampness. Cem hurled himself down on the bed fully clothed and turned his face to the wall. He stayed there for days, with and without hashish.

I measure the days by the dirty light that breaks through the ceiling of the room. You have to stand beneath that funnel to glimpse a round scrap of sky, cloudy or starry, above your head. Most of our light comes from the fireplace—they keep it lit around the clock. I sit in front of it, staring at the flames, sunk in silence. Only Cem's sighs or ravings disturb the quiet. The hashish often makes him ramble incoherently, yet from single words caught here and there I can figure out what dreams visit my friend. Karamania, of course, the red mountainous desert of Lycia, blindingly white Rhodes framed in bright blue, the colorful tumult of the coast of Savoy...

God Almighty, I think, *thank goodness you have blessed us with hashish.*

November 4, 1487

Here in Bourganeuf, I have more freedom than Cem; he is allowed only as far was the fortress wall, where he goes to stretch his legs sometimes. "No strolls outside the tower." The monks claim Bayezid has made attempt after attempt on his brother's life. When Cem is out on the wall, guards watch over him from one end and the other, and yet more guards keep watch up above from the roof of the tower. In Bourganeuf eyes are always on Cem; when he wants to escape them, he spends whole days in his room, lying on his bed. Sometimes he tolerates my presence, other times he asks me to leave. I prefer the latter—I find it endlessly taxing to keep vigil over a person who does not speak for hours, who is absent.

I leave not only Zizim's Tower, but the fortress itself. I slowly make my way down the hill—very slowly, so it lasts longer. I set out through the streets of Bourganeuf, a half dozen streets about 300 strides long. I already know their every cobblestone, every window box full of geraniums. I know the working people of Bourganeuf by sight. They study me carefully from behind their counters, between their various sacks and jars; their gazes pass me from shop to shop, they follow me all the way along my short path to the city wall where the royal guard sends me back, again only with their eyes. Then I again retrace my steps, under those working people's same gazes.

In the beginning I dared to start conversations—could I really live like this, staying silent twenty-four hours a day? I would stop in front of a shop and start asking questions about their trade. They would give me one-word answers—here people always seem hurried, businesslike, they look upon you as a dangerous loiterer. Their answers imply I have it easy, I'm fed by the king, after all. It's more than reproach—there is hostility in their words: I am a Saracen. A suspicious character.

I climb back up the hill to the fortress, even more slowly to make it last. I walk around the church two or three times, I even go into it now and then. Through its colorful stained-glass windows the northern light does not look so turbid, the sun practically shines in that narrow nave. I contemplate the clay statue of John the Baptist, painted in three colors, with his glassy, hate-filled eyes. Once I caught myself sticking my tongue out at him—this is the most I can do to harm Brother d'Aubusson's patron saint.

I go out into the courtyard and circle around the church. I surely resemble a bat in my quiet, aimless wandering. I put off the moment when Zizim's Tower will again swallow me up. But it inevitably comes, and I start up the stairs. They creak more loudly than ever—the wood is still drying, drying up and cracking. I go into Cem's room. He is lying there, staring up, as if that sharp funnel of a ceiling has absorbed all his attention and thoughts. He is once again dreaming while awake, so I know it is pointless to speak to him. He no longer needs anyone, the bridge between us has been broken.

I sit down and stare at the flames in the fireplace—fire and the sea contain inexhaustible variation, gripping your gaze for many long hours. I stare at the flames, and since I don't smoke hashish, I am obliged to think. And I think: *God, why have you made time so long?*

November 10, 1487

Today we received a thoughtful gift from Brother d'Aubusson: a monkey and a parrot. Cem peered at the monk who brought them with suspicion. "In his striving to provide entertainment for His Highness, Brother d'Aubusson offers this modest present," the monk whispered. He set down the two cages and slipped out.

After spending a half hour contemplating the new additions that had disturbed our solitude, Cem got up. He walked around the cages with a distracted air, before sitting down on the floor in front of the monkey. I was amused as Cem tried to find a common language with the little creature, making funny faces and gestures, silly sounds. Meanwhile the monkey was studying him, its new companion, in great detail. It apparently came to some conclusion, because it finally stuck its paw through the bars and grabbed hold of Cem's finger.

Cem laughed aloud with the new, not-quite-sane laughter hashish brings on; he opened the cage and picked up the animal. The monkey tolerated this and began playing with Cem's buttons. Then it jumped onto the bed and entertained us with some real monkey business.

"Saadi," Cem asked me, still laughing, "do you think I can teach it to play chess?"

"Why not?" I replied, glad I would now be entirely freed from Cem's silent, heavy presence.

"You can have the parrot," he said magnanimously. "I can't stand the smell of birds."

Thus, I became the proud owner of a parrot, exactly what I had so long been missing. I dragged the cage into my little room, where there was just enough space for the two of us. I

VERA MUTAFCHIEVA

dumped it onto the floor, thinking I would let the parrot starve to death—perhaps that would infuriate Brother d'Aubusson? I was almost out the door when it hit me: "There is no God but Allah!" I shouted at it. If I repeat those words to it every day, will it learn them?

December 3, 1487
"There is no God but Allah!"

Every morning, as soon as I start to stir in my bed, my parrot greets me with our creed.

"There is no God but Allah," I reply to the only creature in France that speaks my language and believes in my God. I would have been foolish to let it starve.

Cem's companion is even better than mine. I often see them sitting in front of the chessboard. They move pawns, knights, and rooks with almost the same skill; they behave in almost the same way: from time to time one of them gets up, paces around the room with the same meaningless movements before returning to the game. It's funny: the animal is supposedly doing everything its owner does, supposedly imitating him completely, yet in the monkey I see something more human, most likely a striving toward humanness. While Cem is still struggling to destroy his humanity. With every passing day his behavior grows more immoderate, with no concern for rules or decorum, as if he is satisfied by the fact he is degenerating and losing the qualities that once made him a brilliant man, an idol to the intellectuals and armies of an entire empire.

Yes, in fact, this is very likely Cem's true essence—Cem, whom I always considered an actor equally good in every role. But on the most fundamental spiritual level, he is an extremely spoiled child. Cem was handsome and charming, talented, magnanimous, generous, attractive, and inspiring, when that brought him some kind of satisfaction. The six years during which he fought against the encroaching despair were also easy years—everything and everyone fed Cem with hopes, and so Cem did not turn his back on his good qualities, since he believed they would soon dazzle the crowds again. But the first moment when Cem needed to fight to preserve his personality, now only for his own sake and not as a means but as an end, Cem let it fall to ruin. And in that ruination he found some perverse delight—the delight of torturing someone who either loves you or needs you.

I am the former, I who saw a deity in Cem; how could I not be tormented by the fall of my idol, how could I not risk everything to save him? The latter is the world as a whole. What harsher revenge against d'Aubusson or Innocent than the destruction of their precious bargaining chip?

This is likely what Cem is thinking, to the extent he's still thinking at all.

Yet my friend's calculations are fundamentally off: he cannot scare his jailers with his spiritual self-destruction, nor can he exact revenge in this way. Not as long as he is physically alive. But perhaps he can at least get his revenge on me, so long as he stubbornly presents me with the broken image of my former idol? This is a good question. But why on earth does everyone overestimate the love another has for him? Why do we overestimate its durability and inviolability?

It's true—I once loved Cem above all else. I would swear this even with my dying breath. But I loved the Cem whom I carried in my imagination, and only insofar as the living Cem did not wage war against the image I had created. When the tasks of our daily life hindered me from belonging entirely to my imagination, I came down to earth and collided there with the nonimaginary Cem. Then there was no room for self-delusion: Cem the man now inspired pity. This pity tempted me and flattered my ego: when you pity, you are better, stronger, more active. You can help.

Yet how long can such a feeling last? Pity, I mean. I still don't know the answer—for the time being, my pity, my service, and my help are compulsory. I am also a prisoner.

December 25, 1487
Last night was a holiday, their Christmas. Down below, in Bourganeuf, things were livelier than on other nights. For a long time, the bells of both the city church and the fortress chapel rang out dully, because their clanging was absorbed by the thick falling snow. The windows down in the city stayed lit up until late, all the windows. I heard a song, a sad song, even though it mentioned that greatest of human joys: birth. As I crouched on the wall huddled in my fur coat, I got the sense that on this night, the working people of Bourganeuf were not as sadly alienated from one another as they were on every other day. They were united by faith in the same god, by hopes for one and the same new year shared by all working people, whether filled with bounty or drought.

I am the only one outside this shared joy, huddled in a fur coat bought with the king's money on the wall of my prison—I don't count Cem anymore for some reason. I am an infidel, a foreign body landed among all this Christianness. I am wearing French furs and tight French pants, I abandoned my turban way back in Bois-Lamy. Even if they were to change my very skin, which they flay from me piece by piece, I would still be foreign.

I hate them. I hate the burghers of Bourganeuf with all their geraniums and jars of Eastern spices. Yet I would like for them to love me. To see me not as a suspicious foreigner, to welcome me for at least this evening behind the curtains of their lighted windows. Then surely I could sit for an hour or two at the feast table and sip a bit of weak French wine alongside them.

Drinking with someone, having them speak to you and speaking to them in turn, being together... Had I ever thought when I praised my luck at being a citizen of the world that around such a citizen of the world reigns a crushing and insurmountable chill? *People, I'm cold*, I wanted to scream last night.

"There is no God but Allah!" the parrot greeted me, my only fellow Muslim in France.

February 4, 1488

I write only rarely, because all our days are the same. I wonder why Cem, in his final lucid moment, asked me to write down his story; what would he want me to write? Our deep and meaningful conversations? We go days without exchanging a single word, not counting the mundane trivialities: "Where is my robe, Saadi?"; "Pass me the pipe"; "Throw some more wood on the fire, Saadi, I'm freezing." I walk between the fireplace and our trunks, sometimes I reach for a sheet of paper. At first, Cem would look at me in alarm at such moments: I would write while he was lying on his back or playing chess with the monkey.

How would I present Cem Sultan to posterity? Now I notice no such alarm—Cem spits upon posterity, just like everything else.

But I cannot do that, no. When all is said and done, I live without hashish, there is no one to replace the world for me, with its countless people, cities, conversations, and roads, thus I find myself starting up conversations with the guards ever more often. I know they will reply to me with filtered words, perhaps even words learned by heart in advance from Brother d'Aubusson's letters, but I am counting on the fact that even the guards are bored in Bourganeuf.

They are not silent; likely d'Aubusson hopes to keep Cem conscious by tossing him scraps of news. This is how I learn of the war between Turkey and Egypt. For this reason, the West is once again swarming with envoys; Corvinus and Qaitbay would now be happy to see Cem sent either to Hungary or to Egypt. It doesn't matter where, as long as he would be closer to Bayezid, otherwise Bayezid will unleash his forces.

"The last Egyptian envoy offered a million ducats for Cem," they tell me.

What a fairy tale! Not only is Cem now a legend, his price has also become legendary as well. Has the world ever seen a person appraised to such heights? The same person who now sits upon his rumpled bed moving knights, pawns, and rooks across a chessboard.

I couldn't help myself, I went in to him; I knew how I would find him—unwashed since yesterday morning, bloated, grayish yellow. In a robe he had not taken off for a week. Fat. Oh yes. That's the other news here: Cem is getting fat. Besides hashish, food is the other thing that keeps him occupied. Our only semirational conversations are on this topic. Every day, Cem describes in great detail what he would like to eat; the cook, who is called in every morning and again around noon, listens to my translation and nods. Sometimes it takes me a long time to find the French word for some spice of ours; here they are different, so I have to make substitutions. In such cases, Cem frowns while he eats, and this is precisely when I hear his most colorful curses against our hosts: pigs, omnivorous rabble, tasteless mutts, and so on. Then I convey new commands to the cook, without Cem's commentary, of course.

April 8, 1488
I bathed him yesterday. He had refused to bathe for five whole months—he was freezing, he claimed. For five months I had not seen him, god of the Karamanian poets, undressed.

In yesterday's steam sat a middle-aged man. His legs were the only things about him that reminded me of Cem—still firm, but even they had lost their sturdiness. Yet another layer of fat covered his back and chest, his stomach hung in several folds. And all of that reddish fur, like a wild boar. Was he not beginning to resemble the Conqueror, with his disfiguring obesity? No, in the Conqueror every feature had been alive, unbridled impulses shook his short, rounded body. This man here is taller, yet with no vital spark, as if dozing off. An animal that has come out of its winter hibernation with reluctance, lethargic. And why is one of his eyelids sagging more heavily, opening more slowly than the other? How much damage this winter of hashish, immoderate eating, and lack of hunting and riding has done.

While the guards keep pushing news on me. Corvinus and Qaitbay didn't get anywhere, I found out, which means the pope's chances are looking up. On the Royal Council, attitudes in favor of Rome are gaining ground. How could they not? I thought, imagining what promises the papal legates were making, how many cardinals and bishops France would gain. After all, the working people always end up footing the bill.

April 30, 1488
It took a great amount of coaxing for me to get him into decent shape for this year's envoy—Cem, in his languidness, stubbornly resisted. I kept telling him that as soon as Bayezid found out his brother had given up his fight, this would reduce his price immediately and they would treat us even more poorly.

We hadn't spoken this much for months. Or rather, I hadn't. Cem shot me hateful looks out from under one eyelid; he was angry at me for disturbing his peace. "Everything is pointless," he said more than once.

He was right. I realized I was going to all this effort only so as not to give Bayezid the opportunity to gloat—I don't want anyone to suspect what Cem has become. I hinted at this to him. "As if it matters," he hissed. And a short while later, after I had slipped on his ceremonial furs: "Let them see, let them! Let Bayezid find out everything, then he'll crush their ugly mugs."

"So now you're rejoicing at Bayezid's victories?" I asked caustically, drenched with sweat from the effort of fighting that heavy, flaccid body.

"At victories over d'Aubusson and all this murderous scum." The first sensical answer I had heard in months.

The envoy was waiting for us in the church—there was no reception hall here. He was standing with his back to John the Baptist, as if sullied by the saint's presence. An elderly desiccated man, who had likely risen up through the army's ranks; his weathered face reminded me of a soldier's. He has surely ridden for years through conquered lands, bearing wounds and loot; he would go back home to catch a glimpse of a newborn child; he has gained experience, gossiped, crawled, and strode; he has passed bribes and committed murders to get where he is now, I thought as images raced through my mind. A general impression of a thoroughly male existence. So far from mine.

Could I not be in his place now, with my quick wit, knowledge, agility? What devil goaded me into serving inspiration, amidst a court of half men in Karamania: a poet, a citizen of the world? Why did I myself not narrow that world to a single empire and a single master such that today I would know I belonged to someone and he would protect me so I could continue to serve? Why did I not choose one city and one woman, no matter which one, among the thousands of women, as my own?

If I had... today some sipahi from Aintab would say, "Saadi is our colonel." Some woman would say, "Saadi is my husband. I am waiting for him to come back from war, to bring our children gifts, to dress me in new clothes, and to buy me perfume. And I will wait for Saadi not for a year, not for six years, but for twenty, because I am his wife and my children are his."

If... if! Somewhere—in some regiment, in some home, an empty space would be left when Saadi the sipahi, when Saadi the father died. But how would the burghers of Bourganeuf react to my death? The guards would bury me outside the city walls so I would not pollute their sacred ground with my infidel corpse. During that time the city would go on living with its workaday sounds, and after three days the parrot would fall silent and forget "There is no God but Allah." Someone else would toss logs on the fire, would bathe the flabby layers beneath which Cem rested, and underneath those layers Cem would not even realize his servant's face had changed.

They had led my master into the church. White and gold—cursed colors. Cem stood, his gaze fixed in the distance above the envoy's head. Perhaps I was seeing things, but he seemed to straighten his shoulders, suck in his stomach. Attempting a regal stance at the last minute. The envoy was peering hard at him—I can only imagine the flood of questions Bayezid Khan showered his messenger with every time, how he insisted on him describing every change in Cem. This gaze was torture for Cem—the world had not had a glimpse of his degradation in a long time, and Cem surely believed it remained hidden, unknown. He tolerated it somehow, yet his shoulders slumped slackly on his way back to his room; every effort he was forced to make cost him ever more agony.

I realize—since I don't smoke hashish, I now come to realizations far too often on the whole—that recently I have been feeling more bitterness than pity toward my master. I sense in recent days something forgotten has awakened within me: my selfishness. My shared cause with Cem has ended in failure, my love for Cem has also burned out, those two human aims in my life no longer exist, and I am slowly but surely turning into an animal. And like every animal, I now want my animalistic right to freedom and pleasure—for myself alone. I am now naked in spirit—I have come to realize this, without feeling any pangs of conscience; it is not my fault. The singing, sublime poet was simply strolling down the streets of the world when he was set upon by thieves; they covered his mouth and left him naked. "Stop, thief!" I wanted to scream. "Stop the thief who stole away from me the lie that I am not an animal."

I sense my animalistic struggle beginning. It finds me during my empty hours, and I have far too many empty hours. It reminds me these hours could be filled: with action, with satisfaction, with success. Yes, I must toss away the final fig leaf covering my nakedness—my sense of duty toward a drowning man. Cem is drowning, he sinks deeper with every passing day. I know my presence does nothing to stop this—no one helps anyone in the world we live in. Step beyond yet another lie—the duty to help— and you're already on your way, completely nude, completely free and alone under the stars.

Free! Indeed, no one is guarding me. Those scumbags, to use Cem's phrase, are counting on the fact that strong reins hold me—the knowledge that someone needs me—so they are not afraid I might escape. They don't guard me.... And why should they guard me? After all, Saadi is not a sultan's son and has never had the advantages of a born ruler, so why should he suffer the curse that hangs over every born ruler?

I have suffered it out of empathy, that much is true. I was tied to a person with whom I shared the same thoughts, the same taste, and the same will. He no longer exists, that person. Am I obliged to serve a memory?

July 18, 1488

It seems I am obliged. The news is bad. If I had run away from the deadly monotony of our days, I would have been justified —it wouldn't have made a difference if it were me or anyone else by Cem's side.

Lately, the guards have been showering me with news. The commander Brother Blanchefort himself even called me in. "Saadi," he told me, "I'm counting on you, given the prince's current state. You must be ready for anything, Saadi."

It struck me that this is how they prepare a dying person's loved ones for the worst. Yet I insisted upon clarity.

"What do you mean, Your Grace?"

"As we informed you, the papacy was hoping to finally get their hands on Cem Sultan. Even up to two weeks ago this seemed very likely. But at the beginning of the month the king gave audience to Bayezid's emissary, who reminded the Council his master would uphold the contract regarding Cem only if Cem did not leave France. Otherwise Bayezid will make peace with Qaitbay and declare war on all of Christendom."

I tried to play down the news. "We've heard this same old song many times before, Your Grace."

"Not exactly," he corrected me. "Bayezid Khan offered the king help against any of his enemies, no matter who, as long as Cem never leaves France. And Charles VIII has been seeking a powerful ally for years so he can reclaim his lawful inheritance: Naples. How does an alliance between France and Turkey sound? Unless we foil it by stealing Cem away for Rome, that is."

"I don't see how that would change our current situation, monsignor. We are in France now, are we not? Yet I constantly keep hearing that our true place is in Rome."

Blanchefort was left unsatisfied by our conversation. But what did he expect? Had he perhaps wanted to reawaken my master's dead hopes through me?

"Cem," I began as he ate his dinner, "it appears a new journey awaits us."

"Hm." His invariable answer.

"They will move us to Rome." I deliberately exaggerated the news to see whether I could evoke in Cem some human gesture.

"Let them move us to the ass end of beyond! Sooner or later Bayezid will crush their skulls. For the glory of the Conqueror." What turns of phrase, no?

His eyes (one half-closed) slid over the roasted round of beef to his cup; they took on a fierce expression, because some bit of gristle had lodged between his teeth; impatient fingers, accompanied by an impatient growling—Cem now gave free rein to such sounds quite often—tossed the gristle in the fireplace, then they prowled over his robe until they were no longer greasy and could better grip the bone. Cem swallowed noisily, poured a full cup of wine down his throat, and wiped his mouth with his sleeve. Then he reached out again—aimlessly, he no longer knew what he was seeking, those hands now knew only to grasp and swipe; they caught a crust of bread and reduced it to crumbs; they carelessly brushed against the tablecloth. Cem snapped his fingers—one of his new, insufferable habits—as if to say even if he wanted to, he could eat no more. He sat there for a short while longer, gazing over the table as if with regret—he had finished his only task for the day. He pushed himself back along with the chair—the intolerable shuffling and groaning of a gorged sluggard; he fixed one open and one squinted eye on the fire—what on earth could Cem be thinking about now?. Why do I get the sense he is less apathetic than usual?

He belched, begging your pardon. He scratched the reddish hairs that filled the space from his nose to his chest (he had chased off the barber). For a moment his hand reminded me of Cem—how could it not have changed, too? What is Cem's hand doing here on this grubby foreigner?

"Rome," he said in a hoarse whisper. "So what? Let it be Rome. Only before winter, do you hear? I hate the cold. Do you hear?" He was shouting at me because I wasn't answering.

That's the other new thing here: the shouting. When he's not silent, that is. The first few times it drove me berserk. I hate yelling. If a person wants to listen to you, you can whisper, even, and if he doesn't want to listen, every shout is powerless. I could not recall Cem ever behaving like this during my nearly decade-long service with him. Now he shouted about the littlest things: my movements irritated him, my presence or absence, my brief comments about the weather or the food.

Why doesn't he admit he hates me? I wondered today. Why indeed. And why don't I admit I hate him, this stump dumped in the middle of my path, the cause of all of my misfortunes? Compassionate scorn, empathetic irritation, spiritual alienation —what complex words we have come up with for something so simple: hatred.

Yes, I admit it: without Cem I would be someone different, somewhere different. It is pointless to list who and where, every human life offers countless possibilities if you yourself—yourself!—do not sacrifice them to some imaginary god. Call it art, unity, love—it doesn't matter. The common trait between the gods we serve is the fact they are imaginary.

I am thirty-two years old. It is still not too late, perhaps.

December 27, 1488
For some days now, one Antoine de Gimel, a young petty nobleman, has joined us. *Could they be strengthening the royal guard?* I wondered. Incidentally, this Antoine did not join the guard, but rather the brothers—I often see him with them. The brothers are extremely cautious with the newcomer. What could this mean?

This—figuring out what something could mean—has become for me a need on par with monkey chess for Cem. Every miniscule change in Bourganeuf feeds my musings for weeks.

Take this riddle: last night, after the church service, everyone except the guards on duty gathered in the church, monks and knights together. Afterward Brother Blanchefort swept past me as if I were a tombstone. *Something is worrying them*, I sensed.

Actually, why am *I* not more worried our end is near? There is no way our daily life could change for the worse—imprisonment is the final step before death. On which of these evenings will the decision to kill us be made? And is some general decision even necessary? Such things are usually best done by a single person. They will surely kill us without a pang of conscience. Our jailers are heartily sick of us as well.

Shall I write my will this evening, then? I would, of course, if only I knew what I had to bequeath. The only thing I have in abundance are my own missed opportunities.

Wonderful.

I, Saadi of Isfahan, bequeath—to whom? this is the painful bit—the possibility of becoming the leading poet of the East; or a pirate who sails the seas for five decades before finally retiring to Cyprus with two sacks of gold to enjoy Greek women and heavy wine; or the aleybey of Peni Shehir, whose life comes to an end at the battle for Vienna, for example, and whose soul flies off to heaven unencumbered; or the simplest option: a master coppersmith from Edirne who awaits the end of his life in his own home in his native city, beneath the wailing of three wives, eight fine sons, and as many daughters, all as beautiful as the moon.

And so, I bequeath to humanity—I am a citizen of the world, after all, right?—my irrevocably missed opportunities. Amen.

December 29, 1488
No, say it isn't so—I'm alive. This night, too, shall be added to the incalculable empty nights during which I neither feasted, nor wrote poetry, nor made love. The morning penetrates the arrow slit in my room very late, and I wait for it awake. I did not want to die in my sleep. Yet another empty morning.

February 8, 1489
Unbelievable: we are in Villefranche. An unbelievable mockery: after seven years of imprisonment, we leave France through the same port where we glimpsed the country for the first time— back then we were convinced we were coming only for a brief, historically momentous visit filled with celebrations.

I can't believe my eyes—we are no longer in Bourganeuf. So there really is a life beyond monkey chess, the mournful reticence written on monkish faces, the tricolor statue of John the Baptist who so loathed me, the insulted indifference of the town's burghers, and every day the tripartite creed: "There is no God but Allah."

Our departure resembled an escape. Incidentally, I took it as such and only today found out it was lawful. But since the Royal Council had announced its decision to allow us to sail away a month earlier, only to follow this a week later with a prohibition on that same departure, Brother Blanchefort—vanity spurred him to reveal this to us—deceived the royal guard with the first letter, making sure the second never reached the knights' leader.

Clearly some subsequent Antoine was now lying in a ditch outside Bourganeuf: Blanchefort had called the knights together that night in the church to read the king's decision aloud to them and then threw himself into feverish preparations. As we are now finding out—it is finally safe to speak, after all Villefranche is a pirate stronghold, and pirates and papists are practically brothers—a series of rather noteworthy individuals were involved in our escape, starting with two bankers from Lyon, passing through the Duke of Bourbon, and ending with the members of the Council to whom Rome had been generous to the point of bankruptcy. And yet a week later Charles VIII had taken the words back, far too late.

But is it still too early for Blanchefort to rejoice? Because it is winter—the sea thrashes Cap Ferrat fiercely, its roar echoes off the sheer cliffs above the harbor; sky, mountain mist, cold, damp splashes, howling—all of this creates an impenetrable huddle above Villefranche, as if France refuses to let us slip quietly out of her hospitable embrace.

They have put us up in a wealthy home. Cem immediately found the fireplace and curled up before it, shivering. "Didn't I tell you?" he complained. "I knew they would drag me around in the winter." This time he wasn't shouting, as if by going out into the world he once again sensed how much he needed me.

"Saadi, tell them to mull me some grog. With a lot of pepper and sugar. All my joints are aching."

How could they not? For almost a year and a half he hadn't poked his nose out of his room—the fortress wall had infuriated him with its thirty steps back and forth, after all. He had lain in the stuffy room, tattered and musty—and now we had ridden for a whole week through a snowstorm. I watched him as he sucked down his mulled wine in deep gulps. The neck and shoulders of an elderly, broken-down man clutching his cup with that pointlessly strong grip only old men and babies use. I grasped the cup to take it away, and Cem suddenly latched onto my hand.

"Saadi, will they at least heat my bed properly? Go see, give them orders."

He had not touched me in a long time. I had avoided it. Hash smokers are unpleasantly damp, clammy with cold sweat. I drew my hand away, simultaneously revolted and guilt ridden, the way we hurry to leave a dying person's room. I put more effort into readying Cem's bed than was necessary, because the dozen or so papist soldiers who manned the Vatican's ship in Villefranche were now scurrying anxiously around their precious guest.

Their precious guest did not wish to get undressed before going to bed; he was afraid his sheets would be slippery. *How else should they be?* I wanted to shout at him, but good thing I contained myself, because otherwise we would've gotten into a squabble.

I finally got him tucked into bed and was hoping for some time alone. After the hunger my consciousness had been subjected to in Bourganeuf, I now felt as if I had gorged on a heap of impressions, as well as a premonition. God Almighty, is there really a chance I might not die a prisoner—would you truly let me escape?

I slipped out between the shoulders of the guards. They let me go—even a bird couldn't fly free of Villefranche. I found myself on the street along the harbor. I wanted to listen to the waves, their roaring, which the sky passed to the cliffs, and which the cliffs passed to the sky. After the somnolent silence of Bourganeuf I was drunk on this rumbling: something was making noise, something was pounding, something was living. You are flowing into life once again, Saadi!

I didn't hear the footsteps, likely they were lost amidst the winter storm. I startled only when the hand was already on my shoulder.

"Saadi," an unfamiliar voice said.

You never know who you'll meet in a pirates' port.

"Saadi," the voice repeated. "Don't you recognize me?"

He took off his hat. In the dim light from the harborside windows stood Renier. The troubadour who had arranged our first escape attempt. From Rochechinard, I believe it was.

"Brother!" I hurled myself against his chest like a widow. I was crying. Clearly I was not in my right mind either at this point.

VERA MUTAFCHIEVA

"Saadi, I'll be damned." Renier awkwardly wiped the tears and snot from my face with his hat. "Are you well, Saadi?"

I think I said yes and slowly got ahold of myself.

"After all, Rome is better than Bourganeuf, is it not, my friend?"

"It's better, Renier."

We fell silent for long stretches in between these brief words, both of us ashamed of our emotional outburst.

"Saadi," Renier said suddenly, as if finally having worked up his courage, "a month ago I came across some of your poems. In Italian."

I stared at him, thunderstruck. "My poems? What poems of mine?"

"No, no, I know a translation is very far from the original, as far as the pope from Sultan Bayezid," Renier continued impetuously, as if I had made some objection. "Yet nevertheless, Saadi, I am astonished. I mean... that which I have been striving to achieve with all my might... which is a model for... for the new challenges our poetry now faces—everything has already been done to perfection in your work, Saadi. And not as an innovation that shows clear signs of experimentation and imperfection, but polished, refined, translucently clear... I envied you, Saadi. Surely this does not offend you—you know the noble envy one master has of another."

I could not utter a word, I was deeply moved. My poems, mastery, innovation, refined development. How long ago had these concepts disappeared into some very deep, very dark corner of my consciousness? Had I ever really created, was I really Saadi, whose songs flowed through the ports, markets, and army outposts? Was this me?

Villefranche. A damp street, lapped by the tongues of countless winter waves. Low-hanging fog and cold, in which several solitary lights shivered—the house where the royal, papal, and Rhodian guards crowded around my fat master was lit up.... While two poets stood absurdly in that little world, which did not wish to know them and which they did not wish to know—they stood there freezing and discussing the laws of poetry.

No, nothing is impossible—everything is possible, and perhaps even rational. Some rational Providence wanted me to meet Renier last night.

"Saadi," he went on, "please hear me well: get out of here. Cem Sultan may be worth not one but three million ducats, but even then he is not worth your sacrifice, Saadi. Centuries after his name has been forgotten, people will read your poems. You, you deserve to be served, not him. Cem Sultan should wash your feet and bring you cups of wine. He should rejoice in knowing how to write so that he can write down the verses you utter when drunk, Saadi."

"I haven't uttered a verse in years, Renier," I said timidly.

"Now therein lies the sin of the world." Renier spoke as if pronouncing a verdict. "Who will take humanity's revenge for the fact that the poet Saadi—something far rarer on this earth than all sultans, real and self-proclaimed—has fallen silent for seven years? Saadi, you must get out of here. Go home, where every tree and rock inspires you to song, where thousands of ears wait for that song. I beg you, Saadi!"

"I've thought about it, Renier.... But how can I leave Cem? He is helpless, you have no idea how helpless he is. It gets worse with every passing day."

"You are sacrificing something that does not belong to you, Saadi. You are merely a vessel for God's gift; you do not have the right to die until you have been drained down to the dregs. Your songs belong to humanity—give them to their rightful owners so that you may die an easy death, Saadi. Otherwise on your death-bed they will torment you; your suffering will be like the death throes of a pregnant woman."

"Do you really believe there is anything left in me, Renier? For seven years now I have been ailing, transplanted into foreign soil."

"Oh, Saadi," Renier said very knowingly.

I needed to get back, they would be looking for me. I bade farewell to Renier without even asking what had brought him to Villefranche. I was still stunned. But Renier grasped my hand.

"Saadi, last night Charles of Savoy passed away, Little Charles, as you called him."

"Little Charles," I cried. "How? Who? Charles was our only real friend here."

"They say Charles had arranged for Cem to be kidnapped on the journey to Villefranche—everything was ready. Eighty loyal knights were supposed to set out from Chambéry yester-day morning, heading for the coast and planning to attack your guards south of Avignon.... But in the morning Charles didn't wake up. Poisoned, they say."

"The Order or the king?" I shook Renier by the shoulders, as if he had borne witness to the haggling between the spiritual and physical killers of that wonderful, pale-faced boy with en-raptured eyes.

"Isn't it all the same, Saadi? Whoever it was belonged to the powerful conspiracy of darkness.... While Charles... All the troubadours of France are now orphans, Saadi, my brother-in-song."

"I can't take any more of this, I don't want any more of this. Renier," I groaned into the impenetrable storm. "Too many people have already died because of Cem, each more honorable than the last.... If only you had known them as I knew them." And then I began to whisper as if telling a secret and the darkness might have ears, "Years ago I thought their sacrifice was worth it; hundreds might die in the name of a cause, but why bother trying to save human lives when the goal is to bring about the victory of a heretofore unseen kind of ruler: the high priest of poets and progressive thinking? But today... Renier, you haven't seen Cem today, have you?"

Renier shook his head.

"Now I am the one who envies you. Be on your way this very night, Renier, because tomorrow they will likely load Cem onto the ship for Italy and will show him in broad daylight. Take your leave now without seeing him, my friend. It will be easier for you, for Charles of Savoy's sake, for the sake of us all who believed we were not suffering, but rather serving."

"Yes," Renier said, then after a pause, "All the more reason for you to leave, Saadi."

Thank you, Renier, I thought as he melted into billows of fog. *Thank you for giving me the right to leave.*

March 28, 1489

The events of the past month ran me so ragged I could not find a spare moment. In brief: we have again gone out into the world and we are at the center of world affairs. We are living in the

Vatican—the heart of the West, in chambers meant for kings. The provincial castles of the Dauphiné and Auvergne are but a bad dream; my cell there, the deathly dullness of Bourganeuf are but a dream.

For a month now I have witnessed how Cem's erstwhile dreams have come true. Innocent VIII has hurled himself into preparation for the big crusade; his messengers, armed with letters signed by Cem, are making the rounds of the European courts; Cem is present almost every day at decisive conversations with representatives of this king or that duke; they offer him aid, exchange promises. We are stewing in the great cauldron that is politics.

Is this really possible? After all, we were the deeply buried treasure of the Order of St. John or the French king—we never did find out whose definitively. Today I'm working myself to the bone to organize high-level meetings, to translate and negotiate—in my master's name, but often without his knowledge. What wind has swept us up and how long will it carry us?

The first few days I felt endless exhaustion. I had grown unused to voices, noise, stress. The whole of Rome—actually, I have not yet seen the city, that's how round-the-clock my work is—the whole of the Vatican with its marble, tapestries, gilding, and statues fused before my eyes into one painfully bright, clamoring blur. Then everything fell into place and I, too, found my place—I, Saadi, the sole lord in service to Cem Sultan, most honored guest of the Vatican.

If I have to recount a more-or-less coherent tale of our arrival and settling in to Rome, I must begin with Civitavecchia, where our ship dropped anchor. This occurred on March 13, after a week of storms at sea. The brothers had hurried along our departure from France, because, as I later found out, as soon as the king learned Bourganeuf was empty, he sent an army of two thousand men after us. This force surely clapped its hands in astonishment and froze with a foolish stare when it burst into Villefranche: we were already at sea. But the sea took its own revenge on us; the storm tossed us hither and thither, separating our trireme from the accompanying ships, thus we washed up in Civitavecchia alone, like repentant pirates in search of shelter.

From Civitavecchia, our ship took us to Ostia and sailed up the Tiber. We set foot on Italian soil for the first time on the very threshold of Rome: at the Porta Portese. I was so dazzled by the multitude of colors and sounds splashing around us that I cannot find words to describe our welcome. I only recall a festive crowd coming toward us, a plethora of ceremonial horsemen in bright clothes. I later learned these were the cardinals' and pope's honor guards, led by senators, foreign heralds, and the Vatican's masters of ceremonies—a heap of titles with unknown meaning. I was all eyes and ears—only now did I feel I had truly come face-to-face with the West. Everything until this moment had been provincial castles, petty noblemen, the rural penury of southern France. It had been easy for me to judge it from the heights of Constantinople, Nicaea, Bursa, Izmir. But here in Italy, things were different: this is the pinnacle of Western architecture, and I still cannot fathom its scope.

As I stood there, flustered before such unexpected magnificence and deeply convinced I would soon awaken from my dream, a disturbance rippled through the crowd of welcomers.

A man on foot shoved his way between the horsemen. They tried rather roughly to deter him—on the whole Italian sounds to me like constant brawling. Just then some lord, lustrous to the extreme—they later told me it had been Franceschetto Cybo, the illegitimate son of Innocent VIII—intervened and cleared the man's way. What a surprise: he was one of ours. Amidst the Roman aristocracy stood ten true believers, without ceremonial armor, disconcerted and offended.

"No, you shall not speak to Cem Sultan." The translator relayed Cybo's command to them.

But they did not seem to hear. They stared at Cem—their eyes drank him in, wonderstruck, as if blinded; they saw in him the son of the great Conqueror, all in white and gold—they had not known Cem seven years ago, thus his new image did not upset them.

I only now thought of him. Even this sight of a dozen of our fellow Muslims being humiliated amidst the splendor of Rome did nothing to alter Cem's expression. Stupid tired, he gazed at his brothers in faith as if their ecstatic agony had nothing to do with him. And he remained still until one of these unfamiliar Muslims stepped forward and, after bowing low three times and kissing the Roman pavement, reached our master's horse, and pressed his face first to the horse's right front hoof and then to Cem's boot. These were not exactly Turkish customs, so whose were they?

"Get up," Cem snorted. These were the only words he spoke to Sultan Qaitbay's messenger.

Afterward this messenger hung on my shoulder. Shattered from the insult and filled with alarm, he poured out onto me his three months of anguish—his fruitless attempts at the Holy See to receive Cem in exchange for a price that would bankrupt the caliphate, but which might nevertheless protect it from the Turkish threat. This poor wretch had spent three months in Rome, and for three months various cardinals had bamboozled him with half promises and nuggets of political wisdom. He was now at the end of his rope.

"I must get Cem Sultan." He spoke to me feverishly throughout our entire journey to the Vatican, and for this reason I didn't even notice when we arrived, everything was spinning before my eyes. "Bayezid's ships are in the Mediterranean—Rhodes is under threat, as is the Italian coast. The pope likely moved Cem here to protect Italy, and Italy alone. Bayezid will be careful with the Italians, since he knows his brother is in Rome. But what about us? What about Corvinus? How could the West not realize this is not about one scrap of land or another being protected from conquest? We need an offensive against the Ottomans, a battle to the death. A campaign led by Cem would destroy Mehmed's empire from the inside—otherwise all is lost."

Tightly packed crowds lined our way, all of Rome was jostling to see the legend Cem. The legend was drooping in his saddle with an indifference that infuriated me—could Cem at this point be truly unable to make even the smallest effort? Now, when we are at the heart of the action that so much depends on, when our obligation is to call forth will, meaning, and strength so as to emerge from the dead end where we had been floundering for seven years?

I felt like shaking him to hurl the hashish from his blood and to snap him out of his daze. *Cem, our day has come, the day we*

suffered so much for, the day that was our greatest hope. That day is
here, Cem! I may as well have been talking to a corpse, I know now.

And so, even weeks after our arrival, after they installed us
in the most luxurious chambers of the papal city, after accept-
ing visits from ambassadors and envoys, Cem had not changed
his behavior one iota from Bourganeuf. He lounged in bed until late in the morning and chased away anyone who attempted
to dress him for public display with indecent insults. Now I
was not the only one tending him; an army of servants bustled
around Cem. Finally, using tactics for handling madmen, with
childish tricks, coaxing, and outright lies, I somehow would
make him presentable. Then Cem would fall completely silent,
and my daily torment would begin.

Someone would arrive—the Venetian ambassador, for example. He would inform my master of something and ask for
his consent or instructions. Fine, even I knew all this was a the-
atrical performance no more real than those I had witnessed
on the squares in Izmir or Nice; I also knew they were playing
us for fools and that things would be decided without Cem's
consent whatsoever—the world was following its course and
its laws. Fine.

But the game has rules. Years ago, we thrust ourselves into
the game, and now we needed to play it out—otherwise we may
as well go and off ourselves. So what sort of ridiculous behavior
was Cem serving up to me?

I now understand: he is firmly declaring with his shouting
or with his silence, with his stuporous sloth or rowdiness, that
he has quit the game, and we can all tie ourselves in knots from
effort, but he, Cem, will no longer take part.

But of course. After all, he announced this to me way back on our journey to Bourganeuf: "Whatever happens from this point on *will happen without me.*" Yet the original push of Cem's actions has been passed on from wheel to wheel during all these years until it set into motion something terribly heavy and complex, and only now are we witnessing the consequences of that forgotten original push. What a story! Was I truly lucky to remain in my right mind, to be left to deal with the mess made by my beloved Cem? Because I truly stand like a curtain between the whole agitation of the world and Cem's madness. Why do I call it that? Perhaps there is a meaning to it, even a deep one: Cem's refusal to play the game? A curtain that will withstand the wild pressure from this side and that for only a short while longer. How they press in from all sides!

Various papal dignitaries come every hour, wanting to know whether Cem Sultan has signed some letter to Qaitbay or some corrupt Janissary commander in Bursa; the Venetian ambassador with the most delicate of hints wants to convey to Cem Sultan that Naples's betrayal would be fatal to the upcoming crusade; the French herald appears before Cem Sultan to express deep regret that we left France without having a personal audience with the king. What, were seven years too short for the king to get around to it? People, people and words. And I, Saadi, called to spread God's gift among my people—as Renier recently explained to me—spin like an unhinged courtly top between all these gentlemen, relaying to them my master's supposed opinion, assuring them the letters will be signed as soon as can be, I am officiously polite and dying of vexation.

Enough. In the evenings, when the abovementioned insistent statesmen go home to their palaces and—with the full knowledge that today they have completed a job crucial to the fate of the world—give themselves over to feasting, extravagance, and debauchery, I sit in my room. Just one lacquered and gilded door away sleeps Cem, who has dozed off while it was still light. I can hear him snoring; that is from the hashish, but likely also from his fatness. Finally, the curtain can calmly fall—until tomorrow morning, when a new act begins in the comedy entitled "The Case of Cem."

During the first intermission between acts, my first evening at the Vatican, I thought I would burst into tears; all of this was too much for me. On the second evening I laughed. Indeed, I leaned my back against the door and laughed like a crackpot. *How right you are, Cem,* I thought. *You yourself have no idea you are doing the only thing the world deserves: you spit on it.* And tonight, the fifteenth night, I don't feel like crying or laughing. I suppose I have grown used to it.

April 20, 1489
Only yesterday did we finally meet the pope. For us, life has become such constant ceremony, we are always either welcoming an audience or going to visit someone. I would not be the least surprised if some morning they told me, "Saadi, today you will be presented before his lordship God himself."

I walk behind Cem through the corridors of the Vatican, musing that this is precisely where the Minotaur should live. I walk and think my own thoughts. I am now convinced my mind cannot grasp the complexity of these relations, interrelations, moves, and countermoves, which the masters of the world weave around that which was once Cem. That same thing, again in white and gold, trudges ahead of me with drunken dignity—only a drunk acts this way, simultaneously comical and stately. We are going to see the pope.

Of course, magnificence—my oversatiated senses take this in as if it were bread and salt; we have seen Constantinople, after all. Of course, the Holy Father resembles both d'Aubusson and Blanchefort, as well as that whole tribe of monks with their mistresses, children, and grandchildren. Innocent VIII offers us the polite empathy that could wrest tears even from stone if we hadn't been so used to it, from way back on Rhodes.

This time I will not stand as a curtain between Cem's madness and society—here Cem must speak for himself. Let us hear what he has to say.

Innocent lays out to him the full plan for the crusade. They are well on their way, he says, to settling all the discord between the Christian rulers; this has turned out to be—in his words—child's play. In the coming spring, a special congress will be called in Rome, at which all European powers will declare how many troops and funds they will dedicate to this great undertaking. And the crusade will start immediately after this congress. Previous crusades will not compare with it: a supercrusade. I listen to Innocent VIII, an experienced and wise man, or so I've heard. Why do I take Cem for a madman? The pope's ravings are no less mad than Cem's. Agreements, a congress, a supercrusade. Just from my tiny inlet onto the sea of politics—my little room in the Vatican—and in just a month's time, I have become all too familiar with the "unanimity of Christian Europe" he speaks of. Around me, Saadi, servant to a living corpse, spies and secret messengers from a dozen states swarm. In the course of a single month I have been offered eight bribes to betray, to denounce, to insinuate, to influence; my belongings have been rummaged through, Lord only knows when, since I supposedly never leave Cem's rooms—yet at least ten different pairs of hands have done so, I surmise this from the disorder they leave in their wake. It is suspicious and perfidious, the impudently fraudulent unanimity of Christian Europe.

"What will your master say to this?" Innocent VIII turns to me, despairing at Cem's blank face.

I ask Cem. I expect his answer to be "Hm." But he peers so intently at the Holy Father that he even raises his second eyelid. And very distinctly utters something, which I translate—which I translate with delight, perhaps Cem's madness has infected me, too: "I will not take part in your crusade, Your Holiness." Oh, how can I take back the words describing Cem as a living corpse and a fat animal?

"What?" If self-control is a monkish virtue, their supreme leader should possess it to a stunning degree, yet Innocent VIII looks to me like a freshly bankrupted banker. "What?" he repeats weakly. And after some time he turns again to me. "Surely your master is unwell."

"He is well," I reply. "And fully in his right mind."

"But... why? How?" The holy old man is spinning in a circle of bewilderment.

I translate. "Because I do not want to fight on the side of the infidels against true believers." Short and sweet.

"But whom did you surrender yourself to eight years ago? What did you seek among us? Why did you offer us an alliance and support, mutual advantage?" Innocent has forgotten himself, and his shouts will surely haunt him on his deathbed, reminding him how a wreck of a man brought the pope, the master of the whole Christian world, to what I would describe as the coarsest, most vulgar of tantrums.

"Do you have any idea what you're saying?" His Holiness goes on, shouting all the louder. "Do you realize you will be double-crossing kings, princes, cardinals? I myself dedicated years of work to this crusade and suffered countless humiliations. It is to be the crowning glory of my reign! And you think you can ruin it?" Good thing he has clenched his jaw, as I sense he is about to let loose with the crudest of sailor's curses.

I again translate. Reclining deep into his seat, Cem stares not with indifference, no—this is gleeful malice, the first emotion I have discovered within Cem in two years.

"Go ahead and curse, Your Holiness. Please, don't be ashamed. Even then you will not find words offensive enough for a man who surrendered to his own enemy. You cannot find the right word, hm? It does not exist. It has not been invented yet."

I again translate, not knowing whom to look at. At Innocent—he suddenly goes cold, clearly stunned that this puppet with the thunderous name has suddenly turned out to be a human being—or at Cem.

Enough already, God! I need to leave, yet I cannot. Cem is not yet dead. Somewhere in that paunch poisoned by hashish and hatred lives a particle of Cem. It surfaces ever more rarely, but they are moments of divine reward for me, the designated sacrificial victim. Cem is not dead—I have seen him today, not the snoring, cursing, flabby sluggard. With a single phrase, Cem has defended all his forgotten dignity. Cem has taken revenge for himself and for me, for our men imprisoned on Rhodes, for our dead.

"Take him away, for God's sake." Innocent pours out his ire on me. "We'll make due with Cem's name, if without Cem himself. You're not taking that back as well, are you?"

"No," Cem says with an exhaustion so unfathomable it shreds my soul. "I cannot take my name back."

September 22, 1489
To think I had complained of the ceremonies, audiences, and important conversations we had been inundated with during our first days here. Up until that conversation between Cem and Innocent, which was a watershed for our way of life in Rome. Once again everything was quiet around us, once again we saw only our guards. Once again I grew close to some of them—Antoine de Gimel, for example. Because the French king had reserved the right to place one of his own men among our guards. Since France was now the defrauded side in the case of Cem, it was trying to take its revenge. Antoine kept me abreast of the latest news; he told me about the Order's machinations to prevent a meeting between Cem and Charles VIII during our seven years in France. The brothers had convinced the king Cem hurled himself with shouts and blows at every unfamiliar Christian—because we're Moors and savages, after all. Antoine told me this with a highly conspiratorial air, hoping this would win me over. While I wanted to ask him in turn, "What kind of a savage is your king, since he believes in fairy tales?"

Antione, a very chatty, lively, dexterous young man with shifty eyes, also told me that in Rome practically every other day they executed someone sent by Bayezid to poison his brother. Such executions were a grand spectacle. Just yesterday they killed Cristofano of Ancona as an example. He had actually turned himself in months ago and confessed his own dastardly plans, and that would have saved his skin if the pope had not learned that another man, Giovanbattista Gentile, had been sent to Rome with the same task. And since they had not discovered the latter, yesterday they dragged the former out of prison, loaded him onto a cart, and paraded him naked through the streets while the executioner tore off chunks of his flesh. On the Capitolium they unloaded his trimmed-down body and subjected it to further treatment with vises, red-hot tongs, and the like, after which they ran him through in nine places, sliced him up, and hung his four quarters above four of the city gates. "What a pity you can't see them, Saadi."

What a pity, indeed. As if enough people have not already voluntarily sacrificed themselves in the case of Cem, now they have come up with poisoners? I wonder how many of them are real and how many invented. Incidentally, as I look at chatty Antoine and his shifty eyes, I am fully convinced he would poison both Cem and me for fifty ducats. To say nothing of the rest of them, the big and small fish that swim around us. And so I arrive at the only plausible conclusion. Bayezid does not wish for our death. Not yet.

November 17, 1489
Today Antoine told me news I dare not share with Cem. Lately he has been in a constant stupor, and I am worried about him.

Antoine told me envoys from Egypt arrived in Venice a week ago. They asked the Council there to plead with Rome to allow the Conqueror's widow to visit her son. Clearly wise to the West's ways in such matters, she offered twenty thousand ducats for such a visitation.

A mother... Surely news of her son's sorry state had reached Cairo, or else Sultan Qaitbay had lost all hope of wresting Cem away. So she, his mother, begs for mercy: she wants to see her child. They will not allow it—I would bet on that even now. There is no room for a mother in the case of Cem, to everyone here she is merely an agent of Qaitbay or Corvinus—on the opposing side, in short.

It is decided: I will not tell Cem this news.

March 26, 1490

Yesterday marked the opening of the congress Innocent had been working toward all year. All signs indicate the congress will last at least a year; from the very first day it has been obvious this business around the crusade is exceedingly entangled.

Neither Cem—whose participation in the crusade had been announced—nor I are allowed to join the sessions. Not that this matters; far too many people find it useful to keep us informed. I feel as if I am not only there, but also following the very thoughts of the European delegates. If I must summarize their viewpoints, I would say: every king is prepared to support the crusade so long as Cem is surrendered to him in exchange for that support; it is already clear to the rulers that Cem is a symbol of unprecedented power; Cem is an inexhaustible font of gold. The king of France, the German emperor, Corvinus, the Neapolitan king, and Venice all want him—these are Cem's most serious suitors. The runts are simply pressing their luck, with no real prospects for success. Which of the big players will wrest Cem away? Because they are offering prices history shall wonder at. Charles VIII has promised to renounce his claim of ownership over his patrimony in Italy, the kingdom of Naples; Venice has offered the papacy a military alliance; Naples has proposed peace to the papacy, which it has been fighting for twenty years now. And so on. If Innocent could divide Cem into a dozen pieces and hand them out far and wide, he would secure Rome's absolute supremacy.

In any case, the game continues. Even though it is clear Cem cannot be sliced into ten, and thus nine of the rulers who insist on him as a condition for taking part in the crusade will refuse to join it, the plan for the war against the Turks was nevertheless discussed at the congress. They decided three large armies should be mustered. The first will include troops from the German states, Hungary, and volunteers pouring in from southeastern Europe. The second will be French. The third Italian. The papacy has been charged with contacting the enslaved Balkan peoples and settling the question of their participation in the struggle.

From what I learned, the only point of contention was who would be generalissimo of the crusade. There were two main contenders: the pope and the Holy Roman Emperor, Maximilian. No decision was reached; Maximilian's envoy declared his master would not lift a finger until he had received Cem Sultan. The debate continues.

As far as I see it, not merely a debate but a true fight would have broken out yesterday if anyone had raised another, far more important question: Who will the lands liberated by common efforts belong to? Doesn't the heretofore unseen supercrusade aim to liberate certain territories from Turkish rule? Who will control them after this liberation? No one knows. And who would be crazy enough to throw away troops and money without knowing what he was getting in return? For this reason, I, Saadi, today lay a bet that there will be no crusade. This is absolutely certain.

April 8, 1490
I am starting to believe Providence itself is meddling in the case of Cem. Or someone is carrying out its orders to the letter. Two days ago, on April 6, ten days after the opening of the congress, King Matthias Corvinus went to his eternal rest in God.

I already rule out coincidence in everything relating to Cem, thus I do not believe King Matthias, our only real ally and the leader of the struggle against the Turkish threat, died a natural death; forty-seven is no dying age.

This death was completely unexpected, and completely opportune for someone. For the German emperor, for example, who had just learned Innocent was more inclined to give Cem to King Matthias—after nine years of haggling, but who's counting?—rather than him. I must note the Holy Father suggested this on April 3, in front of the congress. By the sixth King Matthias was already dead; some folks waste no time getting down to business.

I can imagine what a blow this would have been for Cem, if Cem was still sensitive to blows—the same as with Charles of Savoy, another loyal ally is no more. Of course, I shield Cem from this news, even though I am convinced it would penetrate his consciousness only with the greatest difficulty; Cem is still living in a complete stupor, always dazed. This is no longer just the hashish, but the consequences of it: the dissolution of his will, the decaying of his mind, the damage to all his bodily parts. How long will that demolished body hang on to this quasi-life? His body is still quite young, that is the worst thing. Cem drags it with difficulty from one corner to another—for months they have not even allowed us out into the Vatican gardens, so great was the supposed danger of assassination. In agony he seeks a place for his body; his face is twisted as if in pain, but I don't know whether Cem is hurting or whether this is simple irritation at the fact he is still alive. Alive so that those twenty-some statesmen who convene, compete, threaten, and promise from morning till night have something to do.

No, I cannot imagine a more terrible mockery.

June 21, 1490

What have we come to? Yesterday Bayezid's ambassador arrived in Rome to take part in the congress. A Muslim representative at the Vatican! Christian God, how does that strike you?

The pope, it seems, was taken aback by such brazenness; however, our man was met in Ancona by ambassadors of France, Scotland, Naples, and Venice. They led him to the Vatican with such honor that Innocent didn't dare say a word. Incidentally, I didn't need young Antoine to tell me all this. Innocent wanted to talk to the Turk, but using intermediaries so he could reserve the right to his shock and wounded pride.

Our man was eloquent and brief: Sultan Bayezid offered to leaved united Christendom at peace—absolutely at peace, until the end of his days—as long as Cem remained in the Vatican until the end of *his* days. Bayezid's offer shook up the congress, which in any case had begun to resemble a wrestling match, such was the word on the street. Since Bayezid was willing to maintain the status quo, the crusade was clearly unnecessary—that was the general opinion. As if it really would have happened if Bayezid decided to attack the West.

Last night Antoine delighted me with another bit of news, there is so much of it I can't manage to note everything. After his appearance at the congress, the Turk requested a private meeting with Innocent. These "private" meetings are usually watched by dozens of unseen eyes and by evening, it was as if I myself had been present at the conversation between our man and the pope. Incidentally, the Turk informed His Holiness that Brother d'Aubusson was quite the shyster; that very same d'Aubusson had been receiving over the years not forty-five, but sixty thousand ducats annually, not counting other gifts, and had pocketed the difference. What might His Holiness think of that?

While His Holiness was considering what he thought of that, the Turk sprang yet another surprise on him. That palaver before the congress was only for the congress, he said. In fact, Bayezid Khan has no intention of promising peace to all of Christianity for merely holding Cem in the Vatican—that would be too much. But he would sign a secret agreement with the pope guaranteeing nonaggression against Italy. Only against

Italy, he emphasized. In short, if Innocent secretly gave up on the crusade, which in any case was never going to happen, Bayezid would not menace Italy.

Of course, Innocent put on a show of convincing indignation, he flounced and called upon all the saints, declaring he would continue his preparations for the crusade. But our man could not have expected anything else—after all, hadn't he himself suggested Innocent keep his agreement with Bayezid a secret? And now what do you know, Innocent was not making it public. Innocent kept up his playacting, because he knew Venice and France and at least Naples were present at his "secret" meeting.

Antoine grumbled in dissatisfaction last night—his king would not accept such a turn of events, he said. Where does the papacy get off negotiating independently with Bayezid when Cem is the rightful property of the king? Now there would be yet another bone of contention between the pope and Charles VIII.

How little any of this affects me. Today Cem has nothing to do with the case of Cem, nothing whatsoever. I think more and more often about my own escape from Rome. Why haven't I tried yet? I must still want to see where this whole game my master has set into motion will end.

February 2, 1491
The congress died down little by little; the envoys left Rome one by one before the new year. I won my wager with myself—the crusade would not happen, that was clear from the outset. Especially after Bayezid promised peace with Italy.

Now Christianity has set about strenuously fighting among itself. King Matthias's heirs are locked in a struggle to the death, which only Maximilian will win; if you ask me, the end of Hungary is in sight. Half will go to the Ottomans, the other half to the Habsburgs. To think what could have been. Matthias could have won back all his conquered territory, if only they had given him Cem....

The papacy has new worries: Ferrandino of Naples is pressing harder than ever. The French are fighting the British. Only in Spain are Christians fighting Muslims; the Spanish are kicking the Moors back into Africa.

And we are sitting here in the Vatican. Cem has not left his chambers for more than a year and a half. Bourganeuf is repeating itself. But at least here we have certain comforts.

January 28, 1492
The Roman winter reminds me of ours. No snow, only slush, a warm gray sky, trees black from dampness. The weather is the only thing that changes for us in the Vatican's luxurious prison. No, something has to happen; their watch over me will falter for an hour or two, and then—good luck finding me! I've made up my mind, I've long since made up my mind, but I don't want to awaken suspicion with some clumsy escape attempt. After all, they consider me an infinitely devoted servant who would crouch beside his master until his dying breath. Let them think that.

I will leave without any guilt. I wanted to be sure of that, too. Cem won't even notice I am gone. We haven't spoken in months. I know all his needs and wants so well I fulfill them without orders. He leaves himself in my hands, doesn't give me any commands or any thanks—to Cem, I am an object, just as Cem is to me. Sometimes, sitting in my room, I hear him shouting and thrashing about: Cem now takes more delight in communicating with the door, with the heavy armchair, or with the trunk than with me, which is why I avoid his presence. Cem curses his bed because of some lump in the mattress; Cem kicks the door because the lock sticks; he topples over the armchair with effort; he thrashes about and shouts himself hoarse from cursing. While I sit here just beyond the door; what business is it of mine, this relationship between a feebleminded sluggard and his ebony armchair?

Yesterday a major announcement shook Rome: peace with Naples. Ferrandino delayed the treaty for a full six months in hopes he would get Cem as a guarantee. Childish fancies! Innocent would wage war for ten more years before he would give his wealth, Cem, to anyone else. Moreover, Ferrandino tipped his hand nine long years ago with his promise to hand Cem over to Bayezid; he has also tried six times since then to kidnap Cem, using all manner of underworld adepts.

The long-awaited peace is bolstered by the marriage of the pope's illegitimate daughter to Ferrandino's illegitimate son. Rome is now celebrating the marriage of two bastards in very glamorous style. How long will I ponder these morals so foreign to my mind? God, when will I return home?

February 1, 1492
For the fourth day in a row, Rome has abandoned itself to unprecedented, savage revelry. They are celebrating the first Christian victory over Muslims in centuries—the Spaniards' recapture of Granada and Sante Fe. For this occasion, King Ferdinand and Queen Isabella have poured lots of money into Rome, funds

reclaimed from the Moorish treasures of Granada. The Spanish ambassador arranged for wooden fortifications to be built in two places in Rome. Beggars were hired to reenact the battles. Half were dressed as Spaniards, the other half painted as Moors. The wooden fortifications were set alight, the crowds howled in delight, people got killed and burned.

An hour-long parade passed through the entire city, including the Vatican. At its head we spied Ferdinand and Isabella in a gilded carriage, that is—costumed buffoons. A darkly painted man in a tattered robe and dingy turban was tied to their carriage—this was supposed to be the Moorish emir Abu Abdallah. Carts piled with weapons followed along behind the carriage with other supposed "Moors" trudging alongside them, each a sorrier sight than the last, bloodstained and half-naked. And the "Spanish" army, of course, along with thousands of dazzled spectators. With cries and curses, the inhabitants of Rome poured out their hatred of Islam in blows to the painted paupers, who would receive a small coin from the Spanish ambassador. Their job was not easy, I could see—they would be bruised for at least a month.

The procession passed beneath our windows, I don't know whether this was a coincidence or not. For the first time in many months, I saw something catch Cem's attention. He shuffled over to the window, dragging along his armchair, and sat down with his chin propped on the sill. Cem's single eye expressed astonishment, then mindless amusement, and, finally, anger. It struck me as unbearable up close—because I was also staring out the window—that twisted face gnawing its lower lip, the animalistic fury that took away his last trace of humanity. Yet somewhere deep down beneath all this, I sensed human pain. Or rather, affront.

I also felt it. Why did these conquest-hungry Romans not show their savage bravery in Hungary or Bosnia? Isn't it a little too easy to hurl garbage at painted paupers? *Come on,* I would have liked to have yelled at the crowd. *Let's see you in battle.*

Distracted, I didn't notice Cem had gotten to his feet. He was pressing with both hands, leaning his whole bulk against the window; I held him back at the last moment—he wanted to break it, to get outside. Cem struggled clumsily, shoving me with his palms and pushing with his head like a dead-drunk brawler. I was revolted by the scent of mustiness and sweat, the hoarse growling, the grip of those cold and clammy hands.

I wrestled him to the floor. Cem stared at me in surprise; I had never used physical force on him before. "Ha, so it's you?" he said. I didn't catch the rest. I turned my back and left. Are my troubles so few that I have to be disgusted by myself as well?

I barred the door as if afraid Cem would try to follow me. A short while later I heard him trying the handle. I kept silent. Cem was muttering something. He was not angry now, but pleading, pathetic.

"Bayezid will take revenge on them, Saadi, that's what I'm trying to tell you. My brother, my older brother. Bayezid will drive all of them into the ass end of beyond. First, he'll fight Innocent, then Corvinus and Qaitbay, in the end he'll crush them all. They'll learn all right how to treat tied-up true believers, just you wait. My brother Bayezid..."

Cem shouted these words through the keyhole, the only words he has spoken to me in a long time, but I kept silent. I am disgusted. God Almighty, why did you choose such an ugly fate for the poet Saadi?

March 4, 1492

No, he is not completely mad. Cem was the first one in Rome to realize his older brother was going on the offensive. Indeed, it was high time, but Christianity had decided it possessed a miraculous panacea against the Turkish threat. Never have the Christian rulers felt as unconcerned with respect to the Turks as in the past three years when Cem has been in Rome. After all, they can scare Bayezid at any moment with a crusade led by Cem, can't they?

Well, yes. They had decided we really were those painted Roman beggars you can hurl stones at for a coin a day. No, most honorable sirs. We would not have reached deep into Europe if besides strength we did not also have brains, and if we had not been fighting such a shortsighted enemy. What, did you think a single person—even if Cem had remained a person despite your deliberate and solicitous efforts to turn him into a beast—would scare off our forces for a whole century? The fact that Bayezid, narrow-minded, fearful, petty, base Bayezid, assumed you had common sense—that alone you can thank for a decade of peace. Like every scoundrel, Bayezid only bets on a sure thing; and he gained his surety right after the congress—there, both your singularity of mind and your singularity of purpose really showed. Your holy congress untied Bayezid's hands.

For several weeks a large Ottoman fleet has been cruising the Adriatic; Venice is shaking in terror, Dubrovnik is in danger. Bayezid has personally led his army toward Hungary, he has invaded Croatia. Those are Habsburg holdings. Push has come to shove, my dearest hosts—let's see what you can do. Wasn't haggling over Cem and Bayezid's gold more important to you than the subjection of half of Europe, because you were getting rich in the other half? Well, now you're on your own. Now you will feel on your own backs the suffering of the Greeks, Bulgarians, Serbs, Bosnians, Hungarians. Didn't you once think such suffering weighed less than forty-five thousand ducats a year?

"Cem." I couldn't remember the last time I had addressed him. "Cem, our men are on the attack."

He needed time to surface and meet me in the fog of hashish. Cem lifted his face to me with painful irritation: What do I want from him, and why?

"Cem." I embrace those soft shoulders and feel myself melt with pity. I remember Cem's build—back then he reminded me of a pearl diver, broad shouldered and slender, taut as a bow.

"Hear me, Cem. Our men are winning. Your brother is avenging you, Cem."

I am crying, I haven't cried in years, and the tears burn. Cem does not move beneath my hands. It's like crying over a grave.

My room is very quiet, Cem does not try to stop me, he does not ask questions. When I come back in to bring him his dinner, I find him still sitting the same way, in the armchair. One lonely eye is fixed on the window, looking toward the unspeakably delicate, greenish Roman evening.

March 10, 1492

Last night Antoine gave me a good laugh. He arrived with the news that the Vatican had sent a messenger to Bayezid: he must stop his campaign against Hungary and his cruises around the Adriatic immediately, or else Innocent will release Cem. Is this not truly hilarious?

March 21, 1492

A second Vatican messenger to Bayezid with the same threat. The first disappeared without a trace. Turkish troops are scorching Croatia only two days away from Venice. Venice, ha! Wasn't it playing the slyest game of all in the case of Cem, wasn't it precisely Venice that betrayed the West to Bayezid ten years ago, assuring him Cem Sultan's crusade was an empty fabrication, that both France and the papacy were struggling to take possession of Cem only to receive his annual upkeep and nothing more? None other than Venice finally convinced Bayezid he could be sure of his brother's forced inaction—this certainty has now led Bayezid within two days' ride of Venice. But will he stop there?

March 25, 1492

Aferim, or as they say here: bravo, Bayezid! Today we learned that as an expression of his deep goodwill toward the Holy Father, Bayezid is sending priceless gifts: the lance that pierced the side of Christ as he hung on the cross and the blanket beneath which Mary gave birth.

A terrible uproar in Rome. According to the Church's verification, the lance in question has been housed in the cathedral of Nuremberg for the past two centuries. Which of the two is the real one? How could the pope accept a possible fake?

March 28, 1492

Today we have been informed that the lance in question has also been housed in Paris. Now there are three, a lucky number. Lucky for Bayezid. The pope is obliged to be touched by his amicable gesture and thus only with difficulty can he send a third messenger to the sultan to threaten him; there has been no mention of Innocent's two previous messengers. Now here's a case where the number three has not brought luck to Innocent.

March 31, 1492

This morning a very solemn procession set out from the Vatican. A Turkish ship has entered the Tiber carrying the precious lance, upon which there are still traces of Christ's blood, or so they say. Innocent VIII himself is personally heading the procession. His hands will receive the Christian relic, even though Innocent will know the whole time this is not the lance that...

Antoine has been avoiding me today, pouting. I am flattered; Antoine transfers the indignation of all Christianity onto me as well; after all, Bayezid is making a fool of all Christianity, while the latter is forced to pretend it does not realize this. I am flattered that today I am the proxy for the Vatican's hatred of Sultan Bayezid.

April 2, 1492

Providence continues to meddle in the case of Cem. How else can you explain the fateful coincidences that have dogged us for years? On his way back from celebrations for the lance in question, Innocent fainted. As of today, he still has not regained consciousness; this will be the end of Innocent, who made his life's goal the crusade against the Ottomans and who secretly gave up on that same goal for reasons I understand all too well.

April 16, 1492

His Holiness has dragged out his death throes far too long, which has thrown life in the Eternal City into the utmost confusion. Frightened someone might take advantage of the interregnum, the cardinals have decided to move Cem to the Castel Sant'Angelo. A new prison—and what a prison it is. I wager even if the whole Christian world went to hell, Sant'Angelo would survive—it's an enormous hunk of rock with a deep moat and three rings of thick walls. Truly impregnable.

For the first time we find ourselves in a prison designed as such. They torture prisoners in Sant'Angelo; hundreds of unsavory and inconvenient inmates are left to rot in oblivion in its dungeons. Here we truly are living atop bones, and a very thick layer at that. I don't want to know.

April 30, 1492

We leave Sant'Angelo to return to the Vatican. A new pope has been elected: Alexander VI, or rather, Rodrigo Borgia. Yesterday, Antoine told me such vile things about him I would have been shocked if I had not been living among clergymen for the past ten years. Half of his children have unknown mothers, while the others are from some semirespectable Roman lady. He squanders mind-boggling riches on them, he would stop at nothing to secure power and luxury for them. In the end, this is not so reprehensible, in my opinion. The new pope will have at least one human emotion: fatherly concern. He is mixed up in all the shady schemes of his day in Italy, he has made a deal with the devil himself. Unlike whom? I wondered because, rummaging through my memories, I couldn't find a single European ruler for whom the same did not hold true. In short, the world should prepare for the Second Coming, which will surely be brought on by Borgia and the Borgias as a whole—this was Antoine de Gimel's conclusion. But I saw Alexander VI in a somewhat different light during his meeting with Cem: bold, adroit, clever, charming, decisive, and quick—that was Alexander Borgia, besides all the qualities described by Antoine. I don't believe his reign will bring about the Second Coming.

Who knows why, but I get the feeling Borgia will resolve the case of Cem once and for all.

September 15, 1492
The new pope is exceptionally kind to us. For the first time in three and a half years, Cem can leave the Vatican and ride his horse around Rome. Almost always with the pope himself and one of his sons—Cesare, the cardinal of Valencia, or his fourteen-year-old by-blow, already Duke of Gandia. They take Cem around to famous churches, showing him the holy Christian relics. Cem keeps silent, letting them load him on and off his horse; he lumbers with heavy steps through the church naves and keeps his eyes squeezed shut painfully when there is sunlight. Alexander Borgia and his sons do not despair of him—they invariably accompany Cem, showing themselves with him before the crowds, before ambassadors and envoys.

Antoine de Gimel has expressed a definite opinion in this regard: Alexander VI is showing Bayezid that his brother is alive, able-bodied, and very close to the pope; now Alexander is threatening Bayezid with a crusade. *The time for that has long since passed*, I would reply to Antoine, who in any case has been on edge lately. After the election of the new pope, the French have stubbornly insisted on taking charge of Cem.

To be frank, all this talk now passes me by without affecting me. Gone are the days at Bois-Lamy or Bourganeuf when I would eavesdrop for the slightest hints, interpret the movement of the guards and monks, and try to organize escape attempts. I really don't care, not in the least anymore. Let them pass Cem from master to master—I only hope I can escape.

November 8, 1493
I'll escape—in my dreams. Ever since it became clear Bayezid has begun a major new offensive against Christianity, ever since it became clear there is no one to stop him—where is Corvinus now, what can Qaitbay do?—they guard us so closely that we are not left alone, even in our rooms. I am forced to tolerate some foreigner hovering over my lunch and my sleep—I've stopped even trying to tell their clothes apart. We have guards from all the world's courts, from the Vatican and from the Order. The guard stands there up against the door, unblinking, while I chew, get undressed, or write. Another one stands in Cem's room.

The other day it was Antoine's turn to guard me. He is no longer cheerful, even if his eyes have become even more politely shifty. Things are about to happen, he tells me. The French king is incensed by the vileness of the papacy. The pontiff is not working for the good of all Christians, but only for the Holy See. *Of course, and why not?* I thought. *Cem is no longer enough of a danger to his brother to guarantee such far-reaching peace. In exchange for Cem, somebody could still negotiate a much smaller peace, say between Bayezid and the Vatican.*

"My king fears for Cem Sultan's life," Antoine says knowingly. He says this and peers at me hard; he is amazed I don't pass out from horror.

"Cem Sultan's life has been in danger ever since Rhodes," I reply. "Reassure your king with that."

"But how can I reassure you, Saadi, when Bayezid has offered the Holy Father three hundred thousand ducats for Cem's head?"

"No, Antoine," I reply. "Cem has long since ceased to be worth even half of that. The pope should be happy he still receives Cem's annual upkeep—even that is a gift."

"You're not looking upon things with a level head, Saadi, because of your master's condition. But that doesn't matter to global politics. Cem Sultan's role is only just beginning."

"His role! He can't drink without dribbling all over his chest. But that's not the point, you're right. The great tragedy for you lies in Bayezid's firm conviction Cem will never lead a crusade. Who would waste three hundred thousand ducats when he was sure of that?"

In fact, I am putting on a show—I am afraid. If these people here are indeed shortsighted to the point of idiocy, Bayezid for his part is fearful to the point of idiocy, so I could easily see him stupidly throwing around big money to assure his brother's death, to finally be freed of that ghost. From what I know of him—stargazer, superstitious, moody—he must be terrified of ghosts, too, right?

January 1, 1494

Let us at least mark the new year with a few words. I feel revulsion even at writing with these eternal guards hanging over me, peeking and snooping. I write, question, and ponder only because

Cem's fate scares me—I am afraid of falling as low as he has. I must hang on, perhaps my day of freedom is not far away. After all, if they kill Cem—if Bayezid really has offered three hundred thousand for that—I will be free, no? For this reason, I fight against my own degradation.

I read over my words, and they horrify me. Does this mean I wish for Cem's death? Fine, now is not the time to pretend, at least not in front of myself: if Cem's death is my only escape, then I desire it. Besides, Cem has been dead for years already. What would it cost him to die completely so as to save me? He owes it to me after everything I have sacrificed for him—my thirteen most potent, most active, and most promising years.

I don't even want to mention current affairs, every bit of news drives me mad. How long will the world be interested in Cem and thus keep narrowing his prison? Now Alexander VI is also talking about a crusade. Bayezid isn't too worried and continues his raids into Hungary, Transylvania, Croatia; Venice is wagering all its long and sordidly earned cash trying to buy Cem. What, are they thinking to display him from the fortress walls before the Turkish troops who are already flailing their way through the bogs around the city? That would be amusing: they would dress Cem in white and gold, and a dozen or so men with plenty of blood, sweat, and tears would lug him up to the crenellated wall of the fortress. I wonder if they would even make him shout: "Here I am!"

Merciful God, I think I am going mad.

September 10, 1494
I am witnessing events Antoine prophesied months ago: King Charles VIII has invaded Italy with an army of thirty thousand

men. Not a bad idea—at a time when the Turks are on Italy's eastern border, France has remembered it was illegally deprived of its Neapolitan patrimony and has started a war. Very quickly, on the eve of the war itself, Alexander Borgia put together an alliance including the papacy, Venice, and Milan to oppose them. When we add Naples as well, Italy might just have forces enough to resist the invader. But Charles also has his allies on the peninsula—the Roman senate counts among his friends; he even has his own bribed cardinals in the Vatican. France's victorious campaign in Italy is proof enough of that.

Charles VIII is advancing toward Rome. Here his partisans and supporters await him; Rome is starving, since French ships have blocked the mouth of the Tiber; Ferrandino of Naples has fled his capital.

One by one the participants in the case of Cem are dying off: Corvinus, Charles of Savoy, Innocent VIII, Ferrandino of Naples. A week ago, we learned of Lorenzo Medici's death. Who is left? D'Aubusson and Qaitbay. And me, if history has any room at all for a sultan's servant and former poet.

November 29, 1494
Yesterday Charles VIII set out from Florence for Rome. Hunger and terror, accompanied by round-the-clock crimes and murders, fires, looting, and kidnapping, reign here in the city. French supporters are taking revenge on their enemies, while petty bandits are taking advantage of the unrest. Last night I counted six fires from my windows.

The Vatican is gripped by such fear that no one is allowed to leave or even come close to it. Because it is assumed Charles will not stoop to take the Holy See by force, preparations have been made to transfer the Vatican's inhabitants to the Sant'Angelo fortress. A large squad of guards has been appointed for Cem and me. Four hundred guardsmen will escort us just a stone's throw away.

This morning Antoine came to say goodbye—I won't miss him much. What's one less informant around us?

"See you soon, Saadi," he said.

"Why soon?"

"Because in three days at most, Antoine de Gimel will be head of Cem Sultan's guards, I'm willing to bet. As soon as King Charles takes Rome."

"I only hope you find us alive, Antoine."

"Rest assured of that, Saadi. Yesterday my king sent a message to the pope: Rome will be spared and Alexander VI will keep the Holy See despite all of his revolting crimes, if he voluntarily hands over Cem Sultan to the French crown."

"So Cem is still the winning card in the big game, is that right, Antoine?"

"You've always made me laugh whenever you've doubted that, Saadi. Like I told you, Cem Sultan's role is only just beginning. My king has decided—in an alliance with Rhodes and Qaitbay—to organize the crusade Alexander VI failed to launch. This truly is a secret, but you have no one to blab it to. From this night onward they will forbid you from even talking in your sleep, Saadi."

That's how Antoine and I parted. We also parted from our variegated guard—now only the pope's mercenaries protect us. For the first time in thirteen years, I don't see any Hospitallers' cassocks. They got rid of them, too, thank God. One more page has been turned in the endless story of Cem Sultan. No hint of shared possession of Cem; this night we belong exclusively to Alexander VI. This night, I say, because the vicissitudes of our life have become my daily routine. I believe from tomorrow morning on, King Charles VIII will own us indefinitely.

They ordered me to gather up Cem's things so they could once again move us to Sant'Angelo. There is not much to gather up. Cem has not changed clothes in months; he sits, lies, or paces around his room in his same old wine-red robe.

The front of it is adorned with souvenirs from many an intemperate lunch and dinner, its elbows are worn from the ebony chair. Three ducats a day—that's the Holy Father's daily allowance for his ward, while he receives two hundred a day for him. With those three ducats we feed the guards—even though we never asked for such protection—and ourselves; we warm ourselves with this sum and drink. Surely they steal from those three ducats as well, since Cem for years now has doddered about always in that same wine-red robe.

I gather my books into two trunks, along with Cem's blankets. I leave everything else—to hell with those white and gold garments, those yards of silk for festive turbans. I hope the nocturnal battle sets fire to them, too, along with the papal palace —I hope the world catches fire this night, God!

I will carry my diary with me. I know it's dangerous, but I will try to escape tonight. Across a stone's throw, between one and another of our prisons, across those several hours of interregnum before the wars rolls in. I remove the final fig leaf—duty toward one who suffers—from my animalistic nakedness so I can set off alone and free under the stars.

VERA MUTAFCHIEVA

I will not go in to Cem before the guards come. I expect them any moment. They will lead us away to Sant'Angelo. I don't want to see that bloated, grayish-yellow face again with its drooping eyelid, the sagging shoulders, the helplessly bent back, the hands that have not moved for hours. I am afraid of pity; more than once it has hindered me from acting.

I sit like a man convicted. I, Saadi, have come to know this about life: I do not delude myself—no matter what happens after this night, I am lost. They will either kill me for trying to escape, or else in all my dreams, in every song, cup, laugh, or triumph, I will be haunted by a grayish-yellow face—I will be haunted by Cem's perfect isolation.

No, I won't change my mind, my decision has been ripening for far too long: this night I will leave you, Cem. I don't ask for forgiveness, just as you do not ask me for forgiveness for giving you my best years. Whatever we sacrificed for each other was willingly given. Now I will go, Cem. If you still understand anything, you will understand this: a person can give much to another person, too much, inconceivably and excessively much. But not absolutely everything. There is no such thing, Cem. Farewell.

December 24, 1494
Gently, so gently it rocks me—what delight, my God above! As if my mother, the universe, is rocking me in the enormous cradle of the sea. My mother wants me to sleep, to rest after thirteen years of torment.

Only now do I feel the depths of my exhaustion; it has penetrated every last cell in my body, making me lie all day and night on the pallets in the hold, rocked to sleep by the sea. As if I am not thirty-seven years old, but seventy-three. I am starting to understand why a person loses his despair in the face of death if he has lived long enough: exhaustion. Rest in peace—how right that phrase is.

For days now I have been gathering my strength to write about my escape—even the thought of it wearies me. In brief: I broke away in the gardens of the Vatican, before we were to go to Sant'Angelo. I hid there for two days. It was not hard. Rome was in complete turmoil. Everyone knew Charles VIII had set out from Florence accompanied by crowds whipped into a frenzy by Savonarola, a fierce enemy of the Borgias. All the indignation of a people who had tolerated the pope's and the cardinals' outrages for too long now escorted Charles VIII on his journey to Rome. But at the same time, the Duke of Calabria, the brother of Ferrandino of Naples, was heading toward Rome with a large army to defend the Eternal City from foreign invaders. This gave Alexander VI courage, and he refused France's offers.

I picked up this news from the streets—I snuck out in the evening, dressed as a Frank, an ordinary citizen—I heard it in the pubs where locals discussed the situation, drank down two or three carafes of cheap wine, and then went out into the night to take advantage of it, of the interregnum and the papal guards' fear. A lawless city—that was Rome in November 1494.

Just as a killer always returns to the scene of his crime, I could not leave Rome before things settled down. I spent the night in unfamiliar hovels, I struck up conversations with random passersby—I joined the whirlpool that was dragging down the Eternal City.

During those days I learned the Duke of Calabria—his soldiers were the most dangerous bandits in the city—had promised to protect Rome from the French if he received Cem Sultan in return. Of course, Borgia refused. So the duke immediately withdrew his forces, who looted Rome on their way out as it had not been pillaged since the barbarian invasions a thousand years ago. I doubt this upset the pope much. Rome is Rome, but Cem Sultan remained with the Borgias, despite everything.

New days of lawlessness followed. Each of them brought new French messengers to the city. Charles preferred not to take the Holy Father by force; he was convinced his victories were already sufficient and his supporters in Rome were strong enough such that he could enter the city as a liberator. While Alexander VI was playing for time—the pope did not at all want to give up Cem, that's what it came down to.

Exactly at that time, I left Rome. No matter how curious I was about how the whole story would play out, I was afraid Charles would impose strict order on the city and thus foil my escape. Early one evening in the middle of December, I glommed onto a band of raucous looters. I did everything that needed to be done right alongside them, to seem like one of them; afterward we skirmished with the guards at the Porta Portese and left the city to divide up our loot. I took advantage of the fact that they were drunk and retreated into the darkness, I hid and let out a deep breath—that was my big escape, plotted for so many long years. When you spend so much time planning something, it always happens exactly as you have never imagined it could.

I walked, following the Tiber, making for the sea. From there, I went from port to port. It took another two weeks until I found a ship promising enough—in other words, dubious enough. I finally found it two days ago: a ship with no flags, which was taking on fresh water somewhere north of Naples. Its masters were Levantines—let's just leave it at that. They were supposedly carrying cedar, but such a small ship could not carry a load of cedar. They had supposedly just unloaded it in Naples; however, trade was surely the last thing on Naples's mind, seeing as how it was on the verge of being conquered by France. They were supposedly sailing for Beirut; I don't deny this, because only God knows where it's heading, this ship that took all the gold I had: thirteen ducats—my wages for thirteen years of service to Cem Sultan, one ducat for each year.

I immediately spilled them out in front of the captain, suggesting he rummage through my pockets to make sure I didn't have any more—I didn't want any of the killers on the ship to think they could find so much as an aspron on me, since they would kill me for a single aspron. In exchange I got clothes in our style—surely worn by at least two other men, now deceased—as well as a promise of food during our journey.

So now I'm a Levantine. I am again wearing a turban, quite a filthy one to be honest. I changed my tight Frankish pants for wide-bottomed trousers fitted above the calves. I'm barefoot from there down. We're going where it's warm, after all. Above the waist I have a vest that used to be blue years ago. I am no longer dressed as a European—that means I am practically home.

Two nights ago, as the sailors were eating their bulgur—they often dish me up seconds—I took down the saz that was hanging over the pallets. I felt a thrill I don't remember even when playing my first song in front of an audience; I have not sung for anyone in thirteen years. I held the saz. It was simple, rough, with no decoration at all. I stroked its strings lightly so they would not sound; I was afraid they were out of tune. I called up words from my memory, but they scattered and fled, while a painful lump swelled in my throat. "Words of mine," I begged them. "My song and my thoughts, joy and sorrow! Come back, so I can return to my people with you!"

The sailors were scarfing down the bulgur, the wick in the bowl of oil was giving off more smoke than light. I'm sure I looked ridiculous to those husky, half-naked, dirty backs, as if I were excluded from the circle of men who work, gorge themselves, and hurry off somewhere. Excluded yet again. If only for the fact that bulgur now makes me sick.

I stroked the saz—no, the saz will not refuse me, I have served out my sentence for abandoning humanity, and even the vengeful God must be satiated by my suffering. We have settled our scores, insulted humanity and I who insulted it by depriving it of a poet. "In the name of Allah," I whispered, as if conjuring; that is how every true believer must begin.

The saz started to sing under those fingers that did not seem to be mine, not with that voice from years ago; it sang differently, intemperately, too high and hard for words such as these: "Once I met a devout man, mad with love for another. He had not the strength to wait, nor the courage to declare his love to the object of his affections. No matter how I rebuked him, he would not give up his mad passion, it possessed him fully, thus he replied to me:

Even if you pierce me with a sharp sword,
I will not let go of her skirts.
I have no refuge, thus if you drive me away,
I will again seek shelter in her scorn..."

Very slowly, my voice reached the sailors. Perhaps because it was too unsure, it did not carry. All of my timidity rose up in a burning plea. I was not singing, but moaning, "Don't say you don't hear me. People, brothers! Let me in among you. I want to come back."

One by one they lifted their eyes from the bulgur. One by one they dropped their spoons, and I caught those sounds: clink, clink, clink—in the total, breathless silence. The sailors watched me sternly; like all bandits, they were afraid of a sham, and is there any more reprehensible sham than a fake poet?

"So," their captain said dully, "are you a şair or what?"

"I was."

"For a şair, there is no 'was.'" My candor put all his doubts to rest. "Since you were, that means you are. Why didn't you tell us?"

"Is it important?"

The captain dug into his pocket and counted out ten pieces of gold. "Your journey costs three, no more. You should've said you were a bard."

"I don't want that gold, it's cursed."

"There's no such thing as cursed gold."

"Bayezid Khan paid for the suffering of his brother, Cem, with it."

The faith of a dozen brigands had returned my faith in all people; I gave away my terrible secret so simply, without fear of betrayal.

VERA MUTAFCHIEVA

"Cem, you say?" The captain wrinkled his brow. "Old news, gone like last year's snow. Few folks back home even remember anymore. Hold on to your money." And when he saw I would try to resist again, he ordered me, "Take it in payment for the song about Layla and Majnun. It's my favorite."

So I sang about Layla and Majnun. I skipped over some of the verses because I had forgotten them on my long journey from Karamania to Bouganeuf. "Hey, you forgot about the doe," the pirate reminded me. He had paid, after all. The others were happy just to listen. They were lounging on the pallets, some on their backs, others on their sides; the sailors looked through me with solemn faces. Art made them fall silent, purified by the story of that great love.

Since then, they have added dried fish to my bulgur; they don't allow me to roll barrels when we go ashore for fresh water. I sing every night, but I know if I were to refuse, they would not badger me—they understand inspiration. The saz is once again obedient beneath my fingers. I now make it whisper in the sad parts and use it in place of my voice when I grow tired. I am once again a master of saz and words—I hadn't dared to hope.

When I fall silent, all of them doze off as if I have given them hashish to smoke, and then I go outside. The nights are cold, the sky is pitch dark. Only three of us are awake: the sea, the helmsman, and I. The other two tend to their work, while I stare into the darkness. I feel as if I can guess the part of the sky where the sun will come swimming up. The east. Home. Lately I have become so accustomed to miracles that I can now believe in this as well: I will make it home.

I still don't know what I'll sing on the squares and the ports—songs about Layla and Majnun, about Hafiz's disputed gazelles, or about Shahnameh, who was so endlessly rich he could fill a singer's days until the end of his life? Or my own verses, born somewhere amidst Karamania? I don't know whether I will find the words and the strength, but I would like to create a new song.

A song about homeland and exile, that's what I want to write —I who thought I did not have a homeland and that my home was the world; I who thought exile was simply a journey, a change in place. For the price of thirteen years, I have paid for one piece of wisdom, which I would like to leave to my people. I want to tell them—and to warn them. The world is not only large, I shall sing, it is also hostile. Hide away from it in a single homeland, a single city, a single home; fence off a small part of that big world so you can master it and warm it; find yourself one trade, one sipahi commander, one line of work; have your own children. Cling to something amidst the boundless current of time, amidst the boundlessness of the universe. Choose one truth as your own.

I would sing something like that to the people, if I find the words. Perhaps then Cem would cease to haunt me in his perfect isolation. It was rather unfair of me to say just now that I have paid for that song with thirteen years. In fact, Cem was the one who paid for it. With his whole life.

TESTIMONY OF NICHOLAS OF NICOSIA, WITH NO SPECIFIC OCCUPATION, ABOUT THE EVENTS OF JANUARY 1495 IN ANTALYA

MY NONSPECIFIC occupation came in very handy when serving the powerful and, more importantly, well-paying lords, that much I can say about myself. I was born in Cyprus, but I don't count that as my homeland—the whole Levant is my homeland; I knew it like the back of my hand. For this reason, I was much sought-after; I think I've made myself clear. Even though I died rich, I would argue few worked for their living with more effort or risk than me.

You've already come across my name once in the case of Cem—in 1482, when I was caught in Venice with a letter from Qaitbay to Cem Sultan. Likely you were struck by the fact they didn't kill me; likely you came to your own conclusions why not. Nevertheless, I'll confirm your suspicions—I was set free after swearing an oath to serve Venice, while also continuing my service with Qaitbay. Because of this, I frequently had dealings with the Ottoman authorities in the Levant. Venice maintained its relations with Bayezid through men like me;

they insisted on total secrecy around things that were well-known to all of Christendom: their treacherous behavior not only in the case of Cem, but in the larger Christian struggle against the Turks.

I'll spare you the details of all the difficulties a double agent faces; time and time again, your life hangs by a thread. But even danger, like everything else, has its price: they paid me well.

In December 1494, a secret messenger visited me in Antalya, a port on the Asian shore across from Cypress. I forgot to mention I spent every March, July, September, and December in Antalya, where I would receive my instructions from Venice; otherwise it would've been hard for them to find me, as my work took me to many far-flung places.

The stranger found me at Abu Bekir's, where I stayed when in Antalya. He was a Frank, that much I'm sure about, even though he was dressed like a Levantine. As soon as they led him into the room, he suggested I lay all my weapons on the table. I knew he would search me, so I obeyed the order.

"Don't wait for instructions from the Republic this month," the stranger started in without any small talk. "Bayezid is at their doorstep. But that means you have the chance to serve a power even greater than Venice."

I didn't even ask which power—such questions are unthinkable. I feigned reserved reluctance: I'd think about it, I hinted.

"We'll decide on the price afterward." The stranger caught my drift. "Just so you know, it's not high, since your job isn't dangerous."

"Easy for you to say," I scoffed. For the one paying, jobs always looked easy.

VERA MUTAFCHIEVA

"Five weeks ago, a certain Saadi, a close companion of Cem Sultan, escaped from the Vatican. In the unrest that gripped Rome in those days, no one had kept watch on Saadi, even though his absence was noticed that very same night. Now that Alexander VI's position has been reconfirmed thanks to his treaty with the French, this Saadi must be found. It stands to reason Saadi ran away under orders. In recent years, Cem Sultan has stubbornly refused to cooperate with the Christian powers; on several occasions he has expressed his delight over Bayezid's victories. In short, there's been a change in the brothers' relationship, that's what we suspect. But is this some passing mood on Cem's side? Has he, despite being under close watch, managed to contact Bayezid Khan? These are the questions that remain unanswered.

"But now," the stranger continued, "Saadi has secretly escaped from Rome. Saadi is fully in his right mind, unlike Cem. We suspect his mission to Bayezid could complicate the already difficult circumstances Italy finds itself in. We must stop Saadi from reaching Bayezid at any cost. We cannot even allow him to make contact with the Ottoman authorities in the Levant."

"Easier said than done. When and where will Saadi come ashore? What are his distinguishing features? You want me to find a needle in a haystack."

"If I knew myself, why would I come looking for you, Nicholas? You pass for an expert on Levantine ports, especially their darkest corners. Find this Saadi as soon as possible."

"Find Saadi and rub him out—simple enough. But how can I be in twenty places at once?"

"You're overcomplicating your task, Nicholas. It's winter, few ships sail this season. We have reason to believe Saadi took a pirate ship—he wouldn't dare try to board a Turkish, Rhodian, or Italian vessel. Pirates prefer Antalya, as you know far better than me—Antalya is practically lawless. That's why we're entrusting Antalya to you. You'll send your people to the other ports. With a description I'll give you."

"OK, so I take Antalya. Then what?"

"This is where things get complicated. We suspect Saadi escaped with a significant amount of gold, and he likely is counting on coming into more, so we must assume he'll be well guarded; that means you can't do this alone. You need to go to the Ottoman authorities and share this intelligence with them. Every local agha will want to make a name for himself by catching Cem's messenger. Give them that chance."

"But didn't you yourself say the brothers might be conspiring, that Saadi is coming here as someone who might be of use to Sultan Bayezid?"

"That's what we suspect, so that's what we're telling you. But how would the governor of Antalya know about any change in the brothers' relations? The whole world assumes Cem and Bayezid loathe each other—use that to your advantage."

"My dear sir"—I decided to put an end to the conversation—"you are offering me a job that will cost me my head. I'll have to make the rounds of every tavern and every brothel in the city accompanied by Ottoman guards. This means every pirate with half a brain will take me for an Ottoman stooge—and as you know, the Ottomans are not so popular here in Antalya. Even if I do find this Saadi, three days later some pirate will kill me: the fewer Ottoman spies in Antalya, the better. If I don't find Saadi, which is the most likely outcome, I'll have to answer to the authorities: How did I know Saadi was here, how did I know how he got to Antalya? Arrest Nicholas of Nicosia, give him three hundred lashes, and he'll tell us the rest, because of course they will assume I know the rest. Is that your idea of a safe job? I've got a wife in Cyprus with three kids, plus a wife in Antalya with another two. Do you want them orphaned, is that it?"

"Everyone is orphaned at the end of the day," the stranger reassured me. "But the question is: with what inheritance?"

"Let's talk rationally about my orphans' inheritance, my dear sir."

So we talked. If you ask me, I think the pope was paying. I must admit I wasn't hoping for even half of what I wrung out of him. Especially considering the fact I didn't have two, let alone even one wife—marriage doesn't fit in with my line of work—while my children, if they exist, are scattered under other surnames across the whole of the Levant, so I'd end up with all of the profits from this job. As long as I survived. *I'll survive*, I told myself. *We've seen far worse than this.* I planned to leave Antalya for good afterward.

By that evening I had gone to the Ottoman governor of the port. He didn't show himself much on the streets; the Turks had only recently taken Antalya, and they felt insecure, as well they should. With thousands of assurances of loyalty, I told him my news and of my desire to see things through. He never doubted me for a minute. First, because he very much wanted to make a name for himself with the sultan, and second, because Turks are very gullible, simpleminded people. The governor gave me six soldiers, but I wanted them in disguise—why should we announce from a mile away that the guards were coming?

First, I found out whether any ships had arrived in Antalya or any of the nearby inlets in recent days. No, it turned out. The December storms plus the coastal cliffs and tall waves frightened sailors, so ships were waiting for the sea to calm down. That was a good thing. As far as I could figure, Saadi had not yet set foot in Asia.

The only thing that worried me in those days was the soldiers' growing impatience. I had roustled them out of their warm winter digs, so they were growing surlier with every passing day that I sent them around to various inlets. I was afraid they would bump me off some night to have done with this business, and then somehow lie to cover it up.

And so, it was December 26, probably just a few days before my subordinates would have done me in, when one of them brought news that a ship with no flag had dropped anchor north of Antalya. Only eight men had disembarked; the rest had stayed on board to guard it against their own ilk. They headed for the city, of course. My man lost their trail, of course—a soldier's mind is not cut out for my line of work.

Never mind. It's not as if the earth swallowed them up. In the evening we went around to all the taverns and hash dens. When I put it so simply, don't assume it was simple at all. You've got to have a death wish to barge into a brothel at night where dyed-in-the-wool brigands are smoking hash; you don't want to tangle with these types even when they're sober.

I didn't find anything that would pass for Saadi the first night. But to be honest, the description I got was worthless: medium height, slight build, pale face with dark hair and eyes, clean-shaven. Every third man in these parts looked like that.

VERA MUTAFCHIEVA

Was I supposed to catch them all? And what was I thinking, for Christ's sake? That this Saadi would not be disguised as a sailor, a soldier, or a beggar, that he would not play a role, that he somehow would give himself away?

I started feeling like a fool for having taken their bait. What's more: why would Saadi go out in public? If he was smart, he'd hide underground until he found a horse or a ship to Istanbul. Was I supposed to search every house in Antalya? Of course, I didn't share my worries with the governor; instead I told him I had picked up Saadi's trail. And Christ Almighty, what a trail it was. I kept making the rounds of Antalya's whorehouses every night, somehow hoping, but no luck. Good thing the weather was terrible, so I didn't think he would try to travel—he'd wait. During that time no other ships arrived, which meant he had either come with the one we had found or not at all.

Like every bachelor, I ate my meals out at various inns and the like. Then I would go drink coffee elsewhere—I didn't have a fireplace at home, so I'd wait for night to fall in the warmth of coffeehouses.

One day—God bless that day!—I was at a coffeehouse where a scruffy crowd of a few dozen men huddled around the brazier, and I heard a şair. In threadbare clothes too light for the winter, pale faced and dark haired. The şair sang whatever they paid him to sing, and he sang for a long time. The scruffy crowd listened to him with a reverence you find only in the Levant; Muslims have great respect for all poetry, whether spoken or sung.

I listened—or rather, I didn't listen but thought it over. If someone sent a poet on a secret mission, he would never act like a poet. That was the first thing. Second, why would he pick such a public place for his song, the coffeehouse on the square in front of the big mosque? In my line of work, the most important thing is to not look like yourself, and if you don't have faith in your ability to disguise yourself, you'd better find a nice dark place to hide.

I was making ready to leave. Night was falling, and I needed to go look for my men so we could start the evening's rounds. I wasn't in a great hurry, since cold sleet was falling outside; the rain was downright horizontal thanks to the sea wind. *Great job I've got*, I thought, envious of the twenty-odd loafers who would spend the whole night listening to cock-and-bull stories while sitting toasty around the brazier.

I was just standing at the door, deciding where to head off to, when the şair spoke.

"I won't sing about Rustem tonight, you've heard enough about Rustem. Would you lend your ear to an unfinished song?"

"We don't pay for unfinished songs," someone joked.

"This one has already been paid for," the şair said softly.

"Then go ahead. While you're singing, you'll figure out the ending."

"No, I'm having trouble finding it, my friends. Haven't you noticed when you speak plainly, without inventing or embellishing, it's always harder? As if words were given to us not to reveal our hearts, but to hide them... But nevertheless, listen."

To be frank, it was a bad song. The şair repeated over and over how happy he was to be here, to finally be home, because the worst thing in the world was exile, and once someone had been exiled, he was no longer a person, something along those lines.

I got the sense the other patrons of the coffeehouse didn't like it either. Who cares about someone else's heartache, their regrets and the like? People like their songs with more action. But since it was free, and since the şair himself had admitted he hadn't finished it and it still needed work, they listened to him. And I started thinking things over again.

I was already completely convinced this was not the Saadi I was looking for—such obvious coincidences aroused my suspicions. Not only did the şair admit he was a şair, but he was also singing a song about exile. In short: hey look, I'm coming back from exile and I'm dying to tell you how terrible it is.

Ha, I thought, *there's something fishy going on here.* Most probably they duped me, saying some poet would arrive on a mission for Cem just so I would be overly cooperative with the Ottoman authorities, and in so doing show I was a foreign agent. The authorities would kill me, and in this way, someone would be rid of me, because I knew too much, and besides, I was serving two or more masters at the same time, which was the honest truth.

They think they can fool me, I fumed with anger and fear. This business really was getting dangerous. I was already thinking how I would make my escape right away, so those behind this scheme wouldn't be able to finish what they started.

I opened the door a crack to slip outside unnoticed, when the şair called out to me, "Why are you leaving, my friend? Don't you like my song?"

"Of course, I liked it." Now I was truly flustered. *This means the şair is in on who I am and what I'm doing, and he's trying to keep me here with his banter.* "It's a really wonderful song, but I've got work to do."

"Everyone has work to do in this world." The şair had gotten up and come over to me, where I was on the verge of passing out; now he would open the door and call someone in. "Every-one, except the poet Saadi."

"Who is he?" I said stupidly. Clearly, they were on to me.

"Who? Me. Why am I the only one no one is looking for, the only one not rushing off somewhere? Now *that* is exile, my friend. My song didn't do it justice, I know. Exile breaks all ties between you and other people."

I stood there, thunderstruck. Saadi! Was it possible he would admit it freely, that he would rush toward his death with a confession? What the hell did they want from me?

"So you're Saadi?" I tried a desperate trick, simply because I was stunned. "I've heard that name somewhere, but I don't remember where."

"In stories about Cem Sultan, right? Yes, I am the Saadi who spent thirteen years in exile with his master. I suffered more than any living person can bear, but now I am again among my own people. Finally."

What was I to make of this? I glanced around like a trapped beast. A low-ceilinged, bare room with bare couches; the bra-zier that spilled reddish light out into the dark gray of the winter evening; two dozen sunken, bearded, scruffy faces, and this poet. What was I to make of this? He was standing in front of me just as described, telling me his name, his trade, admitting he was newly emancipated from thirteen years of exile.

"Well," I said, drenched in cold sweat, "how can you prove you're that Saadi?"

"Why should I prove it, my friend? I don't want a prize or fame for what I went through. Forgive me for stopping you. You know, it's because of my suffering; I'm afraid someone might turn their back like you did on my great warning."

He stood there lost in thought. I also sank into thought for the brief moment it took me to decide: What if this really was Saadi? Is it really so strange? Poets are crackpots—I wouldn't put it past him to brag and whine once he'd found himself a listener. Very well, then. Could this stroke of luck really have fallen into my lap? And if I'm wrong, so what? He said he was Saadi, and I had my orders to rub out none other than Saadi, so here he was. He shouldn't have pretended to be Saadi if he wasn't.

In that brief moment I made a bold decision. "Your Grace, why not let others hear your song as well? We're nearby, just two streets away. Will you come?"

Snapped out of his reverie, he looked at me. His eyes lit up; his whole face, exactly as it had been described, lit up. The one who called himself Saadi—I swear to God, not only that night, but never have I once believed that singer was Saadi—went over to the brazier, took his leave of the scruffy audience, and picked up his saz.

"Won't you be cold? You are very lightly dressed," I said. There is decency even in our line of work.

"No," he replied. "Let's go."

He was impatient. I wasn't carrying a weapon, as I wasn't officially working, after all. For that reason, when we turned the corner into an empty street, I had to clobber him with my fist. The şair was walking one step ahead of me, so I hit him in the back of the head as hard as I could. After he fell to the ground, I kept punching him so he wouldn't come to anytime soon. Then

I tossed him over my shoulder. He had a slight build; in this, too, he fit the description. Such sights are not rare in Antalya, so I didn't make too much effort to be stealthy. I carried him to the port; there are always guardsmen there—I needed at least two witnesses. Together we shoved him in a bag along with a rock.

If the weather had been warmer or it had been morning, we would have done things properly, taken a boat and tossed him out at sea, but even that was unnecessary—all you really need is a good five feet of water. I've noticed that on winter nights, you do everything without any flair. So we simply rolled the bag to the edge of the pier and pushed it over the side.

Why didn't I first take him to the governor to be identified, taken in for questioning? Well, I was almost certain—insofar as there is any certainty in such cases—the şair was only pretending to be Saadi.

Yes, you're right: thus ended the very long return of the poet Saadi.

TESTIMONY OF ANTIONE DE GIMEL, HEAD OF THE
FRENCH ROYAL GUARD AROUND CEM SULTAN, ON THE
EVENTS FROM NOVEMBER 1494 TO FEBRUARY 1495

YOU HEARD IT: I foresaw I would take up this post as soon as
my king wrested Cem Sultan from Alexander VI Borgia. I never
doubted it: King Charles VIII could not but win. Italy was too
decimated from internal wars, too many traitors lived among
its rulers, and the plight of its people was too dire. What right
do I have to drag the word "people" into the case of Cem, you
ask? Begging your pardon, but it has already been dragged into
far more vile cases.

Incidentally, my king entered Rome on December 31, 1494,
just an hour before midnight. The stars had prophesied great
successes for him during that year, so he was hurrying to win
his last and greatest conquest, Cem, before it ended.

That sly old fox, Alexander VI, got his way. He made my king
take Rome by force, for which all of Western Christendom reproached him. He also made him do one other thing: treat the
pope with endless courtesy, after he had wreaked violence on
his capital. King Charles saw what he was up to and deliberately

did not poke his nose out of his chambers for two weeks—we had installed ourselves in the palace of San Marco. He was waiting for envoys from Alexander. But the pope was pouting as well—he, on his part, was waiting for an apology. In the end, we were the ones who sent messengers.

The negotiations between Alexander Borgia and the king took another two weeks. On all the other treaty conditions, the two parties came to an agreement within two hours: Charles would lawfully take control of Naples; he would post his troops in six papal fortresses; he would lead the crusade against Turkey. But Cem! What headaches Cem caused for our cardinals and lords.

No, not Cem, most likely. Charles VIII had not seen him yet, so, in fact, the one causing the headaches was the pope. Just hear what he wanted in exchange for Cem Sultan: first, a guarantee of five thousand ducats; second, sixty French aristocrats as hostages; third, for Cem to be held within the borders of the papacy, albeit under French guard. And, finally, for Cem to be returned to the pope after six months. At which time we would receive our money and our people back, and *arrivederci*.

All the Frenchmen and French supporters in Italy thought my king would be mad to agree to such terms after our brilliant successes. But just imagine: Charles VIII accepted them. "Cem Sultan is still in the Sant'Angelo castle," he told the Council. "That means he's in the pope's hands. If we drag out the negotiations around Cem and Alexander doesn't see any benefits he can get in return, he might kill the Turk and render our victory pointless. We must receive Cem alive at any cost—and I do mean *at any cost*. You can see for yourselves: Europe is on edge over our expansions; it might only be a matter of days before the Germans attack us from behind. Or Britain. How can we obtain a lucrative peace unless we have Cem to offer in exchange?"

What the king said about the cost again gave rise to objections: we could wait a bit longer. The king wouldn't budge; he truly feared receiving a dead body instead of a living corpse.

"Cem has been living in the West for thirteen years now, Your Majesty," someone reminded him. "What causes Your Majesty to fear for his life precisely now?"

At that point Charles VIII presented to the Council the letters caught with a certain Hüseyin Bey. Twelve letters, the full correspondence between Alexander VI and Bayezid regarding the "final resolution of the case of Cem."

You don't need me to come to your own conclusions about what a "final resolution" entails. The correspondence began with the news, personally conveyed by Borgia, that King Charles was coming to Italy to wrest Cem away from him and put him at the head of a major crusade. The pope had thus far honored his obligations to Bayezid, but the French did not intend to do so—the time had come for a decade-old chimera to become real: the great Christian crusade. In this letter of his, the Holy Father seemed terribly afraid of such a turn of events, as if he himself were a fervent Muslim. Later, Borgia underscored that the papacy's resistance against France required enormous funds and demanded that he receive the money for Cem's upkeep for the next five years in advance. This money would secure Cem's confinement in Rome, since it would secure Rome itself.

Bayezid's response was reserved. The sultan practically ordered the pontiff to appoint Niccolò Cybo as the bishop of

Arles—take note, Bayezid was now appointing Christian bishops—because he had proved to be of invaluable service to Turkey in the case of Cem. This means certain high-ranking clergymen were working as Turkish agents right under the pope's nose. On the subject of the five years' advance payment, Bayezid remained silent, simply reiterating his wish that his brother not leave Rome.

Unsurprisingly, Alexander VI's next letter was desperate—he wrote it while my king was already sitting in Florence. The pope whined that France was at his doorstep and nothing could save the papacy and Turkey—oh please, those allies so united in thought and action, the Vatican and Turkey—but a miracle. It was either the five years of Cem's upkeep in advance, Alexander VI sobbed, or a crusade.

Bayezid Khan's reply arrived in Latin, in perfect Latin, and, as his imprisoned messenger attested, the sultan had written it personally to prove he was not a barbarian. In his perfect Latin, Bayezid refused to be a puppet any longer in a play he had long grown weary of. His armies were victorious, he declared, so he was not concerned in the least about the prospects of a crusade. He was almost looking forward to it because it was high time—he was sick and tired of all these false promises and lies. So he offered one final opportunity to Alexander Borgia; he gave him the chance to earn some gold so he would not be left completely broke: "Since my brother will die sooner or later in any case, and since his life among infidels is a terrible torment to him, Your Holiness could release him from his years-long agony and allow him to pass into a better, more just world. If Your Holiness shows such mercy to my wretched brother and delivers his body to any port under Ottoman control, those who deliver him will receive three hundred thousand ducats in cash and my imperial gratitude."

I have never heard a more sinister silence than that which followed the reading of those letters.

Here's the thing: the Council was made up of thirty-odd noblemen, every one of them mixed up in the case of Cem to a greater or lesser extent. For thirteen years that case had been deliberated in our circles—its possible developments, its advantages and risks. Each one of us, thirty-odd noblemen, had quite a bit weighing on his soul or, if you prefer, his conscience. It was the fifteenth century, after all, and not a cloister for young maidens. But that which we had just heard surpassed even the fifteenth century with its Borgias, Medicis, Savonarola, Inquisition, and Machiavelli—it surpassed all human imagination. The sultan of the world's most powerful empire was offering Christ's representative on earth a fortune to commit a murder.

No, I phrased that too tamely, and inaccurately to boot. Islam —the greatest threat to Western civilization—was suggesting that the West—in the person of its spiritual leader—destroy its own best weapon in exchange for three hundred thousand ducats.

No, that is still too tame. Incidentally, if you find the words, you can say them yourselves.

We sat there silently during that hour, as if glimpsing into Tartarus, as if witnessing the suicide of an entire civilization.

"After everything you have heard, I'm sure you need no convincing that Alexander Borgia has accepted Bayezid's offer."

I also have no words for the disgust with which the king uttered those words.

We clearly understood that if we did not receive Cem Sultan immediately, he would soon be sailing away, well salted, toward some Levantine port. We agreed to the pope's terms. We didn't plan on abiding by them, but then again, we knew Borgia would not abide by ours either. Consequently, we sacrificed five hundred thousand pieces of gold and sixty Frenchmen. For a lucrative peace with the whole of Europe.

On January 16—after we delivered the gold and handed over our hostages—Cem Sultan's guard was changed. I entered Sant'Angelo at the head of two hundred knights; my long and risky service as France's champion at the Vatican in the case of Cem gave me this right. The papal guards let down the drawbridge, and I crossed its iron-plated planks with my boys, thinking as I walked, *Good thing we are getting in, but even better if we get out*. Because the drawbridge shut behind us. We were in charge of guarding Cem's chambers, while the papal guards manned the whole rest of the fortress. It looked very much like a trap. My only consolation was that beyond the papal guards stood again our men—all of Rome was in French hands.

I found Cem the same as I'd left him two months earlier: sitting in front of the fireplace, drowsing, with no candle lit. The very thought of spending my days with him made me sick; after all, I'm not some Saracen, I'm not Saadi, so as to remain unmoved by that sight. I was present at all his lunches and dinners; I carefully supervised the taster's work—remember, we were expecting a poisoning. Sometimes the Turk would turn to me; I understood nothing of his words except "Saadi." Clearly he took me for his former servant. I knew Saadi's job; I hadn't spent six years with him for nothing, so I could get by even without a translator. It was very simple: the sultan either wanted his pipe or wanted to be tucked into bed. There was no third option.

I spent barely ten days of my service with Cem at Sant'Angelo, and I can assure you I felt all the emotions Saadi must have experienced, if Saracens are even capable of feelings: endless irritation; the fear that somewhere real life is happening and I am missing out on it; and, above all else, disgust. I, the twenty-eight-year-old son of a good family, a man with a future and potential, was wasting away serving some quasi animal. *I hope they do poison him*, I often caught myself thinking, forgetting I myself would pay dearly for Cem Sultan's death. I thought this not only with hatred. Indeed, was Bayezid entirely lying when he said he wanted to deliver his brother from this wretched life?

Fortunately, I did not have much time for such rumination. On February 6, my king left Rome to continue his conquest of Naples. Because he was afraid Alexander Borgia would immediately snatch away the fruit of our victory, Charles VIII decided to take Cem with him everywhere. Under heavy guard.

You should have seen the Turk when we readied him for the journey. Cem had not left his chambers in years, he had not worn any decent clothes. The hardest thing was getting shoes on him—his feet were so swollen, the servants had to try four different pairs of boots before they found ones that fit. They draped a wolfskin cloak with a hood over him. As mollycoddled as he was, we were afraid he would catch cold. At the last minute I realized even that might not be enough. I looked around; there was nothing else at hand, so I grabbed the blanket off his bed and threw that over him too.

We led him out. Our footsteps echoed through the fortress's long corridors, soldiers' footsteps, and mixed in with them, a plodding shuffle; with difficulty the Turk dragged his new, too-big and too-heavy boots.

Many of our men were outside. We stood in formation, waiting for the king. From all the fanfare it was clear King Charles VIII wanted to show his guest great honor. So while we waited, I watched Cem Sultan. He simply stood there, his chin resting on his chest, as if he did not notice anyone or anything. The woolen blanket had slid down one shoulder and its edge was soaking in a puddle. I took the liberty of lifting it and tucking it nice and tightly around Cem—despite my annoyance I felt something like responsibility for his health. Sensing my fingers, the Turk lifted his head. His eye looked at me in bewilderment. Or a question, "Hm?" was all that exhausted, cloudy eye asked.

"We are setting out on a campaign, Your Highness, on a campaign. We're going to war. You shall lead our troops, along with the king of France."

I spoke needlessly loudly, and I must have used gestures as well, as if speaking to a deaf person. Cem shook his head; he wanted to say he didn't understand or that he didn't care. Then he lowered his head again, breathing heavily.

At that time, a fanfare rang out. On each horn a banner with a crest fluttered—the French nobles were greeting their king. Amidst the trumpeters lining the drawbridge, Charles VIII appeared. Our ruler was still very young then, barely twenty, but military life in Italy had invigorated his slightly sickly, pale face. With an authoritative stride, yet without hiding his curiosity, King Charles headed toward us.

"Long live the king!" the knights roared.

Charles greeted them, the tuft of crimson feathers on his helmet bobbing to and fro like a small flame in the gray February day. The cardinals who supported France followed him with their suites; after all, Charles was considered the liberator of Rome.

Slightly puzzled by the strange appearance of his ally, the king glanced around for assistance. Cardinal Saint-Denis, who was responsible for Cem, whispered something to His Majesty, and Charles jumped off his horse. They called over the translator.

"I am happy to meet you in our holy city, my brother," the man translated. "May God support us in our great deed. Today the victorious French army, under my and your leadership, sets out for Naples."

Like a frightened animal dragged out of its lair, Cem glanced up at the king with a scowl. I could see he wanted to step back, but he gave up on the effort and the entire bulk of him swayed. I thought he would stagger, so I rushed to grasp him. Cem was muttering something, but the translator understood. "His Highness says he is a prisoner, only a prisoner. Lead him where you will—he cannot stop you."

This was clearly foolish on the translator's part: we could all see the king flush crimson from the insult. Is that how one speaks to a king, and a conqueror at that? Charles VIII turned on his heel and started giving orders. Cem Sultan was left standing behind him. The blanket had once again slipped off his shoulders.

If you ask me, the smartest thing would have been to load him into the carriage. But the king insisted Cem actually lead the campaign. Italy and the whole world had been hearing about this crusade for so long that Charles wanted to show its beginning.

With the full knowledge we would never get past the beginning—and let's hope that is truly the case, because there were already serious rumors of a European alliance against the French king, fomented by Alexander Borgia. In short, we needed to conquer Naples quickly and go home to defend France.

So Cem rode on Charles VIII's right. The winter dampness caused him to huddle down in his wraps; besides the first blanket, they had now piled more on him. I rode close to him as ordered, since Cem might slip from his saddle. Good thing that didn't happen, as I wouldn't have been able to catch him, given how much he weighed.

A rather large crowd saw us off through the streets of Rome, since the king had given food to the starving city. Farther down the Tiber it thinned out—the spectacle was over, everyone hurried inside where it was warm. While we rode all day. And the next, and the next. We spent the nights at various small castles: Valmontone, Castelfiorentino, Verona, Lord knows where else. The very first night they gave me some documents for Cem to sign. I glanced over them. They were letters to the bishops of Dalmatia and some bishops in the Greek and Slavic lands. In them, Cem Sultan urged them to rise up in rebellion, as he was at the head of an innumerable force. In early March, the letters said, allied Christian armies would invade. Let the enslaved Christians greet them as liberators, let them rebel to the last man against Muslim rule!

We'll be in France a month from now, I thought. *The king is trying to cause some minor inconveniences for Bayezid because he suspects him of being in league with Borgia. Clever.*

I brought the papers to Cem. He was again sitting motionless in front of the fireplace in some room. I think it was the quarters of the Valmontone fortress guards. I put the papers on his knee. Cem didn't budge; his breathing was disgustingly loud. How could I explain to him? I dipped the quill in ink, took Cem's hand, and thrust it between his fingers.

"Here, Your Highness." I pointed to the blank space. "Sign here, please." And I showed him as if I were signing.

"Saadi." He breathed on me the only word the both of us understood.

"Your Saadi is gone!" I shouted. "To hell with Saadi and everyone who dumped you in my lap, you stupid Moor, you imbecile! Sign!"

He understood, if you can believe it. With a shaking hand, like a drunk, he drew some curlicue at the bottom of the first page, then the second. Then he dropped the quill. He was muttering something, very agitated, as if feverish.

I grasped his hand again, forcing his fingers to curl, struggling to grip the quill between them. Then I realized with a start: this hand was very hot.

It struck me: the Turk is ill. What would happen to me if he kicked the bucket? I felt his forehead, which was bathed in cold sweat, overcame my revulsion, and stuck my hand inside his shirt to feel his chest—very hot as well. What was stirring beneath my fingers, unevenly, in crazed desperation or breathlessly quiet: Cem's heart.

"Guards!" I shouted as I rushed through the unfamiliar corridors until I ran into someone, I don't remember who. "Sound the alarm! Cem Sultan is ill."

As if through a fog, I saw people gathering. I was afraid the king himself would come, although I later found out he was already asleep. Several of them lifted the now-even-heavier body and carried him to the bed. Cem was unrecognizable. Flushed bright red, almost purple, shiny with sweat, he gasped for breath as if the air was too thick.

I heard anxious voices calling for a doctor. One guard ran out, several others followed him, yet others came in. While I kept wondering what would become of me, since I had failed to keep the most valuable person in the world safe.

The doctor arrived an hour later; they had brought him from the city. He chased everyone but me out of the room, as he wanted to ask me about the symptoms of the illness. I mumbled something, since everything was spinning before my eyes. I heard the doctor's voice as if from afar.

"It looks like poisoning. A slow-acting poison. Someone forked out quite a bit of money; such poison is very rare—they import it from the Far East. For that reason, it is astronomically expensive." The doctor seemed delighted by his own knowledge.

"Don't worry about the cost, Your Grace," I replied. "There is someone happy to pay it."

We must have been an odd sight, two completely foreign witnesses to an unknown crime. At first we spoke with great difficulty, but then it grew easier, the words flowed. The doctor begged me to keep his name a secret, as he was afraid of the unknown poisoner. "Surely it is not just anybody, right?"

I promised, thinking to myself it would be best to detain him, if not kill him outright, as the king would surely want to hide Cem's illness. Or rather, his death, considering the most unfortunate timing for France. I ordered him to wait for me so I could

VERA MUTAFCHIEVA

pay him, then I left the room and called the guards. But the doctor disappeared like a puff of smoke. Clearly he was far more familiar with the fortress than I was. *Things are going from bad to worse,* I told myself. Tomorrow they would ask me about the doctor.

That night I sat up alone with Cem Sultan. Despite my fear, I also felt relief: he would finally be gone from my life. Cem Sultan would free the world from the great intrigues, the great concerns, the greed, and the guilt. The king would immediately return to France because he would no longer have anything with which to bribe or threaten his enemies. I, Antoine, would also go home, to Brittany, where they had likely forgotten me; it had been six years, after all. And what had been the point of all this—the lies, the rivalry, the outbidding and outsmarting? Who actually won in the case of Cem and who lost?

No one, I daresay. Bayezid Khan remained sultan, just as he would have without all the absurd expenses; Qaitbay lost as much territory in war against Bayezid as he would have even if he hadn't helped Cem; the Turks conquered as much land in the Balkans and Hungary as they would have if they hadn't been threatened with Cem; my king had to go back to France, abandoning his high-flying hopes—he had to go back from whence he came. What about Borgia, d'Aubusson? They ran themselves ragged handing out bribes to nobles, bishops, and cardinals, to say nothing of spies and guards, spending at least as much as they received from Bayezid for Cem's imprisonment.

What was the point of all our vanity, God? I wondered. *If not for this, I would now be home in Brittany, I would have children already toddling about and my own path in life.... Why do we torment others when it doesn't make us any happier?*

Cem did not die in Valmontone, nor in Castelfiorentino, nor in Verona. Now he really was lying in a cart; the carriage was unsuitable because Cem was slowly growing stiff as a board and was unable to sit, getting worse every evening. I could not even force a spoonful of antidote between his clenched jaws; I could not pour in any water. In four days the Turk wasted away so quickly it almost seemed as if sweat wasn't dripping off him, but strips of lard. His skin—grayish yellow beneath the reddish flush of fever—bunched up in deep folds. Now Cem looked almost fifty, although they say he was thirty-five.

At night I watched over him with a heavy head—the king kept the illness a deep secret and did not allow anyone else to guard him—my eyes burning for an hour of sleep. I thought back over the words that had seemed so monstrous to me months ago: "Let my brother be delivered from life and allow him to pass into a better, more just world." *Let him,* I thought. *The sooner, the better.*

Cem died in Naples, our final Italian conquest, in the palace that Alfonso, Ferrandino's son, had abandoned just days earlier. A Pyrrhic victory, as Charles VIII knew it would bring him nothing—storm clouds were gathering in the north, at any moment we expected the Germans to invade France and to force us to abandon our all-too-easy conquests. My king commanded he be crowned as king of Naples as well, but Alexander VI did not promulgate this; the pope had pinned his hopes on a quick change of circumstances.

Perhaps I was the only one who knew where his hopes lay: in Cem's death. It came on the evening of February 25, while a drenched crowd welcomed its new sovereign on the streets of

Naples, and while that sovereign was in a terrible mood—in a week at the latest we needed to leave Naples if we didn't want our retreat to be cut off.

Cem died so quietly I didn't even realize it. I was standing by the windows, watching the fireworks and listening to the music. Down below in the palace gardens, colorful flames were flaring up. They rose in wondrous spheres, lines, and curves, and faded sorrowfully against the winter sky.

That's our whole life, I thought, disgusted. *Our whole life is just fireworks and vulgar songs; a celebration, which you know will be followed by retreat; suffering, which you know is not worth the effort.*

I lit the candles. With the candlestick in my hand, I went over to Cem. The fever had passed; his face looked the color of a headstone. An old face, indifferent to everything. Not entirely, perhaps; in death his face was more expressive than it had been in life during these last years. Some fully human exhaustion and bitterness weighed in the wrinkles around his mouth, yet beyond that exhaustion there was a quiet relief.

"Let my brother be delivered from life...." I recalled, pressing the cold eyelids shut.

The next morning, the king ordered Cem Sultan to be secretly sealed in a lead-plated coffin. We were still keeping his death a secret, which guaranteed that everyone who needed to know of it already knew. In the evening—a terrible rain was pouring down and the city looked dead—we loaded the coffin onto a cart and took it to the Gaeta fortress. We left him there on the ground floor. We had no idea what a Muslim funeral should entail, yet we didn't dare allow an infidel to be buried in our holy ground, and we didn't want to drag him along with us—the king was superstitious, and the presence of a dead man among his troops could not possibly be seen as a good omen.

So we left Cem there and snuck out. I was the last to go, so I could lock up. Although I myself couldn't explain it, it seemed awful to leave him there just like that, abandoned to fate, like a forgotten possession. I turned the key in the lock twice, and ran to catch up with my comrades.

The knights were walking in step, as all soldiers under the sun march. They were silent, not speaking—they were leaving. I fell in step as well—I came back into formation, now no longer a jailer or a nurse.

Over the past few months I had expected something terrible to happen at that hour: fiery rain, an earthquake, a flood—some portent, in other words. But there was no sign, none at all, that a long chapter in world history had finally come to an end.

TESTIMONY OF AYAS BEY ON THE EVENTS FROM
JANUARY 1499 TO MAY 1499

SURELY EVERYONE WILL find this testimony unnecessary; after
all, is death not the end of everything, and did Cem not die? Yet
God, as if unsatiated by my master's suffering, has wished for it
to continue even after his death. Cem's body did not find peace
for another four years. His wanderings continued.

Perhaps it is unnecessary to report whom Sultan Bayezid
heard the happy news from. From Venice, it goes without saying. The Venetians were surely scared as hell—we were beneath
their walls, after all. Thus, to curry favor with Bayezid Khan
and to emphasize that any trifling misunderstandings between
them were purely accidental, while their friendship was eternal,
Venice sent a swift ship to Stambul. From this envoy we learned
not only about the main event, but several smaller ones as well.
Preparations for the uprising in the Balkans, for example; the
names of Christian clergymen with proven ties to France.

Bayezid Khan would not be Bayezid Khan if he had taken
all this at face value. He expressed his doubts and continued

expressing them for three whole months, until Charles VIII went back home and gave up on his Italian patrimony once and for all, which made it clear Cem was not in the game any longer.

"God is great," Bayezid Khan proclaimed, throwing himself down and making twenty bows in all the cardinal directions. "We did not dare believe such an auspicious turn of events could be true."

Then he gave orders to be dressed in black, which he wore for three days, after which he accepted an audience with his viziers, who congratulated him on this joyful occasion. Only in 1495, fourteen years after his ascension to the throne, did Bayezid truly feel like a sultan. Because later, in 1506, he was overthrown and killed by his son Selim the Grim, as you likely know. I wonder whether Selim ever wished, *Let my father be delivered from life and pass on to a better, more just world*? We do not know.

As you know, my visit to France upon the Order's instructions was fruitless, so you will ask what my role was in the case of Cem after I was taken back to Rhodes and was again locked up with the other survivors from Cem's suite. D'Aubusson handed us all over to Bayezid after Cem's death. Bayezid Khan liked to flaunt his piety and virtue. He paid dearly to get back those who had loyally served his brother, and he showered them with titles, houses, and money. And so, after fourteen years in a dungeon on Rhodes, I returned to my homeland at the age of fifty-four.

The other pious act Bayezid swore to carry out when he learned of his brother's death was to bury him with full honors in the Ottoman family tomb. He'd have done better to keep that oath a secret, so as not to raise the price of Cem's corpse.

Five thousand ducats—that's how much the king of Naples demanded for the corpse left to him by the French. But the time had come for Bayezid to laugh, and since he was laughing last, he did so a little too loudly. The sultan refused to pay for Cem's remains. Their surrender to Turkey would only help strengthen the friendship between our two peoples. In short: it's up to you.

But the West had grown so accustomed to gifts relating to Cem that it could not believe its ears and decided to keep the corpse until its price rose. Besides, five thousand was a drop in the bucket compared to the sum Cem's former owners were supposed to receive as a reward for Cem's murder. Three-hundred thousand—isn't that what Bayezid himself had offered? And so Alexander Borgia asked for it, in accordance with their agreement.

Bayezid did not answer his letter. Borgia sent him a second, a third, a fourth, I believe. All without success. Bayezid Khan felt well within his rights not to pay for this final service rendered by the West, since he considered the previous services far too pricey. Tit for tat, as they say.

If you'd like to feel some satisfaction at the end of this hearing of the case of Cem, just imagine Pope Alexander VI at the moment when he realized the full implication of Bayezid's silent refusal.

Wonderful, isn't it? You yourself have slaughtered the chicken that lays the golden eggs in hopes that in its death it will lay a final egg, this time not gold but a pure diamond, but it lays nothing, not a thing. You are left with a sad consolation; you can sell the chicken to someone to cook it up for the price of any old bird. That's what the pope was trying to do now, along with the king of Naples; they asked of Bayezid as much as any well-to-do man would pay for the body of his brother. If not five thousand, then at least three; very well, let it be one thousand.

"No," Bayezid replied, if and when he deigned to reply at all.

I have no love lost for Bayezid Khan, so don't accuse me of partiality when I declare: Bayezid did not do this out of stinginess. A thousand ducats are nothing compared to the mountain of gold Cem had cost him. Here we simply run up against something inexplicable: Bayezid Khan's behavior after his brother's death.

It would be easy to explain it away with the difficulties that arose for the sultan around Cem's death. Indeed, all opponents of the rulers in Turkey—and there were still more than a few; Bayezid's son Selim the Grim later built his rebellion on them—claimed the sultan had disgraced them with his shameful negotiations with infidels and their ringleader, the pope. They accused Bayezid Khan of abasing the House of Ottoman's honor by letting nonbelievers meddle in Ottoman affairs through Cem Sultan's murder. And Bayezid was forced to give them proof, to defend that honor.

But that is only one side of the story. To be fair, let us say the aforementioned unpleasantries were not insurmountable to the sultan; malcontents can be found everywhere and always, and rulers take them into account in one situation only: when they sense their own weakness. Between 1495 and 1499, Bayezid Khan no longer felt weak. So we must seek elsewhere for the reasons behind his actions at that time.

Before, when Bayezid had trembled at the thought of a victorious Cem, his opponents had blackmailed and threatened him with Cem for far too long. So just as when you have a tooth pulled that has kept you from eating or sleeping for a week, you continue to feel as if it is there, even when it is not, and it still pains you. In the same way, Bayezid could not get his mind around the idea he was now free of this threat. As unbelievable as it may sound, he missed Cem.

Pangs of conscience, a sense of guilt, likely added to that emptiness. Count in a desire for revenge as well—those Westerners had actually tortured and killed an Ottoman royal. Perhaps we could also include grief for his only brother, now dead, though I'm not sure about this part. No matter what else he may have been, he was a brother. On the very same day Bayezid Khan saw his authority confirmed, he found himself alone. No matter what else he may have been, he was alone.

For the reasons laid out above—let us call them internal and external—Bayezid turned to the world and declared: "I paid blackmailers to look after my brother, but I have no dealings with killers. What's more, I will punish them." In all negotiations around the case of Cem after 1495, Bayezid Khan used sharp, even imperious language. And so, the years passed until 1499, the last year of the fifteenth century. As if to commemorate this, Bayezid Khan announced an event heretofore unseen in history: he declared war on Naples because of Cem's corpse. Tell me, have you ever heard of a war between two kingdoms for bodily—or better yet, by this time, bony—remains?

The world seized up in astonishment. This business seemed impossible. Yet Bayezid Khan sent his first ships through the Straights, headed for Naples. "Good God," the world thought. "How could the sultan start a war over the dead body of his brother, who was killed on his orders?" Well, don't look for much logic in history—it's made by people, after all. So there you have it: Bayezid Khan—the very portrait of prudence, fear, and perfidy, cautious and cold-blooded to a fault—started a war inspired by feelings, and beautiful feelings at that. Here I have one piece of advice for you, if I may dare to be so bold, because I lived too long and saw too much: when you try to explain history, leave a small but essential part of it unexplained. It is inexplicable—resign yourself to this.

Because I witnessed the final act in the case of Cem, I can assure you there was a hint of madness about it. Our heavily armed, powerful triremes, packed to the masts with troops, suddenly dropped their sails. Naples was already in sight from the crow's nest. But we stopped because we saw coming toward us not a war ship, but three magnificent little galleys covered in gilded carvings, with colorful sails and bright banners. *That's how a king would send his daughter off to marry another king,* I thought. Yes, this, too, was absurd, just like everything having to do with Cem Sultan: with great fanfare, even joy, our enemy was delivering to us a corpse.

I had been tasked with confiscating it; we thought we would have to shell Naples at the very least, if not worse. Now we would have to negotiate; once again we were negotiating over Cem. The Neapolitans were polite yet firm: they would transport the body themselves to our port as an expression of their warm friendship with Turkey. "Fine, you've already expressed it," I replied. I was worried they would try to pull something on us again.

"No, no, we wouldn't want to burden you unnecessarily." Politeness incarnate.

So as not to burden any of our ships—which a dozen cast-iron cannons, trunks full of cannonballs, eighty oarsmen, and two hundred soldiers had not managed to weigh down—with a lead casket, we led the decorative Neapolitan vessels toward Valona on the Adriatic.

We sailed past the coast of Italy. Cem Sultan had passed by here eighteen years earlier before disembarking at Nice; back then I, too, had sailed with him. I remembered how my master had delighted in these shores—at that time they seemed unparalleled to me as well. Where was their beauty now? *No, beauty does not exist in and of itself,* I thought. *If there is no person to delight in it and feed on it, it slumbers.* Cem the poet was no more, so all the rest of us—sailors, soldiers, statesmen—would have to make due without beauty.

In the evening, I leafed through his books. Naples had given us all of Cem's earthly possessions: well-worn clothes, a monkey gone mad from its lonely imprisonment, a parrot, a cup, and quite a few books. Here and there, my eyes lingered over a verse—Saadi, may he rest in peace, had copied them down: "Let Bayezid have the crown. My crown is the world," I read. From 1482. *Master Cem, would you have repeated those words at the end of your exile?*

We were nearing Valona when they stopped us. Not just a ship or two, but more than twenty: Venetian, papal, French. Why, you ask? This, too, is another of history's inexplicable events. Perhaps Europe had seen Cem as a guarantee of its luxurious safety, as a talisman against the Turkish threat for so long that it was afraid to part with his corpse. I'm telling you the truth: none of the various lords who arrived here with their ships was able to give us a sensible answer. They did not want anything from us, they didn't want money or a fight. "Just wait," they said. "But why?" "Could Cem truly be leaving us for good?"

Believe it or not, that little city of ships rocked in open waters for three months. Where did our strange, dreamlike indecisiveness come from, the feeling that every one of us owed somebody something such that we either ran like thieves being pursued or blocked the way like burghers who had just been robbed? Every morning nearly a thousand men awoke on the now sixty-odd ships. They went about their daily tasks; some went in skiffs to get food and water, others kept the ships in good repair. Yet others did nothing. As if some unknown marine spirit held us captive until it received a ransom.

I had heard Christians have the custom of falling silent for a moment when a loved one passes away. Well, we fell silent for three whole months—that was Cem Sultan's funeral. He deserved it. It was not a person who had died, but something immeasurably larger: a myth.

One morning as I was dully hinting—as I had done again and again for some time—that we at long last needed to figure out what was going on, only to keep receiving the same answer—"Just wait; do you really need to know?"—a small boat approached our spectral city. It had been sent by the governor of Valona and carried a letter from Bayezid Khan: he would have the head of anyone who dared delay Cem any longer.

This wind billowed all of our sails. Sixty ships loaded with regret and guilt reached Valona in a day. There, they were expecting us. The city leaders welcomed the simple lead casket with all the honors due a sultan; true believers and nonbelievers had streamed in from near and far to witness the ceremony. We set out for Stambul the next day. All of us together. Among us were Franks speaking their various tongues, all escorting Cem to his capital. Who had invited them, why did they come? Who forced the illiterate peasants, the Christian priests, and the impoverished soldiers to crowd the roads along our journey?

If Saadi had been alive, he would have explained it thus: Cem was a legend, and legends have incredible magnetism. I interpreted it differently, however, because among all of Cem's torments, I knew which was the worst: exile. Thousands of people had a hand in it, thousands of human wills contributed to turning what had simply been a carefree step into irrevocable exile. This turned out to be very advantageous for part of the world; those hundreds of Franks now represented that part of the world during Cem's final journey. It was as if they were thanking Cem Sultan for sparing their comfortable, newly reordered world from ruin. By right, Bayezid's governors should have been walking next to the Franks: Cem Sultan's martyrdom had led to the first true alliance, not only on paper, but one of true mutual benefit, between Turkey and Europe.

You'll ask what drew the dark masses of the people to Cem's coffin. It's hard to say. On the whole, the people experience emotions an individual cannot express. I would say the people were drawn by another alliance, very old and very strong, between all the defeated in history. To them, Cem had suffered the ultimate human misery: exile. They came to pay their respects to that suffering. To set Cem's soul at ease with their presence, to show him he had really come back to his own people.

Despite Mehmed Khan's decree that all Ottomans after him should be laid to their eternal rest in Stambul, we buried Cem in Bursa. From Valona to Bursa, Cem Sultan crossed the entire empire he had dreamed of ruling; Cem Sultan rests in Bursa, where he had reigned for eighteen spring days.

Next to the grave of Şehzade Hasan, Mehmed Khan's brother, strangled on the latter's orders so there would be no dissension in the country, lies the grave of Cem, Mehmed Khan's favorite son. When a man makes a law, he does not know who it will strike down.

"Cem Sultan, son of Mehmed the Conqueror"—I feel like his tughra is copied from the blank sheet of paper that Cem had signed, and which Brother d'Aubusson had filled with his sentence to a life of exile. Thus, d'Aubusson's hand also rests heavily upon Cem's body.

Gifts are often left on the marble slab, even more than on Osman Khan's grave. In life Cem was a foreigner everywhere: a Serb or nonbeliever here, a Saracen or Moor among Christians. Who knows why, but in his death, Cem belongs to everyone. Likely because there is nothing more universally human than suffering.

Sofia, 1966–1967

VERA MUTAFCHIEVA

ABOUT SANDORF PASSAGE

SANDORF PASSAGE publishes work that creates a prismatic perspective on what it means to live in a globalized world. It is a home to writing inspired by both conflict zones and the dangers of complacency. All Sandorf Passage titles share in common how the biggest and most important ideas are best explored in the most personal and intimate of spaces.